Falshed came hurtling out of the wood like a demon from hell, his infernal machine belching flames and spitting sparks. He roared down the slope towards the river, his round glass goggles gleaming in the moonlight. Nothing could stop him now. He was as the devil on the back of some fiery monster from the underworld. Master of speed and distance! Dread minister of the law! Wonder stoat of the age of new police enforcement!

Monty raced alongside a drystone wall, gasping for breath.

'I've got you now, you blackguard!' cried an elated Falshed. 'I'm going to run you down like a rat. Let's not worry the judges. It costs money to send weasels to prison. I'm going to squash you under my iron-clad wheels . . .'

www.booksattransworld.co.uk/childrens

GARRY KILWORTH

GASLIGHT GEEZERS

A WELKIN WEASELS ADVENTURE

CORGI BOOKS

THE WELKIN WEASELS: GASLIGHT GEEZERS
A CORGI BOOK : 0 552 54704 2

First publication in Great Britain

PRINTING HISTORY
Corgi edition published 2001

1 3 5 7 9 10 8 6 4 2

Set in 11/12pt Palatino by
Phoenix Typesetting, Ilkley, West Yorkshire

Corgi Books are published by Transworld Publishers,
61–63 Uxbridge Road, London W5 5SA,
a division of The Random House Group Ltd,
in Australia by Random House Australia (Pty) Ltd,
20 Alfred Street, Milsons Point, Sydney, NSW 2061, Australia,
in New Zealand by Random House New Zealand Ltd,
18 Poland Road, Glenfield, Auckland 10, New Zealand
and in South Africa by Random House (Pty) Ltd,
Endulini, 5a Jubilee Road, Parktown 2193, South Africa

Made and printed in Great Britain by
Cox & Wyman Ltd, Reading, Berkshire

For my granddaughter Chloe
who knows that animals talk

CHAPTER ONE

The Right Honourable Montegu Sylver was sitting in his study sucking on a chibouque: a very long tobacco pipe which curved like a sabre down to its empty bowl. The pipe was empty because young Monty had never actually taken up smoking, but he had the habit of chewing on the pipe stem when he was in a thoughtful mood. Tonight, in his flat above Breadoven Street, with the fog nosing at the window, he was deep in thought. His distant cousin, a weasel of few summers like himself, was up to his old tricks. Someone at the Jumping Jacks club had learned that Spindrick Sylver was planning to bomb Muggidrear city, the capital of Welkin. Spindrick was an anarchist and had been wrecking property from a very young age.

'What was that sigh for?'

The weasel who had spoken was sitting at a card table playing stoatlitaire, an innocent game with the same scoring system as the notorious seed-dice gambling game, hollyhockers. She was a young veterinary surgeon, Bryony Bludd, who treated mostly the down-and-outs and sick mustelids who slept under the bridges of the river Bronn, which flowed through the centre of the city. Bryony lived in the flat across the landing and the pair often visited each other of an evening. Both were lonely souls in need of company, though neither would admit it. It helped matters that they liked each other and enjoyed each other's company.

The area in which they lived, Gusted Manor, was mostly populated by stoats. Being weasels they were not exactly welcome and their snooty neighbours let them know that fact by refusing to acknowledge their existence. Under normal circumstances Monty and Bryony would be living in Poppyvile, the poor area of the city, where most of the other weasels had their hovels. Since they both came from well-to-do families they could afford to live in Gusted Manor, never mind their aloof stoat neighbours.

'It's my cousin again,' replied Monty, taking the chibouque out of his mouth to answer the question.

'Spindrick?'

'Yes – he says he's going to blow up the city. Blow it to matchsticks, if I know him.'

'Oh, what? Not *again*.' Bryony watched as a steam-driven red stoat queen about three centimetres high shot forward and knocked the clockwork black stoat queen into a gutter around the board with a triumphant hiss of hot vapour.

'He's always letting off bombs all over the place. I suppose that's what anarchists do?'

All the red pieces were steam-driven, all the black pieces, clockwork. It was a fair reflection of the views of Muggidrear's population, some of whom were for steam, others for clockwork. In reply to the red queen, a black knight whirred and clicked and leapt across the board to avenge his defeated monarch. He hit the red queen so hard she flew upwards and struck the ceiling like a bullet, chipping the plaster before ricocheting into the water of a vase of flowers, where her tiny boiler exploded.

'Bother,' muttered Bryony. 'These new pieces are too enthusiastic for a quiet game . . .'

Monty said, 'This time it sounds serious – Spindrick, I mean.'

Bryony clucked. 'I suppose now you're going to go off and do your famous detecting and unearth the whereabouts of the bomb.'

'I suppose I have to try.'

'You'll be taunted all the way by Spindrick, of course. He loves to get you running around doing your detective work.' Bryony paused again and looked up at the ceiling. 'His mother should never have given him that black cloak for his seventh birthday. It did something to his weak mind, you know.'

Monty tapped out some non-existent tobacco from his pipe bowl by force of habit. 'That's just the vet in you talking. He's a very intelligent weasel. Probably a genius, if an evil one. Look,' he stood up and stretched his forelimbs, 'I think I'll go for a walk on my own. I need some fresh air to clear my head. I'd rather it was a solitary stroll so that I can get some serious thinking done. Do you mind?'

'Not at all,' said Bryony. 'Wrap up well. It's pretty cold and damp out there. That fog gets into a weasel's lungs.'

'I shouldn't worry. Jis McFail, our landjill, won't let me get further than the front door without my cloak and top hat.'

That much was true. Jis McFail heard the flat door open and with her beady eye ascertained that Jal Sylver had on his thick volehair cloak, not to say hat and gloves. With silverknobbed cane (which contained a sword-blade) in paw, Monty stepped out into the cobbled streets of Muggidrear and set out through the swirling fog for the river. Mustelids were not all that keen on clothes and most tried to wear as little as possible, being furry already. However, some covering was needed in such inclement weather. Monty's cloak sufficed.

The streets were poorly lit by gas lamps, but at least there were these island glows in the fog to comfort the evening stroller. Few mammals were about, however, most preferring to remain by a fire. Those he saw were hidden beneath swirling cloaks and hats of many kinds.

Muggidrear was a city split into two by the murky river Bronn. On the southern side there stood the old Castle Rayn, now called Whistleminster Palace and the home of Queen Varicose, a human with no real power in these democratic times. Humans lived on the south side, while on the other side of the many bridges, the mustelids – weasels, stoats, pine martens, polecats, ferrets, otters and one or two others – had their homes. Humans and mustelids did not really mix, mostly because of the difference in size rather than any dislike of each other. Some of Monty's best friends were humans, but while he could fit into their houses, they could not fit into his. On the south side carriages and carts were drawn by horses. On the north side they were mostly pulled by teams of snorting yellow-necked mice, though steam-driven and clockwork vehicles were beginning to appear on the streets.

Both parts of the city were split into roughly three areas. On the human side of the river was The Dreggs, where the poor people lived; Spiffin Place, where the rich had their homes; and Scatter Green, the commercial and business district. On the mustelid side there was Poppyvile, Gusted Manor and Docklands. The two largest buildings in both places, which faced each other across the water, were the grim, grimy-walled prisons, with their mean and narrow windows where pale inmates drifted by like furry ghosts in another world.

In truth, the mustelids tended to be more energetic than the humans, and far more was going on the north side of the city. It was a bustling place, full of trade and commerce, run by the locally elected Mayor Poynt. There were rumours that the elections had been rigged, since there were far more weasels than stoats to vote and no weasel would have voted for the descendant of the notorious Prince Poynt of Rayn Castle. It is true we inherit the social crimes if not the sins of our forebears.

The corpulent stoat mayor, Jeremy Poynt, had recently appointed an old crony of his as chief of police: one Zacharias Falshed. These two stoats between them ran the northern half of the city. The word on the streets was that a bribe would get you further at City Hall than any properly submitted request. Six centuries had passed since Monty's ancestor, Lord Sylver of Thistle Hall and County Elleswhere, had fought a bitter battle against Prince Poynt and his court of stoats. Although Lord Sylver, once an outlaw, had in a sense won that battle, very little had changed in the land of Welkin. The stoats still had the upper paw and the weasels and other mustelids were kept poor and ignorant.

These thoughts went through the head of the Right Honourable Montegu Sylver as he strode briskly through the narrow winding streets down the promenade which ran alongside the river.

Suddenly there came the sound of something monstrous heading towards him from through the fog.

Monty was in a narrow alley. He could hear a hissing, snorting sound as the dark shadow of a large moving thing passed under the light from a gas lamp. This *thing* lumbered rapidly forwards, virtually filling the whole alley and almost touching both sides. Clearly there was not room enough for Monty and the snorting brute. Its jaundiced yellow eyes and leering face drew ever nearer. Luckily Monty was close to a gaslight lamppost and he leapt agilely for the iron cross on top of the lamp which the lamplighters used to steady their ladders. He grasped it with one paw, pulling himself up and out of reach of the monster. It passed underneath, its hot breath going up his flapping black cloak and causing him a little discomfort in that region. Then it was gone, hissing and clanking, into the fog which rolled around it, swallowing its form.

'That was a close thing,' muttered Monty, dropping from the lamppost, his cane still in his left paw. 'These mouseless carriage-drivers ought to look where they're going . . .'

The 'monster' was one of the new steam carriages which were still quite rare as a means of transport in the city. The steam and coal-smoke they threw out did nothing to help the problem of fog in the damp streets around the river. Better, in Monty's opinion, were the clockwork carriages. At least they were clean, though admittedly they had enormous, curled, metal springs which tended to fly out wickedly when they snapped, threatening to decapitate innocent passers-by.

There was a war going on between the city's two inventors – Wm. Jott, the inventor of the steam engine, and Thos. Tempus Fugit, the inventor of clockwork – for control of the city transport. Mayor Poynt was making the most of this battle, taking bribes in both paws and promising victory to each of the warring parties. The longer it went on, the richer Poynt became.

Finally the dark stones of the river parapet came into view. Here there were one or two strollers, like Monty, taking in a breath of air, fog-laden though it was. They walked along the promenade which followed the river, past statues of stoat generals and stoat politicians and old stoat kings and queens. There were seats there too, of wrought-iron, a material which was becoming almost as popular as wood had once been.

The strollers, mostly stoats, regarded Monty with great suspicion. What was a well-dressed weasel doing in *their* district? Monty had borne these stares long enough to be able to ignore them now. Instead of glaring back he leaned on the stone parapet and stared over at the human side of the city, equally shrouded in fog, then down at the river traffic which was busy on both sides of the water. Boats, barges, sailcraft, went to and fro, plying their various trades on the great commercial river.

'Evenin' guv'nor!' called a voice from below. 'Ain't sin you for a while now.'

Monty looked below to see an otter in a rowing-boat. He recognized him instantly as an otter named Jaffer Silke, one of those mustelids whose job it was to keep the river surface free of flotsam and jetsam. Jaffer was dressed in a ragged old coat, scarf and greasy cloth cap. Monty was horrified to see that Jaffer had a body stretched out long and wet-furred in the bottom of the boat.

It was a foreigner by the look it, since the corpse belonged to a lemming. Though Jaffer had arranged its torso and limbs as elegantly as he had been able, the evidence was that the crea-ture had drowned, a victim of the cold hard river. It was bloated and glassy-eyed and there was mucky river water trickling out of its half-open mouth.

'What have you fished out there, Jaffer?'

'Ar, this geezer?' growled Jaffer, nudging the corpse with his hind paw. 'Found him floatin' downstream not more'n an hour since. Drowned away, I'd say. Not a farthin' in his pockets, neither. City morgue'll give me a penny for it though, when I turns it over to 'em.'

'What? What do they do with them?'

'Gives 'em to the vets, they do, for practisin' cuttin' up. Gruesome if you asks me, which not many mustelids do. S'pose they've got to get their knowlidge from somewheres, eh? This geezer's bladder's full of honey dew, 'e is. Look 'ow he wobbles when you kick 'im.'

Jaffer nudged the body a second time and it did indeed wobble like a balloon full of water.

Monty wanted to say something about respect for the dead but he didn't think Jaffer would understand. A corpse was much the same as a log or a lump of driftwood to Jaffer: it was a danger to river traffic and best dragged out and thrown away. Jaffer did not recognize any rites that might be accorded to a nuisance lump of wood.

'Has he got any identification? Perhaps his family would like to know how he came to his end.'

'Nary a sausage skin in 'is pocket, mouse or vole. Nuthink. Anonimousey, that's what 'e is. Could be the police will draw 'is pitcher and post it up somewheres, but it's my guess no-one'll ever know 'is name. Sad but true. Them lemmin's, they're allus goin' off and gettin' drowned anyways. I hear tell they jump off the cliffs in their thousands where they comes from, just for the drop down to the sea.'

'I think that's a bit of a myth, Jaffer – at least the part which says they do it for fun. Overbreeding is their problem. Still, the poor fellow would no doubt have wanted to live. I wonder which ship he

15

was off? Was there nothing at all in his pockets?'

'Not a forin grote.'

'Ah, well,' said Monty, drawing back from the parapet. 'Sad, as you say. Good evening to you, Jaffer. I'm glad to see you're busy, even if your task has been rather grisly tonight. Just a minute,' Monty bent down and stared at the dead lemming's breast, 'this creature's been stabbed, before he went into the river. Look at that bead of blood on his fur. I'll wager there's a hole underneath in his breast . . .'

Jaffer wiped away the blood and sure enough there was a puncture wound, very small, in the corpse's pelt, right above the heart.

'You're right as usual, guv'nor. I'll mention this to the police.'

Monty walked back home, still no nearer to solving the likely whereabouts of his cousin's bomb. He had no doubt it was lying somewhere, round and black and fizzing; ticking away, due to explode in a week, a month, a year from now. But where that place was remained a mystery. He determined to pass on the warning to Mayor Poynt in the morning and the city's officials could take up the search.

When he arrived back at the flat Jis McFail was waiting for him.

'Youm got a visitor,' she whispered in the hallway. 'A foreign jill, from across the seas.'

'Foreign you say, Jis McFail?' replied Monty, taking off his hat and cloak. 'What sort of foreign?'

'Lemming,' came the whispered reply. 'If ever I saw one.'

16

CHAPTER TWO

The creature who was pacing the rug before
Monty's roaring coal fire was not large. Moreover
she was swathed from head to clawtip in robes of an
exotic design which Monty recognized as be-
longing to the mammals of the Ice Islands. They
were held together by an enormous brooch the
shape of a harp with a long sharp, broad-bladed pin
where the strings would be on a real instrument.

Only a pair of the most beautiful eyes Monty had
ever seen were visible below a brow of the softest,
most silky fur imaginable. Monty was lost in those
eyes for a moment. Then they changed, subtly,
perhaps with the light. Despite their great beauty
there was something behind them which sent a
chill down Monty's spine.

Yet even with this hint of evil in her eyes, this

lemming's features remained the most attractive the young weasel had ever encountered and he found himself wishing Bryony were not there to witness his involuntary fascination with a female of another species. Normally Monty was immune to the charms of others, whatever their gender. In this case he did not trust himself to be his normal impartial and clear-thinking self.

Monty then noticed that Bryony was still sitting at the table, her game remaining half-finished. She was looking tense and awkward. The red-brown fur on her neck was bristling and her white bib looked ruffled.

'Perhaps I'd better go now,' said Bryony. 'I thought to keep you company until Jal Sylver here came home, but I actually have work . . .'

'No. Please stay,' said the lemming, interrupting her. 'You may be of some assistance too.'

Her voice was deep and husky and bore an attractive accent.

Jis McFail was hovering somewhere on the landing. She was one of those stoat landjills who are more in the nature of a housekeeper and mother to her tenants than someone who just minds their own business and takes the rent. Jis McFail could not mind her own business to save her life. She *owned* the place, after all. She felt she was entitled to know what went on in her own house, even if she had not been invited to listen.

Monty knew Jis McFail was there, but he merely encouraged the visitor to speak.

Clearly agitated the lemming said, 'My name is Sveltlana and I am newly arrived from Slattland.'

Slattland was a large cold island out in the green

seas to the north of Welkin. It was a place covered in ice and snow half the year. Both Monty and Bryony shivered involuntarily on hearing the name.

'So, Jis Sveltlana, you came in on one of the steamships tonight?'

'How do you know? And what is this "Jis".'

'Jis? I'm sorry, it's what we use as a form of polite address. *Jis* for jill weasels and *Jal* for jack weasels. Female and male. Just as the humans use *Ms* and *Mr*. I'm afraid here in Welkin we take the human model for much of our culture and society.'

She nodded. 'You said you knew I had come in on a steamship.'

'You have the faint signs of salt-water stains on your robes and fur. It's nothing more dramatic than that, I assure you. You could have been walking on the quayside, but I doubt that in this weather. Also there is that freshness of complexion one gets from an exhilarating headwind, such as one finds in the bows of a fast ocean-going ship. And finally, you have traces of oil on your claws, probably picked up from the deck. Oil is associated with engines, not sails, and I assume it is a steam engine.'

'Quite extraordinary,' said Sveltlana, looking at her claws. She was obviously impressed and Bryony beamed with pleasure at this compliment to her friend.

'Basic, very basic,' demurred Monty with a wave of his claw. 'Nothing remarkable in it. But please, you haven't come here to praise an ordinary weasel. You obviously have a problem you wish us to help you solve. May we get down to the facts behind your visit?'

Sveltlana allowed herself to be settled in a chair at last and she stared into the flames of the fire as she recounted her reasons for being there.

'We need your help, Jal Sylver. I have heard from many sources that your powers of detecting are more than unusual. We came on the ship – perhaps I should first explain the circumstances of our country at this present time . . .'

Monty interrupted gently with his soft voice. 'Your country, Slattland, is in a state of upheaval. It is strongly divided between those who wish to keep the monarchy and those who wish to do away with the royal family and declare the island of Slattland a republic.'

'You are a remarkably well-informed weasel.'

'Yes, isn't he?' murmured Bryony, proudly. 'We read the newspapers together, every morning and evening.'

Sveltlana ignored this intervention.

'So, you know the circumstances,' continued the foreign rodent, 'now we come to the purpose of my visit here. I came on the steamship with the Prince Imperial of my country, Prince Miska . . .'

'What was the cargo?' asked Monty.

'Cargo? What has that got to do with anything?' said Sveltlana, peevishly.

'Please, if I am to help I must know the answers to my questions. I have good reasons for asking, I assure you. Can you remember what the cargo was?'

'Of course I can. It was winter cabbages.'

'Fine, excellent. And the name of this vessel?'

'I – I've forgotten.'

'All right. Please proceed.'

'Well, the prince and I arrived together, around

midnight – last night – when suddenly he disappeared. Simply vanished. I left him packing in
his cabin and when I returned he was gone. We
would like to find him. He may be in danger from
those who do not wish him to return to Slattland.
Can you help?'

'We?' repeated Monty, who had picked up his
chibouque and was chewing on the stem.

'I beg your pardon?'

'You said "we". Who accompanied you?'

Sveltlana looked a bit uncomfortable for a moment, then she seemed to recover her wits. 'Oh, I
have one or two servants with me. I left them on
the dockside. Naturally I would not come alone. I
am of noble blood, you see, a distant cousin of the
prince. In these uncertain times one needs a pro-
tector. Now, can you help us trace the whereabouts
of the prince? We – I – would be most grateful. I
have money to pay for your services.'

Monty put down his pipe and waved away the
leather purse which was being offered him.

'No, no. No payment. I have enough wealth to
worry about as it is. My ancestors were rich
lords, you see. I have forsaken the title recently and
have taken on a lesser one: Right Honourable. It's
enough to open a few stoat doors without being
pretentious. One needs a little edge. Of course I
shall help. You have asked me and I accept. Where
can I reach you?'

'I shall be staying at the Mink Hotel, in Barkly
Square.'

'A very striking address. I wonder – that's a
remarkable brooch you have there? Could I look at
it more closely?'

The lemming's paw flew to her brooch and her eyes narrowed to very sinister slits in her face fur.

'No – no, you may not. This is of particular value to me. I never let anyone else touch it.'

'Fine. It's just that – the pin appears to be stained with something; I simply wondered what it was.'

She looked down, quickly, once again. Her paw covered the brooch as she said, 'I must go now . . .' and promptly left the room and went swiftly down the stairs.

Once Sveltlana had left the flat, Jis McFail came into the room.

'Funny these furriners, aren't they? Got a funny way of talking.'

'I'm sure we sound just as peculiar to them, Jis McFail. One can't judge a mammal by his accent. After all, how many of us in this room can speak Slattlandish Lemming?'

'Well, you for a start,' said Bryony. 'And you've been teaching me in your spare time.'

'Apart from us two?' he said, looking pointedly at Jis McFail, who simply sniffed and left the room.

'Come,' said Monty, picking up his cane and heading for the landing. 'There's more to this than meets the nose.'

Bryony stared at her friend. 'You know something, don't you?'

'I know that beautiful lemming was telling lies, if that's what you mean. Big fat ones.'

'You think she's beautiful? Oh,' said Bryony, with a sideways look at him. 'Anyway, enlighten me as we go along.'

Suitably dressed against the cold fog in thick cloaks, they walked the slick cobbled streets, heading towards Docklands. Grey shapes like phantoms passed them by in the mist, almost always in a hurry. Mammals did not like to stay out late in such inclement weather. Occasionally there was the rumble of a mouse-drawn carriage in some nearby street.

Once, a clockwork sedan chair passed them at frightening speed, the legs of the mechanical weasels carrying the chair going ten to the dozen. The occupant looked pale and ghastly inside the chair, her claws gripping the edge of the window-hole. Whoever had wound up her transport had done it to the springs' utmost capacity. The automatons were unwinding too fast and the chair was running away with its passenger. There were cruel tricksters amongst the doormen of hotels who would do such a thing if they were not tipped lavishly for the winding service.

There was not surprisingly very little traffic abroad. In such conditions it was only the pawsom cabs which braved the night airs, hoping to earn a shilling or two from theatre-goers, and gentle-mammals on their way home from their clubs.

'Come on,' Bryony said, impatiently, 'spill it.'

'Well, our Jis Sveltlana said she came in on a ship with a cargo of winter cabbages. I just happen to have stock-market shares in winter cabbages and the last ship which entered the port carrying such fare was three days ago. Moreover you must have detected that faint whiff of dried vole-meat on her person? It's my guess that the ship which brought her was carrying not cabbages but vole-scratchings, destined for the taverns along the waterfront. Why would she lie, that's the question.'

'You never fail to amaze me. What was all that about the brooch pin?'

'Ah, there, I think I detected something rather nastier than the average. Earlier tonight Jaffer Silke showed me a body he had taken from the river. It was a lemming, stabbed through the heart. My guess is that Sveltlana is the killer of that lemming.'

'You saw blood on that wicked-looking brooch pin!'

'No, I did not. I simply spoke about a possible stain. There was no stain. Of course, if she had done the killing she would have wiped the pin clean afterwards. She is, I believe, an efficient creature. But for one second there she doubted herself – she wondered whether she had left some residue blood on the pin. Her reactions gave her away. And immediately afterwards she knew she had been tricked. She was furious with me. Did you see how she looked at me? That look could have killed a badger at twenty paces.'

Bryony shuddered. 'A murderer.'

'Well, a killer, at least. We can't judge her because we don't know the circumstances. We don't even know for sure that she *did* kill that lemming, though I have a feeling she is responsible. It may have been self-defence.'

'Or it could have been in cold blood,' muttered Bryony.

'Whatever – we need more evidence.'

'So what do we do now?'

'Naturally we go to the harbour-master's office and find out which recently arrived ship was carrying vole-scratchings and make some enquiries of its captain.'

'Naturally.'

The waterfront, despite the weather, was a place of energy and activity. Welkin was in a time of doing brisk trade with many other island states. Its merchant fleet was ahead of its time, having been pioneered by pine marten sailors. It might seem strange to an outsider that it was the pine martens who were the open-water sailors and not otters, who tended to stick to coast-hugging boats and inland-water craft, but in the beginning – when all ships were sailing vessels – what was needed was an agile creature who could scramble up and down the rigging with confidence and ease, not necessarily one good in the water. Otters tended to prefer fresh water to salt, and so as the merchant navy grew it tended to be the good climbers not the good swimmers who crewed it.

After enquiries, Monty and Bryony found the name of the ship they required. It was a steamship called *The Hairstreak*, so they went looking for a vessel with a butterfly painted on the prow. Since most mustelids – even clever ones – were still not able to read, their society worked better with picture language and colours than with letters and words. When they found the craft they saw that the dockworkers, who tended to be weasels, were still unloading barrels of vole-scratchings.

The captain turned out to be, as predicted, a pine marten. He seemed an amiable enough mammal with little to hide. Monty's questions were answered in a forthright manner.

'Prince Imperial? Not to my knowledge,' said the captain, scratching the fur on his head. 'I did have a bunch of passengers from Slattland, it's true, but there weren't no prince among 'em.'

'You're sure about that?' insisted Bryony.

'Well, o' course, royalty don't always wear badges to say who they are, but as a sea captain I'm a good observer of mammal nature. They looked like a load of roughs and scruffs to me, led by this female lemming. Admittedly she seemed more genteel than the rest of them. Now what was her name?'

'Sveltlana?' suggested Bryony.

'No, no, it weren't that.' He frowned. 'Wait a bit, I could look it up on the passenger list but I want to remember it. Sveltlana, you say? Now, it wasn't nothing like that at all. Ah, yes, Bogginski, that were it. Her name was Countess Bogginski. Now why would she call herself Sveltlana?'

Bryony said, 'Wouldn't you, if you were a slender, serpentine female with a name like Bogginski?'

'Nope,' replied the captain, emphatically. 'I'd call myself Captain Clapperbell, which is the name my parents gave me.'

Further enquiries along the taverns of the waterfront revealed that the Prince Imperial had indeed arrived two days earlier on a clockwork vessel with a cargo of winter cabbages. The night the ship landed he had vanished into thin air. Some said he was fleeing hostile forces in his own country and was seeking asylum in Welkin. Other said he was mad on the army and had come to join the Welkin mustelid soldiers in their battles against the rats of the unnamed marshes, a large area to the north.

'Most provoking,' said Monty, as they made

their way back through the narrow alleys towards 7a Breadoven Street. 'Half the story is true and the other half floats in the ether. I shall indeed search for the whereabouts of the Prince Imperial, but what we do when we find him is not yet apparent. I'm loath to pass on such information to the mysterious Sveltlana, since I don't know what her game is yet. Perhaps all will be revealed.'

It was at that moment that a large gang of pawpads came out of the darkness of the alley and advanced to the unsuspecting pair of weasels.

Chapter Three

The geezers who fell on the pair were a mixed gang of club-wielding weasels, ferrets and stoats. There were many gangs around Docklands, made up of ferocious creatures with low morals and bad sleeping habits. Such areas of activity – where gullible boat passengers from abroad step ashore with their wealth in their pockets – attract gangs of this sort with stealth in their hearts. This gang all wore red neckerchieves with white polka dots: obviously their badge of recognition.

'What? Ho! Villains!' cried Monty, unsheathing his blade from its wooden swordstick scabbard.

Bryony got ready with her formidable fangs and claws, the traditional, ancient weapons of the weasel.

The pawpads came in, swinging their clubs,

grunting and snarling, trying to get past Monty's flashing blade. The redoubtable right honourable kept up a magnificent flurry of strokes, creating a barrier between himself, Bryony and the thugs. All that could be seen was the whirling and whirring of his blade through the shafts of moonlight. He might have been a dozen Montys given the tremendous effect of his sword. The thugs certainly thought so, because they were shy to advance. They were very good at taking one step forward and jumping two steps backwards.

'Give us yer purse 'n we'll let you go,' growled their leader, hopefully.

'Give me your body and I'll run it through,' cried Monty, delighted with the evening's action.

This infuriated the thugs who redoubled their efforts, forcing Bryony and Monty back towards the end of a blind alley. The pair were now trapped. One of the ruffians had fallen, having been stabbed in the shoulder by Monty's blade, but there were still seven or eight more of them bearing down on the hapless duo. All that could be heard was the laboured grunts of the thugs as they surged forward and the swishing of their tails which tended to get in the way of themselves.

'You're for it now,' snarled the leader of the pack, a particularly nasty-looking ferret. 'I'm goin' to pummel you good, weasel. I'll 'ave that cloak off yer back and that fancy hat.'

'I want 'is swordstick,' cried a weasel in the mob. 'I baggsy that for me.'

Monty said nothing, continuing to fend off the blows of the clubs by slashing at the forelimbs of those who carried them. Bryony had found a piece of packing-case wood and was fencing an aggressive-looking weasel with a cudgel as if she were at single-sticks. The battle was now reaching a furious pitch and the thugs looked likely to break down the resistance of the courageous duo very shortly.

Suddenly there was a commotion at the back of the gang. Monty heard the sound of poles striking fur-covered bones.

'Take that, you rotten excuse for a doormat!'

Crack!

'Ow, oh Gawd, that 'urt!'

Someone, or some several ones, were fighting the pawpads from the rear. Bryony and Monty stepped up their efforts. The thugs were in confusion. They did not know which way to turn: whether to battle those behind them, or those in front. They were used to simple battles with overwhelming odds: ten to one against a lone mammal trapped under a welter of blows from their cudgels. They started to break and run, ducking under the strikes from the strangers in the rear. None of them got away free. Every ferret, weasel or stoat that ran the gauntlet received at least one egg-sized lump or bruise for his pains.

Finally they were all gone, having disappeared into the thick fog rolling up from the waterfront. One of them must have run full pelt into the dock, because a splash and a cry was heard. Bryony and Monty found themselves facing two weasels, one bearing a lamplighter's pole, the other carrying a watchmammal's staff.

'Thank you,' Monty said. 'Timely assistance.'

'Think nothing of it, guv'nor,' said the lamplighter. 'Just a couple of gaslight geezers. Me and Maudlin 'ere were just passing and we heard the commotion, didn't we, Maud.'

'Don't call me "Maud", Scruff. I keep asking you not to. And I'm not a *geezer*. I come from a good family, fallen on hard times.'

'Sorry, Maud-lin,' replied Scruff. 'I keep forgettin'.'

Scruff turned to Monty again. 'Me and Maud-lin, 'ere, we're good pals. Our great-great-great-great-grandfathers was pals, see, and it's sort of gone down through the ages, this friendship between my lot and his lot. Our several-greats was outlaws, when Prince Poynt was on the throne. They was in an outlaw's band doin' derring-dos and what not, and that sort of glues mammals together, makes even their offspring fast friends. That's 'ow come we was 'ere together tonight. Him being a night watchmammal an' me bein' a gas lamplighter, why it makes it easy for us to keep up this traditional chumship, don't it, Maud-lin.'

Maudlin raised his eyes to heaven but nodded in comfirmation of this long and detailed speech by his companion.

Monty said, 'Good lord. Wait a bit. Your ancestors weren't Mawk and Scirf, members of a band of outlaws led by the notorious weasel, Sylver?'

Scruff's brow furrowed. 'They was, but you better be careful with words like "notorious", friend. You're speakin' of great weasels.'

'But Sylver was *my* several-greats grandfather. My full name is Montegu Sylver. This is Bryony, by the way. Her ancestor was in the same group. That's how we met, when we were at the city library, charting our family shrubs, and found we were taking out the same books and files from the archives. Well, I'll be blowed.'

They all stood and beamed at one another.

Maudlin said, 'I thought you was a lord or something?'

Monty replied, 'Used to be, but dropped it. Now only a right honourable. Felt a bit uncomfortable, that lord business. I'm basically a very simple weasel. Lords have to do things with pomp and circumstance. I hate those robes and heavy coronets. All a bit too solemn and grave for my kind of work.'

'Which is?' enquired Scruff.

'Solving mysteries,' breathed Bryony, as if this were a sacred duty undertaken only by those who had received a divine call.

'Solving myst'ries,' murmured Scruff, in the same tones that Bryony had used. 'Now that's what I call a profession, Maud.'

'*Lin*. Yes, I agree. Beats watchkeeping and lamplighting.'

'Oh, the city needs both of those too, very much,' said Monty, earnestly. 'I'm – I'm just lucky to have the money and time to follow my interest. But you, you're two stout-working fellows. Dangerous occupations given the number of gangs on the streets and the fog which hides them. You have every right to be proud.'

''An' we are, ain't we, Maud.'

'*Lin*. In our simple way, yes. But I wouldn't *mind* being a gentlejack of leisure with a private income. I always felt I could be good at that, if someone gave me the chance.'

'Come, let's go and have a glass of honey dew at the nearest tavern,' said Monty. 'You two deserve that much. Are you allowed to drink on duty?'

'Ho, yes,' said Scruff, with alacrity, touching his furry ear with a deferential claw. 'Ho, definitely.'

Maudlin looked dubiously at his enthusiastic friend but said nothing. Monty took it that he too was permitted a break.

So the four of them walked through the swirling fog until they saw the lights of the waterfront appear out of the gloom. Scruff, who seemed to know the establishments better than anyone else, suggested that the Polecat's Knuckles might be as good as any to whet their whistles, it being amongst other things the closest.

There was a great deal of hissing and huffing, clanging and clanking, going on around the bar area where the patrons naturally gathered. These were all kinds of mustelids, but mostly pine marten sailors, off the ships with a packet of pay and determined to get rid of a good portion of it by morning. They seemed to spill more honey dew than they drank, as they guffawed at some raucous joke told by their shipmates, or yelled at the bar-mammal for more honey dew to fill their pots.

A clockwork piano was tinkling somewhere in the fug of tobacco smoke. In all four corners of the room there were tables where hollyhockers was being played in earnest, for high stakes, and the intermittent rattle of hollyhock seeds in cups could be heard, followed by groans of 'jabbyknocker' or 'widdershins'. Sometimes the cries were of delight, with, 'Yes, a Molly Maguire!' and, 'Well, well, what about *that* then, gentlemammals. A hurdy-gurdy if ever I saw one!' These were all patterns into which the seeds had fallen and, depending on the bets, fortunes were won or lost on them.

They found seats at a table and Scruff went up to the bar to get the drinks. Here he found that the hissing and huffing sound was caused by the automatic barmammal, which was steam-driven.

Immediately Scruff laid his paws on the brass rail that went around the bar, a conical speaking tube detached itself from a number of others clipped to a steam engine behind the bar. It was thrust into his face with such force it almost knocked into his teeth. A voice hissed out of the steam, 'Orders please! Speak clearly into the tube.'

'Er, four glasses of honey dew, one of 'em topped with icing sugar, if you please, barmammal.' He turned and said to a polecat whose elbows were on the bar, 'That's for me. Sweet tooth.' He ran a pink tongue around one of the fangs in the front of his mouth.

The polecat turned his eyes, but said nothing.

A tray shot out on a jointed metal arm and four glasses hurtled down from a glass-holder in the canopy of the bar. They landed, rattling, on their bottoms and somehow managed to stay upright. The mechanical arm, after much hissing and huffing from the steam engine with its whirling wheels and pumping pistons, whipped the tray underneath a brass tap. Frothy liquid came shooting out of the tap into the glasses, until each one was full to overflowing. Then it moved on to another tap, out of which shot a cloud of icing sugar to coat the surface of one of the drinks. Finally the tray moved back towards Scruff, but stayed just out of forelimb's reach until he had laid the eight pennies given him by Monty in a line on the nose of an iron dog sitting on the bar amongst the honey dew slops and pipe ash. The dog flipped the coins backwards into a bucket. There was a clicking, clacking sound as they were mechanically counted somewhere at the bottom of the pail. Then Scruff got his drinks.

'They've got to do something about this rivalry between clockworks and steam engines,' he said to his companions with great passion in his voice. 'It's all gettin' a bit out of paw if you arsk me. Well, 'ere we all are. Cheers. Past the fangway and down the gangway!'

He took his first swallow and licked his lips and whiskers with his thin pink tongue. There was icing sugar clinging to the fur around his mouth.

'Nice bit of sweetner, that.'

Monty said, 'Well, here's thanks to you both. You saved us from a nasty beating, I'm sure.'

'Oh, you weren't doin' so bad . . .'

Scruff had stopped because a shadow had fallen over the table. They all looked up to see a hard-faced stoat leering at them from behind rows of shiny buttons, two of which seemed to be his eyes. Monty recognized him instantly, since they both belonged to the same gentlemammal's club, Jumping Jacks.

'Zacharias Falshed, our esteemed chief of police,' murmured Monty. 'How unpleasant to see you.'

The stoat sneered. Maudlin almost choked on a mouthful of honey dew and tried to make himself look very small. Scruff scowled, glaring at the official with distaste.

35

'You, watchmammal, aren't you supposed to be on duty, patrolling our streets, keeping them safe from vandals?' said Falshed to Maudlin.

'It's precisely because he was doing his duty that I asked the watchmammal to come in here and partake of a drink,' said Monty. 'It's my fault, entirely, I assure you.'

'I wasn't speaking to you, Jal Sylver,' replied the chief. 'I was speaking to one of my ex-employees.'

'*Ex*-employees?' cried Maudlin in a quavering voice. 'Oh, not, not the *sack*.'

'Oh, yes. And you, lamplighter. Have you finished lighting the gas lamps in your district?'

'I have,' Scruff said, leaning forward, 'but you can tell them top hats at City Hall they can take my job and stuff it. If Maud's got the sack, then I quit too. Me and Maudlin is now working for this gentlemammal, the Right Honourable Montegu Sylver, whose granddad saw off your granddad in no uncertain terms, stoat. I'm surprised you ain't shakin' behind your buttons, standin' here before us descendants of the dreaded outlaw band from Halfmoon Wood. I'm surprised you ain't runnin' through that door screaming blue murder. I would be, if I was you.'

'Sylver of Halfmoon Wood? That blackguard and cutthroat. Didn't Prince Poynt hang him from his own oak tree?' sneered Falshed.

'No,' replied Bryony, quietly, 'that was your ancestor he hung, by his heels from the battlements, because he couldn't do his job.'

Falshed gave Bryony what he believed to be a wilting stare, but Bryony shrugged and took another sip of her drink.

Falshed then took out a nasty-looking black truncheon bearing the mayor's crest and tapped the tabletop with it.

'Listen, I want no trouble from you three tonight, or you'll end up in my prison.'

Then he turned to face the barroom and hauled himself up so that he was standing on the bar counter itself, looking down with contempt at the creatures below him. Falshed knew several of these psychological tricks. He knew how to intimidate mammals. Look down on them, from a height. That was how you kept them feeling inferior. He knew this.

'Attention, you mammal rabble . . .' he began.

Unknown to Falshed the enthusiastic automated steam-engine-driven barmammal suddenly recognized him as a customer at the bar. It shot out a metal arm holding a speaking cone which struck Falshed in the small of the back. This blow propelled him through the air and rapidly across the room. He crashed through three tables on his way to the door, scattering drinks, hollyhocker cups and seeds, and money all over the place. Within moments there was a riot going on in the Polecat's Knuckles, which soon spread out on to the wharves and quays and into the other taverns.

Before long the whole waterfront was a heaving mass of struggling bodies, several of them falling over the dock into the water. Policemammals had to be drafted in by steamboat and clockwork carriages, in dozens, to try to quell the riot started by their own chief. He, Zacharias Falshed, was lost in the mêlée somewhere, his black truncheon having been wrenched from his grasp and sent rolling, crest and all, under a platter bearing sacks of meal. There it was coveted by a ferret who had been sleeping off a binge in one of the warehouses.

Monty, Bryony and Maudlin were ushered out the back door of the tavern by the knowledgeable Scruff, who led them through some warehouses to safety. There Monty expressed his thanks again and said if Scruff and Maudlin *did* want new jobs, they could assist him in his mystery-solving for the grand sum of three guineas a week.

'Accepted with gratitude,' said Maudlin.

'Likewise,' said Scruff, trying to be heard above the shouts and screams and the shrill noises of police-whistles. 'Be an honour, Yer Honour.'

The four new friends then split into two pairs to make their separate ways homeward through the city streets. It had begun raining but the noise along the waterfront had not ceased in any measurable volume. In fact the riot was spreading still further, into the Poppyvile and Gusted Manor districts. No-one had witnessed anything like it since the Gordon Riots of the last century, when a prison warden, Gordon William Abraham Joseph Falshed, ordered a brace of town houses compulsorily demolished in order that he might build new gallows.

Chapter Four

'Falshed,' said Mayor Poynt, his ermine coat shivering and bristling underneath the dinner jacket, 'somehow you can manage to start a riot by your mere presence alone. Everything seems calm and peaceful and then you appear on the scene. All at once tables and chairs are flying, good honest citizens, never before known to become aggravated, suddenly begin punching and kicking other good, honest citizens. How do you do it, you great prune-headed nincompoop?'

The chief of police gave his superior a weak grin. He was loath to point out that those 'good, honest citizens' were mostly cutthroats and murderers simply biding their time in the taverns until they ended their lives on the end of a rope. Bringing the mayor's attention to this fact would not help.

Whistleminster Palace was just across the river from where the fighting had taken place and Queen Varicose had sent a complaint to Mayor Poynt that she had been 'much disturbed' by the noise and commotion from the mammal water-front.

Since the queen's opinion could sway the voters of mustelid mayors, Poynt was also more than a little disturbed.

They were standing in the great ballroom of City Hall. Guests were arriving for the mayor's benefit ball. Most of these were stoats, with a very fine sprinkling of weasels, martens and polecats. There was also a token mink or two: second-generation immigrants. The mayor hid his bigotry and preju-dices as best he could but most knew that the engines of his mind ran on narrow-gauge rail-way lines. He made the right gestures, to satisfy gossip and the queen, but underneath he was a corrupt and nasty old stoat, with steel-hard views on which species was the most worthy amongst all the mustelids – indeed among all creatures great and small. Stoats. In his eyes stoats were superior beings.

The mayor owned many businesses. Some he admitted to, others he did not. All the time he was getting richer and richer on the profits made by his factories and firms. Weasels sweated over looms and lathes, but the mayor reaped the profits of their labour. This is the way it had always been: the stoats running things, the weasels toiling. The workhouses were always full of penniless weasels forced into them by hunger.

'I'm very sorry,' said Falshed, 'it really wasn't

my fault. It was that blasted weasel, Sylver. Can't we throw him in prison on a trumped-up charge?'

At that moment the major dodo at the door rapped his stick and called out into the room of milling guests. 'The Right Honourable Montegu Sylver and Jis Bryony Bludd, M.R.C.V.S.'

The mayor frowned and peered at the two new guests through narrowed eyes.

'Speaking of the devil,' he murmured. 'And what's all that? Mrcvs? Doesn't make sense.'

'Something to do with being a veterinary surgeon,' replied Falshed, who was just a smidgen brighter than his boss. 'She's a nail-clipper.'

Just at that moment Ringing Roger, the city's great clock which stood like a grand sentinel on the banks of the river Bronn, chimed eight o'clock. Everyone fell quiet, for the tall clocktower was only two streets away from City Hall and the whole building reverberated with its tones. When it was over, conversation sprang up again. Montegu Sylver bowed stiffly to the mayor and went to speak to a polecat on the far side of the room. Mayor Poynt glared after him. 'Pompous little pelt,' he murmured.

The major dodo was making another announcement at the door.

'Wm. Jott. Thos. Tempus Fugit.'

'This should be interesting, Falshed,' muttered the mayor, his nasty streak showing. 'The two rivals have arrived both at the same time, dead on the dot. The invitation said eight o'clock and here they are, on the last chime to mark the hour. Just like scientists. Rigid as railway lines.'

The two individuals – one a weasel, the other a

stoat – walked stiffly into the room, each ignoring the presence of each other. By playing these two against each other, the mayor was saving a great deal of money which he naturally salted away in a secret section of the cellar below his grand house. Whenever Jeremy Poynt wanted something for the city, like automatic sedan chairs for the transport system or steam-driven taxi cabs, he made both inventors tender for the project.

'Ah, Jott! And Fugit! How nice to see you both,' he cried, going across to shake their paws. 'And you arrived together? Such good friends, despite your rivalry. How refreshing that is in this world of grasping mustelids. Do please help yourselves to the buffet and drinks. I can recommend the peachdew punch. The princess made it herself, you know. Such a treasure, my sister . . .'

They shook the mayor's paw warmly enough but frostily ignored each other and when no-one else was looking gave one another a quick nasty punch on the shoulder. In one corner of the room was a steam-waiter serving titbits with much huffing and hissing. In another corner was a drinks-waitress run by clockwork, whirring and clicking away. Mayor Poynt had been very fair in his use of each their inventions. The next great project was a machine to keep the whole city warm in winter. He intended to get both inventors working together on this particular scheme.

This monumental device would operate below the city streets, perhaps in the sewers, and would provide enough heat to keep snow from the streets and icicles from the windowsills. He did not want to put it through his council, he wanted a *private* project, so that he could sell the heat to the city himself. Thus he had decided to build the machine in secret, using the fortune he had amassed in bribes and gifts from grateful citizens, not to mention the money he had skimmed off the top of taxes and the charity donations which had found their way into his robe's deep pockets.

Jeremy Poynt hated the cold almost as much as he loved money. His ancestors had hated it too. This had the root of its cause in Prince Poynt of medieval Welkin. The ancient prince had insisted on keeping his white winter ermine coat all through the year. (It made him feel more deservingly royal.) Consequently winter had never been very far from his thoughts. This flouting of nature and natural laws (for stoats should turn brown for spring, summer and autumn) had interfered with the genes of Prince Poynt's stoat descendants. Now the Poynts found it impossible to change to reddish-brown in the fine months and the white coat was a permanent feature in the Poynts, as was the continual habit of feeling cold no matter what the weather.

Mayor Poynt sniffed and shuddered. He had the feeling someone had walked over his grave. In fact it was only the shadow of a weasel falling on his feet. He looked up to find that odious creature Montegu Sylver standing before him. One day he would find an excuse to have this so-called detective chained to Madweasel's Stone, out in the middle of the river Bronn, and let the tide work its drowning ways with him.

'Mayor, I understand you're thinking of building a giant machine to heat the city in winter.'

'Where did you hear that, you meddling weasel?' sniffed Poynt, looking round quickly to see if anyone had heard. 'It's not true. Not true at all.'

Monty ignored the denial.

'Don't you think you'd be wiser using the money to open food kitchens and to distribute blankets to the poor?'

'If they're all warm they won't want blankets, will they?'

'But mammals are cold and hungry *now*. And even when it's there, machines have a habit of breaking down. If everyone comes to rely on the city being warm and it suddenly goes cold, many animals will suffer. I'm not saying it's a bad idea, I'm just wondering if you've thought it all through. And by the way, my cousin Spindrick says he's going to blow us all up.'

Mayor Poynt had been about to walk away from this distasteful conversation, but he spun on his heel on hearing these words.

'What? Who?'

'Spindrick. He says he's planting bombs again.'

'Falshed!' the mayor yelled, making heads turn. Then to Monty he said, 'Can't you control this wicken-headed cousin of yours?'

'In a word, no, but I'll do my best to find him and his devious devices.'

The chief of police arrived at the mayor's side, but not before giving Monty a look that would kill a fully-grown badger.

'Yes, Mayor?' said the policemammal.

'Bombs,' said the mayor. 'Bombs all over the place. Find 'em. Find that scrub-faced whey-eater

Spindrick Sylver and throw him into the river. Don't bring him in alive. I don't want to waste rope hanging mad anarchists.'

'Is that legal?' enquired Monty.

'Who cares,' growled Falshed. 'Your lot have been brigands and bandits since Hey knows when. It's time we got rid of a few of you.'

At that moment Falshed was saved a tongue-lashing when the major dodo opened the doors to admit a long line of very young weasels. These pitiful creatures were covered from head to toe in soot. Their wide little eyes were white circles in their faces. Their pink little tongues licked nervously through their fangs at their grimy lips. They shuffled into the room, herded forward by Mayor Poynt's sister, Sybil, who was trying to keep them on a track of sacking which had been laid down to catch the puffballs of soot falling from the fur of these unfortunate creatures.

'Ah,' cried Poynt, rushing forward, 'the recipients of the mayor's benefit. It is for poor little chimney-weasels like these that we are gathered here this evening, mustelids. These intrepid jacks and jills who crawl up our chimneys, keeping them clear of soot: a necessary job if we want to keep the home fires alight. Soot fires are the plague of our city and these young stalwarts use their very own coats as flue brushes as they wriggle through the narrow passages and bends of our chimneys to pop up, high above the streets, great clouds of black powder before them, great wadges of that infernal soot which stop our smoke escaping!'

Bryony called out, 'Just exactly how is the money for this benefit going to be spent?'

'Why,' cried the mayor in a false hearty voice, 'we're going to build a hospital for these little mites. A place where they can get their lungs unclogged.'

'Really?' Bryony said. 'Wouldn't it be better to ban the practice of using young weasels to sweep the chimneys altogether? They get stuck in the turns and suffocate. They fall down the chimneys and from the rooftops. People forget they're up there and light fires underneath . . .'

'Yes, yes, but accidents will happen, won't they? We have to have our chimneys cleaned or there'd be even *more* accidents, wouldn't there? Serious ones. Fires in which stoats – and weasels of course – are burned to death. Oh no, we have to have chimney-weasels. They're a part of our modern lives. Now, this little troupe have come to entertain us, haven't you?'

Timid nods came from several of the small sooty creatures.

'What is it you're going to do for us?' asked Sybil.

'Sing,' said one, stepping forward. 'We're a choir.'

Falshed shook his head, muttering to Jeremy Poynt, 'A *choir*, Mayor? Bit uppity, aren't they? What happened to good old-fashioned acrobatics? I like it when they make wobbly pyramids and fall over in a tangled heap of legs and tails. That's fun. But *choir*-singing. I don't know about that, Mayor.'

'Well,' murmured the mayor, 'you know Sybil.'

The little choir sang beautifully. They sang about snow on the ground and icicles on the windowsills, and how lovely winter looked, but how cruel was its bite. Wouldn't it be wonderful, they chorused, if we had a great bedpan under the city, a hot-water bottle, to keep away the snow and ice for ever.

'Well done, Sybil,' muttered the mayor. 'Good bit of propaganda that.'

When the young weasels had finished, all the stoats in the room began calling for acrobatics. The youngsters did their best to oblige, running, leaping, frog-jumping. For the finale they built a high weasels' tower out of their bodies, locking claw to claw, twisting tail around tail, until the top-most young jack was touching the chandelier with his head. Then someone – Bryony thought it was Falshed – threw a cream cake at the bottom-most weasel, bringing the whole tower down with a terrible crash, and small sooty weasels flew everywhere across the polished floor.

Fortunately no-one was seriously hurt – none of the guests, that is. One or two of the young chimney-weasels had broken limbs, but as the mayor pointed out, this was one good reason for holding the mayor's benefit every year. Once they had a hospital for these poor creatures they would have somewhere to go to get their limbs mended and – he added humorously as the last one hobbled into line – their *limps* mended too. In the meantime, he said, it had been a jolly good show. The singing was a bit off-key, he thought, but what the jolly hey, the guests were all very tolerant of such things. The chimney-weasels had tried their hardest, that was important thing.

'Let's give the urchins a jolly good paw,' cried Falshed, clapping his claws together. 'Let's hear it for the scruffy ragamuffins with their dirty faces and sooty coats!'

The guests showed their appreciation and then went back to their important chatter as the chimney jacks and jills filed out.

'That was disgusting,' said Bryony to Monty. 'Can you credit those three?'

She meant Zacharias Falshed, Jeremy Poynt and Sybil Poynt.

Monty's lips had been tight with disapproval.

'Well, so long as Queen Varicose keeps confirming Poynt's position as mayor of the city, things won't change. Come on, let's walk back to our lodgings. I want to talk to you about certain aspects of the case I'm working on. Also we're going to have to step up our efforts to find my cousin and his bomb factory. Otherwise there's going to be some very bad happenings in this rotten city of ours.'

CHAPTER FIVE

The day after the ball Monty took himself off to Docklands again to question the captain of the ship which had brought the Prince Imperial of Slattland to the shores of Welkin. On reaching the waterfront he found the whole area in a mess. The rioters had tipped over crates, smashed bottles and split open bales; debris was all over the ground. Doors and windows had also been broken and a whole army of mammals was busy sweeping up glass and tidying up. Monty reflected that probably at least half of those martens, weasels and stoats doing the cleaning and straightening were among the rioters who had caused the damage.

It was a fine winter's day, with a weak sun shining through the clouds. There was a stiff breeze coming down the river from the mouth, which helped to clear Monty's head. He found the early morning was the best time to be in control of his powers of thinking and detection.

There was no trouble in finding the boat. Strolling along the waterfront he simply followed his nose until the smell of cabbages was overwhelming him. There was a ship near the warehouses which stood high out of the water. Its hold was therefore empty so there was a good chance this was the vessel Monty was seeking.

Indeed, once he had made enquiries he went up the gangway to the deck. There on the bridge the pine marten captain was making arrangements to take on a cargo of kindling bound for an island without trees. Monty approached him and the captain listened carefully to what the weasel had to say before nodding his head.

'We had such a passenger,' said the captain. 'Lemming from Slattland. Posh type, by the look of 'im. I just takes the money for passage and asks no questions, if you get my drift. Not my job to enquire into a mammal's reasons for wanting to sail.'

'What happened once you arrived?'

'He left us mighty quick. Could 'ardly wait for the mooring lines to be secured, before he jumped from the deck down to the dockside, suitcase in paw. There was someone waitin' for him. Couldn't see who it was, 'cause he never left the coach.'

'There was a coach?'

'Certainly. A six-mouser. Nice little job, with good springs. Looked like it belonged to someone posh. There was a crest on the side. Leastways, I think it was a crest.'

Monty was interested. 'Crest? What was it?'

'Dunno exactly. It was muddy. In fact, it looked as if someone had smeared mud on the crest on purpose, to hide it. It was rainin' hard though and the vehicle headed towards the fruit market. By the time it got there some of the mud would have bin washed off. My advice is to arsk in the fruit market. Someone must have seen it racing through. It was going like blue murder. You would have thought someone was chasin' 'em the way they flew off like that.'

Monty thanked the captain and walked straight to the fruit market, which was on a wharf where exotic fruit was unloaded from equatorial climes. However, before he got there he noticed a crowd of rough-looking mammals in a crude ring around two other creatures. It seemed that the two in the middle were having a barepaw boxing-match. There was a lot of cheering and booing going on. Monty would have passed by without stopping except that he recognized one of the boxers; it was Scruff, the ex-lamplighter. Monty wormed his way to the front of the crowd.

A large polecat with a half-bitten ear and a crooked mouth was swinging punches at the spry weasel. The polecat had obviously been in many a barepaw fight; he bore the telltale marks. And although he was a big fellow, he was surprisingly quick. His dark coat contrasted with his pale underfur, which was spotted with flecks of blood. He seemed to have trouble in pinning down his opponent, for Scruff appeared to be hard to hit. The weasel was like some sinewy cobra, flashing and weaving this way and that, avoiding every punch that was thrown at him.

'Go on! Hit him!' cried a stoat toff from the crowd. 'I've got money on you, weasel!'

'Yes,' cried a dock-worker-weasel. 'Me too. Why don't you clonk him one?'

But Scruff did not seem interested in exchanging blows. He seemed quite satisfied just to avoid being hit. After a while Monty could see Scruff's strategy. The polecat was growing tired and weak. There was also a hint of frustrated anger, which helped to drain his strength. The polecat could not understand why a hole appeared every time he threw a punch at the lithe weasel. He could see his target – the white chest of the weasel – but the minute he tried to hit it, it wasn't there. Gradually he was exhausting himself as Scruff became a perfect network of holes for the polecat to swing at. Not one blow landed on fur or flesh.

'Come on then!' said Scruff. 'Thought you could punch. I heard tell you was the best boxer on the waterfront. Can't see it meself. You couldn't hit a warehouse door if you was holdin' the handle with the other paw. I'm disappointed in you. A legend they said you was. Well, if this is the stuff legends is made of, I don't think I'll bother next time.'

This kind of talk naturally infuriated the polecat, who did indeed have a reputation as a brilliant boxer. The polecat redoubled his efforts, reaching deep down inside himself for the last vestiges of strength. *Wham! Wham! Wham!* he thought to himself. It has to be said, he tried hard, but all that came of it was *Swish! Swish! Swish!* Every single punch went whistling over Scruff's shoulder, or by his jaw, or under his forelimbpit. Not one connected. It was an amazing display of dancing. Scruff was everywhere and he was nowhere. Mostly he was nowhere. The polecat's eyes squeezed out tears of frustration. There was nothing he could do. The weasel was lightning fast on his feet, could bend his body into extraordinary shapes, and simply left empty air space for the polecat's blows.

Finally the polecat gasped and croaked out, 'Oh, Gawd,' then keeled over and lay on the ground, his chest heaving and his eyes staring up at the sky. He was too exhausted to even stand, let alone try to punch his opponent. Scruff quietly slipped off his boxer's vest and went to collect his prize from the so-called referee.

'Wasn't a fair fight,' grumbled a ferret who had lost money. 'You got to *hit* the other fighter at some point to win.'

'Nothink in the rules about that, friend,' replied Scruff, tugging the purse out of the referee's paw, since he seemed reluctant to let go of it. 'Nothink says I got to lay a claw on him. You bring me someone who can punch and I'll think about tradin' a few blows with him. But this geezer didn't have a gaslight in his head. He was too easy.'

There were others amongst the crowd who grumbled, but none of them seemed anxious to take it further. It was true that none had seen Scruff throw a punch, but then nothing he had done so far indicated that he couldn't do it.

The defeated polecat was helped to his feet by his friends. They seemed less of an ugly bunch than the clerks and harbour-workers who had lost

53

money on the fight. Monty stepped forward now and tapped Scruff on the shoulder. Scruff, busy counting his money in case the referee had decided to take a percentage, whirled round. When he saw Monty standing there he clicked his teeth: the equivalent of a human grin.

'Well done,' said Monty. 'A marvellous exhibition.'

'You had a wager on me?'

'No, no,' confessed Monty. 'I'm not normally a betting weasel. But I did appreciate the skill with which you avoided being struck.' He pointed with his silver-knobbed cane, which flashed in the morning sun. 'Tell me, why has that polecat got blood on his bib?'

Scruff clicked his teeth again. 'He was snortin' so hard he had a nosebleed halfway through.'

'So you didn't touch him once.'

'Not a hair, nor whisker.'

Monty nodded. 'But why? Why fight at all?'

'Oh, you know . . .' Scruff seemed reluctant to go into it any further, but Monty knew the answer to his own question.

'It's because you've lost your job, isn't it? Look, I meant what I said. I need you and Maudlin to help me with my detective work. That wasn't just wind, you know.'

'I know, guv'nor, but – but it seems like charity, don't it. We don't really have anythink to do.'

'You will, my friend, believe me.' Monty felt he ought to give the position a title, which would probably help Scruff to see it as a real job. 'Besides, I've always wanted a valet. Would you consider filling the position? Right Honourables usually do have valets. What do you say? It's an extra guinea a week!'

'You're just doin' this 'cause of Falshed.'

'No, I really have been considering getting a weasel. The trouble is my mind's always cluttered with odd things. Detectives have too much going on in their heads. I need to find someone who'll remind me to take my umbrella when it's raining – that sort of thing. Jis McFail has a spare boxroom up in the attic. I'm sure she'll be agreeable to letting you have it as a bedroom. What do you say?'

'Why not?' cried Scruff. 'I could be a sort of bodyguard, too. In case you get attacked while you're detectin' things.'

'What would you do, manipulate me like a puppet to avoid me being hit by thugs?'

They both clacked their teeth at this joke.

Scruff frowned, before asking, 'What is a Right Honourable, anyway?'

'Well, it's usually a title given to politicians amongst humans, but we've pinched it as a sort "top citizen" thing. It doesn't really mean anything, unless you have enemies like the mayor, then you need it sometimes to protect yourself.'

As they walked on, Monty now explained what he was doing on the wharf. Scruff said he would help by questioning the fruit-sellers in the market so the pair of them split up and began making enquiries. Eventually Scruff found a ferret who had something to say, so long as his paw felt the cold touch of coin first. Monty gave him a half-crown and then asked him to tell them what he knew.

'I see the coach, racin' like nobody's business

through the marketplace,' confirmed the ferret, who had one half-closed eye due to a fruitfly bite on the lid. 'Rain had washed the mud off a bit. What I could see was the handles of cricket bats on the crest. It looked like a pair of crossed cricket bats to me, but most of it was under the mud. S'all I can tell you.'

'Not much for two shillin's and sixpence,' snorted Scruff, but Monty seemed satisfied, so he left it at that.

They strolled from the fruit market and Monty asked Scruff if he had eaten breakfast.

'Not as such,' said Scruff, 'but I'd like to treat you out of me prize money . . .'

'Not at all. Come with me, I'll give you a treat. Because of our past nobility my family has lifelong membership of a gentlemammals' club. I never go there, ordinarily – they're a load of old stuffed pelts – but I want to have a good look at the coat of arms hanging in the foyer.

'The club's run by an otter called Sleek. Comes from a long line of fashion designers, so I'm told, but this latest Sleek's skill is in the use of herbs and spices, rather than lace and linen.'

'Only thing is, I promised to meet Maud, down by the river.'

'Bring him along too. We'll all sample the delights of Sleek's breakfast platter.'

Thus it was that the three weasels eventually found themselves in Jumping Jacks of The Promenade. There were many twitching whiskers amongst the yellow-bibbed stoats of the club when they saw two weasels being signed in as guests, especially since the visitors looked like scoundrels.

Falshed was sitting in an forelimbchair reading his newspaper and he almost had a quiet fit. Mayor Poynt was there too, working his way through a plate of vole kidneys. He almost had apoplexy. The otter manager, who happened also to be the same person as the chef, was called to the lobby and complaints were made.

Sleek said, 'Jal Sylver has signed in both weasels and that means he guarantees their behaviour. I can do nothing unless one of them breaks a club rule. Until then, gentlemammals . . .'

There was much huffing and hawing amongst the club members but gradually they drifted back to their forelimbchairs under the fronds of mother-in-law's tongue or aspidistra plants and reluctantly ignored the invasion of their private world. There they made great show of rustling their *Scut Times* newspapers.

'Be bringing in jills next,' one grumbled to his neighbour.

'Over my dead body,' came the reply.

CHAPTER SIX

Following their visit to the club, the three new friends went to Monty's flat at 7a Breadoven Street. There Monty asked Bryony if she would begin making enquiries at the army recruiting office located within Smartbib Barracks, in Cakesandale Square.

'Ask them if any jack lemmings have joined recently.'

Bryony nodded. 'What are you three going to do?'

'I've got to start thinking about Spindrick's threat,' replied Monty, taking his notebook and fountain pen out of his jacket pocket and placing them on an occasional table. 'I can't just ignore his warnings. These two are new at the detecting business. I want to show them the ropes.'

'All right,' said Bryony. 'I'll meet you back here later in the day. Say about noon?'

'An excellent proposition,' Monty agreed.

Once Bryony had left them Monty changed into his oldest clothes. Normally he was one of the smartest dressed mammals on the street, but it seemed he had taken it into his head to look ungenteel. He took out his tattiest pair of trousers, his most worn waistcoat and a threadbare jacket. Finally he placed an ancient rabbitstalker hat on his head. He then announced they were ready to go as he picked up notebook and fountain pen and placed them in a pocket on the same side they had occupied in the jacket he had just taken off and hung in the wardrobe. He added to these items a magnifying glass of very good quality, which he took from the drawer of a writing bureau in the corner of the room.

The very last items he put into his deep inside jacket pocket were three gas torches.

'What's all this about?' asked Scruff. 'Old clothes. Shouldn't we get some old togs on too if we're goin' somewhere mucky?'

'Good observation, Scruff. We *are* going to a rather dirty part of the city. But might I point out that you are already dressed in the most dreadful looking rags.'

Scruff clicked his teeth, knowing that Monty was joking with him.

''S'pose I am. This is me dustmammal's outfit. That was before I was a lamplighter. Used to enjoy sortin' through the garbage. You can find all sorts of useful things on a rubbish tip. By the by, what's the magnifying glass for?'

'I'll show you later.'

Maudlin looked down at himself and said, 'I expect you think *I'm* badly dressed too?'

'Well, not as badly as Scruff, but you won't get on the front of *Weasel About Town* magazine in that cloth cap.'

Maudlin was not as amused as Scruff, and he frowned.

'Where are we going, anyway? You haven't said. Where is this dirty part of the city?'

'Beneath our feet.'

Maudlin frowned again. 'In your cellar?'

Monty shook his head and clicked his teeth. 'Sorry, deeper than that.'

Maudlin found this question-and-answer stuff infuriating, but Scruff's eyes opened wide with delight. 'The middle of the planet,' he said. 'We're goin' to find our way to the centre of the earth. Wow! What an adventure. Didn't that writer stoat, Lord Haukin, do a story like that? Where three mammals went down through potholes, caves and caverns to the hot bit in the middle and found tribes of strange mustelids livin' there?'

'Actually, we're only going as far as the sewers of the city,' replied Monty, tiring of the game. 'Just one or two metres down.'

'The sewers?' squeaked Maudlin, his eyes starting. 'There are spiders down there.'

Scruff clicked his teeth and nudged his friend. 'Always pretendin' he's scared, this one, when he really looks forward to a bit of challenging experience, don't you, Maud.'

'Excellent!' cried Monty, grabbing his sword-cane on the way out. 'Then let's go.'

They made their way down the staircase to the street, with a trembling Maudlin taking up the rear. Once there Monty headed for the first jack-hole in the cobbled street. It was covered by a big iron lid which took all three of them to lift off; curious stoat passers-by watched them in contempt, thinking them sewer workers. Mouse-drawn vehicles – coaches and wagons – went clattering round them.

It took them a while to get the heavy jackhole cover off, especially since Maudlin was actually trying to keep it on. Once the way was open, Monty went down first, down the iron runged ladder set into the wall of the sewer. Maudlin was pushed and shoved next by Scruff, urging him to 'Stop messin' about and get down there'. Finally Scruff himself descended. The lid was then pulled back over the hole to stop walkers and traffic falling into it.

The gas torches were lit. The sight that greeted them did nothing to allay Maudlin's fears. The tunnels walls were covered in warnings, such as, *Welcum to the underworld kingdom of the rats! We luk forwud to meating you.'*

'Rats? What rats? Meating us! Jointing us that means, doesn't it? They're going to cut us up and eat us,' moaned Maudlin. 'Let's go back up now?'

The other two ignored him. Monty started walking along the path which followed the course of the sewer stream. He was speaking to Scruff about a mammal he had mentioned, earlier.

'You remember you spoke of Lord Haukin.'

'Yep. The one what writes scary stories.'

'No, that was the previous Lord Haukin. The

present Lord Haukin is a collector of natural objects. He goes to foreign lands to find sea shells, butterflies, beetles, all manner and shape of the earth's bounty. He's what they call a naturalist.'

'How interestin',' said Scruff.

Maudlin snorted. 'You find *everything* interesting.'

Monty said, 'He even collects owl pellets. Lord Haukin has one of the finest collections of owl pellets in the whole of Welkin.'

'What's them?' asked Scruff, bluntly.

'Well, you know owls eat small rodents whole. Their stomachs sort of separate the flesh from bone and fur, and digest it. The bone and the skin are then squeezed into a tight pellet, like a lozenge, and the owl coughs it up, sometimes with such force it leaves his mouth like a bullet from the barrel of a gun. Lord Haukin collects these unwanted lumps of bone and hide for their varied mixtures. He says they can be seen as works of art, if the beholder cares to view them in that light.'

'How interestin',' said Scruff. 'Didn't know that.'

Maudlin said, 'Can we stop talking about rodents?'

'We're talkin' about owls,' said Scruff.

'You're talking about what owls eat, which is mostly rodent.' Maudlin held up his gas torch, the blue flame wavering in the draught which blew lightly down the tunnel, making their shadows stretch on the wet, slimy walls of the sewers. 'We are down here, surrounded by rodents. I shouldn't wonder if they're staring at us right now, from their hidden nooks and crannies. I don't think we should be chattering about the cousins of these watchers being chomped by owls.'

'You worry too much,' cried Scruff, his voice echoing down the tunnels and making Maudlin flinch.

Almost at that very moment shapes appeared on the path ahead. There were flaming torches in the claws of these phantom-like creatures. Maudlin let out a little squeak of fright and looked behind him but similar shapes had appeared in their rear, cutting off all thought of escape. Both groups, those in front and those behind, began to close in on the three weasels. Monty stood his ground, holding his light steady. Scruff took his cue from his new friend and employer. Maudlin was preparing his 'I'm on your side' speech, reserved for tight corners.

When the two groups of torch-bearers reached them the three weasels could see they were besieged by rats.

These creatures were rather curiously, not to say foppishly, dressed. They wore old-fashioned brightly coloured pantaloons with lace fringes around the ankles, and floppy shirts with lace cuffs and collars. They could have stepped right out of the pages of a history book. Two or three centuries previously every weasel in the land had worn such clothes, but fashions had changed dramatically since then.

'Good morrow to thee, gentlejacks,' said the leading rat. 'To what do we owe the pleasure of your company? Many is the hour we have sat with our fellows around the biscuit barrel and contemplated a visit from above, wondering if our fortune could ever hold great. Life in the real world above passes us by without a touch of its paw.'

Maudlin thought this sounded very sinister. Rats were the ancient enemy of mustelids. There had been many battles fought, lost and won between large rodents and mustelids. In the beginning, rats had an almost-language of their own, full of shrieks and screeches which no other animal could understand (except perhaps for Flaggatis, an ancient mustelid sorcerer who had incited the rats to violence). Yet, here was a rat talking as if he were the ghost of one of Maudlin's ancestors. The speech was curiously old-world, very flowery, with lots of flourishes and gestures from the speaker: lots of bows and floating waves of the claw.

'It wasn't my idea,' Maudlin blurted out. 'These two made me come.'

Scruff clicked his teeth in amusement and said to the astonished-looking rat leader, 'He will have his joke. Take no notice.'

Monty said, 'We would like to speak with your elders, if you would be so pleased to receive us?'

'Delighted,' murmured the rat. 'If thee would be so kind as to follow me, we will escort you.'

The rats led off. Maudlin wondered whether to make a quick dash for freedom, but he was hemmed in on all sides by stinking rodents. They would chop him down before he got a metre. He decided the best course would be to go along with the other two and wait for a good opportunity to run. Let Monty and Scruff be taken in by this obviously false show of friendliness. Maudlin knew otherwise. Rats were rats. Full stop.

However, no chance showed itself. Finally he was taken into a sort of creepy room which led off the main sewer. A rat, on seeing his puzzlement, informed him it was a huge crypt, the walls of which had collapsed and had thus opened it on to the sewers.

'Our elders use it as a meeting place now,' said the rat, 'away from the loathsome stench of the sewer flow. It is dank and dark, to be sure, but what is a little dampness in such a place?'

'A crypt?' Maudlin's eyes darted round the stony cells, noting the crumbling pillars and wall niches. 'Doesn't it worry you?'

The rat moved closer as if in conspiratorial mood. 'I have oft,' he whispered, 'seen the ghosts of dead mammals drifting through the cold mists of this underworld. There is one – a King Rat – whose form materializes before the night watch. They say he was murdered by his own brother, who poured poison in his ear while he slept. A murder most foul. The king's phantom cries out, as he rattles his ancient sword and spear against his chest armour, for revenge, revenge, revenge.'

'Three revenges,' said Maudlin, almost choking. 'That's a lot. I hope it wasn't three weasels that encouraged his brother to do him in.'

'No-one knows who was behind the killing, but we have our strong suspicions.'

Maudlin was convinced he was being set up for execution. They were going to be tried for the murder of an ancient king rat. The fact that the three of them had not been alive when such a king had been killed had nothing to do with it. The rats would probably say, 'If not you three, then your grandfathers did it, and you must inherit their sins.'

'We're doomed,' he muttered to himself. 'We're going to be slaughtered in the name of justice.'

'What's that thee says?' asked the rat. 'Mine ears are not what they should be at my age. The rumble of the carts on the street above, thee understand. They damage the hearing after a lifetime.'

'I said "justice",' replied Maudlin.

'Oh, that. Yes, we all wish for justice, do we not?'

In the streets above the sewers a gang of lemmings had hold of one of Muggidrear's most prestigous sign-painters. Curlicew, the name of this stoat, was responsible for most of the coats of arms painted on the coaches of the noble, rich and famous families of the city. Sveltlana stood nearby. She too had learned about the cricket bats on the coach that had taken the Prince Imperial – and she wished to know more.

'Cut off his nose,' she said to one of her minions as the stoat struggled in their grasp. 'Then slice away his ears.'

A bright, sharp blade was produced. Curlicew screamed.

'Please – please don't hurt me. Come – come with me to my workshop. I'll show you my books of designs. Oh, no – please – please don't cut off my nose. Mercy, Jis.'

Sveltlana's eyes narrowed. There was no mercy evident in those eyes. They were cold, brittle eyes, carved from ice. You could see she could just as easily order the slitting of the stoat's throat as the cutting off of appendages.

'You have a book of designs? With the names of the families beneath?'

'Yes, yes,' sobbed Curlicew. 'Even from freshly knighted clients. They come straight from reading the New Year's Honour's list to my signwriting shop. And I keep a record when customers ask me to invent them a new coat of arms. Come with me. I'll show you. There's lots and lots of cricket bats. And some tennis racquets, and footballs too. You can take your pick . . .'

'If this is a trick, I'll have you killed and thrown into the river Bronn without a second thought, you know that. The crabs will be eating you before another day dawns.'

Curlicew looked into those icy eyes and knew she spoke the truth. He knew that he was going to be lucky to escape with his life, even if he gave this lemming all the information she required. He was going to have to wait his chance, and then run for his very life.

He hoped he would get that chance.

CHAPTER SEVEN

Maudlin remained stiff with fear as he expected punishment from the rats for the death of their king.

Scruff was as relaxed as he always was in difficult circumstances. In this he was much like his ancestor, Scirf, who had run with Sylver's outlaw band. Nothing had bothered Scirf, except a desire for learning. Like Scirf, Scruff's personal habits were not all that a queen might desire in a pet cat. He nipped his fleas in public. He neglected his pelt until it was in a condition no respectable doormat would tolerate. He scratched too often and bathed too seldom. But he had a brave heart, a cool head on his shoulders, and was loyal to the last drop of his blood. If his best friend, Maudlin, had asked him to step on the gallows in his stead, Scruff would have raced up the steps and put the noose around his own neck with words such as, 'It is a far, far better thing I do now . . .' on his lips.

While the other two waited and fidgeted out of earshot, Monty talked with the leader of the sewer rats. When the amateur detective saw that his friends were holding back he called them to his side.

'I was just asking Toddlebeck here if he would keep a sharp eye out for any strange devices he sees down here in the underworld.'

'Toddlebeck is my name,' said the rat leader, with a flourish. 'It was my mother's name before me, and her mother's name before her . . .'

He went on at great length, but finally ran out of mothers.

'Bombs!' Monty said, grimly. 'If my cousin the anarchist is going to blow us all up, this seems the most likely place he will install one of his explosive devices: below the city streets. I've explained to – excuse me – what is the correct address for a rat?'

'You mean like *Mr* and *Ms* for humans. Or *Jis* and *Jal* for weasels?' asked the rat.

'That's precisely what I mean.'

'*Sir. Sir* is the correct term. Thus I am known as Sir Toddlebeck. That fellow over there is Sir Spanglebright. And that female by the edge of the sewer flow is Sir Jallywarble. We make no distinction between males and females in our address. We are all equal down here in the sewers.'

The three weasels stared at him and the rat leader felt obliged to explain.

'S.I.R. Seriously Interesting Rat. Some believe it

means Seriously Intelligent Rat, but animal cleverness goes without saying, doth thou not think? Whereas we cannot all be *interesting*, can we?'

'Oh – oh, *definitely*, Sir Toddlebeck.'

The rat leader sighed, his forelimbs behind his back, his right claw clasping his left.

'I am gladness itself that thee have come down here to talk to us,' he said. 'We are sadly behind the times, I know, but that's because we're isolated. We get left behind in the race for progress. We speak a rather antique tongue, I grant thee, for the same reasons. We are neglected by those who walk over our heads, trotting across the ceiling of our dark world. We hear the footsteps, especially during rush hour, of thousands of mammals. We hear the rumble of the mouse-carts and the vole-drawn trams. We are the forgotten race of the underworld. Sad. So sad.'

The leader hung his head and some of the rats close by were weeping soft silent tears for their condition.

'But you're *rats*,' Maudlin could not help blurting out. 'You're our traditional enemies. You can't expect us to be good neighbours with sewer rats.'

He got a rather hard look from Monty for this outburst. Sir Toddlebeck was peering at him with a hurt expression on his rodent features. His rat's whiskers were drooping, his tail lying limply on a slimy wet stone, his shoulders slouched low on his breast.

Toddlebeck said, '*Sewer* rats. Sewer rats, they call us. They've forgotten our real name. Those who are your traditional enemies are the marsh rats, up

70

in the north, not us. Our real name is the "common rat". The northerners are called the "ship rat". Common in this sense does not mean "ordinary"; it refers to our greater numbers. *Rattus norvegicus*, we. *Rattus rattus*, they. We have a good grasp of language. Their speech has improved since medieval times, it's true, but they do not delight in the use of fine words, as we do. To them language is merely a military tool. They have more words for "cannonball" than I care to know.

'The language of the common rat is meant for poetry, for fine prose, for storytelling. It is the language of the courtier, the language of polite address, of praise. *"By waters opaque of no crystal worth, the common rat dwells deep under the earth . . ."* I just made that up. That's what we do, you see. We embellish, we delight in a purple prose, we florate the spoken word. We are warriors only in our quest for beauty. Do not, my dear weasels, place us beside the marsh rats of the north, who are barbarians and war-mongers and bringers of death.'

'Sorry,' whispered a chastised Maudlin, hoarsely. 'I won't ever call you sewer rats again.'

'Quite so. My most emerald thanks.'

Maudlin then whispered to Scruff, 'Is there such a word as *florate*?'

'If there isn't then there should be. It sounds like a good 'nough word to me. Wish I could make 'em up as good.'

'So,' said Monty, 'you will send a message if one of you should spot anything that looks like a bomb? I live at 7a Breadoven Street. Jis McFail will take a message if I am not at home.'

'It would be in our own interest to do so,' said

71

Toddlebeck. 'If some infernal or fantastical device exploded down here, you can imagine the noise. If we were not all blown to kingdom divine, then we would certainly be deafened. Can I give you a tour of the uncelestial world? Thee would see some sights which might surprise thy eyes.'

Maudlin was upset and annoyed when Monty accepted the invitation. However, the tour turned out to be as interesting as the rats had suggested.

There was one place where the roof had collapsed and a hundred graves had fallen through from a burial ground. There were rotting corpses and weasel and stoat skeletons all over the place, along with broken headstones and iron palisades. Unknown to the mourners, mustelids were burying their relatives one day, only to have their loved ones drop like ungentle rain upon the world beneath the next. The bodies were like broken puppets, littering the low-ways and bow-ways.

All over the city, crypts and deep cellars were linked with the rats' world of the sewer and drain. There were parts where gas street lamps had been pulled all the way through and turned upside down, so now they lit the thoroughfares of the underworld, instead of lighting the streets. The rats even had their official gaslighter, such as Scruff had once been, whose job it was to replace and relight the gas mantles, once they burned out.

A whole new city there was, under the streets of the town, where a whole new set of mammals worked and played. They did so a century or two behind their neighbours above, but in the darkness of the sewers contemporary fashions were unimportant. It was a crowded world, with much comings and goings, and politeness was more essential than anything else. If you met someone on the sewer towpath, pulling a barge full of goods along the mucky canal, you stepped aside and bowed with a flourish, murmuring the usual greeting, 'Good morrow to thee, neighbour. May thy ill health be unstirred and thy nose remain blocked.'

You learned in the underworld not to investigate shapeless lumps on the low-way, nor enquire too closely after a neighbour's sleeping habits. At one point they found themselves under the mansion of Mayor Poynt, and found the grease thick on the walls. At least half a metre of fatty deposits covered the sewer at this junction, having come from the waste food thrown down Poynt's kitchen loo. It seemed he liked a lot of butter and lard in his food, which accounted for his hearty condition.

Finally, the three were ready to leave for the overworld.

'Thank you, friends. Now, I bid you good day,' said Monty, and received an equal bidding in return, along with many sweeping bows as he and the other two weasels made their way through the rats. They headed towards the nearest jackhole to the surface.

Maudlin was so surprised and delighted that they had got away with their hides intact that he was virtually bouncing along. Now the gloomy tunnels with their walls running with dirty rainwater did not seem so oppressive. Now the rivers of filth were not so smelly. He stopped short, however, of saying that he wouldn't mind living down there.

They knew it would be raining on top, for the

drains down below were torrents of rushing water. Indeed, when they emerged from the jackhole alongside the river, they found it was night-time and the skies were pouring forth their bounty. The three weasels received one or two curious stares as they kicked the jackhole cover back in place, then made their way past a drenched policemammal to a cocoa shop where they drank hot chocolate and talked over the day's events.

'I never would 'ave thought it,' said Scruff. 'Fancy them rats all carrying on their lives right under our feet! How did you know about 'em, Jal Sylver? Have you met some of 'em before?'

'No, I never did, but I have heard of them from time to time. I have a friend – Jaffer Silke – whose job it is to see that the river is clear of flotsam and jetsam. He meets with rats from time to time. They swim through the grilles and out into the river on occasion. It was Jaffer who told me of this society below our streets.'

Maudlin said, 'Well, you've left a warning about your cousin the anarchist with them. Let's hope they discover any device before it explodes.'

'Yes,' repeated Monty, 'let's hope they do. In the meantime, let's apply our minds to finding the prince. I just hope he's still alive to be found. There are several dark forces at work and I feel time is of great importance . . .'

CHAPTER EIGHT

The morning after the visit to the underworld of Muggidrear, Monty sent his two jack assistants off to scour the city. He told them to search for a weasel with a lightning flash down his nose, just like the one he himself bore on his own face.

'It's a family birthmark,' he told them. 'All the Sylvers have it.'

'So, we're to look in alleys, under arches, in basements – wherever this Spindrick may be hiding.'

'Just look in all the holes of the city,' Monty said. 'You may find him in one of them. But he's a wily weasel. You may discover some clues by asking others if they've seen him, or one of his devices. I'm going off to see Lord Haukin. You remember, I spoke of him yesterday? Besides collecting everything under the sun, from bottles to owl pellets, he is also very knowledgeable about nobility. He's a dyed-in-the-ermine aristocrat who believes the fall of the great families of Welkin has been the most terrible tragedy.'

'Personally,' Scruff said, 'I'm all in favour of a republic. I don't see why animals shouldn't all work for a living. Those stoats who think they're so special, just 'cause they were born in a bed wiv silk sheets, are living in cloud cuckoo land.'

Maudlin said, 'I think it's a shame we've lost all our noble families. They made this country great!'

Scruff snorted at this and Monty said, 'I'm inclined towards Scruff's point of view here, but let's not argue. Let's get about our business.'

So saying he left the pair and walked briskly to the nearest cab stand. There he took a mouse-drawn cab to the heart of Gusted Manor, where there was a crescent of grand white houses. Some of these expensive dwellings contained successful artists, or politicians, or famous veterinary surgeons, but one – the house right at the end on the left – belonged to Lord Haukin. It was, like the others, a pretty terraced building with a balcony bearing a balustrade of short, white, fat pillars.

In the driveway fronting the elegant crescent was a fountain of natural mineral waters, whose salts were supposed to be mildly healthful. People with both money *and* breeding spoke of taking the waters outside Lord Haukin's place. The fact that the fountain belonged to the whole crescent of some thirty houses did not make any difference. All Welkin's aristocrats felt that if the whole block did not belong to Lord Haukin, it jolly well should do.

Mayor Poynt, whose many-greats-grandfather

had been the ruling prince of the land, was especially of this opinion. Jeremy Poynt was leaving Lord Haukin's place, just as Monty was stepping out of his cab and paying the weasel driver. The mayor frowned, puffed and fluffed himself up, and then spoke in haughty tones.

'I shouldn't have thought weasels were welcome here – Right Honourables or not. This is the house of a noblestoat.'

Monty sighed. 'You obviously have no idea of our family histories, Jal Mayor. The Sylvers and Haukins have been close friends for centuries.'

'Really?' sniffed the mayor. 'Well, some mammals have no sense of decorum.'

Monty watched the mayor's carriage leave the crescent, noting that its crest did not have a cricket bat in it, then turned and rang the bell on the door. A few minutes later it was opened by a tall thin weasel-butler with a nose set higher than his ears. He peered down at Monty through two dark disdainful eyes, as if the right honourable had just emerged from under a mossy stone. It struck Monty that butlers were of a higher breed of mammal than the animals they served; they had to be for they believed themselves to be superior beings no matter what their origins.

'Right Honourable Montegu Sylver, calling on Lord Haukin,' said Monty, pushing past the butler and tossing cane and gloves onto a hallway settle. 'Is his lordship in the library?'

The butler was flustered. 'A weasel? Are you expected? Do you have an appointment?'

'Yes, a weasel. You must be new here. A Sylver needs no appointment in this house. Please do not announce me – your master knows exactly who I am and why I'm here. Just show me to Lord Hannover Haukin.'

There was authority in Monty's tone. This, and the fact that he knew his lordship's first name, persuaded the butler against all his training and better feelings to show Monty to the library.

Monty entered just as Lord Haukin, a young stoat with a monocle jammed tightly in his right eye, was taking a shot on the billiard table.

'What ho, Hannover,' said Monty, using the lord's first name. 'Been thrashed by that sharpster Poynt again?'

'Who the devil are you?' snapped Lord Haukin without looking up, confirming the butler's worst fears. 'What do you mean by striding in here and making such remarks.'

Lord Haukin's cue stick was whirring and clicking, humming and ticking. It seemed to have a life of its own. He simply levelled it at the cue ball and it went TOCK-TOCK-TOCK and shot out its chalked tip on the end of a spring to strike a white ball. The cue ball flew across the table like a mad mouse, missed the red ball the lord was aiming at, hit the cushion, and vanished into a corner pocket opposite. The cue stick then whirred again, chimed the hour in the traditional Whistleminster tune of Ringing Roger, then finally fell silent. It was a sinister silence, broken by the lord himself as he whirled on his visitor.

'Blast! Now see what you've made me do.' This time he looked up and to the butler's relief, said, 'Oh, it's you, whatsisname. It's all right, Culver, I know this fellah. Friend of mine. How'd'y'do, thingummy. Want some coffee? I was just about to have some meself.'

'Love some.'

'Culver?' said his lordship to his butler, 'coffee for two – and stop leavin' those books of poems lying about on my coffee trays. I ain't going to read 'em, so there. You know I don't read those sort of books, whoever's wrote 'em – even those by butlers who think they're poets.'

'Written them, my lord,' corrected his butler, coldly.

Lord Haukin turned back to Monty and adjusting his monocle said, 'You spoke about Poynt? Yes, he took me for a packet at billiards this morning. Fellah's a blasted cheat if you ask me. He's got this new steam-driven cue, which he can't seem to miss with. Offered me this clockwork one, but it don't work half as well as his did. Took me for a whole bag of guineas.'

'That sounds like Poynt.'

'Yes, he's a cad all right. But I need to keep in touch with him. Find out what he's up to. You've got to stay one jump ahead of stoats like him. Now, sit down and tell me what I can do for you.'

They both threw themselves into forelimbchairs which were surrounded by glass cabinets full of 'interesting' natural objects. There were sea shells, of course, and lumps of petrified wood, and a chunk of black lava labelled 'Mount Viviperous', and stuffed dragonflies caught in the act of swooping on an insect, and the fossil of a prehistoric garden slug, and seeds which came in unusual shapes (there was a bean which looked like a frog), and dried sea horses, and a stuffed basilisk which had obviously been frightened to death because of its open mouth and staring eyes.

'Interesting collection,' murmured Monty, nodding at the glass cabinets. 'I was telling a friend about your habit the other day.'

'My habit? My hobby. My life. What Varicosian gentlemammal doesn't have his glass cabinets full of scientific objects, eh?'

'Quite. Now, the reason I'm here, Lord Haukin, is to ask you about noble crests.'

'I see. Just a minute.' The young lord stood up and went to one of the other glass cabinets, the ones that lined the walls of the library and were full of books. He opened one and took out a huge leather tome. With some effort he carried this across the room and dumped it on the coffee table. The little cane table creaked and bent its legs. Dust flew up from the book, having collected there for centuries.

Sitting down Lord Haukin said, 'Here we are. First Lord Haukin's book on royal and noblestoat crests. Did it himself in illuminated text and the drawin's are his too. Hasn't changed much since his time. Fact is, lot of the ancient families are gone now. Some of 'em sold their titles abroad. Others let 'em go for nothing. You know the old stoat who cleans the toilets on Whistleminster Bridge? Actually the Earl of Jessex.'

'No!' exclaimed Monty.

'S'the truth. Father gambled away his estates. Reduced to penury. Rather clean pawbasins than beg.'

'I never would have guessed it – except that

80

he has sort of grand gestures – the way he passes you the paw towel with such flourish.'

'Precisely! You can't hide blue blood. It will out in manners and behaviour. Personally I would fight every jack in the land to keep my title and my estates, you can be sure of that. Can't think why you gave up your title, Sylver. We need the ruling classes. Breeding counts. Well, you know my beliefs. Birthright and all that.' He became so heated his monocle dropped out of his right eye and fell into his lap.

Monty was well aware of Lord Haukin's fierce arguments in defence of the aristocratic class.

'Now,' said Lord Haukin, replacing his monocle, this time in the left eye, confirming Monty's suspicions that it was just for show and not a necessary aid to the lord's sight, 'what is it you need to know?'

'I'm looking for a crest which has a cricket bat as part of the whole.'

Lord Haukin snorted. 'Half the crests in this book have cricket bats in them. It's one of the most commonly used heraldic symbols. Cricket is our national game you know. Even Poynt takes a holiday from being a nuisance to go to the Ovoid cricket ground once a month, to watch his favourite team, Fearsomeshire CC.'

Monty sighed. 'I guessed as much. But what about military families? You know, where the tradition is for the young jack to follow his father into the army? Those families which have portraits of generals covering the walls of their mansions and who use the salt and pepper pots every dining-in night to show you how their grandfather, General Bloater, won the Battle of Stankimoor?'

'Plenty of those too. Get to the point. What d'you need to know all this for?'

Monty explained. 'I'm looking for the Prince Imperial of Slattland. A lemming. They say he's mad keen on the army. He was last seen in a coach with a crest bearing a cricket bat. I'm wondering if he's with one of the noblestoat families who are army barmy.'

'Prince Imperial? Of Slattland? Know his family. Very good family. Very old. Go back to the dawn of time. All them mad about opera and the army. They would eat their own kittens rather than miss a good performance of *Toastca*. But my guess? He's gone to join the hussars. Most famous regiment of hussars? King Redfur's Own. Founded in antiquity. First regiment of hussars to be formed. That's where you'll find your royal lemming, unless I miss my guess.'

The hussars. Monty considered it. Lord Haukin might well be right. The hussars were not mounted. No stoat or weasel regiment rode any other creature. For a start, unlike a human and his horse, the mustelids could not ride a mouse. Mice could draw coaches, but they were not of the right shape or size to be able to ride on their backs.

But the stoats who had first formed the army's regiments had copied the hussar uniform from human regiments. They loved the black furry hat with its floppy silk sock hanging over the edge. They loved the colourful tight tunic and even tighter trousers. They loved the cloak thing, which was actually called a *pelisse*, because it was so flamboyant and dashing, and gave a noblestoat *elan vital*: that special aristocratic energy and look which held him apart from common weasels, ferrets, polecats, pine martens and other such guttersnipes.

'Last question,' said Monty. 'Do you know a lemming by the name of Sveltlana? Probably from a rich or noble Slattland family. Very beautiful. Eyes of a goddess. Fur richer and softer than a mink's.'

'Sveltlana. Sveltlana. No, only as the heroine of an opera. You know the one? About the female lemming who was so comely the god of the sky fell hopelessly in love with her. When she rejected him he cried and cried, flooding the earth, and all the mammals drowned?'

'Yes, I've heard of it. How about Bogginski? Countess Bogginski?'

Lord Haukin drew in his breath, sharply. 'You don't want to have anything to do with her. Nasty. I might even go so far as to say *evil*. Stay well away from that one, thingummy. Or you'll end up floating face down in some dark river, drifting lifeless towards an unknown sea.'

'Thank you,' said Monty, 'for your advice.'

'Think nothing of it, whatsisname. Now, fancy a game of billiards?' asked Lord Haukin, rising hopefully. 'Culver, my butler, will be an age with that acorn coffee. He's an insolent fellah and I'd get rid of him, but the Culvers have been with our family for generations. Tradition and all that. He was with an uncle who's just passed on. I've inherited him. Culvers would die for a Haukin, if we asked 'em to. Not that we would. Honour bound to die for oneself, of course.'

Monty knew that Lord Haukin was basically a

very kind stoat, like most of his forebears, and would not dream of dismissing Culver even if the butler had stolen the family silver. The Haukins kept up this show of being cold-blooded, haughty gentlemammals, but Monty knew that if Scruff knocked on the door that instant and pleaded for work, Lord Haukin would invite him in for tea and biscuits, and later do his utmost to find employment for a destitute weasel in distress. Haukin was hard shell on the outside and marshmallow on the inside.

'All right, I'll take you on.'

Monty was given a steam-drive cue. 'I'll stick to the clockwork,' said Lord Haukin, 'even if it is inferior. You're the guest. See that button thing there, on the base of the cue stick. You just aim and press that. The stick will do the rest.'

The cue stick was hot to the touch. It chugged and vibrated gently in Monty's grip. Every so often steam hissed from little holes halfway up the rod and the whole thing juddered slightly, as if there were a vast amount of contained energy within. Monty sensed pressure building up inside the tiny boiler within the cue stick handle. His first shot was going to be a humdinger, of that he was certain.

He lined up with the cue ball and pressed the release button just as Culver entered the library with the coffee tray. There was a snort, almost a bellow, from the cue stick. It let out a great *clunk*, shuddered violently and somewhere inside a piston powered forward. Instead of striking the ball the end shot out so hard it hit the felt-covered slate table with great force. This caused the cue stick to fly backwards like an arrow, sliding through Monty's paws as if they were a guiding chute. The cue stick flashed across the room and neatly took the coffee pot off the tray in the butler's paws and carried it crashing into a glass cabinet.

Owl pellets were scattered everywhere.

'By cracky!' roared a delighted Lord Haukin, his black-tipped tail swishing the air. 'You hit a moving target. Can y'do that again?'

Culver was still standing stiffly in the middle of the room, holding the tray. 'If he does, my lord, it will not be *me* carrying the tray. I was almost severely injured by the flight of that infernal machine. I suggest, my lord, that if you and your guest wish to play games of this sort, that you do it in the garden, where it is less dangerous to your devoted staff and more appropriate for the type of activity.'

Lord Haukin and his guest duly hung their heads in abject apology as the tall, thin weasel-butler glided from the room.

CHAPTER NINE

Monty left his pal's house and took a cab to
Breadoven Street. On the way the weasel driver
used the whip. Monty took him to task.

'There's no need to treat the mice like that. I'm
sure they're doing their best to get us there.'

The weasel driver, a rough-looking mammal
with matted fur, glared down at Monty. He didn't
say anything in case it would affect any tip he
might get, but Monty could see he was irritated.
'Mind your own business' was written all over
his face. But Monty felt it *was* his business. It was
the lot of mice to be pullers of transport, but there
was no need to ill-treat them. Monty had always
felt that if you showed kindness to mice they
responded well and gave you their best. If you

were cruel to them they could turn on you at the most surprising moments.

Back at his flat Jis McFail was tidying the rooms. She didn't have to do this. She was not Monty's housekeeper, she was his landjill. But she was one of those stoats who think jacks are useless lumps when it comes to housework and keeping things tidy. She had no patience with them and would rather step in and do the job herself. Jis McFail tutted when she found sweet wrappings stuffed under one of the cushions, as if this confirmed to her that all males were about as useful as a mop with no head.

'Jis Bludd is in her rooms,' said Jis McFail. 'She wants you to knock on her door, the very minute you arrive.'

'Thank you, Jis McFail. Very kind of you to take messages.'

'Of course it is, but I don't mind for gentle-mammals like you, Jal Sylver.'

There was no prejudice against weasels in Jis McFail, even though she was a stoat by birth. She had a real soft spot for Monty, who it was to be said was one of the most polite and mannered of weasels when it came to dealing with the gentler sex. As rough and hard as he could be on jacks who annoyed him, Monty was like melting butter around jills.

He knocked on Bryony's door and within a moment she had opened it.

'Oh, Monty. Good. Have you met with any success?'

'Not a lot. But I think we're inching our way

forward. What about you? Did you check at the recruiting offices?'

'Of course and yes, there's a lemming who joined the army recently and has been sent to the battlefront to fight against the rats of the unnamed marshes. He gave his name as Walt Wittering, but I shouldn't think that's real, would you? It could be the Prince Imperial.

'However, there's another thing I came across while I was about town. I saw a poster for a variety show. You know, one of those shows they hold in Musk Hall, with dancers, singers, comedians and the like. There's a magician on the bill. "Miska's Magic Show". Guess where Miska comes from?'

'Slattland,' said Monty. 'But Miska's a common enough lemming name – needn't be our Prince Miska.'

'No, of course not, but it's worth looking into, don't you think?'

Monty nodded. 'Good work, Bryony.'

'Basic, my dear friend, basic.'

'Well, we'd better check these things out before we all go trogging up to the border. Perhaps the Prince Imperial is indeed one of the troupe of this magic show. When's the next performance?'

'This evening, at six o'clock.'

At that very moment the building shuddered slightly as Ringing Roger struck the hour of five o'clock.

'Have you seen Scruff or Maudlin?'

'They're both in Scruff's room, playing a game of hollyhockers. I don't think they found anything when they scoured the city. Scruff had an argument on the bridge with a human who nearly stepped on him. Told the man to watch where he was going. Then the man threatened to throw Scruff over the bridge into the river. Scruff bared his fangs and the human thought better of it and hurried away.'

'Hmm, pity about these confrontations. Queen Varicose is getting quite upset that animals and humans are not living in harmony. Still, there'll never be a perfect world. We just have to try to get on with one another as best we can. Tolerance is the thing.

'Now, I didn't expect those two to find anything, but I had to give them something to do to keep them busy. We'll go and fetch them. Then we'll all walk round to Musk Hall and see if we can get tickets to tonight's performance.'

'Variety show!' cried Scruff, delighted, when Monty advised him of the plan. 'Will there be a talent contest? There usually is.'

Maudlin groaned. 'You're not going to try to sing again. Well, I refuse to play the harmonica for you. Last time you were pelted with tomatoes and a few hit me.'

'It might've bin your playin' what caused the mob to turn against us,' said Scruff, haughtily. He turned to Bryony and Monty. 'It was outside the Palace Theatre. We was buskin'. Just a shame that a greengrocer was nearby – otherwise they wouldn't have had any ammunition to chuck at us.' Back to Maudlin again. 'Anyway, I don't need to sing. I can recite poetry. I'm good at poems.'

Maudlin groaned.

They reached the hall at quarter to six. There was

a young weasel jack on the steps, a bootblack. 'Shine yer shoes, guv'nor?' he asked, touching his whiskers in deference to a gentlemammal. 'Only thruppence farthin'.'

'No thank you, Boots,' said Monty, 'but here's a bright shiny shilling with the queen's head. I want you to do something for me.'

'For a bob? You bet, guv'nor.'

'I want you to watch the side door of the hall. If you see any lemmings leave during the performance, note which way they're going. If they take a cab, see if you can overhear the address they give the driver. There's another shilling in it for you if you're successful.'

'Gotcha,' said the little bootblack with a smart click of his tiny teeth. He wiped his claws on his front where his white furry bib was streaked with black shoe polish, and then, the shilling in his pouch, turned back to his potential customers. 'Shine yer shoes, Jissis?' he asked a stoat with an imperious look on her face. 'See yer face in 'em, I guarantee. Nice face like that oughta be seen by its owner.'

The stoat stopped at this remark and she nodded, putting a foot on his shoe-shiner's box.

Scruff said, 'That little jack'll go far.'

They managed to obtain tickets to the performance, but were right in the middle of the row. Before the gaslights were turned down, Scruff said, ''Ow about this one:

> *There's a little red-eyed jack-shrew to the north*
>   *of Catmandoo*
> *whose throat is full of thunder and a bit of*
>   *lightning too –*

90

he's got a nasty temper and he gets into a stew
whenever he gets tipsy on a jug of honey dew.'

Maudlin rolled his eyes. 'You're not going to say that in here. Look, there's about five shrews I can count in the audience. They won't let you get away with it. You know what shrews are like? They're the meanest, bad-tempered creatures on the planet.'

'That's the whole point,' argued Scruff. 'Tell it like it is, I say.'

Luckily at that moment the lights went down and a stoat came from behind the curtains to announce the first act. This was a troupe of jill singers from a whisker-trimming shop. They were not very good. The audience showered them with rotten fruit. Bryony said it was a shame because they had tried hard.

'Don't matter,' said Scruff. 'You get up on that stage, you have to perform proper, or expect to be pelted.'

'We're all *pelted*,' said Maudlin. He turned to Scruff. 'That's a joke, get it? We're covered in fur. We've got pelts. We're all pelted.'

'Fine,' muttered Scruff. 'You can come up on stage with me and once you've played the harmonica for me, you can tell a few jokes.'

Maudlin shut up after that and tried to enjoy the show, praying that there would be no amateur night tonight and that Scruff would not be able to drag him up on to the stage.

Finally, after several acts, it came time for the magician. This turned out to be a jack lemming, as expected, with several assistants. One of the helpers was a jill whom Monty recognized instantly. It was Sveltlana, the jill lemming who had asked him to find the Prince Imperial of Slattland.

On stage there was a lot of smoke-and-mirror stuff, with lemmings vanishing in boxes and then jumping out of human top hats. There were card tricks and silk kerchiefs and coins that appeared out of nowhere. A flock of butterflies suddenly exploded from a cream jug and flew up to the ceiling amid a lot of 'Ooooos' and 'Aaaaaas' from the audience. Finally, Sveltlana was put into a wardrobe covered with star and moon symbols which was run through with several swords. Blood oozed down the blades and dripped onto the stage. When the box was opened there was nothing but a bag full of tomato sauce, covered with sword slits.

Before he left the stage the lemming magician announced there would be another 'magic' act to follow.

There was clapping. Then the curtains closed and almost immediately opened again. Standing in the centre of the stage was a weasel of average height wearing a leather mask. All that could be seen of his face were two piercing eyes. These bright orbs surveyed the audience. They were the sort of eyes that locked on to your own and held you mesmerized. Scruff, especially, felt the power of that stare. It had him nailed to his seat. He could not move or turn away from that look.

'I'm sure I know those eyes,' muttered Monty.

The figure on the stage spoke. 'Jills and Jacks,' he said, 'tonight you will witness one of the most amazing feats of will-power you have ever seen in your life . . .'

'I *do* know that voice,' muttered Monty.

'. . . and you will go home from here convinced that there is still magic in the world. Dark magic. Magic which can make you do things you would not wish to do. I speak of course of the magic of the mind. The kind of magic whereby one creature – namely me – can control another. Now, somewhere in the audience there's a dog. I wonder where it could be? Rover, Rover, are you out there? Where are you?'

The audience looked around nervously. Mustelids do not like canines. In fact they fear them greatly, which was one of the reasons why the humans stayed on one side of the river and the mustelids on the other. Humans had dogs and cats for companions. Weasels, stoats and their kind wanted nothing to do with such creatures, and while they did not exactly believe the magician, they were just making sure.

'Come on, doggy-woggy, I know you're out there somewhere,' said the magician in a deep hypnotic voice. 'Where are you, Rover?'

Maudlin clicked. Bryony sniffed. Monty shrugged his shoulders, sceptically, still wondering about those eyes and that voice.

'*Woof!*' barked Scruff. '*Woof! Woof! Woof!*'

'Is that you, Rover?' cried the magician, focusing on Scruff. 'Good dog. Come on, boy! Come to heel!'

'*Woof!*' barked Scruff, going down between the seats on all fours, his tongue hanging out. '*Woof! Woof!*'

'Stop that,' muttered Maudlin out of the corner

of his mouth, 'everyone'll think you're serious. Stop messing about, Scruff.'

But Scruff wasn't listening to his friend. He was listening to the weasel on the stage, who was now encouraging him to join him.

'Up here, boy. Come on! Come on!'

Scruff went bounding towards the aisle on all fours, treading on mammals' toes, causing all sorts of commotion. Mammals in his row jumped up to let him past. The audience began to clack their teeth loudly; they were beginning to get it now. This weasel, a member of the audience, had been hypnotized. He thought he was a dog. He believed it.

'*Yap, yap, yap, yap, yap . . .*' went Scruff, as he finally made the aisle and went loping down it towards the stage. '*Yap, yap, yap.*'

'There he is,' cried the magician, 'my faithful dog, Rover.'

The audience clacked their teeth with pleasure. All except Monty. He had now recognized the creature behind the leather mask.

It was his anarchist cousin, Spindrick.

CHAPTER TEN

Monty jumped to his feet and pointed with his cane. 'Hold that weasel!' he yelled. 'Scruff! Capture that weasel!'

'*Yap, yap, yap,*' barked Scruff, delightedly, running around the legs of the mammal he was supposed to apprehend. '*Woof, woof, woof.*'

Monty was trapped in the middle of the row of mammals and knew that he could not reach the stage in time to prevent the escape of the slippery anarchist.

'That creature behind the mask is my cousin Spindrick,' he informed Bryony and Maudlin. 'I recognize the voice.'

Spindrick now whipped off his disguise to reveal his face, which of course had a lightning-flash mark identical to that on the face of Monty.

He clacked his teeth in amusement on seeing his cousin out in the audience.

'Well, well, well,' he said, 'no need for this charade any more is there – we know who we are.'

Maudlin yelled, 'Scruff! What's the matter with you? Get him! Get that evil weasel!'

Scruff's tongue lolled out, as he panted and looked out into the audience, not seeing anything past the gas footlights. He could hear the voice of a familiar weasel though and it got through the haze of his mind. Was that the voice of his master? Scruff was aware he was a dog and therefore someone owned him, someone fed and watered him. He knew he had a lot of affection for the owner of that voice. That surely had to be his master, the one who looked after him and to whom he was loyal. What was it telling him to do? Get him? Get who? There was only one creature to get and its leg was just a metre away from Scruff's jaws.

Spindrick was saying, '. . . so, cousin Montegu, you followed your clues to this theatre, did you? Very clever. I thought I had covered my trail pretty well but I always underestimate your genius for detecting. Ah, I see you're looking surprised. Was it an accident then? Yes, surely it must have been. This is simply a coincidence, isn't it, us being here together? In which case, you do not know the details of my plans, do you . . . ?'

The audience was watching this exchange with open mouths. More than half its members thought this was all part of the show and they were waiting for the climax of the act.

'I shall leave you now,' said Spindrick,

with a smirk. 'Happy detecting, cousin. OW! ARRRGGGGHHH!'

The last yell was because Scruff had finally decided to bite him on the ankle. Scruff then got hold of Spindrick's leg and clung to it for grim death while the performing hypnotist and anarchist tried to shake him off.

'Get away, hound. Desist! Let got of my leg!'

The audience had now risen to its feet and were clapping and cheering, giving the performance a standing ovation. They thought it was wonderful that the hypnotist on the stage could not only make a weasel think it was a dog, but could hypnotize his friends into thinking they were cousins and detectives hunting down an anarchist. This was the best show they had been to in a long time. Look how the dog-weasel worried the hypnotist's leg, hung on to it with clenched teeth, made it look as if the performer were *really* in pain. It was all very realistic.

'Hold on to that bomber,' cried Maudlin, attempting to force his way down the row of seats. 'Don't let him throw any bombs!' Monty winced, knowing what was going to come next.

Bombs?

The clapping died, instantly. The word 'bombs' had been heard. A shrill scream of panic left the mouth of a jill weasel near to Maudlin.

'There's a bomb in the theatre!' she shrieked.

Pandemonium. Panic. Everyone went down on all fours and started scrambling for the exits. Tails swished the air. Whiskers fought for space with whiskers. Some mammals stood still, it had to be said, and called for calm. A jill weasel here, a jack there. But the majority had felt the wind of fear blow through the theatre and they were intent only on getting out. Ushers held their posts by the door, trying to regulate the flow of mammals. They were ruffle-furred but ready to do their duty. They spoke in calm voices.

'Single file, single file, don't panic. Let's get everyone out, but all in one piece. Someone could get hurt if you rush the doors.'

Monty did his best to order calm around him. Bryony did the same. Maudlin too, now called for order. Gradually things got a little better. There was a crush at the doors, but constant reassurance from ushers and others managed somehow to control the pounding hearts and racing brains.

Finally, Monty and the other two managed to reach the stage, where Scruff stood, blinking and staring into the middle distance.

'Are you all right?' asked Maudlin, with concern. 'Are you with us, Scruff?'

He waved a paw in front of his friend's eyes.

Scruff shook his head. 'Yeah, course I'm all right. What's all the commotion? Somebody lost a six-penny piece?'

'Where did Spindrick go?' asked Monty, briskly.

'Spindrick?' cried Scruff, looking round. 'Is he here?'

'Never mind,' sighed Bryony. 'Come on, let's see if the bootblack saw anything.'

They all went out through the side entrance and eventually saw the bootblack. He was speaking with a lemming, standing with some others on the pavement. The boots urchin recognized Monty and waved to him. The lemming questioning him turned – and Monty saw that it was the beautiful Sveltlana. Their eyes locked. Both creatures – Monty and Sveltlana – had finely tuned intellects and sharp instincts. In that instant both instinctively knew they were deadly opponents in this game.

Monty moved forward to intercept her. Without any regard for mammal life she pushed the bootblack violently out into the road, under the wheels of a mouse-drawn carriage. Brushes, blacking and a box full of polishing cloths flew into the air. A female stoat screamed. The moment froze as everyone who looked on in horror expected the urchin to be crushed under the thundering wheels of the vehicle.

Monty moved swiftly. He flashed forward, threw himself across the road, and gathered the urchin in his claws as he did so. The iron-rimmed wheels of the carriage skimmed by their heads. Only the tip of Monty's tail was caught between cobblestone and wheel. He bit his lip as the pain streaked up his spine. Then he felt himself being lifted to his feet and dusted off. The bootblack was standing nearby, looking stunned and shaken. Monty felt the sore tip of his tail and then thanked his helpers before rejoining his friends. Sveltlana was nowhere to be seen.

Bryony said, 'That was brilliant. You're so brave, Monty. Are you hurt? Oh, your poor tail. Let me . . .'

'No, no, leave it for now. It's nothing. How is the boots?'

The urchin was fine – scared and a little upset, but otherwise fine.

'Why'd she do that?' he asked, aggrieved. 'Push me out in the road like that?'

'Because she is careless of any life but her own,' answered Monty.

Monty gave the boots his coin and the four of them went down the alley taken by the lemmings, but they had disappeared into the foggy night, down by the river where the gaslights burned dimly through the dense evening.

The four weasels walked along the pavement following the river. Muggidrear Turret Bridge was lit in the distance. There was little traffic on it, since not much passed from animal to human side of the river, nor vice versa. However, they did see about a dozen willowy shadowy shapes hurrying across, just before the two sides of the drawbridge went up to let a four-mast schooner sail underneath.

'The lemmings have crossed the river,' muttered Monty.

Bryony said, 'I wonder what they were doing? – at the theatre I mean.'

'My guess,' replied Monty, 'is that they hoped the Prince Imperial of Slattland would go to see the performance. I know he's keen on opera. Perhaps he likes magic shows as well?'

'How did you know that?' asked Maudlin.

'Oh, one picks things up, here and there. It's part of the work. Now, I think we'll follow those lemmings over into the human half of the city,' said Monty.

'The bridge is still up,' pointed out Bryony, 'and there's more ships coming up-river.'

'True,' said Monty. 'We'll have to get across some other way.'

He suddenly put his claws into his mouth and let out a shrill whistle, the high piercing note of which had the eyes of the other three weasels popping out of their heads.

After a while Monty cupped a paw to his ear and said, 'Hello, there's a friend of mine. Hi, Jaffer! Over here,' he called out into the fog on the river. He turned to others and remarked, 'In case you're wondering, I have very keen ears and know the sound of his oars. Jaffer has a particular rhythm to his rowing and I'm very familiar with it. He's carrying cargo, too. A body, I shouldn't doubt.'

'How can you tell that?' asked Bryony.

'Again, the measure of the oars striking the surface. The time between each stroke is closer together than usual, therefore the oar is travelling over a short distance. This means the boat is heavy and low in the water. Thus it must be carrying a load. Simple really.'

'Oh, yes.' Bryony clicked her teeth. 'Simple.'

Up until now Bryony had heard nothing, but now there came to her ears the sound of oars splashing in the misty regions of the water below, where night vapours wafted back and forth. A prow lamp swung back and forth, its light appearing and disappearing in the poor visibility. Finally, like a dark ship of some cold-water species of sea raider, the hull of a boat came into the light of the promenade gaslamps. Jaffer Silke was down below on the river, rowing towards them. Monty found the nearest flight of steps leading down to a landing stage and hurried to the water's edge. Jaffer pulled in alongside.

'What's to do, guv'nor?' asked Jaffer, the river

otter. 'I heard yer whistle and came as quick as I could.'

'Could you take us across the river, Jaffer? The bridge is up for a boat. There's half-a-crown in it for you.'

'Well, I don't know as I can take any money, since you've done me favours lots of times,' said Jaffer.

'No, no, I insist. There's four of us, after all. Come on, you three,' Monty called up to the parapet, 'Jaffer's going to take us across the river.'

Bryony and Maudlin came down the steps, treading carefully because the algae on the stone was very slippery. They each held one of Scruff's forelimbs, leading him down. All this while Scruff was still in a state of mild shock. He had not properly been brought out of his hypnotic state and he was still bemused.

Jaffer said, 'You'll 'ave to 'elp me move John Stoat 'ere. We'll dump 'im on the landin' stage and I'll pick 'im up later.'

The four weasels looked and saw that there was a dead stoat lying at the bottom of the boat. It was someone who had obviously drowned, for the body was sodden and still. The eyes stared milkily up into the foggy uplands of the night sky. There was a look of horror etched into the lines of the stoat's visage, which frightened more than one of the weasels present. Maudlin and Monty took one end of the corpse each and carefully placed it down on the landing stage.

'No need to be so pernickety,' said Jaffer. ''E can't feel nothin' now.'

Jaffer went on to explain, once they were all in

the boat and he was rowing across the river, that it had been a suicide.

'Jumped from Whistleminster Bridge,' said Jaffer. 'Saw 'im take the leap.'

'How horrible,' Bryony said, shuddering.

'Yep. Shouted out somethin' about "I hate critics" and then just flew. Cold water kept 'im under. Didn't come up for about a kilometre and by that time all the dear breath 'ad been squeezed out of 'is body. Shame.'

'He was a playwright,' explained Monty. 'Donklin Swaythe. Thought I recognized him. His new play *Riverbank Tales* was slammed in the press last night. Too maukish, they said. Poor fellow. He's out of it now.'

While everyone had been musing on the death of the stoat playwright, Scruff was still recovering from his ordeal on the stage. He felt floppy and uncoordinated. His thoughts were soggy things which fought their way through all the cotton wool in his head. This was a new experience to a weasel who was normally as sharp as a tack.

Maudlin was uncomfortable. He found he was sitting on a piece of driftwood which Jaffer had fetched out of the river. Annoyed, he tossed it out, into the night. It landed with a splash some distance away.

'*Woof!*' barked Scruff, and instantly leapt over the side of the boat and began swimming towards the stick.

Maudlin stood up in alarm. 'What's he doing?' he cried.

'Sit down, you dilly-headed fool,' cried Jaffer. 'You'll 'ave the boat over in minute.'

The boat was indeed rocking violently. Maudlin managed to sit down without capsizing them all, while Scruff swam steadily towards the stick, doggy-paddle. He reached it, took it in his mouth, then swam back to the boat again. Relieved he had not drowned, they hauled him up, where he shook himself, showering them with water. Then he sat and shivered, looking bleakly from one face to another.

'What?' he said at last. 'I couldn't help it.'

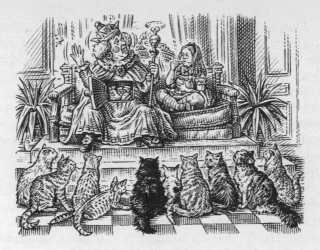

CHAPTER ELEVEN

'I could do with one of the weasel-dogs,' said Jaffer Silke, jokingly, as he rowed steadily towards the distant shore. 'You wouldn't want to hire 'im out to me, would you? He could fetch all sorts of rubbish out of the river.'

'How-w-w w-w-would y-y-you like a th-thick ear!' stuttered Scruff through chattering teeth, his whiskers drooping sadly.

Bryony was trying to dry a shivering Scruff as best she could with some dirty towelling she had found in the bottom of the boat. 'Leave him alone,' she said. 'He's upset and humiliated enough as it is, without you.'

'I'm n-n-not so m-much hoomiliated, as a bit s-scared,' said Scruff, his teeth chattering. 'I mean, when's it g-going to wear off?'

No-one could answer that question.

The four friends were eventually deposited on the far bank. They climbed up the steps from the landing stage to find themselves on an identical promenade to the one on their side of the river. The fog was just as dense here too, and the gaslights just as weak. However, there were humans walking the stone flags and not mustelids. They clumped back and forth alongside the river like clumsy giants. They *were* clumsy giants.

Monty always forgot how large human beings were until he encountered them again. They were massive creatures with feet longer than a weasel's length from nose-tip to tail-tip. Humans weighed almost a thousand times more than a weasel. Human was to weasel as tyrannosaurus rex was to human. There were other things about humans which made them like the dinosaurs. They were great gallumphing creatures with tiny brains, who were fast trying to become as extinct as the prehistoric giants. The power of their senses had dropped almost to zero, so they rarely noticed anything smaller than a dog.

'Speaking of which,' said Monty, now thinking out loud, 'we have to be on our guard for cats and dogs.'

'Thank you for reminding me of that,' said Maudlin, his fur standing on end as he searched the night around him. 'I had forgotten those delightful creatures.'

'I'll be all right,' Scruff said. 'I'm one of them.'

A human crunched by without looking down and seeing them. Gravel spat from underneath the soles of its boots and the stones zinged through the air like bullets. Monty hurried away, along the cobbled ways, towards Whistleminster Palace. The others followed. Monty was trying to think the way Sveltlana was thinking. The Prince Imperial of Slattland was royalty. It therefore followed that he just might visit Queen Varicose while on Welkin. There were so few creatures of royal blood they tended to stick together, whatever their species. If the prince had come to this side of the river it would be to visit the palace and the queen.

In the main streets of the city, herds of humans lumbered by. The four weasels were dodging everywhere. Dogs eyed them suspiciously, but since there were four weasels, the canines thought better of attacking. While you were chasing one weasel two more might be biting you on the nose; it wasn't worth the trouble.

Everything was so much larger on this side of the river: the roads, the pavements, the houses. It was like being in a land of giants with voices booming out in the fog like the bellowing of monstrous beasts. There were rats in the street here, too, who mostly went unnoticed by the humans with their lack of alertness. The rats filched from dustbins or hung around the gutters where the garbage was thrown. These were common rats, like those in the sewers, but street-wise. They stared hard at the weasels and muttered, 'Watch it! Watch it!'

'Ignore them,' said Bryony. 'They just want a fight.'

Massive carriages thundered by, their steel-rimmed wheels causing sparks to fly from flintstone cobbles.

'It's a wonder there're not more fires over here,' said Scruff. 'I'd hate to think what happens when they get a gas leak.'

They passed through the area known as The Dreggs without incident. When they reached the commercial district, Scatter Green, they found it empty at that time of night. Finally they came to Spiffin Place, the posh area of the human city. Here, down by the river's edge, they found Whistleminster Palace, all lit up from the inside with gas lamps and candles. Its many hundreds of windows glowed in the night. They went through gates and doors, passing many bored guards who failed to notice four small weasels slipping into the palace.

'I've been here once before,' said Monty, 'when the old king was on the throne.'

'What for?' asked Maudlin.

'It was when I renounced my lordship. You have to do in front of the king. He was a nice old man. Now of course his daughter is ruling the country. Not many people know very much about her, since the old king kept her presence a secret. No-one knows when she was born, or who her mother was. The king, as you know, had about six wives in all. They kept dying for one reason or another: mostly of boredom. All anyone really knows is that she came to the throne on the death of the king last year, and the palace staff have kept her hidden here since then.'

Bryony said, 'Surely there must be something wrong with her for them to do that?'

'I don't know,' replied Monty, 'but I think we're about to find out. Look, here's her private apartments – that's her crest on that door. You'll notice it hasn't got a cricket bat in it. We'll go in through the mouseholes in the skirting-board, rather than bother those guards to open the door.'

There were two large mouseholes. They took the one furthest from the sentries, even though the pair guarding the door looked half-asleep.

They found themselves in the cavity within the wall of the queen's apartments. A mouse saw them enter, became alarmed, and started running this way and that until it found an escape hole further along the wall. On entering the queen's rooms the weasels found a young woman with a golden-haired child sitting by her side, looking out of the window watching the boats going up and down the river. The young woman – the four weasels presumed she was the queen – was surrounded by at least sixty cats, all comfortably staring at her with unblinking eyes.

'Excuse me, Your Majesty,' said Monty, clearing his throat.

The little girl jumped in a startled manner. 'Goodness! Weasels!' she said.

'Sorry, child, I did not mean to upset you. I'm afraid we rather crept in. We're here to speak to the queen.'

In all this while the queen had not moved a muscle. However, there was a whirring sound, then several clicks. The queen turned her head in a jerky manner. In a very metallic and rasping voice she said, 'He-llo. Who have we here, I won-der?'

Her face was stiff and stern and Monty could see where the steel brow joined the hairline and where the bronze rosy-red cheeks were fitted, one either side of the nose. The mouth opened and closed with a clacking sound and every time she moved she whirred and clicked.

'Are you – the queen?' asked Monty, hesitatingly.

'Yes. I am the qu-een,' replied the obviously mechanical figure. 'What is it you want?'

Monty was shocked. So were the rest of the weasels. The queen was not a real person but an automaton. The king had died leaving this strange clockwork figure to rule Welkin. For a rare moment Monty was thrown into confusion. Then something dawned on him.

'You're not the queen,' he said to the mechanical woman, '*you* are!'

His last two words were directed at the child, a golden-ringleted girl of about six years, whose chubby face immediately registered anger, turning her into a brat for a few moments.

'No I'm not. I'm really not. How could you think such a thing. Leave us, immediately, or I'll call the guard. You could be thrown into prison for the rest of your natural life. All I have to do is scream.'

'Please don't do that, Your Majesty,' he continued, speaking to the child. 'If you give me a moment I'll explain why I think you're the queen, and not that automaton. It's because of these cats here. Cats are drawn by human royalty. They would risk anything for a glimpse of a ruling king or queen. I remember the cats that surrounded the old king.'

'Oh,' said the child, a tear coming to the corner of one eye, 'you knew my daddy?'

'I had occasion to speak with him. While I was here I asked two or three of these cats what they were doing here, and they all replied, "A cat can look at a king!" They never went further than that sentence and I suspect that the cats do not even know their reasons themselves. They *have* to be in the presence of royalty – they have an irresistible need to look upon the monarch of the land – and that's the sum of it.'

Scruff turned to the nearest tabby and said, 'What're you doin' here?'

And the tabby replied, 'A cat can look at a queen!'

Monty went on, 'Cats would *never* come to see a mechanical queen, a clockwork doll that whirred and clicked and made metallic noises. Only the real thing, a flesh-and-blood monarch, would draw them from their homes to sit at royalty's feet. Thus I deduce you *must* be the queen, Your Majesty, even though you're but a child.'

The child-queen drew in her breath sharply. 'Oh, you won't tell anyone, will you? The people who pass the palace every day, while I sit here looking out of the window, think this automaton is the queen. It's all for the best, you know.'

'Hmm, I think you're right,' continued Monty. 'There are many unscrupulous creatures who would take advantage of a child-queen. It's best that as few mammals as possible know. These weasels will keep your secret, Your Majesty, I guarantee that. They're absolutely trustworthy.'

'Are they?' cried the child, brightly. 'Introduce me to you all.'

'Right Honourable Montegu Sylver, at your service, Your Majesty,' said Monty, bowing very low.

111

'Veterinary Surgeon Bryony Bludd.'

'Scruff, uncommonly good lamplighter, secretary, valet and expert at many other things, Your Majesty.'

'Maudlin. Ex-watchmammal.'

'So nice to meet you all.' She dropped down off the automaton's lap and skipped across the floor to look down at them. 'I don't get to meet many animals these days – except these cats of course.'

A general purring went up from the furry creatures scattered like lumpy cushions around the room. The queen had mentioned them! They were honoured. They looked at her even harder.

'What can I do for you, weasels?'

'Well, we wondered if you'd had a visit from a royal lemming – the Prince Imperial of Slattland? But you seem to be kept away from visitors here, so I don't suppose you have,' said Monty.

'There were some lemmings here, asking the same question,' said the queen. 'I heard my uncle telling them in the next room that no such royal creature had made a visit on me. He let them glimpse the queen – my big dolly – sitting at the window. Then they left. You *promise* you won't tell anyone about me? My uncle will be very cross if everyone finds out I'm only six. He doesn't shout or anything, but I hate it when he looks sternly at me and says, "Well, that *is* a disappointment."'

'You need have no fear, Your Majesty. Now I think we ought to be going . . .'

The queen smiled at him. 'You will come back some time, won't you? I get so lonely here. I like weasels.'

'Certainly, Your Majesty. We'll pay you another visit when we are able.'

She clapped her hands, delightedly, went to the automaton, opened a panel in its stomach and put her hand inside.

'My secret sweetie store,' she confessed. 'You won't tell my uncle, will you? He keeps on about my teeth rotting.' She flashed them a white smile. 'But what are teeth for if not to eat sweeties? Anyone want some liquorice allsorts? Or dolly mixtures? Or lemon bonbons?'

'I'll have a lemon bonbon,' said Maudlin, scampering forwards. 'Thank you, Your Majesty. And perhaps one or two of those dolly mixtures? And a stick of liquorice? And perhaps . . .'

'Maudlin!' said Bryony, sharply.

'Yes? Oh, right. No, the lemon bonbon will do fine, thank you, Your Majesty.'

Suddenly the cats began meowing all at once, whining softly, 'We want bonbons! We want bonbons!'

The sound of a multitude of cats meowing did something to Scruff. He went down on all fours and, glaring at the nearest whining cat, growled softly in the back of his throat. Bryony noticed the trouble too. In one minute Scruff would be chasing cats all over the room, barking like a mad-weasel. He *was* a mad-weasel.

'Heel, Scruff,' she said, sharply. 'Heel!'

Scruff's attention was taken away from the feline worshippers of the child-queen, who was now crunching a boiled sweet with her strong little teeth. Bryony marched towards the mouse-hole in the skirting-board and Scruff dutifully followed, with Monty and Maudlin close behind.

'Goodbye, Your Majesty,' the weasels called over their shoulders, 'long may you reign!'

'I think it goes without question,' said Maudlin, 'since she's only six years old.'

Chapter Twelve

Jeremy Poynt, Mayor of Muggidrear, sat in his forelimbchair and sipped a mixture of hot honey dew and golden syrup. His body looked pudgy and slack. Under his mayoral robe the white-furred mayor was a mammal wreck. Good living and a very sweet tooth had taken its toll on his health and physical appearance. He didn't care a hedgehog's hawk for any of that, except when his liver headaches were bothering him. Then he cared – but not enough to give up his thickly stirred sweet drinks and large sticky-fruit puddings with lashings of cream and butter on top.

This morning, however, he was feeling particularly good. His tar-tipped tail stuck out behind him radiating extraordinary energy. Mayor Poynt was on the verge of becoming very rich.

The Poynts had always maintained that there were only two things worth having in life: wealth and more wealth. All other desires were satisfied by having wealth, including enough power to do as one pleased. This is why they had renounced their royal status, put it aside, become common stoats and ordinary citizens – although the Poynts could never be common or ordinary; they were far too clever for that.

It might be thought, by the casual reader, that if they wanted power the Poynts should have clung on to their royal status. Not so. Jeremy Poynt's grandfather, William Poynt, had realized that kings and queens had had their day. Their power was gone. They were simply figureheads, good for the tourists, but mocked in private. They relied on the state for pocket money, which everyone resented forking out.

Mayors, on the other paw, had quite a lot of power and countless opportunities to make pots of money. If you were a prince you couldn't become mayor, because that was to all intents and purposes a step down the ladder. Any taxes one had to raise could be blamed on the human royal family. Thus William Poynt ordered his grandson, Jeremy, to give up the princeship.

Zacharias Falshed, Chief of Police, came into the room.

'Mayor, I have it on good authority that those weasels visited Whistleminster Palace last night. Do you think it has anything to do with your guest?'

Jeremy Poynt pushed a lever on his steam-operated chair. It *shwooshed* steam out of holes in

116

the arms as it swung jerkily round to face the doorway through which his weasel-servant had gone only a few seconds before. Thankfully the doorway was empty and the servant nowhere to be seen. Another twist of the lever and the chair swung back again, hissing scalding steam onto the legs of the policeman. Falshed hopped and jumped out of reach of the tendrils of hot vapour.

The mayor said, 'Falshed, you are far too incautious.'

The chief of police looked uncomfortable. 'Sorry, Mayor. There's only the two of us here.'

'You never know who might be listening. That cockroach on the wall, for instance, crawling over that rose pattern. How do you know it's not a clockwork bug, able to record our conversation?'

'That's impossible, Mayor.'

'Well, it is in this day and age, but perhaps one day . . .'

Falshed acknowledged the mayor's far-sightedness. 'I came to tell you that the vet jill, Bryony Bludd, is organizing a movement to do away with chimney-weasels.'

The mayor sat bolt upright in his chair, causing his back to twinge.

'What?'

'She says that if clockwork-waiters and steam-drive bartenders are possible, you should be able to sweep chimneys without sending little weasel jacks and jills up with a brush and dustpan.'

'She did, did she?' fumed the mayor. 'Oh, yes. And where would I get my acts from if that happened? My choirs are famous throughout Welkin. Parties are organized around the fact that

117

my little choirs will be on the list of entertainments. It's a nice little earner, that one. Who does she think she is?'

'Well, lots of mammals are listening to her. Look, Mayor, why not form a proper little weasels choir? You can go into the schools and get nicely scrubbed jacks and jills. They sing just as well.'

'Oh yes,' cried Mayor Poynt, 'they sing just as well, but do they *look* the part? The whole idea is that these young weasels come straight from crawling up chimneys. They're black from head to toe, soot dropping off them in lumps. It's *appealing*. Don't you know the value of publicity, Falshed? It wouldn't be the same having clean, ordinary little brats from good homes. There has to be something about them that makes the audience go "Aaaahhhh, sweet" – and reach into their purses for a good wadge of money. I've got seventeen orphanages scattered around the city, supplying chimneysweeps with chimney-weasels. How am I going to keep those orphanages running if mammals don't go "Aaaaahhh, sweet" and give me mousecart-loads of guineas for my charities?'

Falshed shifted uncomfortably. 'I hadn't thought of that.'

'Well, you'll just have to come up with another scheme to replace my singing chimney-weasels, that's all,' said Poynt. 'Something that brings in just as much dosh.'

Falshed was alarmed. 'What? I'm no good at this sort of thing, mayor. It's Sybil who's got the brain amongst us.'

'Yes, well, Sybil is going soft on me. She refuses to think up any more of these schemes if it involves young weasels. She says they've got as much right to a decent life as anyone else. I can't believe it – a Poynt developing a conscience!'

'She does?' cried Falshed. 'That's monstrous. She spouts an awful load of rubbish sometimes.'

'That's my sister you're talking about. Though I must admit I don't know where she gets these strange ideas from. Weasels were put on this earth to provide for stoats, and that's all there is to it. Anyone who thinks differently needs his brain tested by a vet.'

'By a *weasel* vet? Click, click – that's very funny.'

'So,' replied the mayor, unimpressed. He began pouring himself another portion of honey dew laced with golden syrup, saying, 'What's this scheme you've come up with?'

Falshed was aghast. 'Not yet! I've got to have time to think about it a bit, Mayor. I can't do it just like that.'

'So, think! I'll just finish my drink.'

Falshed hopped from one paw to the other on Mayor Poynt's living-room carpet, as he desperately tried to come up with a scheme for making a lot of money. When Poynt was down to the dregs in his cup and was making slurping noises, sucking up the final glob of syrup sludge, Falshed at last had an idea. All he did was reverse the scam they were already working. Instead of having little weasels crawling up the inside of chimneys, why not have them going up the *outside*? What were such creatures called, who climbed factory chimneys? Steeplejacks. That was it. They'd run a scheme involving steeplejacks.

'Steeplejacks!' he cried.

'Steeplejacks,' repeated the mayor. 'And?'

'Apprentices. We pass a law saying that all new young steeplejacks – and steeple*jills* I suppose – have to pass a final exam. They have to climb the outside of Ringing Roger. We could charge crowds to watch them do it, creeping up the brickwork of that high clocktower, clinging on by their very claws. It could be a very good money-spinner, that one. And we wouldn't have to cheat by calling it a charity. Climbing Ringing Roger would be a necessary step to gaining a steeplejack's licence and becoming fully-qualified to climb factory chimneys!'

Mayor Poynt frowned. 'I could object to your use of the word *cheat*, Falshed – we *never* cheat. We simply keep secrets. However, your scheme sounds quite sound. Let me think. Yes,' he mused. 'Yes, it might work. Well done, chief. However, we must of course ensure that from time to time one of these little creatures fall.'

'Fall?'

'Yes, from the top of the clocktower – or halfway up – but it would be better from the top. More dramatic. There's nothing like a desperate infant's scream, a dying fall followed by a thump on the pavement to bring the crowds in. After watching the first little weasel drop they'd be back in their droves for more excitement. How moving too, that the fallers would be innocent little weasels with everything to live for. There's nothing like the death of a small creature to move the crowd to the compassionate release of their purse strings. We could run a collection for the funeral expenses . . .'

'And keep the money?' cried Falshed, aghast.

As usual the mayor had taken a rotten scheme to make money and taken it so much further it was now a crime against nature. Falshed wished Sybil were here. He always got tongue-tied in her presence because he liked her a lot (though she showed nothing but contempt for his simpering enquiries after her health and well-being), but she would have tempered the mayor's greed a little. It might be that she would approve the original scheme, but the mayor's variation on it was nothing short of evil. Even Falshed wasn't as bad as that.

'. . . and if none of them fall after the first couple of climbs, we'll just have to grease the tower or something. Otherwise watchers will get bored and just stay away.'

'Won't there be some objection to that?' said Falshed, the voice of reason.

'Yes, I suppose so, but it's just an example. I know! Maybe we could insist they climb at noon. We'll think of some reason why it has to be at that time: something to do with lunch-time. You know Ringing Roger judders quite a bit when it strikes the hour. Twelve strokes might be enough to shake off those little clinging lumps of fur and send them hurtling to their death. What do you think, Falshed? Am I a genius or not?'

'Genius,' muttered Falshed, faintly. 'Indeed.'

'Good, it's settled then. My building firm will begin throwing up a few false chimneys here and there, in order that the demand for steeplejacks increases. In this day and age, where poverty is part and parcel of life, there'll soon be loads of young weasels begging for a job, no matter how dangerous the work. We'll start off with a few of my orphans and by the time we run out of them there'll be some others ready. The chimneys won't cost much. Just a few bricks. I don't pay the brickies more than a few pence a week. They're all weasels too, you know. That's what building firms are all about. Maximum profit, minimum outlay.'

'Oh, yes, your building firm,' said Falshed. 'What's it called again? The name keeps changing. I can't keep up with you.'

'*Weasel Building Contracts, Ltd.* Can't have anyone associating it with the mayor's office, can we? If anything goes wrong, I'll just tell everyone it's nothing to do with me; it's these blasted weasels who try to run firms when they're not competent to run a rabbit's burrow. My manager's a weasel. So are all his clerks. If there's any blame around, it'll fall on their shoulders. Everyone knows all the problems in the world are caused by weasels, so my back will be covered.'

Chapter Thirteen

'As far as this group is concerned, I shall be the weasel who is "Tuesday",' said Spindrick.

One of the two men present nodded and said, 'All right, my false name is Saturday.' Being a human he towered over Spindrick, even though he was sitting down. Spindrick was in no way intimidated by the size of the men present, however. He was one of those creatures who take little notice of bulk.

'I'll be August,' said the second.

Spindrick scoffed. 'You can't be August, that's a month. You have to be a day of the week. It's usual. Anarchists are always named after days of the week.'

'Sunday then.'

'Well, I think choosing "Sunday" isn't right or

proper,' said Saturday. 'Sunday is a holy day.'

Sunday protested, 'We're supposed to be anarchists. That means we're atheists too. We don't believe in holy days.'

'Well – *I* don't, it's true, but my mother did, and I don't want to upset her memory.'

'All right then, I won't be Sunday. I'll be Friday.'

Spindrick said, 'You can't be Friday. Friday was a man-servant. You don't want to be thought of as a servant, do you? That's the sort of thing we're fighting against.'

'Well then, what about Wednesday?'

'People might think you're a member of the football team,' pointed out his companion. 'Shuffield Wednesday's supporters would.'

'Thursday?'

'Could be confused with *Thirsty* in an emergency, when everyone's not paying close attention to what you're saying. When you say, "I'm Thursday," we'd all be thinking you want a glass of water.'

The second anarchist was getting frustrated. 'Well, there's not many days of the week left, are there? How about Monday? Any objections to washing-day? Would that upset your mother? Would that confuse the football fans? Any characters in a book about castaways on desert islands called *Monday*?'

The other two looked at each other and finally nodded. 'Monday's all right,' agreed Spindrick. 'You can be Monday.'

Ruffled, Monday nodded hard. 'Well I'm glad that's all settled then.'

Spindrick had crossed the river and was meeting

with two humans in the crypt of St Pompom's Cathedral. The men were both dressed all in black: black broad-brimmed hats, black long-flowing cloaks, black thigh-high boots. They cast big shadows from the candles in the niches around the walls. The three sat on stone coffins which contained the bones of saints and princes. The men were contemptuous of the dead, especially the revered ancestors of princes and prelates. They also sneered at their surroundings. They cared not a fig for St Pompom, a long-dead jester weasel who had sacrificed his own life in order to save the lives of a party of archbishops out on a picnic when a mad pigeon attacked them.

As the bishops were being punctured by a lightning-fast beak, St Pompom had bravely jumped into a fast-flowing stream. Going for help, he used his inflated mouse-bladder as a float. He was sadly washed downstream into an entangling sargasso of mustard-and-cress. Drowned and martyred, his sacred remains lay in the coffin under the broad bottom of the second cloaked figure in this sinister group. He had been buried with his precious inflated mouse-bladder-on-a-stick – the same instrument with which he used to playfully beat the bottoms of kitchen weasels to amuse the first Prince Poynt, while singing witty songs, such as *'Fie diddle-de-dee, a weasel's life for me! I scrub, and scrape, and cook and bake, and yet I get no tea. Diddly-diddly fie, a weasel lives to die! There's food enough for everyone, except for you and I.'* This brilliant satire, which he had made up himself – a monument to his creative genius – was etched upon the side of his stone sarcophagus.

'So, fellow anarchists,' said Spindrick, 'can you help me with making a large enough bomb to destroy the city?'

'It all depends on how many humans and animals you want to kill?' said Saturday, in a gruff voice. 'If you can tell me that, Tuesday, I'll tell you how much gunpowder we need and how to pack it tightly enough so that there'll be an explosion which will rattle the letter-boxes of the gods.'

'Humans? Animals? I just want to destroy property. I don't want to kill anyone. I want everyone to return to the green fields and shady woodlands with no heavy-handed authority telling them what to do – no totalitarian governments or librarians to corrupt their way of life.'

Monday shook his head, his hat flapping and his cloak rustling.

'Not kill anyone? That's not an easy task.'

Spindrick said excitedly, 'Well, here's my idea. Once the bomb's in place I'm going to announce it, so they clear the city.'

'Won't they go looking for it and defuse it?' said Saturday. 'I would if I were them.'

'We'll tell them they only have ten minutes to clear the city.'

Monday said, 'That might work, especially if you tell them they'll be blown to smithereens. I've not yet found out what a smithereen is, but people get terrified when they're told they'll be blown to them.'

Saturday said, 'What if no-one goes?'

'Then,' replied Spindrick, 'I'll spit on the fuse and put it out.'

'If you're forced to do that,' said Monday, 'you'll

lose all future credibility as an anarchist. No-one will ever believe you again. You'll be washed up in the maniac bomber circles. You'll have to hand in your black cloak and hat and black boots and wear ordinary clothes again.'

'I *do* wear ordinary clothes,' pointed out Spindrick, 'it's you human anarchists who wear all black.'

'You've got to have a sense of fun,' argued Saturday.

'And a sense of style,' added Monday.

'Now, about this gunpowder,' asked Spindrick, 'can you let me have enough for my needs?'

'Seventeen barrels of the stuff. Just stack 'em all together somewhere under the city and I guarantee it'll blow everything to Kingdom Come,' he said, gleefully adding, 'wherever that is. I've often wondered if there's a Kingdom Go. It would more appropriate, wouldn't it, to say "blow everything to Kingdom Go" because that's what's actually happening. Things are not coming, they're going, right up into the air.'

'I'm not really interested in smithereens, Kingdom Comes or any other scientific state or place,' Spindrick said, primly. 'I just want the stuff to work efficiently.'

'Oh, it'll do that all right,' said Saturday. 'It's been kept nice and dry.'

Spindrick asked, 'And where is it?'

'Where's your money?' said Monday, grinning.

A glowering look came from Spindrick. These two appeared to be anarchists and assassins, but they were far too interested in money to be genuine political agitators. Any self-respecting conspirator and rebel was more interested in the cause rather than how many coins were rattling in the purse. He suspected these two treated gunpowder plots as business arrangements. Spindrick wasn't so sure he approved of his. He preferred dealing with mammals with high ideals, like himself, out to change the world.

'It's here, in my pocket,' replied Spindrick.

They did the exchange, then left Spindrick with seventeen barrels of gunpowder – on the wrong side of the river.

'Hey!' he yelled after the two men. 'Saturday!'

Monday turned round, thinking that Spindrick was making a date for another meeting at the weekend.

'Can't make it,' he answered, his words echoing around the stone walls of the crypt, bouncing off petrified lord and lady, ringing in the iron grilles and brand-holders. 'Not at all.'

Spindrick thought he meant now, because he had something wrong with his legs or back or something.

'Well, what about Monday?'

'Monday's no good, either,' said Saturday. He was about to say, 'Dentist appointment,' when Spindrick interrupted with:

'Well, course he isn't. None of us are up to any good. We're gunpowder plotters.'

The men only caught the tone in Spindrick's voice and they didn't like it. This was not the sort of place they enjoyed doing business, amongst old bones and ragged corpses. Who knows what these dead creatures had died of: perhaps something nasty and catching, the germs of which lasted over the centuries. If they had to meet in such places they might as well be nice to one another and get out as soon as possible.

'What about Tuesday?' said Saturday, sharply. 'Is Tuesday all right?'

Spindrick snapped, 'Of course I'm all right. What *about* me?'

Monday said, 'Well, what about you? We don't know if you can make it or not. We can only decide whether *we* can.'

'I'm not asking you to help me *make* it. Just to carry it across the river,' said an exasperated Spindrick.

'Well, why didn't you say so,' grumbled Saturday, 'instead of messing around trying to fill the blasted calendar with meetings?'

To Spindrick the barrels were huge objects, being man-sized, and he appreciated help in getting them through the crypt to the grilled window which dropped down into the river. They removed the grille and yelled for a boatmammal. It just so happened that the otter, Jaffer Silke, was the one they yelled at. He rowed slowly over to the outlet and stared suspiciously into the darkness within. 'What's to do?' he muttered.

'We need to get these barrels over the other side of the river Bronn,' said Spindrick. 'Come over here and help us.'

Jaffer shook his head slowly. 'Not till you tell me what's in 'em. I ain't taking salt herring. They make my boat stink.'

'It's not salt herring,' said Spindrick, patiently.

'Well, what is it then?'

'Pepper. Black pepper.'

Jaffer still wasn't sure. 'Black pepper, eh? They look big barrels. I could only take one at a time. What's anyone want wiv all that much black pepper?'

'What do you care?' growled one of the men in black cloaks. 'It's a shipment just in from Jamaycky Island, but they dropped it on the wrong side of the river by mistake.'

'In a crypt,' said Jaffer, and added sarcastically, 'because they wanted to pickle the dead.'

'No, no, it was a mistake,' muttered Spindrick. 'A mistake that's all. We just used the crypt to get them closer to the river's edge, so we could get a boat like yours to take them across. Are you going to help us or not? Come on, we haven't got all day.'

'All right,' said Jaffer. 'Cost you a bob a barrel.'

'What?' cried Spindrick, but then he quickly changed his tune as soon as he saw there was no other vessel within calling distance. 'Oh, all right – a shilling a barrel it is. Now bring your craft in closer so we can lower the first one onto it.'

Jaffer did as he was told, mooring on an iron ring set in the wall of the river. As the two men and the weasel struggled to get the barrel of pepper into his boat he took out his old clay pipe and went to light it.

'NO!' cried Spindrick, almost letting the barrel drop into the water. 'Put that out!'

Jaffer blinked. 'Beg pardy?'

'Sorry, didn't mean to yell,' replied Spindrick, greasily, as the two men suddenly backed away from the river's edge. 'The, er, pepper is very – very sensitive to smoke. Rare spice, you understand.

Don't want its fragrance damaged by tobacco smoke. Hope you don't mind.'

'Why didn't you say so?' he muttered in reply, tapping out his pipe on the gunwales and letting a wadge of red-hot tobacco fall into the bottom of the boat, 'Stead of just yellin' at me like that.'

The three creatures on land watched wide-eyed as the glowing tobacco fell slowly downwards – then relaxed in an uneasy sweat to see it sizzle in the bilge water under the middle seat.

Spindrick had an unhappy two hours while Jaffer rowed his barrels over the river, one at a time, until they were all piled on the other bank of the river. He paid him seventeen shiny shillings, then got a carter to take the barrels, one by one, to a cellar in Limpole Street.

There he took out the blueprints of his mighty bomb.

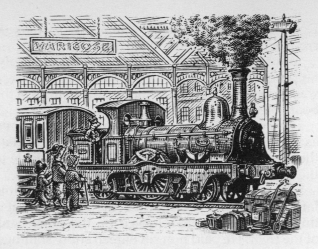

CHAPTER FOURTEEN

'There's nothing else for it. We'll have to go north to see if the Prince Imperial has joined the army,' said Monty. 'It'll probably be under an assumed name, but there can't be too many lemmings in our regiments. We'll look very closely at the hussars.'

They were gathered at Monty's flat at 7a Breadoven Street. It was evening. A bank of fog was pressing its cheeks against the window. Outside, the street lamps were balls of hazy light in the dense vapours coming up from the river. The noise of the day had died and the evening sounds were muted. Smells lingered from the aromatic markets. And the rumble of mouse-carts, the chug of the occasional steamcar, the whirr of various clockwork motors, all added to the evening's dull cacophony.

Cobbled Garden had now closed, leaving the poorer street mammals – mostly weasels – to root around in the gutter for cabbage stalks and carrot tops. Rotten apples and daffodil flowers were snatched up and eaten with equal gusto.

Further along the river Smudgerfield Meat Market was still busy, but then it hardly closed at all. It simply slowed down to an almost-stop in the middle of the night, then picked up speed again. Mouse, vole, rabbit and other carcasses were carried from wagons and hung on hooks, ready to be butchered for the following morning's trade. The mice which were slaughtered for the table were of course a different type to those which were beasts of burden. It was the large field mouse which drew the cart and plough, and the smaller harvest and wood mouse which found its way to the plates of the carnivores. Similarly, the bank vole was raised in herds for its meat and the field vole for its milk. The water vole of course, as large as a rat, was not used for any domestic purpose.

The shrew however, was different. Same size, but different. It was a savage and intelligent animal.

On the human side of the river, the Swift Street presses were being oiled, ready to go into action on the following day. Reporters were already out gathering their copy. The mustelids did not produce any newspapers. They were not on the whole fond of reading though a few of them could do so if they moved their lips. Monty and other mustelids bought *The Chimes* or *Scut Times* in specially printed editions – small and wieldy – for him and his kind. Stoats such as Lord Haukin and one or two university professors, were unusual in their love of books and the printed word.

'Bryony,' said Monty, 'I would ask that you remain here, in Muggidrear, and keep a weather eye open for anything unusual. It could be the Prince Imperial is still here, somewhere, though I've heard not a whisper from our usual sources of information. Do you mind staying behind while we take the train up to the front line?'

'Not at all,' said the vet. 'I have no desire to see cannons blasting away at rat defences.'

'Oh, I have,' cried Maudlin, eagerly. 'I've often thought I should join the army. I think I'd make a fine cavalry officer. Those hussar hats! Wouldn't I look grand?'

'You'd look a treat,' said Scruff, generously. 'For meself, I'd probably be a common soldier and stuck in some trench or behind some rock or somethink. Not my idea of a good time. You, though, Maud – you'd look like a prince, wiv a fine uniform on.'

'Yes, I would, wouldn't I?'

At that moment there was a tapping at the door. Monty opened it expecting to find Jis McFail with a tray of mugs full of hot chocolate, only to discover Jaffer Silke. The otter stood, cap in paw, and indicated that he would like a word with Monty in private. Monty stepped outside the door and closed it quietly behind him. Those in the room heard a low whisper but could not make out what was being said. Finally there was the sound of goodbyes and Monty came back in again. Jaffer had gone. They could hear his paws on the wooden stairs which led to the street.

'What was all that about?' asked Bryony.

'I'll tell you later,' said Monty. 'I don't mean to be secretive, but this is family business.'

'Fair 'nough,' Scruff said, pinching one of his fleas between two claws. 'Family business is private business.'

Maudlin wanted to argue. He hated secrets. No, that wasn't altogether true. He didn't mind them if he was privy to them, but not when he was on the outside of them. They seemed monstrous things then. Quite unacceptable. Those who kept them lacked manners and breeding. When there were secrets around he always imagined they were there to provoke him, that he was the target.

'Don't you think, if we're a group, that we should all know what's going on?' he said, stiffly.

'It wouldn't do any good,' said Monty. 'It doesn't involve you.'

If there was one thing Maudlin hated more than secrets it was things that didn't involve him.

'I wonder you want us involved at all,' he said with a good deal of starch in his tone. 'I suppose we're too common to be let into anything more than basic footwork. That's our lot, I suppose, as ordinary street weasels? To be used then cast aside.'

Scruff clicked his teeth and put his forelimb around the shoulders of his closest friend. 'Don't be so dramatic, Maud. We're not bein' pushed aside. Let Jal Montegu do things the best way he sees 'em. You an' me, we don't need to know every nut and bolt. Look, we're on our way to see the army in action! That's good, ain't it?'

Maudlin cheered up. Yes it was. Moreover he'd

never before been on a steam train. That would be exciting in itself.

The following morning the three jack weasels went to Varicose railway station where there were various huge trains half-hidden in clouds of steam. Most of these were for transporting humans but the last three tracks had what the humans called 'model trains' and were constructed especially for mustelids. These engines and their carriages ran on narrow-gauge lines, had weasel drivers and fire-mammals. The engines were painted either green or red and the carriages in cream or yellow with black markings. On the engines there were shiny brass pipes and taps, brass handles and plates, and it was all too much for Maudlin.

'They're beautiful!' he breathed.

'I have to agree with you there,' said Monty. 'They have a certain beauty combined with power which makes the heart race in pleasure.'

They went up to the engine and watched a fire-mammal feeding the great steel beast with coal. Sooty smoke was issuing from the chimney, covering everything within its reach in smut. The firebox glowed red from within. The driver was opening and closing valves, letting steam out, trap-ping steam in. Glass-fronted gauges showed that pressure was building within the boiler: energy waiting for release through the great pistons, round and round pipes, tunnels and bores, and eventually into the steel wheels.

The firemammal looked up and clicked his teeth.

'Want to know the names of things? I allus think the names of things is like unfoldin' bits of wrapped magic, like sticky sweets out of a paper bag. Looky here . . .'

He began pointing to various tubes, pipes, grates and iron doors, telling the wide-mouthed weasels what they were called.

There were smoke tubes, fire tubes, steam tubes; a mud drum; sand pipes and blast pipes; feed valves and safety valves; an ash pan with damper doors; a whistle valve handle; a drop gate lever; an automatic lubricant pump; firehold shield and fire-hole door; firewater preheater and top feedwater tray; and a host of other wonderful bits of language which altogether made up this fairytale metal monster.

'O steam locomotive!' cried Maudlin in his most poetical voice. 'I am entranced by your beauty! O steam locomotive, what base tongue can tell of your mystical parts? I will ride you into the wide and whistling mouth of the wind! I will breath your smutty breath! I will stand in your steam and stare at your manifold taps and wheels and gauges and levers and pumps! You are made in the forge of the gods and given to mustelids, that they might know something of each of heaven and hell. I bow before your majesty, your might, o iron dragon, o steel-muscled mouse.'

'Wery nicely said,' the firemammal stated, with a nod of approval. 'Couldn't 'ave put it better meself.'

The driver suddenly pulled the chain on the steam whistle and the engine let out an urgent shriek of joy.

This was a signal for the three weasels to get themselves aboard, which they did in unseemly haste. Once in the carriage, they settled down together, facing a stoat bishop, a pine marten and her two kittens and a travelling sales weasel with a cardboard suitcase who seemed nervous and distracted. The bishop stared straight ahead; the pine marten's attention was on her young; but the salesmammal's eyes were darting everywhere, one second staring out of the window, the next into Maudlin's face.

Another poop from the engine, the weasel guard waving a green flag, a hissing and grinding, and they were pulling out of the station. Soon they were rattling over the points, and clackety-clacking northwards along the rail which would lead them to the unnamed marshes.

Maudlin rushed to the window, opened it, and put his head outside to see where they were going. One of the young martens tugged at his leg.

'You're not supposed to do that,' said the young-ster, primly. 'There's a notice there.'

Maudlin glowered at the youngster and then looked to see where she was pointing. Sure enough there was a notice below the window which read: DO NOT PUT YOUR HEAD OUT OF THE WINDOW.

'Don't see why,' muttered Maudlin.

'Because,' said the prim little marten, 'it might get knocked off by a bridge or a train coming the other way. Isn't that so, Mamma?'

The kitten's mother nodded emphatically. 'Quite right, my pet.'

'It's my head,' argued Maudlin. 'If I want to knock if off, I will, so there.'

He put it outside again into the rushing wind, only to be covered in ash from the locomotive's chimney. Coughing and spluttering he stayed where he was as long as possible, so as not to lose face. The air was full of little bits of soot and ash which got into his eyes, mouth and nose, and was layering his collar slowly and steadily with grime, turning it into something slate grey and unseemly.

The countryside sped by, green and beautiful with fields full of grazing voles and high-banked streams running twisting through them. Out here, out of the great city of Muggidrear, nature was beginning to turn its attention to spring. Blossoms were settling like snow on the bushes and trees and yellow-headed flowers were everywhere.

It was all very lovely, but the smoke became too much. Finally Maudlin retracted his head and went and sat down. The two marten kittens clacked their teeth in amusement. Monty looked at him and shook his head sadly. Scruff winked, as if to say, you and me are like two peas in a pod now. When he stared at himself in the oval mirror, just below the netting which held the suitcases, he saw that his face was covered in soot. Only his white eyes peered out, as if from behind a dark screen. They looked sore and bloodshot.

'Serve you right, Maudlin,' he said to his reflection, on seeing the humour in it all. 'Teach you to pay attention to notices.'

The mother pine marten nodded her approval of this remark.

Later they sped through several grim-looking northern towns, full of fabric factories, where the houses were in back-to-back rows and their rooftops and chimneys swept up and down in graceful columns, following streets which finally led them out of their dingy environment into a world of light and colour. There were weasels in their thousands in these towns, weaving a living from their labour. Finally, there were no more towns, only single dwellings like lonely cast-away boxes, stuck in amongst the crags and gulleys of a rugged landscape. Even these were not to last, for they turned to turf-roofed crofts shaped like a rough dome, the smoke curling up from a drystone chimney in the middle of each mound.

Chapter Fifteen

The steam train sped on until it was night. The
bishop had said nothing. He simply sat there and
stared at the three jack weasels. The mother marten
and two kittens got out at a small country station
called Hoppingononeleg, halfway to the marshes.
Monty and Scruff got up and went out into the
corridor to stretch their limbs. The weasel salesmammal with the cardboard suitcase leaned
forward and asked Maudlin if he was interested in
the music of the ocarina. The salesmammal had a
haunted look. He seemed not to have slept for
a month by the look of his eyes and the trembling
of his paws. Maudlin wondered whether this was
because he had been particularly unsuccessful at
selling things lately.

'Ocarina?' said Maudlin as more night went by

outside the window. 'What's that?' His voice revealed his wariness. He thought the weasel's cardboard suitcase might be full of these objects and he knew he was weak when it came to a hard sales pitch.

Shaking like a leaf in the wind the weasel stared hard into Maudlin's eyes, making him feel rather uncomfortable. It was the stare of someone close to madness. Surely it wasn't that bad for the sales-mammal? And if it was, he should change his job, quickly.

The salesmammal croaked, 'They're musical instruments. You look like a musical weasel. Do you play?'

'Do I play what?'

'Anything. Any instrument at all.'

'I can whistle quite well, through my two front fangs.'

'Good. Excellent!' The salesmammal took down his suitcase. 'What about an ocarina? They're really the vogue at the moment. Everyone's playing an ocarina.'

He opened his suitcase and withdrew a crude shape of unglazed pottery which looked like a lemon with a tag on the side. The salesmammal showed Maudlin that when you blew into the tag bit, which was the mouthpiece, and played your claws down the holes in the hollow lemon, an eerie hollow-sounding tune could be played. He only played a few short notes, then glancing qiuckly at the window, he swiftly took the instrument from his mouth. He seemed to be looking for something and when it failed to come he turned again to Maudlin and resumed his encouraging sales-tone. 'It's easy to learn. I couldn't play a note two weeks ago. It sort of teaches you as you go along.'

'Really?' said Maudlin. 'Let me have a go.'

'No, I can't do that. It's unhygienic.' He glanced towards the door. Monty and Scruff were just outside, talking, framed in the blackness of nowhere and anywhere. 'Look, if you want it, you can have it. No charge. Do you want it?' There was a certain anxiousness to the weasel's tone, which bothered Maudlin every so slightly. 'Say you want it and you can have it.'

'Yes,' said Maudlin, stretching out his paw.

The salesmammal held back. 'No – you must say – "I want the ocarina". Say it. "I want the ocarina".'

By now a desperation had crept into the sales-mammal's voice. It was almost as if he were on the edge of a nightmare. He stared into Maudlin's eyes with anxiety pouring from every follicle on his coat.

Maudlin felt sorry for him. 'Oh, all right, *I want the ocarina*. There, I've said it.' He took the instrument from the other's paw. 'I must say you have to be new to this job. You're too eager for a sale – much too desperate. You must try to be a little less fervent in your approach. Not everyone's as soft as I am when it comes to these things.' Maudlin reached down and felt in his pocket for some change. 'How much is it?' he asked, looking up.

But the salesmammal was gone.

Maudlin asked the bishop, 'Where did he go to?'

The bishop was reading a black book, his lips moving, saying the words very slowly and carefully. It seemed he did not like to be interrupted in this exercise. He huffed. 'Who?' he said.

'That sales weasel. He gave me this ocarina, then he seemed to vanish . . . Oh, did you see that weasel pass you?' Maudlin asked, as the other two came back in to their seats.

Monty replied, 'What weasel? Oh, that sales fellow. Yes, he hurried along the corridor, carrying his cardboard suitcase. Why?'

'Well, he sold me this, but he didn't wait for any payment.'

Maudlin held up the terracotta instrument.

Scruff groaned. 'You bin wastin' your money again? You remember what happened when you bought that mouf organ.'

'It was a harmonica,' said Maudlin, huffily. 'Anyway, it was faulty.'

'It wasn't faulty. You got no ear for music, that's what it was. You spent three weeks drivin' me barmy, running up and down the scales, and never a tune did I hear from you.'

'Huh!' exclaimed Maudlin. 'Well, I didn't pay for this one. He gave it to me.'

'What's that that's wrote on the side?' asked Scruff. 'Under the holes.'

Maudlin, who had not seen anything written on the ocarina, now turned it over in his paw. Sure enough there were some words etched into the baked clay. He read them, slowly, his lips moving with the rhythm of the words: **Play a tune and I'll drop my lune**.

'What's a lune?' asked Scruff.

The stoat bishop looked up, glad to be able to show off his learning. 'A lune is a hawk's leash or lead.'

'Drop the leash? That means let it off the lead.' murmured Monty. 'That sounds a bit ominous, doesn't it?'

'Not really,' replied Scruff. 'It would be if Maud could get anywhere near a tune, but he can't play to save 'is life.'

'Huh!' muttered Maudlin. 'So you think!'

He put the ocarina to his mouth and blew. Without knowing how he did it, his claws flew over the holes. What came out of the instrument was one of the most uncanny tunes any of them in the carriage had ever heard before. It was a ghostly sound, as if from somewhere beyond the natural world, beyond the ken of weasel or stoat. It crept into their bones, an ancient, mysterious melody – primitive, primal, uncivilized – each eerie unnatural note carefully shadowing the next. It was a hollow, mooning sound. Folk music, perhaps roughly composed by savage owls deep in Welkin's past, and never refined? For some reason it chilled the very blood of every occupant of the carriage and all wanted the sound to stop, yet could make no actual protest. Finally one of them found the strength to make his mouth work.

'Stop!' protested the bishop. 'This is a fiendish music. I feel it in my very bones. We are playing with the very forces of evil here . . .'

'Hey!' cried Maudlin, delighted, taking the instrument from his mouth, 'I didn't know I could play like that! I must be a natural. I must have ocarina talent packed into my face and claws. Maybe my father played one? Or my grand-mother? It's a family gift.'

He was full of himself.

145

But even as he spoke, something wicked, something quite evil which resembled a black ragged bedsheet, came hurtling out of the night to flap against the window of the carriage. Blown in by a malignant wind, the evil entity billowed and twisted out in the darkness, buffeting the pane as if trying to force an entry. It had a face so strange and chilling it would have made a grown man's heart stop beating and cause him to drop dead in his tracks. Weasels – and stoats – were made of sterner stuff, however. They simply screamed and threw things at the window to make the fiend go away.

'What is it?' shrieked Maudlin. 'Is it after me?'

Monty, the calmest of all those present, said, 'It wants all of us by the look of it. Horrible, most horrible. I don't think I've ever witnessed a supernatural creature like that since that case I solved of the devil-hound on Bosky Moor. See how its maw opens as if to swallow the night. See how its eyes reveal the horror of the grave. See how it wails and thrashes at the window, keeping pace with the train without effort.'

'I can see, I can see, 'cried Maudlin. 'I don't want to, but I can.'

The ever-practical Scruff said, 'Well, what are we goin' to do to get rid of it?'

'Light,' murmured the bishop. 'We must have light.'

It was true that the light in the carriage was very dim, coming from the gas mantles above the luggage racks on either side. Scruff rushed off down the corridor of the train. All the while he was gone the creature fought the rattling pane of the

146

window, trying to break through. Its form seemed very soft, however, or without much physical strength for it could not summon the power to break the glass. Monstrous eyes glared at the occupants and a horrible mouth stretched and gaped. Arms like twisted, knotted towels fresh from the washing-tub sought to embrace the mustelids.

Scruff finally returned, swinging the guard's lamp. It was a much brighter light than the one in the carriage. He rushed to the window and swung it back and forth before the phantom's eyes. The wailing outside got louder and louder but thankfully the creature began to drift away. Then suddenly, *whap*, the atmosphere changed. Maudlin screamed sharply. But all that had happened was they were in a tunnel. In fact the spectre had gone back to the hellish place from whence it had come – for the time being at least – and they were safe.

The bishop looked shaky. He sat down on the seat, his forelimbs were trembling. He was a very old stoat and incidents like this were not good for his heart. Scruff shrugged and went off to return the lamp to the guard. Maudlin collapsed in a heap in the corner. Monty applied his brain to the problem.

'We must get rid of the ocarina,' he said to Maudlin. 'It was the tune which brought the ghost.'

'You think it was a ghost?' cried Maudlin.

'I'm certain of it. Something from beyond the grave. We called it forth with music composed by ancient mustelids who were closer to dark secrets than we are. Tooth Age weasels, perhaps? Or primitive stoats whose shamans could reach into the world of the dead? Who knows? A mammal community who probably painted their fur with blackberry juice and danced themselves into a trance on moonless nights. I've heard such tribes inhabited Welkin in the distant past. They must have made the ocarina, fired it in some earth oven, and invested it with powers to summon such creatures as that ghastly spectre from some deep pit which can only be imagined by civilized weasels such as we.'

'I fear you are right,' said the sweating bishop, running his claws through his matted fur. 'I am *sure* you are right.' He shuddered. 'If I were you I would toss that evil instrument out of the window and rid yourself of it for good.'

Maudlin snatched up the ocarina and the bishop obliged him by dropping the carriage window so that he could throw the object out into the night. However, before the window could be closed, the ocarina came sailing back in again to land on the seat beside Maudlin. They tried closing the window very fast, but even this did not work. No matter how quickly they did it, the ocarina seemed to beat them.

'In that case,' cried a desperate Maudlin, 'we'll smash it!'

He threw it with great force at the floor. The ocarina shattered into a dozen shards. Scruff was back by now and he helped kick the bits into various corners of the carriage. The group of mustelids then watched mesmerized – and terrified – as the broken pieces swiftly scuttled together – a family of parted crabs – and joined to form the whole again. Twice more they tried to break the instrument and each time the pieces came back together and re-formed into the hated ocarina.

Maudlin said, 'I know. It was *given* to me. I'll just give it to someone else. Pass on the problem.'

'You can't do that,' said Scruff.

'It's not moral,' said the bishop.

'It's not ethical,' said Monty.

But Maudlin did it anyway and no-one tried to stop him. The very next passenger who passed along the corridor on their way to the toilet was offered the ocarina. It was a weasel nurse, and she refused, thinking something was not quite right. Why would anyone want to give something away? Sell it, yes. They would probably ask her for payment once it was in her paws. No. She refused it. So did three more passengers. Desperate, Maudlin dropped it into the open bag of an elderly jill stoat as she stumbled along, her concentration on the rocking of the speeding train as it hurtled into the night.

'That's that,' said a relieved Maudlin, dusting his paws. 'Gone.'

'That poor jill,' said Scruff, feeling guilty. 'It'll frighten her to death, y'know.'

But when Maudlin reached into his own bag, he found the ocarina snugly ensconced within.

'I suppose the mammal who takes it off me has got to *want* it,' he said, mournfully, recalling the circumstances in which it was given to him. 'Well, I'll hang on to it then. But I won't play it. Ever again. I'll just keep it safely tucked away in my bag. Now, I'm hungry and thirsty after all that excitement. Has anyone got anything to eat?'

'I have some biscuits here,' said the bishop,

opening a folded kerchief on his lap. 'You're all welcome to share.'

He held one up between two claws. Scruff immediately went into a doggy-begging position and said, '*Ruff. Ruff.*' Then, to the astonishment of the bishop, he leapt forward and snatched the biscuit from the clergymammal's paw with his teeth.

'Good gracious!' said the bishop, astonished by this strange behaviour.

'Oh no,' moaned Maudlin. 'Not this again.'

Monty said, 'Scruff, heel. This instant!'

The bishop looked from one resigned weasel face to the other. Were they all quite mad? He was beginning to think he had chosen his travelling companions very unwisely.

CHAPTER SIXTEEN

The next station was the end of the line. Here the three companions would have to alight. The place was called Howling Hill because wolves had once inhabited the shallow rise behind the little village. The wolves had moved out of the area long ago, complaining about the noise from the battlefront, which was only three kilometres down the road; they said it interfered with their choir practice on a Thursday night. It is not generally known that wolves take their singing very seriously.

They are a species which believes they are born with good voices and an inbred sense of note and scale. One of them, Dai-the-entrails, once said, 'Every wolf has the voice of an angel and it's a wonder we don't come into the world with wings as well as a good set of teeth, look you.' The other creatures of the forest and field were profoundly glad that there were no flying wolves around to swoop down on them like eagles, especially mother sheep with early spring lambs to watch.

As they drew into the railway station at Howling Hill, Maudlin suddenly thought of something.

'Hey,' he said to the bishop, who was getting a carpet bag down from the fishnet rack above his head, 'why don't you *exorcize* my ocarina? Get rid of the ghost?'

The bishop placed his bag on the seat and looked puzzled. 'Exorcize it? How would I do that?'

'Well,' said Scruff, having recovered from his few moments of playing copy-canine, 'you're the religious mammal – you should know how to do that. Don't you sort of thump a holy book with your fist and yell fire-and-brimstone prayers at the ghost? Or swing an incense-burner between lighted candles while shoutin' what's what in the latest incantations?'

'But,' protested the stoat, 'I'm not in the least religious. At least, I am a little bit, but not enough to be a clergymammal.'

Monty interrupted. 'Scruff, Maudlin, I think you have this all wrong. Never judge a book by its cover, or a bishop by his robes. This gentlemammal is not a clergymammal, nor is he anything else connected with the Church. I thought you had noticed he had his mitre on back to front. No true bishop would make a mistake like that.'

'Have I really?' said the stoat, turning his pointed hat round the right way. 'Thank you for telling me.'

'He oughta be ashamed of hisself,' expostulated Scruff, 'goin' round, pretending to be a clergy-mammal.'

'No, no, you have me wrong,' said the bishop who was not a bishop. 'This is merely the trappings of my interest.'

Maudlin growled, 'Talk sense.'

'He means,' said Monty, who had gauged the situation accurately, right from the first moment he saw the bishop, 'that he is dressed as a bishop for a reason, but it has nothing to do with the Church.'

'Ho, and what might that be?' cried Scruff, in his policemammal's voice.

'Chess,' said the sweating stoat. 'I'm a chess-piece. I'm here for a convention of chess-lovers, who are staying at the hotel in the main street. We all gather here annually for this event. It's close to the battlefront, you see, and chess is essentially a game of war. Look out of the window . . .'

They were just drawing into the station and the three weasels stared out onto the platform. There, milling around, were stoats dressed as knights, as kings and queens, as common (but old-fashioned) soldiers and as castles. One poor fellow, his first time at one of these conventions, seemed to be dressed as some sort of blackbird. He was looking miserable and out-of-place and was definitely being shunned by others.

'A gatherin' of chess-pieces,' said Scruff. 'Well, what was that black book you was readin'?'

'If you had looked more closely,' said Monty, 'you would have seen it was a book on chess moves. I believe this gentlemammal was studying opening moves. Your particular interest was in the opening move known as *La Défense Belette*, am I right?'

'Quite right,' said the stoat, looking astonished. 'How did you know?'

'Fundamental, my dear fellow, fundamental. You were crossing and uncrossing your hind limbs in the manner of Gallic weasels while you were reading. I therefore deduced the subject matter had something to do with Gallic mustelids. There is only one set defence which has its origins in that far-off land, and that is *la défense belette* – the weasel defence. *Voilà!*'

'Remarkable,' murmured the impressed stoat.

Maudlin was still staring at the stoat dressed as a bird.

'Well, what's *he* doing here, then? Has he got the wrong fancy-dress party, or what?'

Monty shook his head. 'My guess is that he's dressed as a rook, which is another name for the castle piece in chess. He's just taken it literally that's all. By the look of the others they don't approve.'

They opened the carriage door and stepped out one by one onto the platform. The bishop hurried off to greet a friend he had not seen for a year; it was a stoat who had come as a king. 'Check, mate!' cried the bishop, rushing up to his pal. 'Wonderful to see you.'

The three weasels made their way through the stoats to the exit, with the words, 'Check,' and 'Check, mate,' in their ears all around them, as stoats greeted each other all over the station.

'Load of anoraks,' muttered Scruff.

'What are those?' asked Maudlin. 'Anoraks?'

'It's a penguin word, meanin' "They who gather in groups to discuss the meanings of the scratches on dead elk bones",' replied Scruff.

Monty then decided that since there was only one hotel in the frontier town of Howling Hill, they would have to stay there.

'The alternative is to camp out in the woods,' he told the other two, 'and I've been told there's a manless horsehead who roams these parts during misty evenings. These stories of the supernatural are often false, but you never know.'

'What's a manless horsehead?'

'It's just the disembodied head of a riderless horse which floats through the night and bites any traveller foolish enough to be out after midnight, especially near the village of Sleepless Hallow, which is just over the rise. It has eyes of fire and jaws of iron, and its teeth are black with the smoke and soot of the underworld. They say whenever the horse's head bites a mammal, that mammal becomes a horse's head himself, one of the living dead, roaming the moors eternally in search of flesh to bite.'

'In that case,' said Scruff, 'definitely the hotel. Is it expensive?'

'Don't worry about that,' said Monty, 'I'll meet the bill.'

'S'very kind of you, guv'nor.'

'No, no, it's not. I asked you to come along. I can't very well leave you both out in the street while I sleep in a comfortable bed.'

They found the hotel – the lobby full of chess-pieces, all talking excitedly – and booked into two separate rooms; Monty had one and the other was shared by Maudlin and Scruff. All three were so exhausted they skipped dinner and decided to go straight up to bed, even though the chess-pieces were all partying downstairs. Maudlin said he hoped the noise would not keep him awake.

'Tomorrow,' said Monty, 'we must go looking for the Prince Imperial. I'm sure if he's army-barmy he'll be in the middle of the fighting, so we'll know where to begin. I've met the type before. They're not satisfied with all that being royalty brings. They want to be heroes too, with lots of medals on their pelts . . .'

They separated, going to their rooms.

However, because they had gone to sleep so early, they consequently woke very early. In fact it was about three in the morning when Scruff's eyelids suddenly flew open. He found himself staring at the ceiling, illuminated by the full moon glowing through the glass.

'You awake?' he asked Maudlin, nudging his friend.

'I am now,' growled Maudlin.

'Fancy a walk?'

'A walk?' Maudlin went up onto his elbows. 'Are you mad?'

'Nope. I thought we might do a bit of work for once. Save Monty the trouble, see? We could walk to the battlefront. S'only about three kilometres. Then look for this Prince Impertinent. Find 'im. Report back to Monty before breakfast. Surprise 'im, like.'

'I don't know. What about this manless horse-head?'

'Nah. Probably just a story. Anyways, Monty

said it came out at midnight. S'gone that now.'

'I think Monty said it appears *after* midnight.'

'Nah. It'll be all right.'

Maudlin shrugged. 'Anything to get this trip over with as soon as possible. I don't like the countryside much. It's full of nasty surprises. Give me the good old city every time. There might be horrific murders and sordid grave-robbings every night, but there's no spooks.'

The pair dressed and left the hotel, slipping past the sleeping polecat clerk. Maudlin had his back-pack on, with water and sandwiches saved from lunch-time – he did not want to find himself peckish halfway to the front. Scruff took the lead, striding out in front, his tail following stiffly behind him. At the end of the village they found a signpost which said '*To The Battle Zone – Blood and Gore Unlimited*' and continued on along that way. The dirt road was full of grooves and ruts caused by the cannons which had been dragged that way. It was not easy walking on such a surface, which was also muddy and covered in puddles.

The walk started out with a clear night, beamed down upon by a contented moon, but after a while the morning mists began to drift in. Soon they were walking in the swirling vapours, the moon having vanished behind a thick cloud, making it hard to see the road.

'Are you all right, Maud?' said Scruff, from time to time. 'The black bat night will soon fly off, once the sun comes out.'

'Don't mention bats to me,' said Maudlin, shivering and looking around him. 'I've heard they get tangled in your fur.'

After a long walk they came to a rickety-looking bridge over a stream. Here the morning mists had collected in abundance. There was a coldness about this hollow which seemed to have nothing to do with climate or weather – a chilled air which collected there, heavy and oppressive. All that could be heard was the soughing of the breeze in the branches of the chesty trees, and the babbling of a mad brook which had lost its reason up in its craggy source when tumbling over rocks and dashing its head against stones. Halfway across the bridge, Scruff suddenly stopped and held up a single claw. 'Listen!' he whispered. 'Can you hear somethink?'

'What?' asked Maudlin, shuddering.

They both stood there, stock still, listening.

'I thought I heard a sort of low whinnyin' sound,' said Scruff, after a while. 'You know the sort of sound I mean.'

'No I don't,' protested Maudlin. 'And what's more I don't want to.'

'Yeah, you do, Maud. A sort of – horsey sound.'

At that moment the moon came out from behind its screen. Maudlin saw a sign, half covered in green mould, sticking out of the boggy marsh beyond the insane brook. The sign read 'SLEEPLESS HALLOW'.

'Oh, no!' he shrieked. 'We're going to get bitten.'

From out of the night, heading towards the bridge at a speed which made its mane flow out like a flag behind it, came a disembodied horse's head. Its eyes blazed with fiery wrath. The muscles on its neck stood out like iron bands. Its jaws were wide with fury, revealing two rows of thick ugly teeth, rotten with the smoke and ashes of the underworld. Strangely, the pair of terrified weasels standing on the bridge could hear the thunder of the creature's invisible hoofs as they pounded on the hard-earth road.

Nearer and nearer it came, and when it was just a few metres from them, it whinnied insanely, its jaws snapping the misty air in front of it. The sight was so terrible to mortal eye that the two weasels were frozen in terror. They could not run, they could not hide. They were trapped by this fiend of a severed head, bearing down on them with great speed. It seemed to gather all the forces of darkness as it came: they swirled in eddies about its dilated nostrils, its flattened ears. This was a stallion straight from depths of the nether world, intent on attacking the two defenceless weasels standing on the wobbly bridge.

Chapter Seventeen

'Quick!' yelled Scruff. 'Play your bit of china.'

'My what?' cried the terrified Maudlin.

Scruff grabbed his pack and took out the ocarina. 'This lump of pottery. Quick, play it.'

The spectral horsehead swept down upon them at great speed. Maudlin had no idea why his friend wanted him to play the ocarina, but it was no time for questions. This was a time for action. He put the mouthpiece to his lips and blew. As before, miraculously a tune came out, as magic a sound as Maudlin had ever heard. The notes wailed out into the early morning. Mists scattered, as on the other side of the bridge from the horse's head, came the raggedy phantom, hurling itself along. Thus the two weasels seemed to be attacked from two sides.

'What good was that?' yelled Maudlin. 'Now if one doesn't get us, the other will.'

'Or each other,' said Scruff.

And he was right. As soon as the two spooks were aware of each other they went into battle. Spectres are jealous creatures and guard their territories fiercely. The raggedy phantom flew at the ghostly horsehead. It seemed intent on wrapping its weird form around the spectral head. But instead the horse opened its mouth wide – very, very wide – until it was like a small red cave. It swallowed the ghost of the ocarina as if it were a blanket escaped from a washing-line. Then the blazing eyes turned their attention on the two weasels.

'It didn't work!' wailed Maudlin. 'It's still coming for us.'

Scruff said, 'Wait a minute!'

The untidy weasel was right to wait. A few moments after the raggedy ghost was swallowed it came out of the end of the horse's neck. Of course, the horse had no stomach, nor in fact any body at all, so there was nowhere for the swallowed ghost to go, except to come out of the horsehead's food pipe at the other end. Once more it tried to wrap itself around the stallion's head, only to be gripped by those strong teeth and drawn into the monstrous mouth again.

Yet again, it appeared out of the end of the horse's neck, like a silk handkerchief from the fist of a magician.

Maudlin and Scruff slipped away, heading for the hotel, leaving the two ghosts to their endless battle which neither of them could win. Both exhausted weasels went back to bed for some well-earned rest. Being terrified can be a tiring business.

Monty woke them both at 8.30 a.m. After trying to get into the bathroom on the landing and being checkmated half a dozen times, they all went down to breakfast with one another. The two weasels said nothing to Monty about their escapade. They didn't want to appear foolish in front of him.

Once at the table they ordered a full Welkin breakfast of mouse sausages, vole rashers and pigeons' eggs on fried bread. Maudlin had dandelion juice, but Scruff said that always made him want to go to the toilet too much. He had acorn coffee instead. Monty finished off with fruits-of-the-allotment. In all, it was a substantial meal which would last them until they got to the battle-front.

Monty hired a mouse-cart with a driver to take them up to the front. Maudlin and Scruff were surprised by this, but they really shouldn't have been. The roads were rough and dirty and Monty was, after all, a gentlemammal, a city weasel with a pride in his appearance. They crossed the same bridge that the pair had reached in the early morning. High above, the horse's head and the raggedy phantom were still battling it out. Monty looked up and said wryly, 'My, you two *have* been busy, haven't you?'

'How did you know?' asked Maudlin.

'It doesn't take much nonce to guess. It's my belief that if you tried throwing away that ocarina now, you'd be successful, but I suppose you don't want to.'

'Not now,' confessed Maudlin. 'It might come in useful again.'

The carter was an elderly country weasel.

'You city folk up to see the fightin'?' he enquired.

'We are visiting the front, yes,' replied Monty.

The elderly weasel clicked his teeth and said, 'Ar! Didn't think you'd come up here to take the waters.'

Lying next to the road were scummy pools full of chickweed and rotting elder branches. It was a dreary landscape covered in broken trees and shell-holes. Up ahead the guns were pounding. Soon they could see the shells bursting in the air ahead, like fireworks exploding with fierce lights. Two lone shapes slipped by the cart, casting long shadows in the early morning sun. Deserters from the front, the carter told them. Every day weasels, stoats and ferrets got fed up with the war and decided to run away.

The three visitors were not prepared for the grandstand!

When they arrived on at the front, on the edge of the unnamed marshes, there was a great stand there, built from timber. In the stand were jills and jacks in the finest clothes, watching the battle in comfort. The jills twirled their parasols. The jacks pointed with their umbrellas. It seemed that the war was a spectacle which provided entertainment for travelling mustelids. Some were sketching, others painting, others still were recording high-lights in the battle in goldplated notebooks with silver pencils.

Just ahead of the grandstand was a line of bronze field cannons, some of them with clockwork motors, others with steam-driven mechanisms, according to which general they belonged to. They were firing round shot and shells into the marshes. No rats could be seen. There were no shells or shots coming back from the rats, either. In fact nothing at all was coming from the murky outlands with its peat hags and tall reeds on the other side of the river. Except words. Every so often, after a particularly fierce barrage, rat jeers could be heard.

'*Missshed! Can't hitttt a barnish doorrr!*'

Phrases like that did not seem to perturb the stoat generals in the least. These individuals strode back and forth behind the cannons, their hats sprouting waving sparrows' feathers, their chests jangling with masses of medals, their boots clinking with heavy spurs on which the rowels spun and flashed gloriously in the sunlight. They barked their orders at colonels, who shouted at captains, who yelled at lieutenants, who finally got to shriek at sergeants. The sergeants, being the only ones who knew what they were doing, rolled their eyes and gave rather more sensible orders to their troops than had been passed down.

There were messengers who ran hither and thither with what looked like long shopping lists. Nearby stood several extra colonels and majors with reinforcements, some paw soldiers, others cavalry, and most important of all, the artillery. The cavalry had no mounts, but were expected to run faster into battle than the paw soldiers who marched in long straight magnificent lines, colourful in their red coats, their bayonets pointing enemy-wards and glinting evilly in the sunlight.

It was a grand parade of soldiers along that front. As the morning went on one or two rats began to show themselves on the other side. They popped up, fired a musket, and then ducked down again. Monty caught a glimpse of hard rodent features, their eyes narrowed and whiskers twitching, then a blaze of fire from the muzzle of a musket. Occasionally these shots would ping off metal or embed themselves in wood, but in all the long day Monty did not see one person actually hit.

'It was a stoat called Flaggatis who originally stirred up the ship rats to a frenzy of hatred against the mustelids,' Monty told the other two. 'The rats invaded south Welkin, were pushed back north again, and the war has been going on along the border ever since. It's all very silly really, since each of us has all the territory we need. We don't actually want the unnamed marshes and I'm sure the rats aren't interested in the towns and cities of Welkin where the common rat lives. But the war's been going on so long no-one knows how to stop it.'

'Who's leadin' 'em now?' asked Scruff. 'They got their own leader? One of them?'

'Yes, Dakk Makkintashhh. He's a middle-aged rat who wears a pink bandanna around his head. A very *big* rat. Dakk Makkintashhh has sworn to drive the mustelids out of Welkin altogether, but one wonders whether this hatred has any roots. Perhaps if he were given the chance Dakk Makkinstashhh might be agreeable to peace?'

Monty looked at all the stoat generals, and the officers of paw and cavalry regiments and could not see them giving up their illustrious careers for a few rats. They needed rat unrest in order to keep their smart bright uniforms with the rows of shiny buttons. They needed the war so that they could fire their noisy guns. There were some stoats, and weasels too, it had to be said, who loved the glint of the burnished bronze cannons; the sounds of muskets in the early dawn; living under canvas with wood fires and camp stoves; the splendour of a smart uniform, with its fine sword and tassels dangling from the hilt. They loved it. And peace would mean they had to give all this up, along with any chance of glory.

'Watch this,' said Monty to the other two. 'You see how they would hate to give it all up.'

He left the pavilion behind the lines and walked up to the nearest general.

'Sir,' he said, 'my name is Montegu Sylver. The Right Honourable Montegu Sylver. With your permission I shall cross the river and speak with Dakk Makkintashhh. I'm sure he's a reasonable rat. Perhaps I can get him to lay down his arms and enter peace talks?'

The stoat general turned in alarm at these words, his multiferous medals clinking against each other.

'Ooooo, no,' he said, pursing his lips. 'Too dangerous. You're a civilian, sir. A civilian. Couldn't let you go over there without seventeen certificates from the Minister of War, all duly signed and stamped. More than my job's worth to let you cross that river.' He looked Monty up and down, the sparrows' feathers in his hat flopping back and forth. 'Even a weasel. Even a weasel, sir. Not on. Not on at all.'

'But what have you got to lose?' protested Monty. 'If I don't come back, you can deny you ever saw me. If I do, you'll be a part of history, the making of a peace treaty between the rodents and mustelids.'

'Not my decision to make. You go to the Ministry of War in Muggridrear and get those certificates. Then, if they're not out of date by the time you get up here, I'll let you cross that river.'

'Out of date?'

'They only last twenty-four hours.'

'But it takes a day and a half to get here.'

'Not my responsibility. Speak to someone at the ministry.'

Monty came back to the other two. 'You see what I mean?' he said. 'They don't want the war to finish. They want to keep it going so that they continue to get promoted and can get campaign medals pinned to their chests and enjoy their jolly lifestyle up here amongst their comrades.'

That evening, when all the officers were in their tents, the three weasels went back and forth, enquiring after lemmings. There was a new lemming in the cavalry, it was true. He was a tall arrogant fellow with a habit of looking down his nose at smaller creatures.

When Monty demanded that his papers be inspected they found he was not who he claimed to be. It seemed he was the son of a cobbler, back in Slattland, but certainly not the Prince Imperial. He had told the recruiting officer he was of noble blood, but it was all a lie to get officer status. Now they knew he was only a cobbler's son, they demoted him from lieutenant to sergeant in one quick movement. He was furious with Monty and his friends.

'What did you have to come up here interfering

for? I was quite happy. The army was quite happy. Now you've stirred it all up and I've lost my commission and have ended up a non-commissioned officer!'

'Sorry about that,' said Monty, 'but you shouldn't have fibbed in the first place. We're really looking for Prince Miska, the Prince Imperial. I don't suppose you have any idea where to find him?'

'That opera-mad idiot?'

'We'd heard he was keen on the army, too.'

'Oh, well, yes – but that's different, isn't it? I mean the army's a jack's life. Opera's for jills and tone-deaf jacks who want somewhere warm and cosy to go to doze. The army, well, there's nothing like the army. Guns banging. Lots of lusty singing around the fires at night. Yelling and charging with bayonets. Sticking things. Shooting things. Nothing like it. Makes a jack feel he can breathe.'

The lemming calmed down a little after that. In fact, he said, he didn't object to being a sergeant so long as he was allowed to stay and fight rats. It was all he asked of life, to be allowed to sleep and kill things, and be paid to do both. That was what army life was all about. He invited the weasels into his tent where he was cleaning his kit for a parade the next morning.

'I'd heard that Prince Miska was coming to Welkin, before I left,' said the ex-lieutenant, now a sergeant, huffing on his brass buttons as he spoke. 'There was a rumour that he wanted to demote himself from a royal to a commoner.'

'Why would he want to do that?' asked Monty.

A furious polish with a soft yellow duster, before answering. 'Something to do with politics. Who knows how these mammals think? I'm just the off-spring of a lowly cobbler. I do know that Slattland is ripe for revolution if something doesn't happen soon. The lower classes have been poor for too long. They want some share in the country's wealth. There's some dangerous creatures about, hoping to benefit from the change – hoping to grasp power.'

'Countess Bogginski?'

The lemming's eyes opened wide and he stopped polishing his buttons for a moment to stare at his boots, glazed to perfection and mirroring the inhabitants of the tent.

'You know her. You know the Bogginski? She is mad, that one, like a monk we once had. Rumplesputin. It was said the Bogginski poisoned all her brothers and male cousins, because jills can only inherit if there are no jacks left in the family. Nothing could be proved, of course, but it was thought she sent them invitations to a party, with stamped, addressed envelopes included so that they could reply . . .'

'And the poison was in the envelope glue? When they licked it, they went into convulsions?'

The lemming said, 'How did you know?'

'I guessed,' replied Monty. 'Was that her only alleged crime?'

'No, there were many. Even as a child she was suspected of drowning her governess by pushing her down a well. She is a bad lot. And she hates Welkin. She holds this country responsible for all Slattland's ills, saying that Welkin drains international trade away from Slattland by controlling the seas. If she ever gets into a position of power, there will be war between your country and mine, no question about it.'

'And whose army will you be in then?' asked Maudlin. 'Yours, or ours?'

The lemming declined to answer this question.

The three friends left the front in the early evening, heading back to their hotel. Guns were still booming along the line, hollow-sounding in the still of twilight. Up here no birds sang at the close of the day. As darkness fell, the shells bursting over the marshes were like fireworks, sending sparkling, fizzing whizz-bangs into the air. Monty swore he could hear 'Ooos' and 'Aaaahhhhs' coming equally from the grandstand and from the depths of the marshes themselves. It seemed that even the rats were enjoying the display of pyrotechnics.

They had decided not to stay the night on the front because of the invasion of midges that were swarming in now that the day was over. Everyone in the grandstand had beekeepers' hats which they hastily donned, letting the veils fall over their faces. Out of the marsh came the midges, a particularly vicious biting kind of insect which buried itself in your fur. The three weasels were soon scratching away like mad, trying to pick the maddening creatures out of their pelts. When Monty breathed he took a dozen or so midges down with each breath. They got into the corners of his eyes and stuck there in the moistness. It was not pleasant.

'Well,' he said, as the carter took them back over the bridge, past where two phantoms lay draped

170

over the bushes like damp washing, exhausted by their all-day battle, 'at least we know the Prince Imperial is not with the army. It seems we shall have to look elsewhere.'

At that moment the sound of a shrill steam whistle hit the evening air, followed by a shout billowing with terror.

'The wolves are coming back! The wolves are coming back!'

CHAPTER EIGHTEEN

When the three weasels entered Howling Hill town its citizens were rushing around with hastily packed suitcases, running for a waiting steam train, or mouse-drawn buses. The chess convention was piling into both, eager to get out of town before the wolves descended upon the defenceless populace like Assyrian humans. Mothers were clutching kittens to their breast; visiting businessmen were stuffing guineas into velvet carpet bags; groups of youthful mustelids were tearing out of town on bicycles. It was chaos. Tails were tripping mammals up. Whiskers were becoming entangled. Paws were being trodden on. Noses were being knocked.

From the hills came the sound of wolves crying for want of the distant moon, distressed that it was ever out of their reach. Once they reached the point where they were sickened by their complete helplessness to possess the golden disc – maddened by hopeless love of that far-off prize – they would fall upon the hapless town and wreck it. When wolves were in this state of frustrated frenzy they set out on a crazy path of wanton destruction. They might regret this later, but for a time there was no reasoning with them.

Thus the citizens and its many visitors were leaving town fast.

'There's more to this than meets the eye,' said Monty. 'I think we ought to go up into the hills and discover what is going on there.'

Maudlin's teeth began chattering. 'Go up there? What for? Let someone else go up. It's nothing to do with us, is it?'

Scruff put a forelimb around his friend's shoulder. 'There you go again, jokin' as usual. You are a card, Maud. We know you better than that. Well, guv'nor, how are we goin' to do it?' The last remark was addressed to Monty, who looked deep in thought.

'I think we ought to take bicycles,' he said at last, 'and ride up into the foothills to see what's making that noise.'

'Wolves,' said Maudlin, quickly. 'Everyone says so.'

Monty said, 'Never listen to everyone. Only to yourself. Come on, there's a bicycle shop over there. We'll hire some machines.'

The shop had been vacated, the front door wide open and its owner on his way to the already overpacked train. Monty told the other two to sort

173

out a bicycle each and he would leave a note to say that the machines had been borrowed by Jal Montegu Sylver, 7a Breadoven Street, Gusted Manor, Muggidrear, Welkin. Then he left some money in an envelope to pay for the hire.

Scruff was more than excited, having never ridden a bicycle before. These machines had lovely big gas lamps on the pawdlebars, fat comfortable saddles, well-oiled chain and pedals, and nice swishing wheels. Scruff immediately jumped on his and tried to ride it, falling off at least a dozen times. Finally, after twenty minutes, he was able to make a wobbly hundred metres without crashing down into the dust. Monty already had riding skills, learned of a Sunday afternoon on Wasters Way, which ran through Muggidrear's largest park. Maudlin had once been a postmammal and had ridden with the mail.

The three then set off for the hills, the sound of crying wolves echoing in the valleys.

There was a bell on the front of each bike. Monty wished there weren't, but there was. Scruff could not resist dinging his at every opportunity. Finally, Monty had to ask him to stop.

'But there's creatures in the way,' explained Scruff, reasonably. 'We don't want to run over 'em, do we?'

'I'm sure that deathwatch beetle you were so worried about back there was well out of the way since it was halfway up a tree trunk,' Monty said. 'And in any case it must have heard you coming from at least a mile away.'

'It might have forgot we was there and run out

174

without thinkin' into the path of these lovely shiny machines.'

'I don't think so,' said Monty patiently, 'and I would appreciate it if you let the bell alone now.'

'Half the fun,' grumbled Scruff.

'I might point out,' interrupted Maudlin, 'that this is not supposed to be fun. We're in wolf territory on a moonful night. We'll be lucky to get away without having our throats torn out. Moons like this one are apt to make a wolf loony.'

Scruff could see the point. It wasn't that he worried about having a torn throat so much as the fact that they were warning the wolves of their coming. It seemed clear that Monty wanted to catch the wolves at their choir meeting and if they heard bells dinging in the night the pack might well consider calling it all off. Wolves were good at laying low and slinking about unseen, as well as warbling and crooning. It was better they were unaware of the coming of the three weasels.

As they came nearer to the howling, the three cyclists looked up to see a wolf standing on a stark crag. It had its head arched upwards, its nose pointed at the distant moon, and it was letting out the most mournful howl the world had ever heard. From behind it, in the timber forest, came further accompanying yowls and cries. Harmony, it seemed, was not the most important thing here. To make as much howling-noise as possible seemed to be the main idea, with a few blood-curdling yips between.

It was indeed a frightening sight. There is nothing like a fully-grown wolf to put the fear of savage teeth into a mammal. This creature looked big enough to swallow the three weasels and their bicycles whole. He was deep-chested, with broad shoulders, and his coat glistened with droplets of evening dew. Around his large paws, set firmly on the rocky crag, a mist was curling. The coolness of the night had arrived.

Maudlin shivered. 'Look at the size of him!' he whispered. 'Now perhaps you'd think it best to go back down and catch the train?'

'I might agree with you,' said Monty, grimly, 'if there were not something strange about that wolf. Look at him. He hasn't moved a muscle in the whole time we've been watching him. Singing like that takes a lot of effort. He'd be filling his chest with air, setting himself for a good yell, lowering his head between yowls to get the best out of his throat box . . .'

'He'll get the best out of our throat boxes, if we don't go now,' said Maudlin. 'You mark my words.'

But Monty insisted they went on. They hid their bicycles beneath some undergrowth, and crept forward on paw. Once they had entered the tree line, they could smell woodsmoke. A little further on a lighted fire could be seen between the trees. Hunched figures were seated around the fire, with great shields or masks set beside them. These gathered creatures were far too small to be wolves. In fact they were smaller than the three weasels creeping up on them.

There were, it seemed, over a score of the campers. They were clicking their teeth and chattering away to each other, but with an edge to their voices as if they were not used to sharing camp fires, not used to being in company, and didn't enjoy it all that much. These were mammals who, unlike wolves, were entirely unsociable and only got together for a purpose.

'Rannies,' muttered Scruff. 'A whole crew of 'em together. A ranny doesn't even like another ranny, so what's this lot doin' all cosy as jack-scouts, round a communal camp fire?'

Scruff was using the nickname for common shrews, who were sometimes called 'rannies' though no-one knows why. In ancient times it had been thought that, like mice and voles, shrews did not own any intellectual capacity. Yet Monty had recently read in *The Chimes* that strange markings had been found in shrew regions – scratched into the surface of rocks or in the baked clay ground – which were proposed by one stoat professor of Muggidrear University as being victory songs of shrews during a period when mustelids did not have the power of speech themselves. 'The symbols,' he wrote in his paper, 'are unmistakably those representing the triumphant warrior and the defeated foe. We have found similar markings in the holes of ancient rat warlords and I would stake my reputation on the theory that the shrews of antiquity recorded each battle, whether as individuals or as a group.'

The 'wolf' standing out on the crag was obviously a dummy. Now that they were closer Monty could see it was made out of a potato sack stuffed with straw and using twigs for legs. Its tail was fashioned from a teasel and its ears from rhododendron leaves.

The weasels soon found out about the howling too.

Just behind the crag, out of sight in the bushes, was an enormous conch shell. Standing by the end of it was a shrew who kept putting his lips to the tapered end and howling. This would have been a very thin sound if not for the megaphone effect of the shell trumpet which magnified the volume and gave the shrew's call a wolf-like sound. These were creatures who were playing at being wolves. But for what reason, asked Scruff. Why go to all this trouble to trick a town?

They soon found out the answer to this question.

Grumbling and moaning, all the shrews except the howler got to their feet. They picked up the almond-shaped 'shields' and Monty then saw that these were masks made to look like wolves from the front. When the shrews held these shields up before them, from a distance they would look like a pack of wolves coming down the hillside. Indeed, they jostled each other on their way out of camp in order to give this impression.

Avoiding being seen by the howling shrew, who was still doing his business with the conch, the three weasels watched the rannies go down the hillside into the town.

Once in amongst the deserted houses the shrew gang began looting the town. Monty had seen enough. 'That's it,' he said. 'We can't let them get away with this. You two follow me.'

Monty took off his jacket. Then he crept forward until he stood directly behind the howling shrew. He tapped the creature on the shoulder. The shrew leapt nervously into the air, at the same time letting out a deafening shriek through the shell trumpet which could be heard in Muggidrear let alone Howling Hill.

'You made me jump!' he cried, accusingly. 'What's the idea, sneaking up on a fellow like that from behind? You could give someone a heart attack.' He bunched his claws into a fist. 'I've a good mind to punch you on the nose . . .' Then he saw the other two weasels approaching him from the sides. 'Hey,' he said, his eyes narrowing. 'What's going on?'

At that moment Monty whipped his jacket over the head of the shrew and all three weasels leapt on him. The little fellow put up a terrific fight and if it had not been for the jacket tangling him he might have given the weasels a run for their money. Finally they managed to tie him up with the sleeves and left him squirming on the ground.

'I'll kill you!' was the muffled cry from within the jacket. 'I'll mash you into mushy peas! I'll tear out your forelimbs and hit you with the soggy ends! I'll swing you by your tails and throw you into the next county! I'll knock all your teeth out and use them for hollyhocker seeds! I'll . . .' and so it went on, ceaselessly, while the others tried to think.

'Quickly,' said Monty to Scruff, 'put your mouth to the end of the conch shell.'

'What for?'

'Just do it.'

Scruff shrugged and did as he was told.

'Sick 'im, boy!' yelled Monty, into Scruff's ear. 'See 'im off!'

Dog commands.

Scruff immediately began barking and growling aggressively. The sound was magnified and went out into the night. The shrew inside the jacket went silent immediately. In the town the raiding party had frozen in their tracks. *Dogs!* A shrew might not fear a lot in life, but one thing he didn't like was a dog. Especially a dog in defence of property. Also, with dogs there was always the probability that humans were there too, with shotguns and other nasty weapons. The barking and growling continued to grow louder and louder as Monty spurred Scruff on to fiercer sounds.

The ranny raiders let fall their shields, dropped most of their plunder, and began to scatter. They fled towards the unnamed marshes to the north where they knew even dogs and humans would not follow. Finally, the last shrew left town, carrying a biscuit barrel under his right forelimb. This was the chief and he at least was determined not to leave empty-pawed.

Once they had all fled into the darkness of the open fields, Monty released the shrew from the jacket. Like a true fighter he came out swinging and snapping with his sharp teeth. The weasels had anticipated this and had long branches to fend him off. Finally, exhausted, the shrew vanished into the woods at the back of the hill, yelling over his shoulder, 'Next time I see you, I'll knock your blocks off and put them back on the wrong bodies!'

A final swish of his tail and he was gone.

'Well, that's that then,' said Scruff, in a satisfied voice. 'Might as well get back down to the town. S'pect they'll be quite grateful we saved it from being looted, eh?'

Monty said, 'Mammals are seldom grateful creatures, Scruff, you should know that. But we have done our best. We could do no more.'

They gathered up the bicycles and rode back down to the town.

When they reached the bottom of the hill they found the townsmammals coming towards them – pine martens, weasels, stoats, polecats, ferrets – waving their forelimbs in anger. Deep in the middle of the mob was a shrew, muttering into the ears of all who would listen to him. The three weasels from Muggidrear recognized the shrew at once. It was the howler of the ranny raiders. When the shrew saw them, he shouted to the mob, 'There they are, riding the stolen bikes. I told you. They tricked everyone into thinking there were wolves up in them there hills. All they wanted to do was rob your shops and houses . . .'

Monty, Scruff and Maudlin stopped dead in their tracks as the furious mob surged towards them.

Chapter Nineteen

The rabble looked as it were out for blood. Such
ugly mobs were never in any mood to listen to
reason. The ranny had fired them up, made
them deaf and blind to any argument. They saw
the three weasels on bicycles and they assumed the
machines had been stolen. If these newcomers to
town had stolen bicycles, they would steal anything, including kittens from mothers' forelimbs
and walking-sticks out of the paws of grannies.
They were thieves and villains, blackguards and
cutthroats.

'Beat them!' cried the ranny, from the centre of
the crowd. 'Knock them senseless before they can
argue their way out.'

The owner of the bicycle shop, a large fat stoat,
cried, 'They can't argue their way out of this one.

182

They've been caught red-pawed. I say we throw them into the local pond before we pass them over to the police. If they drown, they're innocent, if they float, they're guilty.'

There were shouts of agreement from the rest of the mammals.

Monty surveyed the scene through narrow eyes. 'This is getting ugly. No sense in staying around here. No-one's going to listen, the mood they're in. Split up, quickly, and ride for your lives!'

The other two needed no second telling. They turned their machines and pedalled furiously. Monty did the same. The mob roared and stampeded after them. About thirty mammals followed Monty out of the north end of the town. His hind legs were going ten to the dozen as he sped along the dusty roads to escape the red-eyed beast of a mob. Happily he did not suffer any punctures on the flinty road or he would have surely been caught. Gradually the unfit townsmammals dropped off, one by one, until there was only the ranny who had started it all, still in pursuit.

Monty halted and got off his bike. He stood there in the middle of the road, waiting.

'Ha!' cried the ranny, catching up with him. 'Now we've got you, thief!'

'We?' said Monty.

The ranny, puffed and sweating, looked around him and saw that he was all alone.

'All right,' he said at last. '*I've* got you.'

He came at Monty, trying to butt him in the stomach. Monty skipped neatly aside and clipped the shrew's ear as he passed. The ranny roared and thundered forward again, only to find himself clawing at thin air. Monty had neatly stepped out of the way of this charge, too. In fact it was the same with every attack. Suddenly Monty was not there and the ranny was swinging or biting at nothing but the wind. Monty had studied Scruff's technique closely and knew the moves.

'How do you do that?' cried the shrew, frustrated.

'I learned my footwork from the famous Gentlemammal Gym Corebutt, an artist with pawsicuffs and the best boxer in all Welkin. You should take some lessons yourself. You're far too clumsy and off balance. I could push you over with one claw right now. A puff of wind and you'd be on your back in the dust. You have no artistry.'

The shrew was inclined to agree and turned to go, but before he left he yelled viciously over his shoulder, 'You ruined our raid. I'll make sure the townsmammals send the police after you. There'll be no hiding place for *you*, weasel. You'll end your days in a dark prison cell and I'll be there to clack with satisfaction through the bars. You mark the words of Orgibucket of the shrew raiders. My gang now know it was you who did this to us, too. They're all out looking for you. When they catch you they'll tear off all your fur in clumps and give it to bald water rats to use as wigs. They'll cut off your tail and make it into a mouse whip. They'll chop off your ears . . .'

And so he went on, until his voice drifted faintly into the night, and the sense of the words was lost on the wind.

Monty picked up his bike and, realizing he had no choice, continued to ride in the direction of

Muggidrear. The city was a long way off, however, and he knew he could not reach it for three or four days. His gas lamp had gone out on the pawdle-bars, but he was able to see the road in the moonlight. After two hours of hard riding he felt he was far away enough from Howling Hill to rest a little.

At this point he happened to come across a coaching inn where mail coaches stopped for the night and which passenger coaches used for a staging post. Hopeful that he might find a bed free, he propped his bicycle up against the wall of the inn and went up to the door. From within there was the sound of clacking tankards of honey dew, clicking teeth, and other merriment. It all sounded very jolly. As he opened the door the smell of roast volison hit his nostrils. His tummy rumbled. He hoped the others found this inn as easily as he had. It would be nice if all three of them could put up here for the night.

He stepped through the doorway into the parlour with its roaring fire and jolly occupants.

Instantly, the whole place went quiet. Every head turned to stare at him as he entered the room. Mugs of honey dew were raised but unmoving as the occupants of the room stood like statues, staring at this intruder who had just walked through the doorway. For a moment, no-one spoke – they were all too astonished at their luck.

Monty stood, aghast. Those who stood there with foaming mugs of honey dew poised were the ranny raiding party. Rudely etched in blood on the wall above their heads was a five-pointed figure with the words *'Ware thou the wererat!'*

within its crude form. A single dart flew across the space between the rannies and this weird symbol, and struck the gas lamp which hung from a single cord above their heads.

The ranny who had thrown the dart looked with narrowed eyes at the intruder. 'You made me miss,' he growled.

'Get 'im!' yelled another one, jumping to his feet. 'Don't let 'im escape.'

Two or three more darts flew from the paws of those who had been in the middle of a game. Fortunately they missed Monty's head and stuck in beams and wall.

Monty dashed out of the doorway and ran straight into a thick wood opposite the inn, leaving his bicycle behind.

The shrews chased after him. Once in the wood the undergrowth was dense. It was also very dark. The drunken rannies blundered around, getting pricked by the thorn bushes and brambles. Cries of revenge were soon replaced by curses and yells of pain.

'Help! I'm lost.'

'Ow! Where is he?'

'Dunno, I just fell down a rabbit hole and can't find my way out.'

'Who's that? That you, Filliput?'

'Let me go, you oaf. You got me, not 'im.'

'I've just been sick.'

'Serve you right, Smacker, you ate too much of that worm pie at supper.'

'You can talk, greedy guts – I didn't see you lettin' the snail-n-slug pudding go to waste.'

'I've got burrs in me fur.'

'Get me out of this blackberry bush.'

'I'm *still* lost!'

Monty crept away, finding a path through the trees more by luck than woodland skill. The branches caught on his collar and coat tails, but he was able to get on without being followed. He wondered how much more bad luck he would encounter. He was rapidly becoming very tired. Intrepid mystery-solver he might be, but he had lived in a city all his life and was not used to the outdoors. The forest can be a worrying place to those who had abandoned it, many generations before. Monty's many-greats-grandfather had tried to get weasels to go and live back in the woodlands again, after the humans returned to Welkin, but though they tried it was too difficult to camp out all the time when they were used to houses and all the comforts of homes and beds with sheets.

There were thoughts in Monty's head about finding a hollow oak and curling up inside it to go to sleep, but every likely tree he found with a hole in it was full of rainwater. Sleeping in that would be most uncomfortable for one used to a soft mattress. He tried going into a rabbit hole, but found it was occupied by a duck with a nasty temper who told him in no uncertain terms to quack off and find somewhere else.

It was all very frustrating. He had to gather himself together and get back to Muggidrear where he could continue the search for the Prince Imperial. Monty had a strong feeling that the prince was now in great danger from Sveltlana. It was important to find him before the dark, mysterious and deadly Sveltlana discovered him.

There were dangers in the wood too. Tawny owls were evident by their hooting. Ghostly-looking barn owls were also around. These latter did not hoot, but let out wheezy cries and shrieks which were even more frightening. Both these birds normally ate rodents, but would take a weasel in a pinch. Monty kept treading on their pellets and thinking that Lord Haukin would have a field day adding to his collection if he were to come to this particular wood during the daylight hours.

Finally, very late, Monty eventually stumbled into a ring of gaily painted caravans and camp fires, around which were seated creatures he had quite often heard of but had never met before in his life. One of them got up and came over to him.

'Lost, are we?' said the spiny creature, wearing a red kerchief with white spots tied around his neck. 'What's to do, stranger?'

The mammal who had spoken was, like the other gypsies around the fires, a hedgehog. These creatures were often accused of stealing and being a general nuisance, but in fact as with all things there were no more thieves amongst them than amongst any other set of creatures in the land of Welkin. Simply because they chose to live travelling the highways and byways, they were looked down upon by those who lived in houses. They were known by some as hedgepigs or urchins, but unlike the word 'ranny' for shrews, these were terms of abuse. Monty always felt that whoever the creatures were they deserved respect and dignity.

'I'm sorry to intrude upon your evening,' he gasped, 'but I fear I'm on my last legs.'

'Come in,' cried a jill, in the process of stirring a big black iron pot on the fire, 'make yourself at home.'

'Before I do,' replied the exhausted jack weasel, 'and I very much want to, I must tell you the police are after me. There's also a gang of common shrews searching the woods for me. I'm afraid I've landed myself in a lot of trouble not of my own making.'

'Oh, we don't worry about things like that,' said the jill hedgehog. 'If you say you've done no wrong, then I believe you. Come on. Sit yourself down by the fire. It might be spring but there's still a nip in the air at night which can bore right through to your bones. Have some beetle soup. It's just been boiled up. Just pick out the wings and bits of shell and spit them in this bowl. We like to keep the place tidy.'

'Thank you, thank you. I'll sit by the fire, but I'm – I'm not all that hungry, if you don't mind.'

He found himself a seat on the log beside the colourfully dressed hedgehog gypsies, who looked at him curiously.

'City weasel, by the look of 'im,' said one, as if Monty were not able to hear him. 'Got 'is fancy clothes messed up.'

'Never mind that,' said the elderly jill, who was a portly creature with a sacking apron. 'I've just realized. You prob'ly don't eat beetles, do you? We've got some nice barley mash if you'd prefer?'

'That would do very nicely, thank you,' said the grateful Monty. Then turning to the young jack who had just spoken, he said, 'Yes, city clothes. Not very appropriate for a night in the forest. I suppose you wouldn't have some others that I could swop for these? I don't mind how old or ragged they are. In fact, the older the better.'

Another jill hedgehog spoke up. 'Got some clothes from an old washertoad. She travelled with us for a while, takin' in washing to make a livin', but she went and died on us. Old age, nothing catching.'

'They would be all right. I suppose I could cut a hole for my tail to poke through?'

'I think there's plenty of holes already in 'em. She was a very poor washertoad.'

The clothes were fetched. Monty thought they would make an excellent disguise until he could get back to Muggidrear and clear his name. He put on the frock and mop cap, along with a threadbare apron and some wooden clogs. They were certainly very old clothes, but they had been scrubbed as clean as a whistle and smelled of soap.

Once he was in the clothes and his own were in a neat pile beside him, he relaxed a little. He had to undergo jokes from the hedgehogs, who found the idea of a weasel in washertoad's clothes quite funny, but he took all this in great heart. Just as he was tucking into his barley mash several stoats came out of the forest bearing lanterns.

'Policemammals,' cried a voice. 'Stay where you are, everyone, while we search the camp.'

The jill beside him quietly picked up his city clothes and threw them on the fire, where they burned with bright flames.

CHAPTER TWENTY

Scruff took the road into the hills. He reasoned that the mob would have a harder time chasing him uphill than on the flat. However, he forgot that he also was having to go upwards. So, whereas Monty and his pursuers were flying along level ground, he going fast, they racing to catch up with him, Scruff was pedalling ever more slowly and those chasing him had slowed to a walk. The townsfolk were dogged in their efforts to catch him, but all the heat had been taken out of the chase. Walking after someone is not as exhilarating as running after them. There isn't the same excitement in it. Gradually his pursuers dropped away and wandered back to the town. Only the cycle-shop owner and some of his cronies continued to go after the weasel whom they believed had robbed him.

Scruff passed the spot where the fake wolf was still howling silently at the moon. Eventually he came to the end of the track. Here he found two great wrought-iron gates set in a high wall. This appeared to be an estate of some kind, straddling the saddleback of the hill between two valleys. Looking through the gates Scruff could see a great mansion standing four-square in some beautiful gardens.

A notice on the gate read BEWARE OF THE DOG. Someone rich and powerful lived here. Perhaps a human. Perhaps a wealthy stoat. Scruff was just about to leave and try to go round the great estate when he saw Maudlin's bicycle propped against the wall a bit further along. There were some muddy prints on the wall where someone had climbed over it.

'Maud's gone over the wall,' he muttered to himself. 'I'd better see what's in there too . . .'

His pursuers were now very close behind. Scruff propped his bicycle against the wall and, being very lithe and slim, managed to slip through the gate's ironwork. The stoat shop-owner and his friends eventually reached the gate. Being larger and stouter they did not attempt to squeeze through the bars. Instead they peered at Scruff, standing on the other side. One of them went to ring the bell on the gatepost, but Scruff called out, 'I wouldn't do that, if I were you.'

'Why?' asked the stoat.

''Cos of the sign!'

The stoat read it out loud. 'Beware of the dog.'

'Friend of mine,' fibbed Scruff. 'Listen, take some advice. You've got two of your bikes back.

Leave it at that. When you get back to your shop you'll find a note and some money, which proves we was goin' to pay for the machines when we got back to Muggidrear. If you'd have looked at that note instead of just listenin' to that thug of a shrew, you'd know it was the shrews who was robbing the town, not us weasels. But you stoats was always fickle-headed and jumpin' to conclusions.'

'You watch it, weasel,' said one of the stoats. 'I might just come in there and give you a thick ear, dog or no dog.'

Suddenly, a large shape appeared out of the shrubbery to Scruff's left. It was a huge, golden dog. Like most hounds he still walked on all fours and wore only a collar: a very smart red one with brass studs. The canine soul in Scruff stared at this collar in great envy, wishing he owned it. The dog ambled over to Scruff and looked down upon him.

Seeing him there had acted as a trigger to Spindrick's hypnotism. Once more Scruff believed he too was a dog. And here before him was another hound. Scruff wanted to make friends, in the way that two canines do. His tongue lolled out of his mouth.

'*Woof!*' said Scruff. '*Grrrrr. Woof! Woof!*'

The dog half-closed one eye. 'We don't do that any more,' he said, in a cultured voice.

This matter-of-fact reply to Scruff's doggy greeting shook Scruff out of his hypnotized state.

'What?'

'We don't do the "woof, woof" thing now. Not all of us, anyway. I personally thought it was degrading, all that "man's faithful servant" stuff. Very demeaning. Not on. Not on at all.'

193

'Oh,' said Scruff, stuck for words. 'All right then.'

'Now,' said the hound, 'what's going on here? I've already got one weasel in the house. Now you? What's happening here?' He turned his head to address those who were pressing against the gate. 'What do you stoats want?'

'He stole my bike,' said the shop owner, through the bars. 'I want him thrown in jail.'

'Did you steal his bicycle?' asked the dog of Scruff.

'Borrowed it. We left some money at the shop, in an envelope. Some shrews stirred them up. They just wanted blood.'

'Yes, stoats can be a little short on patience.' The dog spoke to the shop owner. 'Have you retrieved your bicycle now?'

'I've got two of 'em back, but that's not the point. The point is, they were stolen . . .'

'Leave us,' said the dog, interrupting. 'There's no damage, is there? Then leave us.'

'But . . .'

'LEAVE US!'

The force of the dog's voice was like a hot wet blast of air hitting the stoats outside the gate. They hastily scrambled away, taking the bicycles with them. After running some distance the stoats wisely decided to actually ride the bicycles instead of pushing them. Two stoats got into the saddles while two more sat on the crossbars. A fifth, the last, sat on the back mudguard of the bike Scruff had borrowed.

With the bicycles loaded thus, they shot off down the hill at an alarming rate. Smoke was coming from the brakes. Both Scruff and the dog had the feeling that there was going to be a crash soon, probably at the bottom of the hill. Scruff was disappointed he wasn't going to be able to see this crash. It would have cheered him up considerably.

'We only took 'em so we could ride up the hill and see what the wolves was doing,' said Scruff, watching the stoats leave. 'Only they wasn't wolves, they was shrews making out they was wolves. We sorted 'em out for the towns-mammals – and was they grateful? Not a bit of it. Fickle's what they are. Stoats is happier being part of a mob than having to think for themselves.'

'That's been my observation too,' said the dog. 'Now, perhaps you'd like to join your friend in the house? I believe he's taking tea and crumpets at the moment, with the owner.'

'You're not the owner?'

'Good heavens, no,' said the dog. 'I'm simply a companion.' He looked around. 'There aren't any more of you, I suppose? Weasels, I mean.'

'There was one, but he went in the opposite direction.'

'I see. He won't be joining us for tea?'

'Don't think so,' said Scruff, scratching a bald patch on his pelt. 'Monty was pedallin' like mad when I last saw him, goin' for open country.'

'Monty?'

'Right Honourable Montegu Sylver, solver of mysteries. Lives in Gusted Manor in the capital. Famous among weasels.'

'Ah!' cried the hound. 'Indeed. I've heard of him. My cousin had a little run-in with this Montegu Sylver, out on the moors.'

195

Scruff stared at the dog. 'A run-in?'

'Yes. You see this Montegu Sylver, *solver of mysteries*, was responsible for destroying my dear cousin, who shall remain nameless – probably because she doesn't *have* a name, or one that we in *this* world can pronounce anyway. My cousin – a very distant relationship I might add – was once known as the Bitch of the Basketvoles. She roamed Inkly Moor, tearing the throats out of travellers, lost villagers and anyone else she could sink her supernatural fangs into.

'She was a terrifying monster. A creature from the deepest pits of the netherworld, with eyes like blazing coals and jaws of iron – but I liked her. I thought she had spirit. Well,' a click of the teeth, 'she obviously had *that*, since she *was* a spirit. She was greatly feared, especially on moonless nights when the dark oak branches melted into the surrounding dusk and pools became liquid slate. Then she would wander abroad looking for pale-throated victims on the moor.'

'Ho, yes?' said Scruff, wondering where this tale of a horrible hound was leading. 'Was she then?'

'Yes, she was. *Greatly* feared. She was three times my actual size and of course with her supernatural powers she could appear out of the darkness, rip her victims to pieces, and then vanish back into that twilight world from whence she had emerged. But some objected to this pastime of killing innocent wayfarers and wished her gone. They sent for this friend of yours – this Montegu Sylver – and he helped trap my cousin. They – they immersed her in holy water from the church font – of course this had the effect of destroying her powers and turning her into a normal dog just like the rest of us pathetic creatures of ordinary stamp.

'She's now in a home for the feeble-minded, somewhere on the seafront not far from De'athmouth pier.'

The dog's tone had been growing more bitter as the tale went on, but Scruff felt he ought to defend his friend's actions.

'I'm sure Monty wouldn't have done anythink that wasn't right and proper.'

The dog seemed to pull himself together. 'No? Well, I'm willing to see the other side. I had the facts second-hand of course, from an interested party, and may have a few of the details wrong. If you say your friend was acting in the best interests of all concerned, why, I'm certain you're right.'

They walked up to the house. Through the open french windows Scruff could see Maudlin drinking tea and eating hot toasted crumpets. Maudlin was talking to another creature who was behind the muslin curtains, hidden from Scruff's view.

The dog entered the room first, saying, 'Another weasel, Nigel.'

'Eh oop,' cried a high-pitched voice in a north Welkin accent, 'Cynthia *will* be chuffed.'

Scruff followed the dog into the room and saw that the creature who had spoken was a large mink. He was sitting in a wing-backed forelimb chair eating crumpets. The melted butter was dripping onto his beautiful fur, which looked soft and shiny. There was jam on there too, and some honey. The mink waved a paw, indicating that Scruff should sit himself down in a chair.

197

'Eat oop, chuck,' said the mink. 'Get theeself a cup o' tea.'

'This is very nice of you,' said Maudlin. 'Very nice indeed.' He turned to Scruff. 'Glad you got away from those stoats. I've just been saying to Nigel here, it's time stoats realized that there were other mustelids in the world besides them.'

There was a little cough from the large golden hound who had settled on the carpet in the way that dogs do.

'Oh,' said Maudlin, correcting himself quickly, '*mammals* that is – not just mustelids of course.'

At that moment a female mink came into the room, carrying a plate piled high with more toasted buttered crumpets.

'Ah, Cynthia. Look at this,' said Nigel, '*anuther* guest. We're very fortunate. Very fortunate indeed. Come and sit thee down. Have some tea, petal.'

'Ooh, how nice,' said Cynthia, placing the crumpets on the occasional table. 'How very nice.'

Scruff settled down in his comfortable chair and began to tuck into the crumpets. There was a strange atmosphere in the room, a sort of faint menace about the two minks and their companion dog. But for the moment he was too busy eating his crumpets and being sociable to take notice of it.

CHAPTER TWENTY-ONE

Cynthia got up while they were eating and went to a bookcase at the far end of the room and opened a drawer beneath the shelves. Although Scruff was feeling suspicious he thought nothing of this. He kept his eyes on the dog and on Nigel. Cynthia returned after about a minute and said, 'More crumpets anyone?' Maudlin and Scruff both stretched out their paws for the plate of crumpets. Instantly, Cynthia pounced, clamping fetters on their forelimbs. She locked them with a *click* and a *clack*. Scruff looked down aghast, to see that he had been well and truly clapped in irons, manacled, and Maudlin with him. The pair of unfortunate weasels were linked together by a short chain.

'Hey!' cried Maudlin, jumping to his feet.

Scruff, calmer than his friend, said, 'What's all this?'

The dog rose from the floor and finally stood on two legs. It was a frightening sight because in that position he was as tall and as deep-chested as a human. His presence seemed to fill the whole room, his head close to the ceiling. He strode over to the weasels and looked down upon them like some golden giant. Gone was his cheerful disposition: his huge jaws were set in a grim expression and his brown eyes glared malevolently. He yawned, revealing an astonishing set of teeth, then licked the edge of his mouth with a monstrous tongue.

'On your feet,' he growled.

The two minks reacted quite differently. Nigel fell back in his chair and clapped his paws together in delight. And Cynthia clicked her teeth in glee.

'Well done, Cynthia,' said the jack mink. 'Well done indeed!'

'You two,' growled the hound. 'Drop what you're eating and come with me. There's a dog-cart outside. I want you inside it. Now.'

Scruff said, 'Not until you tell me what's goin' on. I can come quietly or I can make a big fuss. I'm not coming quietly until I know what's happenin' here.'

'You're going to the foundry,' said the dog. 'Nigel, Cynthia and I own an ironworks. We need weasels to work in it. It's hard dangerous work, but you'll be fed.' The dog clicked his teeth. 'Not as well as this, of course – you've seen your last hot buttered crumpet – but we'll keep you alive. Now let's have you outside the back door and in the cart.'

Scruff walked towards the doorway. Maudlin took his cue from his friend and followed him. They walked through a maze of hallways until they were taken by the dog through a back doorway, bundled into a dog-cart and the dog hitched himself up to the harness. Soon he was running through the countryside, pulling the cart behind him. They crossed a stone bridge, went up a gradient lined by elms, swept over the brow of a hill, and thence down into a green valley.

In the middle of the valley was a huge dark factory with several tall chimneys belching black smoke. From the cart the two prisoners could see something glowing behind the many hundreds of windows of the factory. The light inside grew bright and faded, by turns, as if someone were turning a gas lamp up and down. Also through the murky windows they could see figures moving: serpentine weasels, bent with the effort of carrying heavy loads, walking back and forth. Their sinewy silhouettes, like certain letters of the alphabet, drifted by the glass panes, sometimes lit bright, at other times simply a dull glow.

'Slaves,' muttered Scruff.

Maudlin said, 'What?' But Scruff was loath to repeat his fear, in case he worried his anxious friend too much.

Soon they were down in a yard running by some long sheds. There were huge piles of coal in the yard, like black mountains. A bucket-conveyer was moving from one of these mountains, carrying the coal through a hole in the side of the factory. There were gangs of weasels on the coal mountain, filling the buckets with shovelfuls of black lumps.

They paused to watch the dog-cart as it rumbled by, only to receive a stroke of the whip from an overseer mink for not paying attention to what they were doing. The worst of it was, they didn't seem to care. They were beasts of apathy, too far gone even to worry about the pain of the lash, only interested in the next meal and their straw beds.

The cart stopped. A mink overseer came out of an office attached to the factory.

'Two more for you, Joe,' said the dog.

'Out!' said the jack mink. 'Quickly.'

Scruff and Maudlin did as they were told, stumbling because they were still awkwardly chained together. The dog went off with the empty cart without another word. Scruff and Maudlin were led through a doorway into the factory – to a place inside which must have resembled the fiery pits of Hades. It was sweltering. In the middle of a huge room was a furnace which threw out a suffocating heat. It was so intense that it was difficult to look at its fire with the naked eye. There was a gang of weasels nearby, shovelling coal deposited by the bucket chain. They were throwing it onto the furnace fire, which spat back sparks and glowing bits onto the coats of the shovellers. Their pelts were covered in burn marks and the stink of singed fur filled the whole of the room.

Other weasels were doing various jobs around the room. Some were transporting glowing ingots of iron. Others were lugging iron ore and dumping it into a great melting cauldron which was lowered onto the furnace then lifted once the metal had turned to white-hot liquid. The bucket was then swung sideways by a chain, tipped, and the molten metal poured into moulds made of sand and brick. The blinding white stream of melted pig iron was both beautiful and awesome to see. Maudlin could not take his eyes off it every time the great cauldron was raised and tipped. It streamed out, yellow, red and white: a waterfall of fire.

'Move yerself,' said the mink overseer, nudging Maudlin with the stick he carried. 'Don't stand gawpin'.'

'Where are we supposed to go?' asked Scruff. 'What are we doin'? I have to warn you, once I tell the authorities about this place, you'll end up doing a hundred years in prison. I feel sorry for you. But if you let us go now, I'll put in a good word for you.'

The overseer hit him with his stick.

'Get on, get on. I ain't got time to waste nattering to the likes of you,' said the mink. 'You're on the tipper, you,' he said to Maudlin, 'since you seem so fascinated by it. It's the most dangerous work in the place. If you get splashed by the melted iron, it bores a hole right through and you're dead as a nail by mornin'. It's like gettin' shot by a red-hot bullet, only worse. It only takes a drop the size of a coin.'

'I don't want to,' said Maudlin, stopping dead in his tracks. 'I'll shovel coal instead.'

'You'll do as you're told,' said the mink, firmly. 'Or you get some of this stick.'

'I'll do it,' growled Scruff. 'I'll go on the tipper. You let him shovel coal. I think I can handle that big old bucket all right. You be careful I don't tip it in your direction, that's all.'

The mink's eyes went pale with fright at the

edges and his nose twitched at the thought of molten iron on his head.

'You try anythin' funny,' he said, 'and you'll regret it.'

'Well, you won't be around to see me regret it, will you,' replied the unrepentant Scruff. 'You'll be a smudge of ash on the floor.'

The two weasels were soon put to work. It was stifling hot inside the ironworks. There were no complaints from the other workers though. If one of them even looked like opening his or her mouth, or slacking in any away, a stoat overseer was soon there with an encouraging stick. They were a poor-looking lot, the weasels. Maudlin attempted to find out what they were doing there. They surely couldn't all be weasels who just happened to wander up to the house on the hill?

'Workhouse,' said one out of the corner of his mouth. 'We were all living on the parish, 'til we was taken out of there one mornin' by some stoats who said they was takin' us to a decent job. Decent. Ha! Look where we ended up. And it's not as if we've got a choice. Someone asked if he could go back to the workhouse the other day and they just clicked their teeth at him. They found it all very funny.'

'How did you end up on the parish?'

'Easy. Lost me job as a clerk on the docks. The guv'nor brought his nephew in and I wasn't needed any more. Couldn't get another job, no matter how hard I tried. Got into arrears with the rent. Couldn't pay. Was threatened with debtor's prison. Threw meself on the mercy of the parish who put me in the workhouse. Got taken from there with a load of others one morning and here I am sweatin' me guts out in an ironworks.'

'That's a terrible story,' said Maudlin.

'Not as bad as me brother's. Same thing happened to him, more or less. 'Cept he went and stole a loaf of bread. They put him on a ship and deported him to an island called Southland. They work convicts there until they drop, diggin' sulphur. This is breezy work compared with diggin' sulphur. The gas fumes get in your nose and eyes so they smart all the time. You can't breathe without it hurts your lungs. No, I'd rather be a slave in an ironworks factory than a convict on Southland.'

'I'd rather not be either,' said Maudlin, shovelling harder as the overseer walked towards them. 'I'd rather be tucked up in my own little flat in Muggidrear.'

'You can say goodbye to those dreams. You won't get out of here. Nigel and Cynthia have never let a weasel get away yet.'

Maudlin shovelled the coal and nursed his hurt and anger. Every so often he looked up to see Scruff tipping the huge cauldron and pouring the molten iron into the moulds. Maudlin could see how dangerous it was. Scruff was already smoking in various places on his pelt where tiny drops of hot metal had splashed. This made Maudlin feel very guilty. He hadn't intended that Scruff should take his place, but once Scruff had made up his mind to help someone there was no stopping him.

At the end of the ironworks, in a separate part of the factory, there were weasels assembling new steam engines and clockwork motors. There were street-cleaning machines with great suction nozzles underneath; there were garden-watering devices with lots of spouts; there were mouse-milkers sprouting tubes; there were steam-driven ploughs and clockwork yachts; there were plum-pickers and corn-cobbers and machines for fermenting honey dew. In fact for any task you could think of, there was a device or machine – of clockwork or steamwork – being manufactured at that factory.

Despite the fact they were slave-workers, the weasels who built clockwork machines were great rivals with those who manufactured the steam engines. They worked on opposite sides of the shed and yelled challenges and insults at each other.

This deadly rivalry even seemed to extend to the machines themselves, though of course they were supposed to be lifeless.

Once in a while, every so often, a newly built machine would go berserk. Maudlin and Scruff witnessed a steam-driven treacle-dispenser suddenly rear up like a beast of prey and go charging around spraying everything clockwork with hot sticky syrup until it eventually crashed into a soup-ladler and was spooned to bits by the stronger machine.

'Ludicrous, this rivalry,' said Maudlin, after another such incident when a clockwork pen-holder suddenly jumped off the assembly line and stabbed a set of steam-powered bagpipes to death. 'Absolutely daft.'

'Yeah, but it's fun though, ain't it,' clicked Scruff, as the bagpipes wailed its death-song, the steam hissing from the many new vents all over its tartan bladder.

Once the sordid, dingy day was over, the weasels were all chained to one another and marched out of the factory. The night shift came on looking just as miserable as the day shift. Maudlin and Scruff were taken with their fellow workers in mouse-carts to a long railway shed still on the factory grounds. They were herded inside and chained to a long iron pole which ran down the wall.

Under the pole were some flea-infested blankets on a straw mattress. Maudlin and Scruff were ordered to sit on these 'beds' while they were each served with a bowl of gruel by a mechanical cook. The blankets were still warm from the bodies of the night shift.

'This is nice,' said Scruff, as he was given his bowl of thin soup by a clockwork dispenser. 'Very nice. Just what I needed – a holiday.'

The mink overseers glared at him. One said, 'You think that's funny?'

'Funny? No. I'm serious. I've been to a place which is a hundred times worse than this. I'm grateful to be here.'

'Where's that then?' asked an overseer.

'Oh, I couldn't tell *you*. It'd turn your stomick. I've seen grown stoats go straight out into a dead faint when I've told 'em about where I've bin. Good gracious, you'd keel over in sheer disgust, you would. I mean, I expect you think you're tough, but you don't know the meanin' of the word.'

'Huh!' muttered the mink, but he was clearly

intrigued by this mysterious place of horror. However, he knew he was going to lose face by insisting that Scruff tell him where it was. He decided to wait until Scruff was ready to tell him. At that moment the weasel in question was lapping down his gruel as if it were vole steak. Once he'd finished the foul meal he lay down on the worn, dirty blankets and stretched out with a great sigh. 'This is the life,' he said. 'Lucky old me!'

The mink overseer said his fellow thugs, 'I'll get it out of 'im, before the night's over, you mark my words. He'll be *beggin'* to tell me in the end.'

CHAPTER TWENTY-TWO

While the three jack weasels had been having their adventures in the north, Bryony had been quietly running her surgery in a condemned warehouse in Poppyvile, the poor area of Muggidrear. While she had some rich patients in Gusted Manor – these she naturally charged – she ran the clinic in Poppyvile with two other vets completely free of charge. The poor mammals, with their various complaints, queued outside the clinic for treatment by Bryony and her two fellow jill vets, Texrose Tuttle and Honeysuckle Jones. They got a stream of mammals with various complaints, from the dreaded 'mad weasel's disease' to watery eyes.

Bryony quite liked the work, except that the single jack nurse/receptionist they employed between them would insist on whistling most of the day long. When he wasn't whistling he was humming or singing. This might have been quite pleasant, except that he only knew one song: *All Things Bright and Beautiful*, and of that song he repeated one line over and over again: '*All humans straight and tall*'. Thus they were trying to work – putting poultices on bruises and bumps, and lancing ugly running sores – with a jack singing in their ears, '*All things bright and beautiful, all humans straight and tall . . .*' over and over again, irritatingly humming the lines he did not know.

When he was told to stop singing, he whistled. Weasel whistling is unlike any other creature on this planet performing the same act. The nurse had two little fangs which honed an ordinary whistle until it was a sharp, high-pitched wind-sound, squeezing through a crack in the doorway to the sky. It had the same effect on the vets' nerves as claws running down a blackboard or squealing brakes on a rusty train. It made their eyes water, their tongues fur and their brains jangle.

'One day,' Bryony told Honeysuckle and Texrose, 'I shall pull out that nurse's teeth and scatter them around Poppyvile.'

'We'll hold him down,' the two replied in unison.

Once the long line of poor weasels and other creatures had gone down somewhat, Bryony and her two fellow vets took a break. They didn't eat anything – Bryony found it difficult to feel hungry after mopping pus out of boils and cutting growths from between the claws of street urchins – but they did manage a drink of cocoa. It was while she was sipping this hot beverage that the jack nurse came into the warehouse and said,

'There's a sewer rat wants to speak to you.'

Bryony recalled that Monty and the other two had been down into the sewer system to speak with the rats there. She got up and went out to see a whiskered creature with a hairless tail standing on the wasteground outside. He was wearing a white silk shirt, loosely tied with ribbons around the wrist and neck and trimmed with lace. His pantaloons billowed, too, over a smart pair of floppy mouse-skin boots. There was a sword at his side and on his head he wore a broad-brimmed, black hat with a sparrow's feather flying from it at a jaunty angle.

Holding the sword hilt with one claw to lift the point from the ground, he swept off his hat with a great flourish and bowed very low in the manner of medieval mammals with jolly nice manners. Bryony was quite bowled over by it. Coming from the mess of gory injuries and yucky bandages, this charming rat was a breath of fresh air.

'M'jill,' he said, softly. 'I am called Toddlebeck, leader of the sewer rats. I come here as a matter of expediency to inform thee of the state of certain mysterious doings below our paws in the sewers of the city.'

'Doings?' she repeated, faintly, wondering if it meant the same thing to both parties.

'Happenings, occurrences, events, et cetera. Jal Montegu Sylver has asked me to keep him abrace of any unusual goings-on beneath the city. I find he has left this jewel in Welkin's crown, our fair city Muggidrear, for more northern climes, but my enquiries have led me to thee, m'jill, here at this place where thee and thine administer physick to the poor and needy.'

'It's kind of you to come,' said Bryony, fighting a strong urge to copy his flowery language. 'What do you have for me?'

'Some fiend is constructing an engine of despair, whose metal limbs e'en now stretch out beneath the whole structure of the city. I fear this device will embrace every corner of the mammal half of Muggidrear, whose turrets and towers, whose spires and steeples pierce the dying sky of evening, while looped by ropes of light from an ochre sun . . . by the way, what *is* the difference between a steeple and a spire? We have discussed this question over many exotic meals, hot with the spices of eastern recipes, of a Friday night. Some feel that a spire has to be smooth, while a steeple should be a structure with many sides. What say thou?'

'Um.'

He sighed. 'Thou knowst not. How sad. I felt certain a jill of your great learning would settle the question once and for all. Never mind. We must concentrate our attention on this device below the streets.'

'Yes,' murmured Bryony, thinking of Spindrick. 'I wonder what that is. Who's actually building it? Not just a single weasel?'

'By the stars hidden above the sewer tunnels, there is a vast army of engineers and the like working on immense networks of pipes leading from this infernal machine. I have heard two names in the speaking – one Thos. Tempus Fugit and one Wm. Jott – these two gentlemammals seem to be the important personages supervising the construction.'

'Clockwork and steam engine, working together?' cried Bryony in surprise. 'That *is* unusual. Thank you, er, Master Toddlebeck. I'm most grateful for your help in this matter.'

The hat was swept off again and the bow followed as a matter of course.

'Thy servant, m'jill.'

'You're going back down again now?'

'Naturally. The sewers are my home.'

Bryony said, 'Don't you ever get fed up with it? I mean, it's virtually a prison, isn't it?'

'In the words of that immortal rat poet Colonel Poisonlace, "*Sewer bricks do not a prison make, nor filter grille a cage.*" '

'Very profound.'

Toddlebeck then left her to puzzle over this strange machine which was being built – secretly – below the city streets. It had to be a secret, for Bryony read the newspapers every day and she had seen nothing about such a device. She would not have put it past Mayor Poynt to be doing something devious in the sewers. It was to be hoped that he wasn't trying to drive out the rats who lived down there. Having now met one of them, a charming gentlemammal, Bryony felt a familiar surge of do-gooding zeal go through her compassionate body. It was like a bolt of electricity, and motivated her to investigate this devious structure.

Her first point of call was Lord Haukin's place. Cutler the butler opened the door, took her card, and asked her to wait in the lounge. Shortly afterwards Lord Haukin joined her, his monocle firmly in place.

'Ah, what's-her-name, isn't it? You're thingummy-jig's friend, aren't you? His flatmate, whatever. What can I do for you?'

'I was wondering if you'd heard if Mayor Poynt was building something under the city?'

A wrinkled brow. A stoatish twitch.

'Something? What something?'

'A device of some kind. A machine. Clockwork and steam engine combined. Have you heard of anything like that?'

Lord Haukin paced the floor, head down, thinking. Suddenly his head came up.

'Yes, of course. Monty mentioned it to me. Didn't he say anything to you? No, perhaps he wouldn't. It's one of those jack things, you know. Machines. Not a jill thing at all. That's why he told me and not you I suppose. You jills don't understand mechanics, do you? Not taught 'em in school, I suppose. Better with dollies and dressing up, eh? Not so hot with a spanner and screwdriver. When we were young jacks we were always given a box of meccano for birthdays and Christmases. M'sister always got a box of ribbons. Different brains, I suppose.'

'Nothing of the sort,' said Bryony, hotly. 'I'm just as good with a spanner as any jack I know. Now what's this machine . . . ?'

Lord Haukin observed her through his monocle. 'Ah, yes, *you* might've been. You're different from the rest of the jills. I find 'em twittering balls of fur. Empty-headed creatures. Full of the stuff and nonsense to be found in milliners' shops. Always on about bright feathers to stick in their tails or on their heads. When you try to engage 'em on a serious subject, like painting in oils, they change the subject to watercolours. Watercolours, I ask you! Insipid art form, if you ask me. Sunday painting, I call it. *Real* painters use real paint.'

Bryony pursed her lips. 'I think you're a little behind the times, Lord Haukin, if you don't mind me saying so. And if I might be so bold, I would say there's been *plenty* of jills throughout history who are equal to the jacks in *all* things.'

'Well, can't say I agree with you, but we'll save it for another time. Yes. This machine. Monty says it's probably a great heating device, a furnace of sorts, to keep the city warm in winter. You know how Poynt says he suffers with the cold. Sounds a good idea on the surface, but actually not a good idea. I can't remember why Monty decided that, but I agreed with his reasons at the time. Now, can I offer you a cup of tea? Some biscuits? A nice new hat?'

'You are impossible, Lord Haukin,' said Bryony. 'Thanks for the information. I will ask Monty why he didn't say anything to me about this, but I'm sure it's not because I'm a jill.'

'If you say, so, m'dear.'

She ground her teeth and left.

Bryony walked the streets to another address. She wanted to find out whether or not Monty's theory was fact. Ringing Roger struck five just as she rounded the corner entering the south side of Gusted Manor. There was a big green door in front of her with a bell to the side. She pulled the brass knob and a steam hooter hooted. A few moments later the door opened and a stoat opened the door. She recognized him as Wm. Jott. Standing behind this famous inventor was another creature, a weasel, and she knew instantly that this was Thos. Tempus Fugit, the clockmaker.

215

'Yes? What can I do for you?' said Wm. Jott, looking her up and down.

'I, er, someone sent for a vet?'

Jott looked puzzled. He turned round, glanced at Fugit, then turned back again. 'No-one here sent for a vet.'

'Oh? I wonder if I have the right address?' She stepped back to look at the number over the door. 'Goodness me, I've made a mistake again. I wonder – are you going out?'

'We, yes, we're on our way out,' replied Wm. Jott, in an impatient voice.

'Are you going my way?'

'Which is your way?'

'Well, I have another call to make and I wonder if you can help me find the address. Someone was hurt in the sewers today. Scalded by some hot steam and then struck by a flying brass cog. I'm not sure how to find my way down to the scene of the accident. A boiler explosion or something, followed by a burst clock spring flinging loose cog wheels all over the place.'

Jott stepped outside, followed by Fugit.

'Accident?' said Jott. 'Sewers?'

'The heating device!' cried Fugit.

There was alarm and consternation on both their faces. It told Bryony everything she wanted to know.

'Oh, never mind,' she said. 'It's probably a crank call.'

But the two inventors were already on their way, hurrying across the street towards the nearest jack-hole cover.

216

Chapter Twenty-three

Monty, with the hedgehog gypsies, was having his own troubles. The local stoat police had walked into the firelight and demanded to search the camp. Monty sat by the fire staring into the flames, disguised in the washertoad's frock, cap and clogs. Luckily the washertoad had been very large and her clothes swamped him. The mop cap came right over Monty's face and the dress covered him from throat to hindleg ankles, where the clogs took over. If he curled up in a tight coil within the old garments there was a chance he could get away with it. He only hoped the police would not look at him too closely.

At that moment there was a roaring, hissing, gurgling sound out in the night. Everyone, including the police stoats, stopped to stare into the darkness. Something was heading towards the camp. Something with one big yellow eye and a fiery tail. Whatever it was, flames belched from its rear while its one fierce eye remained trained on the camp. As it came closer everyone began to shrink back towards the safety of the caravans.

'What is it?' shrieked a hedgehog. 'Is it a dragon?'

The noise increased with every metre the thing drew nearer to them. Finally it roared into the camp, burping steam and water, throwing red-hot cinders in its wake, and coughing up smoke. It was a monstrous machine on two wheels, with pawdle-bars on the front, a saddle halfway down and tubes and pipes going everywhere. It was a maze of metalwork with a glowing fire heating a small boiler in the well in front of the saddle. Hot water hissed and bubbled from valves and taps along some of the pipes while ash dropped from under-neath, burning the grass. Astride the great black saddle was a creature wearing high black boots, rounded-glass goggles, gauntlets, mouseleather helmet, mouseleather jacket, and a long flowing white silk scarf.

'Ho!' said the creature, peering through the muddy, greasy glass of his goggles. 'Here I am.'

Then he began turning off taps and stopcocks, pushing levers, closing boiler doors and finally he switched off the gas lamp in the front. A turn of a tiny wheel and two metal rests sprang out from the sides of the machine so that the rider could dis-mount without it falling over. It rested there, still gurgling and hissing softly as if ready to burst into life again at the owner's touch and roar off into the darkness of the night. Finally the Rider stood away from the device and stretched himself.

When he walked round his machine he did so as if he'd been riding it for a week, with his hind legs wide apart. He was obviously sore in those regions of his anatomy.

'What is *that*?' asked a hedgehog gypsy, bravely stepping forward and inspecting the machine.

The rider raised his goggles up to his brow revealing two pale rings round his eyes which, unlike the rest of his furry face, were free of oil and smut.

'That,' he said, proudly, 'is my new police steamocycle, invented for me, personally, by none other than Wm. Jott.' He patted his bottom, which seemed to be steaming a little. 'Bit hot on the old buttocks at the moment – saddle's too close to the boiler – but I'm going to suggest some modifications when I get it back to the city.'

'Steamocycle!' said a police stoat, excitedly. 'Will'um all get one?'

'No,' replied the rider, coldly. 'Only the chief – which is me.'

The local police stoats in the camp suddenly looked very efficient and conscientious. Here was the boss of bosses, in their own country parish. Yokels they were, but not wishing to appear so. They might chew the odd straw or two, but they wanted to appear keen in front of this city peeler. Several of them jumped, thinking it might be expected of them.

Monty was especially alarmed by the newcomer's words. He peeked out from under his mop cap. Yes, it was indeed Zacharias Falshed, removing his gauntlets and pushing his goggles further up his brow. Sooty face he might have – cinders in his whiskers also – but it was definitely that dratted Falshed. Now Monty was in a pickle. Should he get up and run now, or wait until he was recognized?

He stayed where he was, thinking he might actually get away with it. Falshed had no doubt had a hard ride. He would be tired and not at his best. His eyes looked bloodshot, probably from the smoke and cinders.

'So,' said Falshed, slapping his leather breeches with his pair of gauntlets in military style, 'what have we here? I understand from a message I received that you're searching for three weasels. I know these villains. They're rogues of the first water. Especially that scallywag Montegu Sylver. I want him apprehended and thrown into jail before the day dawns.'

The sergeant of the country policemammals was staring at Falshed in awe. 'You'm got a message?' he said, in his strong local accent. 'But we'm only just a-started lookin' for these 'ere weasels.'

'Telegraph!' announced Falshed. 'Another new invention. Mouse code. Dots and dashes. That sort of thing. All you need is a copper wire going from here to there, what's called a "mouse key" for tapping out the letters, and there you have it – a message can be sent in seconds and received in seconds. Wonder of the age. Criminals can no longer run from the long forelimb of the law. We can cross oceans, mountains, deserts. We can reach out and claw them back to justice!'

One of the policemammals applauded wildly.

'Now,' said Falshed, 'have you searched this place?'

He strode into the camp, his leathers swishing. The police now went through all the caravans, looked underneath, searched some nearby rabbit holes, and then gathered all the occupants into the firelight. All this while Monty had been sitting hunched over the fire. He was stirring a pot of soup so as to look busy. Falshed finally noticed him.

'Who's that?'

'Her?' said the leader of the gypsies. 'Oh, she just wandered into camp a little while ago.' Monty knew the leader had to protect himself and his clan. If Monty were discovered the gypsy leader could pretend ignorance. 'She's a washertoad. Lives up the lane I think. Came to see if we had any dirty laundry but I told her, we do our own. I – I think she's hungry. We did ask her if she wanted some soup.'

'Hmm,' said Falshed. 'You. Washertoad. Have you seen any weasels skulking about?'

Monty kept his head bent, so that the mop cap fell on all sides of it, hiding his weasel features.

'No, sir,' he croaked. 'No weasels, sir. What've they done, sir?'

'Done?' cried Falshed. Monty could almost see Falshed's mind working, as the police chief searched it for a good reason to arrest innocent weasels. 'Done? Why, *murder*, that's what they've done! Their leader, Montegu Sylver, has – has – has assassinated the Prince Imperial of Slattland and disposed of his body.' The chief seemed very pleased with this obviously sudden invention. He nodded violently.

221

Monty felt the blood rush to his head. This was monstrous.

'I've – I've heard of Montegu Sylver,' Monty said. 'He doesn't sound like the sort of weasel who would commit murder. He helps the police solve crimes.'

'All carnivores,' said Falshed in a very low and choked tone, 'are prone to fits of killer madness – especially creatures like us mustelids. Being a frog you wouldn't know – wouldn't understand – there was a time when weasels and stoats had – had the madness of blood in their brains – a red mist falling before the eyes – savage attack was instinctive – our early selves – seeing nothing but red death. Sometimes – sometimes our ancestors rush up inside us – take over our civilized minds – and turn us back into those blood-thirsty brutish creatures we once were . . .'

'Toad,' Monty muttered. 'I'm a toad, not a frog.'

The police sergeant said, 'Stand oop when you're speaking to an officer of the law. Nobody ever teach you'm manners?'

Monty stood, still keeping his head bowed.

'Hmmm? Washertoad, eh?' asked Falshed. 'Where's your dirty little hovel, washertoad?' Falshed stepped forward, peering intently in the firelight. 'D'you normally wear your frocks inside out? What's under that tear? Looks like a furry ankle to me . . .'

Monty glanced down and saw to his dismay that there was a rent in the dress through which his leg was showing. Knowing the game was up, he lifted his head and revealed his face to Falshed.

'Let's see how good you are on that machine,' he

cried, and with a quick twitch of his nose raced off into the trees.

Falshed was soon after him. Goggles down, gauntlets on, he jumped into the saddle. With a few expert flicks of taps and switches, he was off, after Monty. The small furnace roared, spurting flame out of the exhaust. The boiler bubbled. Steam coursed through the pipes, working the well-oiled pistons. The greasy bike thundered over the uneven ground, its iron-banded wooden wheels digging into the turf and sending divots flying at the face of the moon. Gravel and dirt showered the other policemammals who raced on behind, determined not to miss anything in this exciting chase of a villain over their county.

Falshed weaved in and out of the trees, having practised long and hard on his steamocycle. He steered like an expert. In amongst the tangle of pipes and valves and taps his legs were kicking levers and knocking stopcocks as and when required by the steam engine. Every particle of energy possible was being forced from the machine. It strained at every pipe joint, every welded plate, every rivet on its tank. It vaulted hillocks, it ploughed through leaves, it churned up footpaths.

Monty felt his only chance was the river. If he could find a bridge it might not take the weight of the steamocycle. He ran out of the woods and down a meadow, seeing the silver glint of water at the bottom.

Falshed came hurtling out of the wood like a demon from hell, his infernal machine belching flames and spitting sparks. He roared down the slope towards the river, his round glass goggles gleaming in the moonlight. Nothing could stop him now. He was as the devil on the back of some fiery monster from the underworld. Master of speed and distance! Dread minister of the law! Wonder stoat of the age of new police enforcement!

Monty raced alongside a drystone wall, gasping for breath. His frock was flapping violently in the breeze, billowing and filling with air like a sail, holding him back. The clogs on his feet clattered on stones and rocks, hampering him. His mop cap, caught by a ribbon around his throat, acted like a parachute dragging him back.

'I've got you now, you blackguard!' cried an elated Falshed. 'I'm going to run you down like a rat. Let's not worry the judges. It costs money to send weasels to prison. I'm going to squash you under my iron-clad wheels and do the whole of mustelid society a favour.'

As he spoke these words he was thundering by the drystone wall, his white silk scarf flying behind him. There was a stile set in the wall. As he passed this the loose end of his scarf wrapped itself round a post. Falshed was suddenly jerked from his saddle. He landed, half-throttled, on his bottom. His impact with the ground took him into contact with stones and hard earth. All the wind went out of him. He sat there stunned and choking, watching his precious machine shoot past its prey.

'What the . . . ?' Monty was startled to see the empty steamocycle roar by him on its way to the river.

The machine was now on a course to destruction. It crashed over some stones, through some reeds, then flew off the bank of the river. It hit the water about six metres from the edge. There was a loud hissing, spitting, huffing sound, then a second's silence while it sank. This short moment of peace was suddenly shattered as the boiler exploded. Water, river weeds and bits of reed showered both Falshed and Monty. It was a magnificent bang, no doubt heard by those in the next county.

'My precious steamocycle,' cried Falshed. 'The mayor will kill me!'

'I hope he does,' yelled Monty, backing towards a stone bridge. 'I hope he takes it out of your pay.'

Infuriated, Falshed unwound the scarf from his neck. In an instant he was on his feet. Other police-mammals had finally caught up with the pair now and were in hot pursuit. Monty raced towards the bridge and ran halfway across. Too late he saw that reinforcements were on their way and were approaching from the far side. He was trapped in the middle, with no place to go – except over one of the sides.

Without hesitation he jumped from the parapet into the water. Only he didn't enter it. Instead he fell in something soft and mushy, which was silently going about its business. It took him a few moments to realize he had dropped into a barge full of swill. The river was quite swift at this point and the vessel took him quickly away from those chasing him. His last view of Falshed, before the barge went around a bend and behind a screen of willows, was seeing the chief throwing his goggles angrily into the waters of the river which had stolen his quarry from him.

CHAPTER TWENTY-FOUR

Mayor Poynt and his sister Sybil were dining at their favourite gourmet restaurant, *Ring of Bright Cordial*, whose owner was an otter called Tarca. Tarca's place specialized in game-bird dishes. There were many to choose from and Sybil liked to have them read out to her by her brother, who it has to be said enjoyed the sound of his own voice.

'*Amazon Swallow in Blackberry Sauce – a succulent roasted red-rumped swallow done to a turn and smothered in blackberry juice thickened with lark's spit.*'

'That sounds nice,' said Sybil, 'but I'm not sure I like lark's spit.'

'You always say that, but you haven't tried it yet, Syb.'

'I know what I like and don't like, brother. Tell me something else.'

Jeremy Poynt, wearing a black dinner jacket over his soft white ermine pelt, shrugged his shoulders and tried again.

'*Water Babies — mouth-watering young of the red-breasted merganser, fresh from the egg, basted with delicious melted mouse-milk cheese and served with chickweed garnish.*'

'What's a "mangerser"?'

'Some sort of sea duck, I think.'

Instantly, Tarca himself was by their table, having smooled up gracefully with a complimentary bottle of rose-petal wine.

'Quite right, Mayor,' said Tarca. 'Some sort of sea duck it is, but fortunately it lays up to eighteen eggs. We hatch them ourselves from an incubator in the kitchen. They're popped into boiling water the instant they're born, cooked to a scream, and on your plate only seconds after they leave the shell. Fresh, is the word. Fresh.'

The mayor pointed to the menu. 'You're charging five guineas a dish! If you can get that many eggs and hatch 'em yourselves, why is it so expensive?'

'They're an endangered species, Mayor.'

'Oh, in that case. But I think I'll have the swallow. And turn the heating up in this place. It's freezing!'

'I'm afraid there's no heating on, Mayor. It is rather warm weather, you know. The chef is roasting in the kitchen.'

'Blow the chef, I'm cold. Turn on the heating. It's like an arctic winter in here. You must have left the ice-house door open.'

'I'll have the fires lit immediately.'

227

'Good – Sib, what do you want to eat?'

'I think I'll have cheese on toast,' said Sybil. 'I believe I may become a vegetarian after tonight.'

'Why's that, sis?'

She sighed. 'No particular reason, Jeremy. You wouldn't understand.' She pointed to the wine. 'Is that nice?'

Tarka replied. 'Oh, Princess Poynt, the petals have been maturing on a compost heap for at least two seasons. It's delicious. On the house, of course.'

Unlike her brother, Sybil had not renounced her title, and still liked to be called 'princess' by the citizens of Muggidrear.

'Most kind,' said the mayor, who expected complimentary wines and other such frills as a matter of course, but was not too aloof that he could not be gracious in accepting them. 'Plonk it down on the table will you, Tarca, we'll pour it ourselves.'

'Plonk! Ha, I like it, Mayor. You're very sharp tonight.'

'I'm sharp *every* night. And while I'm waiting for the main course I'll have a starter.' He picked up the menu again. '*Deep-fried garden slugs stuffed with blackfly*. Nope. Skin gets too tough and wrinkly when they're boiled in hot fat. *Parasite worms, especially cultivated in the intestines of a dead house mouse, on strips of seagull tripe*. Bit exotic for my taste. *Cockroach shells in squashed weavel sauce*. Nope. Ah, yes! *Warm rabbit's blood*. I'll have a big glass of that, with two straws.'

Sybil said, quickly, 'I don't want any.'

'Oh, all right, just the one straw.'

Tarca clicked his claws at a weasel waiter, made a swift sign, and a tall glass of warm rabbit's blood appeared on a tray.

The mayor continued studying the menu as he slurped the viscous red fluid.

'Jeremy!' said Sybil. 'You're making a noise.'

He took a breath, thickening drops of blood hanging like heavy dewdrops from the tips of his whiskers and bending them.

'Got to drink it fast, Sib – it clogs up the straw when it starts to get cold.'

'Jeremy, could you please pour me a glass of wine?'

The mayor put down the menu and poured the wine. Sybil tasted hers and nodded. All the while there were mammals going past their table, saying howd'ye'do. The restaurant was quite full. It was actually theatre night, but since the play on at the Sphere Theatre was political and anti-stoat in the bargain, most stoats were dining out instead. The mayor wasn't fond of plays anyway. Too much talky-talky for him.

Tonight's play had been written by a badger and was called *Wind in the Walnuts*. Something about a group of nut-eating wood-mammals being turned out of their rustic homes by greedy stoat landlords. Propaganda. A lot of stoat citizens would be boycotting the performance.

In the corner of the restaurant a quintet was playing softly. Weasels were at the instruments. Stoats were not much good at playing music. They listened to it, of course, and were good at critical appreciation, but they seldom played. There was one weasel on the clumpicord – an instrument that mimicked the thud of autumn fruit hitting the forest floor – and three others on wind instruments called wids which were made out of hawkweed stems. The fifth was playing a stringed instrument called an arachnibox which had a real spider's web stretched across a dried, hollow turnip over which the bow was passed.

Left to themselves, the weasels would play weasely folk songs, which the stoats found too weird. These tunes were ancient poems about freedom and liberty and that sort of thing. Stoats were never happy about the lower classes going on about freedom, so the weasels were forced to play happy little ditties instead, all about taking in washing, and blacking the kitchen stove, and scrubbing the front step, and going down to the bread shop and finding only stale buns with currants like lead shot. This sort of song made the stoats click a lot, which they felt was right and proper when you were out of an evening to enjoy yourself.

Suddenly, Mayor Poynt stiffened. His sister looked up.

'What is it?' she asked.

Jeremy nodded towards the doorway. A stoat had just come in. He looked battered and bruised and none too happy.

'My chief of police,' murmured the mayor. 'I expect he's come to tell me that he's not been able to arrest that scoundrel Montegu Sylver.'

When he reached the table Zacharias Falshed said, 'I haven't been able to arrest that scoundrel Montegu Sylver.'

The mayor gained a certain amount of satisfaction for having predicted this sentence, word for word.

'And,' continued Falshed, flinching, 'I've lost the steamocycle.'

'You've *what*?' cried the mayor, leaping to his feet and causing a lull in all the conversations in the room. 'You've *lost* it?'

'Well, worse than that. It exploded. It's at the bottom of the river. I couldn't help it. That dratted weasel tricked me. It was a pretty big bang, I can tell you. I was lucky to escape with my life.'

'We'll talk about how lucky that was, later,' said the mayor through tight lips. 'What's happened to the weasel now?'

'Escaped on a river craft.'

'What sort of craft?'

'A barge.'

The mayor's eyes nearly popped out of his long narrow skull. 'A *barge*? What, did it have winged mice pulling it? Couldn't you catch up with it?'

'It wasn't travelling beside a towpath,' said the chief of police, miserably. 'It was on a fast stretch of the river and it was driven by fast clockwork. There were stinging nettles all along the banks – and brambles. It was impossible to follow the boat on its meandering path through the fields.'

'Meandering,' murmured Sybil. 'I *like* that word. It's euphonic, just like my name.'

'You have a beautiful name,' said Falshed, turning his attention to his boss's sister. 'Sibilant. I've always thought so.'

The mayor snorted. He hated it when Falshed used long words and showed him up. 'Course it's *sibilant*. Her name's Sybil. All you've got to do is add an *ant*. Anyway, never mind her blasted name. What about my steam bike? You'll pay for that out of your own pocket, Falshed. In the old days we princes could hang you from Whistleminster Bridge by your heels, but I'm told I can't do that any more, though faun knows why. Those rushes of blood to the head often do a lot of good.'

'I'm sorry,' said Falshed, hanging his head. He sat down in the spare chair.

'Who said you could join us?' the mayor cried. 'You take a lot on yourself, Falshed. Besides, you look like death warmed up. I take it you've had a bath?'

'I have bathed, Mayor. It's the bruises and cuts.'

'Well, I'd rather you didn't bleed on my dinner if you don't mind.'

Sybil interrupted her brother here. 'Oh, don't scold him, brother. I think it would be nice to have company for once.' She turned her attention to the stoat policeman. 'Chief Falshed . . .'

'Zacharias,' he murmured. 'Zach.'

'Zacharias,' she said, clicking her teeth. 'It must be lonely work, being chief of police.'

'You have no idea. Everyone hates me.'

'Even your boss!' growled Jeremy Poynt.

But then the mayor cheered up considerably. His roasted swallow had arrived. Moreover the place was getting warmer. Other diners and the waiters were beginning to wilt under the onslaught of the fires in the grates, but the mayor found this kind of temperature to his liking.

'Aha!'

The swallow looked delicious. The chef had

used its shape in flight and had stuck it on a small stand on the plate so that it looked as if it were swooping through the air and gathering insects for its supper. Except that it was mostly featherless and a sort of purply colour from the blackberry sauce. It looked like a modern work of art, worthy of any sculptor of the great steam and clockwork age.

'That,' said Sybil, 'is simply beautiful.'

'Ain't it just,' said the mayor, and snapping off a crisp wing he began crunching.

Sybil's face fell. She turned to Falshed. 'You see what a crass brother I have, Zacharias? He has absolutely no soul. He doesn't appreciate art in the least, now does he?'

Falshed was in an awkward position here. If he so much as twitched, and that twitch was recognized as an agreement with Sybil's statement, the mayor was going to take enormous offence. Yet he couldn't just sit there and not reply to this charming princess. He knocked a fork on the floor instead and took his time in retrieving it. By the time he had wiped it on a napkin and put it back beside the mayor's plate Sybil's cheese on toast had arrived and she was tucking in.

Sybil continued their earlier conversation. 'So, you *do* find it lonely – being chief of police?'

'Well,' Falshed replied, philosophically, 'it comes with the job. Even my own family . . . they're afraid of me. Everyone hates me and everyone – except the mayor and yourself of course – fears me. They know how conscientious I am. I would shop my own grandmother if it became necessary,' he added, with a certain pride.

'You haven't got a grandmother,' said the mayor, finding the swallow's wishbone and snapping it himself with left and right paw in order to ensure he alone got the wish. 'And if you had, I'd have appointed her as chief of police instead of a nincompoop like you. Now, are you going to order any food? I'll have seconds if you are. I'm feeling rather peckish tonight.'

'You're peckish every night,' Sybil told him. 'You're getting positively fat. Look at those rolls on your belly. It's disgusting. If you're going to have something else, have salad.'

At that moment Falshed's secretary, a police sergeant, came into the restaurant. He was the token weasel on the mustelid police force and his name was Pompom, after the cathedral's great saint. His many-greats-grandfather had been jester in the court of Prince Poynt and his family had been loosely connected with the Poynts ever since. Pompom looked harassed and upset.

Making his apologies to the mayor, who glared at him as if he were a dung beetle, Pompom said in hushed tones to Falshed, 'Jack the Ripper's back.'

'Jack the Ripper?' Sybil said. 'Who's that?'

Falshed sighed dutifully and got to his feet. 'A jack weasel of wanton destruction,' he said. 'Some say he must have had training in a weasel steam-laundry to perform his crimes so efficiently.'

Sybil gasped. 'But what does he do?'

'It's delicate, princess,' said Falshed. 'I hesitate . . .'

'Oh, for goodness' sakes, Falshed,' said the mayor, chomping into the swallow's drumstick. 'Sybil, the creature simply goes through the city stealing mammals' underwear off washing lines and ripping them to shreds. Mostly jills' frilly panties and jacks' briefs. Sick, if you ask me. Needs catching soon. Falshed, can't you come up with a more imaginative name than *Jack*?'

'Well, the only thing we know about him for sure is that he's male – and that he likes the sound of tearing silk and cotton, of course.'

'Well, hurry up and catch the fellow. I lost two pairs of favourite boxer shorts last week.'

Falshed came to attention and clicked his heels. 'Yes, Mayor. Princess? May I say how charmed . . .'

'Go, Falshed,' growled the mayor.

But Sybil said, 'Goodbye for now, Zacharias, and if you should ever get *desperately* lonely, I'd love a game of hollyhockers.'

'Oh, *please*,' groaned her brother, pushing the parson's snitch to the side of his plate. 'Spare me!'

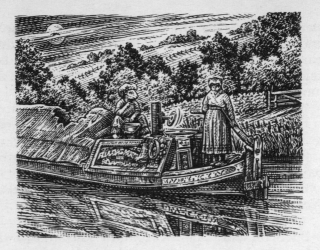

CHAPTER TWENTY-FIVE

If the bargemammal had not hooked him out of the swill, Monty would probably have drowned. It was not a nice way to die, sinking into a bog of sludgy, porridgey waste food. There would have been many unpleasant gulps and swallows before death finally numbed all earthly sensations.

The bargemammal, a jill polecat whose face markings resembled a burglar's mask, regarded Monty with some amusement.

'Hello, washertoad. Two shirt collars missing this week. Try not to let it happen again.'

'Very funny,' said Monty, spitting out slops that tasted suspiciously like school dinner. 'Now, if you'll assist me to my feet, Jis, I would be most grateful. Do you have a bucket of water I can wash in? I should like to get rid of some of your cargo from down the front of my frock. It's oozing into all sorts of unpleasant crevices.'

The jill had not let go of the barge-pole. She stood there, a stalwart meaty-forelimbed female, wanting some answers.

'Look, I let you jump into my barge with the police after you 'cause of that machine he was chasing you on. Steam-driven, wasn't it? Can't stand steam, myself. I'm more your clockwork mammal. The barge motor is clockwork. Everythin' inside the barge has got nice cogs and wheels and a flyspring. Wouldn't have steam if you paid me. Hate the vapoury stuff. But I want to know. Why are you dressed like that?'

Monty replied with dignity. 'It's a disguise.'

'You'll be telling me next you were going to a fancy-dress party.'

'No, I was escaping from the police, as you saw. They believe I have abducted – or murdered – a lemming prince. It's not true.'

The polecat had no love of the stoat police, who were known to be corrupt and unfair, but she was not sure Monty was not a murderer or someone capable of a terrible crime.

'So you say.'

'My name is Montegu Sylver,' said Monty with a certain amount of forced aplomb. 'The Sylvers have been respected amongst weasels since prehistoric weaselsaurus roamed our dear Welkin.'

'So you say.'

'I can assure you, Jis, that I have an honest and respectable background. My friend Bryony Bludd was saying just the other day . . .'

'So you – wait a bit. Did you say Bryony Bludd? Not Bryony Bludd the vet? Describe her to me.'

Monty described his friend to the best of his ability.

The polecat put down the pole. 'Why,' she said, in a more friendly voice, 'Vet Bludd treated me for distemper and cured me. She's a one off, she is. Any friend of hers is a friend of mine. I'll get you that bucket of water. You just stand here by this tiller. If the barge looks like crashing into the bank, just twitch it a bit in the opposite direction. Won't be a tic.' She spelled the word for him and clicked her teeth. 'That's a joke I made up today. I get plenty of time for thinking.'

The polecat disappeared down below aft.

Monty stared out into the night. There was a moon, so he could see clumps of reeds behind which were the banks. It was a pleasant enough evening. Fish plopped on the surface occasionally. Night animals were out on the towpath, their dark silhouettes slipping by without a sound. An owl flew across the face of the moon, startling the weasel for a moment. Monty felt very vulnerable standing on the deck of the barge, exposed to such creatures as monstrous owls.

There were strange sounds too. Screeches and squeals, some sounding like pain was the cause, others hostile. Rustlings in the pond weed. Slithery sounds in the grassy banks. Scratching of bark amongst the nearby trees. Croaks, groans and gulps. Slurps. All manner of sniffing and snorting out in the fields that slid by.

'I'm not a country mammal any more,' he

murmured to himself. 'My family have been in the city too long now.'

He wondered what had happened to his two friends. He hoped that since the police had been so keen on chasing him that the other two had escaped and would be on their way back to the city by now. They would have to clear their names, of course. Bicycle thieves were regarded as just slightly less criminal than murderers since most mammals relied on their bikes to get them to work in the country. Bike thieves had received rough justice in the paws of rough locals in the past, ending up not in the courts but hanging from a jury-rigged gibbet in some lonely wood.

'Ah me, the scrapes I do get myself into,' he mused.

At that moment the barge was travelling through some houses whose gardens stretched down to the river's edge. Untended, the barge had drifted right and was heading towards a boat house on stilts which stretched out over the surface of the water. Monty noticed the danger just a little too late. He grabbed the tiller and wrenched it sideways. The barge swung violently out into the river and towards the opposite bank. He wrenched it again in panic. The barge lurched to the right, ploughed into the bank and on into a small greenhouse on the water's edge.

The barge stopped dead. Panes of glass came crashing down all around the front of the vessel, falling with more than a tinkle. A strong smell of crushed tomato plants wafted to Monty's nostrils.

'What's going on!' yelled the polecat from

below. 'I've just spilled the whole lot and twisted my ankle in the bargain.'

'Sorry, sorry,' said Monty, staring aghast at the damage he had caused to someone's greenhouse. He picked up the barge-pole and began shoving the barge away from the bank. It was hard work. The bows of the barge were buried firmly in the mossy mud. Lights had now gone on in the house. Someone came out with a lantern. To Monty's consternation it was a human. It had a shotgun under its arm and swung the light back and forth, saying, 'Who's there?'

'Sorry, sorry,' said Monty, pushing as hard as he could. 'I'll pay for the damage.'

The human came along the garden path. It was a man. He towered over Monty, shining his light down on him.

'What's this?' he said. 'A washertoad wrecking my fence?'

'Accident,' said Monty, for whom like most animals the powerful smell of human being was still a frightening odour. 'Didn't mean it. Send your bill to Montegu Sylver, Flat 7a Breadoven Street, Muggidrear.'

'Huh, a townie, eh? What's a washertoad doing living at posh address like that? What have you been doing in them clothes? You stink of pigswill.'

'Mouseswill, actually.' The waste food had dried to a crust on Monty in the wind now and he felt absolutely wretched.

The bargee came up from below with a bucket of water.

'Here, you leave this to me,' she said to Monty. Then to the shotgun-carrying human, 'You, you've been told where to send the bill. Go back to bed.'

'Who are you telling?'

'I don't know, you ain't got a label.'

'Good mind to give you what for!'

'Oh, go and play with your gun and leave work-mammals to get on with important matters.'

All this while Monty had been conscious of the human wielding a weapon, but the polecat seemed not to care. She was obviously used to dealing with country humans. She took the barge-pole from Monty's grip and pushed off from the bank with the ease of a skilled bargee. The human stood and glowered at them. Then he shook his fist and yelled, 'Don't think I won't send that bill.'

'I hope you do,' cried Monty, relieved that he had not been peppered with buckshot. 'I'll certainly pay it.'

'You better,' came the voice, drifting over the canal, 'or I'll send Dinsdale to collect it.'

'Who's Dinsdale?' asked Monty of the bargee.

'Search me,' she said, getting the craft to rights. 'Some sort of debt-collector, I suppose.'

They passed silently by a village now. Monty could see the graveyard stones gleaming white in the moonlight. Two more humans were out there, digging in the churchyard. Monty heard the clink of spade on flint. Monty recalled that recently two badgers, Herk and Bare, were up to their old tricks of body-snatching from Muggidrear's Lowgate Cemetery. The bodies of weasels and stoats had been offered to Bryony. Bryony did cut up bodies it was true, to study anatomy, but those were cadavers which had been donated by the creatures themselves when they were alive. In this instance she had realized that these corpses had come from the graveyard since they were half-decomposed.

However, the two badgers were not convicted due to lack of evidence. It was strange to think that humans practised this crime too.

The barge drifted on into the night. Finally it reached the wide part where it entered Muggidrear. Monty saw the gaslit streets with relief, shining hazily through the fog. By chance, and very good luck, he saw his old friend Jaffer Silke, rowing across the waters. Hailing Jaffer, Monty got a lift to a landing stage on the eastern side of the city, though he had to share the rowing-boat with dozens of live ragworms, just piled into the bottom of the vessel and left to wriggle around.

'Nice bit of jelly to go with, and these 'ere rags'll sell for a few bob,' said Jaffer, having received the cargo in part payment for a job. 'Jellied ragworms – you got to love it. I plan to cook 'em up the minute I get back tonight – then take 'em to the south end, where there's loads of jellied ragworm stalls. Would you want one for your supper, guv'nor? You could slip it in the apron pocket of that there frock you're wearin'. By the way, *why* are you wearin' that female clobber? You look like some sort of washertoad.'

'It's a disguise, Jaffer.'

'You're not actually takin' in washin' then?'

'No, I'm not,' said Monty, firmly.

'Pity, these pants and jacket could do with a bit of a scrub.'

Monty was dropped on the jetty and he made his

way back to Gusted Manor. Mammals stared at him in the light of the lamps, as he hurried through alleys and byways, over the slick cobbles of the market squares, under arches, around statues. Finally he came to Breadoven Street where he saw a policemammal pacing up and down outside the house which contained his flat. He avoided going that way, skipping around the back of the building, over a fence, and down the yard, up the drainpipe, in through Jis McFail's landing window and finally, and with great relief, reaching the door of his flat and going inside.

He did not light the gas lamp because of the policemammal outside. Instead he took off his dress and threw it over the dark form of one of forelimbchairs. Then he crawled onto his soft bed with sigh, tucking his tail in behind him. As he rolled over to face the wall, his nose touched something cold and clammy. Gingerly, he reached out and felt something slimy and moist. He noticed, for the first time, a foul smell. Then someone lit the lamp and he found himself face to face with a putrid corpse, rotting and dribbling green fluid onto his sheets. The mouth of the dead body was open and a little grey tongue poked through the gap between the two front fangs. The eyes were missing.

'AAAGGGHHH!' yelled Monty, jumping off the bed.

'No need to shout, yer jillship,' murmured a silky voice, behind him. 'It's only us.'

Monty whirled to face two badgers. One was sitting in the forelimbchair, the frock draped about his head like a veil where Monty had flung it. The other was standing, holding the lamp. They were both smirking in that obsequious way that grave-robbers have with real mammals. It's as if they can only really relate to corpses and have trouble when they have to exchange social chit-chat with live creatures.

'Only us,' said the one in the chair. 'Nuthink to get excited about. Phew! This frock's a bit high, innit? What you bin doin' with it, cleanin' out the water closet?' He still left it there, hanging over his face, the sleeves like ear flaps over his large-domed head.

CHAPTER TWENTY-SIX

'What are you doing in here?' demanded Monty. 'Herk and Bare, isn't it? Turned to burglary now, have we? And what's that stoat corpse doing in my bed?'

'Why, yer jillship, we 'eard you wanted bodies, to cut up like,' said Herk. 'We faund this one in a stagnant boating pool, in the ruins of the kursaal funfair. You can 'ave it for a couple of guineas.'

'Even if I approved of body snatching – even if I wanted corpses – this one's falling to bits. Look! Its nose has dropped off onto my pillow.'

Bare said, 'Granted, she's a bit ripe, yer jillship, but I never knew a vet to be fussy about such things. You can dig out her liver and lights easier now she's gone all soft and mushy. An' her teeth and bones are as solid as the day she was snuffed.'

'This mammal has been *murdered*?'

'Oh, yis, but not by us,' proclaimed Herk. 'Some other begger did it in the park, when nobody was looking. Now she *has* been done, so to speak, it's a pity to waste 'er, ain't it? I mean, all that good corpse would have gone to waste, so to speak. We couldn't leave her there.'

'You keep saying *her*. This looks like a male body to me. A jack stoat.'

'Figure of speech,' murmured Bare.

'It is *not* a figure of speech,' argued Monty, who was hot on such things. 'A figure of speech is an expression used for the sake of emphasis, like a hyperbole.'

Bare went on the defensive. 'Well, what's one of them? A highperbrolly? Some sort of umbrella?'

'It's exaggeration for the sake of effect. I'll give you an example. *There's thousands of books on that shelf.* Clearly there are only a couple of dozen books, but I exaggerated to impress you. Now do you understand what a figure of speech is? Good. Well, don't make mistakes and then call them figures of speech, just to cover up. That's just plain dishonest.'

' 'Scuse us for breathin',' snorted Herk.

At that moment there was a knock on the door. Fully expecting it to be the police, but tired of running, Monty opened it. It was not a mammal in a blue uniform, but Bryony. She stepped inside. Bryony said, 'I heard a shout. Monty, you're back!'

'After many adventures, yes,' said Monty. Then turning to Herk and Bare, he added, 'This is the veterinary surgeon you require. I am the Right Honourable Montegu Sylver, Esquire.'

Herk drew himself up, gathering his indignation in the form of a large stomach which hung over his wide leather belt in rolls of fat.

'So,' he said, looking at the frock, now on the floor, 'you're not a vet after all. You ain't even a female. You talk about being dishonest and honourable an' all that? Goin' about wearing jill's dresses. And that mop cap! It don't even suit you. You look a fright in it.'

Monty snatched off the cap, now aware that he still had it on.

Bare turned to face Bryony. 'Vet Bludd, I presume?' he said, in a deep, echoing voice. 'May I have the honour to make your acquaintance, your jillship.'

'What do you want?' asked Bryony.

Herk said, 'Got a body for yer. Still got its liver and lights. Birds 'aven't got the eyes yet, either. Well, not all of 'em. There's still lots left round the edges . . .'

Bryony turned to stare at the body, then shuddered slightly before saying, 'Half-a-crown. But I don't want it in that condition. You have to deliver it to my surgery cleaned and ready for dissection.'

'Five bob!' came back Herk. 'If we've got to clean it up first, we can't let it go for less than that, can we, Bare? That's prime amatony, that.'

Monty felt it was time to intervene. 'Bryony,' he said, gently, 'the body is of a murdered stoat, found in the old kursaal. As you know, the boating pond in that ancient funfair is a favourite place for getting rid of bodies.'

Bryony's furry brow wrinkled. 'Oh.'

'Yes,' said Monty.

'In that case, drop it in the mortuary first, clear it with the coroner, then take the *cleaned* body round to my clinic. You know where that is. I'll pay you four shillings. A florin each. It's more than it's worth. There are bits dropping off it every other second. Look, there goes a claw. It's rolled under the bed.'

The badgers grumbled, but they gathered the body together in a blanket as best they could and made their way out of the flat and down the staircase. The smell was quite high. It drew the landlady from her living room at the foot of the stairs. Jis McFail stood by the door to the street and tutted at the two scruffy badgers.

'That's something dead in there! I can smell it.'

Herk said, 'Only an old murdered stoat.'

He swung the blanket so that the load banged against the landing wall and made a squishy sound.

'See?'

'You be careful. Don't treat it like a load of rotten cabbages. Even murdered creatures is entitled to respect.'

Once they had gone, Monty went to the bathroom and had a good all-over wash. He found some clean clothes and changed into them. Then he went back to the living room, where Bryony was waiting for him. He picked up his chibouque and began to chew on the stem while staring with great seriousness at Bryony.

'I can't believe you did that,' he said at length. 'How can you buy a murdered stoat from those two body-snatchers?'

'Easy, I pay four shillings for it.'

'Yes, but Bryony . . .'

'Look, if you can go round disguised as a wash-ertoad, then I can buy bodies to further my studies in anatomy. How are we vets ever going to find out the secrets of the mammal form if we haven't any bodies to cut up?'

Clearly they were not going to agree over the body issue, so Monty let it drop.

Leaning back in the forelimbchair he sucked his chibouque and said, 'We've been through desperate adventures, I can tell you. I still don't know what's happened to the other two. I hope they got away from the mob.'

'You were chased by a mob?'

'Then the police. Chief Falshed to be precise.'

'The police?' cried Bryony.

'Falshed will have it that I've assassinated the Prince Imperial. They haven't got a body, of course, and any evidence will be false, but if they catch me they'll jail me until I'm either convicted or cleared, in which case I won't be able to continue looking for the prince.'

'How did you get away?'

'I only managed to escape capture by dressing up in some clothes loaned me by hedgehog gypsies, then jumping into a barge full of mouseswill.'

'So that's what the smell is? I thought it was still the body. What did you do to incur the wrath of a mob and the interest of the police?'

'We borrowed some bicycles, that's all. Nothing too drastic. But things got a little twisted around and heated. I wish I knew where Maudlin and Scruff were. They took another direction. You haven't seen them, by any chance, have you?'

'No,' said Bryony, then a little more coldly, 'I've only seen your friend Lord Haukin. Why didn't you tell me about the mayor's heating machine? The one he's building below the city? I had to endure the bleating of that insufferable Haukin with his monocle flashing at me every time he nodded his head. It was really too much of you, Monty.'

'Sorry, but Hannover's not that bad.'

'He is to me. And why doesn't he make up his mind which eye needs correcting?'

'The monocle is an affectation.'

Bryony snorted, 'You're telling me. Everything about that stoat is an affectation.' She softened a little. 'So, anyway, no I haven't seen your two weasels anywhere. I do hope they're all right. I *have* seen one of your sewer rats, though. Toddlebeck, is it? Such a gentlemammal! Always swooping to bow. We talked about the heating machine, which he has observed being constructed. Nothing about a bomb though. Perhaps Spindrick has given up the idea.'

Monty shook his head. 'Spindrick *never* changes his mind. He's inflexible. Doesn't come from my side of the family.'

'Oh, really?' said Bryony, in a distant voice. She picked up the frock and mop cap.

'You can have those,' said Monty, generously.

'I think they'd look better in Jis McFail's wardrobe.'

'Up to you. Look, I don't think we'd better go searching for Scruff and Maudlin. It'll only confuse things further. Best wait until they come to us. If I know Scruff he'll find his way back all right. I take it you haven't found out any more about Prince Miska?'

'No, how about you?'

'Not a thing, except he hasn't joined the army. It's odd, isn't it, that he's disappeared so thoroughly. One might suspect he's being detained somewhere against his will . . .'

At that moment there was a rapping at the door. Monty went to the window and looked down on to the gleaming wet cobbles of the street below. Sure enough there was a police constable fiddling with a silver whistle on a silver chain standing under a street light. A little further along the street stood a black windowless carriage hitched to two mice. There was a blue lamp hanging on the side. Mist was billowing out of the alleys on the side of the river. Ringing Roger chimed the hour over the city. It was getting late. The knock sounded again.

'Someone at the door,' reminded Bryony.

'I know. I was just checking something.'

Monty went to the door and opened it. A triumphant Chief of Police stood there. He pointed a leather-clawed glove.

'AHA!'

'I beg your pardon?'

'I said, aha!' repeated Falshed in a rather weaker tone than before. 'It's meant to intimidate you. You've been nicked, Sylver. Put out your paws and I'll give you a present of some nice shiny bracelets. The Black Maria awaits, to take you to the ball. Ball and chain, that is. Time to begin your porridge. If you can't do the time, don't do the crime. You lags are all alike. You all get caught in the end. It's no good trying to hide behind that jill. You can't get away this time.'

Monty said, calmly, 'What am I charged with?'

Falshed stepped inside the room.

'*Murder*,' said Falshed, dramatically. 'Also the theft of a bicycle. There are several constables downstairs. The house is surrounded. You can't escape. You, jack, are a murderer and a thief.'

'I hired the bicycle. I think you'll find, when you check, that we left a note and some money for the loan of the machines. You're making a fool of yourself.'

'Making a fool of myself?' hissed Falshed. 'And what about the missing prince? I suppose you know nothing about that, do you?'

'I know very little about Prince Miska's disappearance. I've been trying to find him myself. There's a jill lemming looking for him too. If we don't find him soon, he may very well be assassinated.'

'Never mind the talk, you're for the high jump.'

'Chief,' said Bryony, stepping forward, 'I want you to think carefully here. If you arrest Jal Sylver, your career will be over in a blink, no matter what the mayor has told you.'

Falshed looked unsure of himself and shuffled his feet. The mayor had indeed implied that no harm would come to Falshed over this arrest. 'What – how do you make that out?'

'You know as well as we do that Jal Sylver has nothing to do with the Prince Imperial vanishing. If you arrest Jal Sylver now, when the prince is found – dead or alive – we will sue the fur off your tail. Your name will be splashed across the front page of *The Chimes* and you'll be working as a boot-black for the rest of your life to pay off the costs of the court action, which you will *lose*, make no mistake about it.'

'I – I don't think so, Jis Bludd.'

'Oh, yes you do. You know very well that when the truth comes out Mayor Poynt will abandon you. He'll throw you to the wolves in order to keep his own name clean. *You'll* be blamed for falsifying evidence, false arrest, et cetera, et cetera. You know how it will go. First you'll be suspended, then sacked, then go to prison. There are plenty of weasels and stoats behind bars who would like to see *you* in there, Chief Falshed. I'm sure you'll get a warm welcome from them.'

Something was happening behind Falshed's eyes. There were lights flashing and sparking inside his head. Through those eyes, Bryony and Monty could clearly see his mind working, the messages going back and forth between different parts of his brain. There was a realization in there that Bryony spoke the truth. Mayor Poynt was not to be trusted. There was dirty dealing going on somewhere and Falshed knew that if anything went wrong, he would be the scapevole. He had to at least delay the arrest of Sylver until he was sure it was legitimate.

Finally Falshed glanced over his shoulder at the doorway, and his eyes narrowed before he spoke.

'You never saw me,' he said, in the same dramatic tones he had used when accusing Monty of murder. 'I was never here. I'm going to tell the constables that Montegu Sylver was absent.' He drew in his breath. 'If you ever snitch on me, I'll destroy you both, I swear. The Falshed revenge is not something you want to witness – ever.'

'So far as we're concerned,' said Monty, 'this conversation never took place.'

Falshed nodded. 'I'm gone,' he said. 'But one day, Jal Sylver, I'll have your guts for garters.'

'In the meantime, you'll have to use elastic, like everyone else.'

'Yes, well.' There was not a lot else to say. The chief of police left in as dignified a fashion as he could manage to join his two young stoat constables at the foot of the stairs.

One of them was saying as he descended the stairs, 'I swear I can smell dead bodies . . .' but Jis McFail came out of her room at the bottom and yelled at them, 'Wipe your big muddy paws on the doormat next time!' and the thought was immediately driven from the constable's mind, as he hurried to get out of a house where the landlady stood with crossed forelimbs and glared thunder at him.

Monty watched the chief and his party from the window.

When Falshed reached the street the third police constable who had been playing with his whistle had the instrument snatched from him by his boss. 'They're not toys,' Monty heard Falshed say, angrily. 'I'll keep this until you feel responsible enough to use it for its proper purpose.'

'Aw,' muttered the constable, clearly upset.

CHAPTER TWENTY-SEVEN

'Oh, come on,' pleaded the mink overseer. 'Tell me.'

All through the shift, while Maudlin had been shovelling coal and Scruff had been tipping the great bucket full of molten iron, the mink guards had been desperate to know Scruff's secret. A place which was worse than the iron foundry!

Already Scruff's pelt had singe marks on it where tiny splashes of white-hot metal had burned holes. Maudlin had noticed that the day shift tipper, now off duty, hardly had any fur left at all. He felt deeply for his chum, especially since Scruff had volunteered to do the job in his place. That was the mark of a true friend. Maudlin had heard that the average life-span of a tipper was two weeks. A fortnight! A weasel could only be so careful, then one big splash and it was all over. Yet Scruff seemed cheerful enough. Maudlin too wanted to know this place where Scruff had been: almost as much as the mink overseer and his pals.

'Just give us a hint,' said the overseer. 'Was it on Welkin?'

'Ho, yes, it was on Welkin all right,' replied Scruff with a knowing roll of his eyes.

The other weasel slaves, working in the vast foundry, were grateful to Scruff for keeping the guards busy. The clink and clank of their tools told the story that they were working, but at least they weren't being beaten while they did so. The minks had grown so used to hitting mammals with their sticks they now did it for pleasure. It was a relief to many to be able to get on with the gruelling tasks of hammering red-hot iron rails into shape, or lifting heavy loads, without the added suffering.

'Definitely on Welkin,' said Scruff.

'Near, or in Muggidrear?'

'Oh, *in* Muggidrear.'

The dawn light was slanting through the windows. Gas lamps had been extinguished in the huge workroom. Thin shadows drifted here and there in the dimness.

There was that eerie feeling about the atmosphere which makes one start and look around quickly, thinking something has moved in a corner. It was the time when spiders yawn and stretch and come out to see if they've caught anything in their nets overnight: some fly or moth struggling out its last few seconds of life; the time when doors creak loudest, for no reason at all. It was the time when the dreams and nightmares of animals appear to be real. A strange time. An unholy time.

'Oh, all right,' said Scruff at last. 'I'll tell you. The very *worst* place on earth is . . . Huggermugger's Nursery School.'

'A *nursery*,' sneered the mink overseer in contempt. 'Worse than *this*?'

'It's not the place. It's who runs it.'

'Who did run it?'

'The nursery teacher from the dark side of the moon, Jis Ludgate, a weasel you do not want to meet, my friend, especially if you're only three years of age and innocent as a kitten.'

'I think it would take more than a nursery teacher to scare *me*!'

'Well, you may be made of tougher stuff than me,' replied Scruff, spilling some molten metal on his tummy fur and not even flinching. 'As for me, I never want to see that fiend again. She made my life a desperate state to live in for a while. I managed to escape one day in an empty toy box, which was thrown out as rubbish, but I'm certain if I hadn't I would be marred for the rest of my natural days. *Ludgate!* Even now that name can send shivers down my spine. Two syllables from hell.'

'Huh!' said the overseer, unimpressed. 'What did she do?'

'Her potty trainin' was a desperate enterprise. She used to put the potty out in the snow and ice for an hour before makin' you sit on it. Metal potties! They was frozen so cold the iron rim used to stick to your bottom. I've still got a red circular scar where a potty was pulled off. I'll show it to you . . .'

'No thanks,' said the mink. 'Is that all?'

'Course not. She used to tie our forelimbs at night, so we couldn't suck our claws.'

The mink nodded. 'That *is* bad.'

'And wipe our noses with shiny, 'stead of tissue toilet paper.'

'Oooo. Nasty.'

'An' if she caught us pickin' our noses, she dipped our claws in vinegar which made your nostrils sting when you did it again.'

The mink said, 'Did she ever make you swallow mustard, if you said "Damn" or "Heck"? I had that once. I had to swaller two gallons of water and still my mouth and belly was on fire.'

'I've got a question for *you*,' said Scruff. 'Who *really* owns this foundry? I mean, I know Cynthia, Nigel and that dog run the place, but there's Jal Big behind it somewhere, ain't there? Who's the mammal collectin' all the brass at the end of the month?'

The mink's eyes narrowed. 'You don't need to know that.'

'I'll make it worth your while,' whispered Scruff, with a sideways look at Maudlin, shovelling coal. 'You see if I don't.'

The mink was particularly stupid. 'Are you threatenin' me?' he cried, loudly.

'No,' hissed Scruff, 'I'm trying to bribe you, you idiot.'

'Bribe me?' The mink's eyes opened wide. He moved closer to Scruff in a conspiratorial fashion. 'Why didn't you say? What have you got for me?'

'An ocarina.' Scruff spoke the word as if it were the most precious object on the face of the earth.

'Yeah?' the mink said, brightly, then as predicted. 'What's one of them?'

'It's a very rare musical instrument.'

The mink glowered. 'I don't play.'

'No, no. You don't have to have no talent for it. You just put the thing to your lips and a tune comes out. What's more,' Scruff looked around, 'gold and jewels follow.'

'What do you mean?'

'I mean it's a *magic* flute. You play a tune, say, *Twinkle, Twinkle, Little Star*, and you gets lots of stars, in the form of *diamonds*. They just fall like the gentle rain from heaven on the earth beneath.'

The mink wasn't *that* stupid. 'Why ain't you rich then?'

'I am. We both are, Maud an' me. Own vast estates in Shotland. More in Eyerland. I have a fleet of merchant ships in the eastern seas carrying ivory, and apes and peacocks, sandalwood, cedarwood and sweet white wine. Maud has another fleet in the western isles, with cargoes of diamonds, emeralds, amethysts, topazes, and cinnamon, and gold moidores.'

'Huh! What would I want with apes and peacocks?'

'They're just sort of the trimmin's, see. You pepper your estates in Shotland and Eyerland with them to make 'em look fancy. Lords and earls and whatnot come to visit. "Ho," they say, "lookit all them posh creatures from exotic lands. This bloke must have a bob or two."'

The mink looked sceptical. 'I'd rather have somethin' of *real* value in this modern world. Somethin' that makes *real* brass on today's markets. Solid stuff. Dependable.'

Scruff nodded his head enthusiastically. 'The ocarina can do that. Oh, yes. Easy-peazy. Somethin' more down to earth, eh? Like coal or road-rails, pig-lead, firewood, iron-ware, and cheap tin trays.'

'Now, you're talkin',' said the mink. 'Look, the gaffer that really owns this place is Jem Poynt, Mayor of Muggidrear. Those three up on the hill? They just run it for him.'

'I thought as much,' said Scruff, narrowing his eyes and pursing his lips. 'An' you, my friend, are a rich mink. That weasel over there with the shifty eyes, he's my friend Maud. He's got the ocarina. I'm sorry to have to betray 'im, but this is survival. Just go up there and arsk him for it. He'll give it to you, all right.'

The mink grasped his beating stick more tightly and marched determinedly over to where Maudlin was innocently shovelling coal. Maudlin thought he was in for a thrashing and he dropped his shovel and covered his head with his forelimbs. Other weasels looked on sympathetically, expecting the worst.

'Give it to me!' hissed the mink, his eyes darting round to make sure the other minks weren't watching. 'Give it me, now!'

'What?' whimpered Maudlin.

'The ocarina thing.'

Maudlin looked across at Scruff, who nodded slowly.

'Oh, *that*?' said Maudlin. 'Well, I dunno as I can, really. I suppose that rotten turnip over there told you I had it, just to save his own fur?'

'Give it over,' hissed the mink, 'or I'll thump you one.'

Maudlin reached inside his vest and withdrew the ocarina. He tried to look grumpy as he handed it over. The mink took the instrument eagerly. Before he could help himself he had the mouthpiece to his lips and was blowing. Such a weird tune came out it startled the whole factory floor. Everyone stopped working, dead in their tracks.

The notes flew out of the fat clay ocarina like the songs of witches at a witchguide campfire rally: shrill and sharp, but with penetrating clarity. The mink played with wide open eyes. His claws ran up and down the holes like spiders. Some sounds were so piercing it made eyes water. Some were so deep they stirred the bowels of tummies. When the tune was finally over and the mink lowered the instrument from his lips, his fellow guards rattled their sticks on the ground in appreciation.

'I didn't know you could play,' called the overseer. 'Give us another one . . .'

But the sentence was barely out of his mouth when something flowing and wicked came hurtling through one of the broken upper windows. It was made of green mist and black shadow. Its eyes were fathomless hollows in its shapeless head and its mouth was a cavern from which there was no return. In its slavering jaws it held a limp and exhausted manless horsehead, but there was plenty of room for more victims in there. Since Scruff and Maudlin had last seen it, the phantom seemed to have grown tenfold in size and was now more terrifying than ever in its aspect.

The *thing* hovered in the air above the slack-mouthed weasels and minks below, surveying the silent scene. Its eyes hungrily took in the number of victims it had at its disposal. It decided to go for the ones with sticks first, because they looked the most threatening. The phantom didn't like being threatened.

Someone a long way back on the factory floor dropped a tool. Through metal aisles fantastical, the shovel blade rang faintly. This seemed to act as a signal for the supernatural fiend. The phantom swept down like a hawk and swallowed its first victim, the mink overseer.

Everyone ran screaming for the exits.

One by one the terrifying monster swallowed terrified minks. They went down like so many chocolates into the throat of a bonbon-loving gannet. While the fiend was busy with the minks the weasels scattered, making good their escape. They prised open the locks on the doors with jemmies and ran outside into the fresh air.

The next shift was just coming through the gates. Their mink escort were bewildered by the escaping weasels, but they soon rallied and began to wield their sticks, yelling at the night shift to get back inside the factory. No-one took any notice.

At that moment the ghastly creature from the other world swept through the open doorway of the foundry. Out in the fresh air it seemed to expand even more. Out in the open it seemed to be fashioned of material like scummy pondweed, which trailed and dripped slime everywhere it went. There were curtains of grey-green webby stuff hanging from its limbs, and its speckled pale belly swelled like that of a bloated frog as it ate more and more minks. It seemed ravenous. It sucked minks in through a forest of razor-sharp teeth, mincing them into streaks of red meat. The phantom liked its food soft and spludgy, rather than solid and crunchy.

Once the night-shift minks had all been gobbled up, the horror of the ocarina began devouring the day-shift guards. The day-shift weasels joined the night-shift weasels in scattering about the country-side. Soon there was not a weasel in sight – the slim lithe weasel is good at finding hidey-holes in trees and banks – and Maudlin and Scruff were amongst the best hidden of the lot, in the unplugged knot of an old oak.

The pair emerged once darkness fell again. It had been cramped and damp in the hollow oak and neither of them had slept. They had now been awake over twenty-four hours and were cold and hungry. They crept away over the moors, making their way south, stopping first to relieve some scaresparrows of their overcoats, scarves and hats, to help them against the chilly night air. They wrapped themselves up in the tattered clothes, grateful for any item of clothing which would keep out a keen wind which had found itself somewhere on the edges of the moor.

'I'm glad we got rid of that ocarina,' said Maudlin. 'Good idea of yours, Scruff.'

'Ah, it was you made me think of it.'

'Did I?'

'Yep. You're sort of inspirin', Maud. That's what you are. Look, there's a light on the edge of the moor. I'm hopin' that's my northern Aunt Nellie's cottage. It's the way I've bin heading this last hour. Let's go and find out if she'll give us a breakfast and a bed for a few hours. I dunno about you, but I'm bushed. I could sleep for a week.'

Maudlin yawned. 'Me too. And I could eat some sparrows' eggs and a nice plate of bank vole rashers.'

'Well, I'm sure we'll be welcome at Auntie's place. She's one of the old school. Talks a bit funny, but that's the dialect round here.'

'I don't care how she talks, so long as the beds are soft.'

CHAPTER TWENTY-EIGHT

Finally the intrepid pair of weasels were across the moor and walking up Auntie Nellie's garden path. Scruff seemed to remember that there had been a windmill not far from her house, but it appeared to have gone. He could see the foundations still there on the grassy knoll, but nothing else. Scruff thought this rather strange.

That fine widow-jill herself was busy making supper. All her chores for the day were over. She had done her washing, scrubbed the front step and polished the door handle. The house was spotless. It was always spotless. Over the years Auntie Nellie had hunted down all spots within the cottage walls and ruthlessly done away with each and every one. Where spots were concerned, she showed no mercy. Even had one claimed to be an ally, she would have pretended friendship, then – when it was least expecting it – she would have attacked with duster, mop and floorcloth, until it had been sent to its maker.

Auntie Nellie was just sinking into a soft fore-limbchair, when she heard a knock at the back door. The *back* door. Only familiar tradesmammals and relations came to the back door. Had the coal-mammal forgotten that extra sack?

'Auntie!' cried Scruff, as the door opened.

Auntie Nellie stood there and scowled at the two vagabonds standing on her back step. 'What d'ye want? I 'aven't a sou for the likes of vagrants and no-goods. Where did yer get them hats and coats? Yer look all brussoned, if yer ask me. If it's money yer want, yer 'ave to work for it, like I always has, yer pair of scruffs!'

'It *is* me. Scruff. Your nephew.'

Finally, she recognized him. 'Oh, *you*. Why 'aven't yer bin up to see me, these last 'undred years?'

'I have come up to see you, Auntie. Look, I'm 'ere.'

Her face brightened. 'So you 'ave. Come on in, m'duck.'

'What's *brussoned*?' whispered Maudlin, as he wiped his feet on the scullery mat.

'All bundled up tightly in your outdoor clothes,' explained Scriff, 'usually uncomfortably. It's that dialect I talked about.'

'Oh?'

'Come on, come on,' muttered Auntie Nellie, leading them into a spotless parlour where there was not a pelt hair to be seen. 'Sit yerselves down on the sofa. Not doin' so well for yerself, these days, eh?' she clicked. 'Those clothes look as if they belong on a scaresparrow.'

'They do, Auntie. We pinched 'em out in the fields. The crops will 'ave to fend for themselves.'

'Can't even afford yer own clothes,' said Auntie Nellie, sympathetically, 'yet here yer are, come to see your old relic of an aunt. Come by stage-coach or train?'

'Train.'

'There's posh for yer! What's the matter with yer friend? He's got a face like a portobello kite.'

'He's just hungry – and tired – like me.'

'Hungry?' She went towards the kitchen. 'Why, I'll soon cure that. In half-an-hour you'll be complainin' you've got the gorman ruckles.'

'What's the *gorman ruckles*?' whispered Maudlin as Auntie Nellie vanished into the nether regions of the old cottage.

'Tummy-ache.'

'Oh.'

Sure enough, within thirty minutes there was a feast on the table. Fried bubble-and-shriek, made of leftover elderberries and nettle leaves; streaky vole bacon with the gristle cut off; mouse brains and chitterlings; black pudding; and some northern batter slabs made from acorn flour mixed with mouse-milk butter, baked into a cake, then fried in a liberal dollop of vole lard (in these parts they were known as 'greased cricket pads' and were an acquired taste).

Maudlin tucked into everything, even the greased cricket pads, but not the chitterlings, which he pushed surreptitiously to the side of his plate. Auntie Nellie noticed.

'Eat yer nice mouse guts,' she said. 'I've soaked 'em in special vinegar for almost a week.'

'I – I'm not fond of intestines,' said Maudlin.

'Eat yer mouse guts!' she snapped, her pointed face glowering at him.

Maudlin gobbled them down quickly, trying not to notice the sour taste.

'There's a good weasel,' said Auntie Nellie, her face beaming once again. 'Oh dear, does it bring yer kernels up?'

'Pardon?' said Maudlin.

'Sour face, yer've got. Was them mouse guts asky-tasky?'

'A little.'

'Never mind. Now, off yer both go to bed. You'll find some sheets and blankets in the wardrobe at the head of the stairs. Pillies in the wicker basket in the spare room. Use them twin beds I bought at Widdershin Fair last Crobbletide. Be interestin' to know if they're as hard as they look. Good for yer back, hard beds. Off yer go, off yer go. Get out from under me paws. I'll follow yer up, once the washin'-up's done. It's a wonder we don't all fall down with fatigue – you from travellin' on yer puffer engine and walkin', and me from me chores. Tomorror one of yer can chop me some kindling while the other fetches water from the pump. How's that? Sounds like a lot of fun, eh? Night-night.'

'By the way, Auntie,' said Scruff. 'What happened to the windmill you had next door?'

'That thing?' She snorted. 'Wind wasn't good

enough for 'em, was it? Too slow and ole-fashioned, they said. So they bought one of them new clockwork mill engines to grind the flour faster and make the mill wheel turn quicker. Only trouble was, they didn't take the sails off first. Powerful engine, it was, made them sails spin like nobody's business. Whole windmill took off when them sails started whizzin' round. Shot up into the sky with a great whirrin' sound. Never seen again.'

They tramped up the wooden stairs, found the sheets, blankets and pillows, and made their beds. True enough the mattresses were as hard as navy biscuits. Still, they were exhausted. Just before they fell asleep, to the clinking of dishes in the scullery, Maudlin said, 'Your aunt treats us as if we were young kittens.'

'That's because I ain't seen her since I was six, Maud. She still thinks I'm a young scallywag.'

'Oh.'

'She likes you though. She likes most weasels.' He was silent for a few moments, before adding, ''Cept those who look snirped.'

'What's snirped?'

'Mean face, narrow eyes, tight mouth, pinched nose. Funny how the old dialect comes back, once you hear it. Night, Maud.'

'Night, Scruff. And thanks for getting us out of that jam.'

But Scruff was already asleep. He never heard compliments anyway. They fell off him like raindrops off a water vole's back. Soon he was snoring, drifting away in some always-always land, where he was six again and cutting a river reed to make a flute, shinning up trees to eat ripe plums, and avoiding Friday night baths like the plague. In that land the sun always shone, the summer days were hot and long. In that land the winter nights were as cosy as being in bed with hot-water bottles while there was snow on the roof. In that land hearts were always, always full of joy.

They both woke abruptly to the sound of a cooking pan being struck by a metal spoon.

'Up yer get, yer lazy pair. Rise and shine. Out of sheet lane and down the wooden hill.'

Maudlin lay staring at a white ceiling for a while. He felt thoroughly refreshed. There were angels in his head. There were fairies in his fingers and toes. He wondered if there was such a northern word as 'smungled' because that's how he felt. All warm and smungled. Even when he heard Scruff drag the gerry pot from under the bed and use it, he didn't flinch. But he couldn't use it himself. His upbringing wouldn't allow it. He finally rose and went downstairs and asked to use the toilet.

'Out in th'yard,' said Auntie Nellie. 'Down th'bottom.'

He went down the path, framed by stinging nettles on both sides, to a rickety outhouse at the bottom of the yard. Inside the sun was coming through the cracks in the planks. There was a wild wood mouse hanging from a nail on the back of the door. He knew wood mice were tough and it was the practice to hang the meat before jugging it, but he thought the back of the toilet door was a bit much, considering the smell and the flies. Still, these country weasels were not as faddy as townies like him, he knew, and they rarely got ill, so who was he to complain?

When he got back to the house, Auntie Nellie had breakfast waiting for him. Then he and Scruff discussed how they were going to get back to the capital, since they had no money.

'Can't we borrow some from Auntie Nellie?' asked Maudlin.

Scruff pursed his lips and definitely looked snirped for an instant.

'Not Auntie Nellie. She's as mean as a queen wasp when it comes to brass. Has to be, to survive up here. No, we'll have to think of somethink else, Maud. We'll go into the village this mornin' to see an old friend of my dad's. Prof. Speckle Jyde. He's very bright. A bit eccentric, but very bright. You never know what he's up to in that barn of his. Might have some new machine which'll get us down to Muggidrear. I used to test some of his devices. Nearly got killed several times,' Scruff added, cheerfully. 'Boiler on his steam kite blew up on me. Luckily I fell into the village pond and escaped with nothink but bruises.'

'Where does he live?'

'At the old watermill. By the by, he's a gerbil. Have you ever met a gerbil?'

'No,' confessed Maudlin.

'Well, they're kind of antsy, if you know what I mean, Maud. Nervous, jumpy creatures. Still, you'll like Prof. Jyde. He's a good 'un. Let's go and see if he's in.'

The pair left Auntie Nellie to spot-hunting (even though spots were now extinct in her house) and walked down the village street. There

271

were all sorts of country weasels out there. Some tough-looking (in a rustic way), some slack-jawed and obviously simple, some bustling. They all spoke to Scruff as he walked by.

'Wuppa, Scruff. An't seen you lately. You bin away?'

'On holiday,' Scruff invariably answered. 'Been to see my cousin in the capital.'

Maudlin whispered, 'I thought you hadn't been here since you were a kitten.'

'Haven't,' replied Scruff, 'but time does funny things to these country folk. Nothin' much changes up here, from one year to the next. All they know is they haven't seen you around for a bit. I find it best to just say what I said. Cuts out a long conversation, which we 'aven't got time for at the moment.'

They passed through the village square. Maudlin was charmed by it all. There was an old timber-framed guildhall in the middle of the cobbled square with a mouse trough and a water pump beside it. On one side of the square was a tavern and on the other side a place of worship. In between these was the Jills' Institute and a little further along the Townjills' Guild. The Working Jacks' Club stood in the far corner and the Weasel Farmers' Rural Bank opposite it.

Stalls were beginning to go up on the square. It was obviously market day. Livestock was being led in by the weasel farmpaws. There was the cattle: herds of bank voles and harvest mice. There were also dairy herds of field voles and wood mice. Carts began to arrive, full of grain, drawn by large yellow-necked mice. A squire came in a coach

272

drawn by a matching pair of mice. Gypsy weasels with red-and-white spotted neckerchiefs, nobbly sticks in their paws, led in fine yellow-necked mice for trading. It was a wonderful bustling place of activity.

'Come on, Maud. Stop gawpin'. We ain't got time.'

So Maudlin reluctantly followed Scruff out of the other side of the square.

Chapter Twenty-nine

The gentle and benevolent gerbil who was Professor Jyde had always been the very model of politeness, good-breeding and unimpeachable fine manners. This had grieved him all his life. He longed to be a ruffian who destroyed parties with bad behaviour. Someone with a reputation for drinking too much honey dew and enjoying disorderly conduct. Someone who made others groan when he entered the room and leered and made rude noises and blew raspberries at pompous folk and threw soft-boiled eggs into clockwork fans in a crowded room.

Yet he knew that he could never achieve this ambition as himself, so he set out to make himself someone else, someone who was already there buried deep within him, but who had not yet been allowed to come out.

The professor lived in an old acorn-grinding mill on the top of a hill overlooking the town. It was in a windy spot, naturally, and though the new mill on an adjacent hill had taken over the job of producing acorn flour, the old one still had its sails intact. The professor had put a brake on to stop them whizzing round because the cranking sound they made interrupted his thoughts.

Prof. Jyde's thoughts were very important. He was at this present moment perfecting a formula for a potion which separated bad habits from good habits. The boil-necked Dr Lycus Heck lurked somewhere inside Prof. Jyde and the potion, when taken, let him out.

He had taken it once and a terrible change had come over him. He had shuddered and shaken, gone into convulsions on the floor, smashed several test tubes and glass bubbles, knocked over a bunsen burner and singed his whiskers. What had happened after that, he did not remember, but he did know he felt good about it all once he found himself back as the professor again. He had realized what a wonderful breakthrough he had made in the cause of science.

Animals with over-fastidious habits could now be cured. Those with impeccable manners and charming etiquette could develop disgusting ways for just one night and give all those self-righteous prigs out there something to be indignant about. It had been a wonderful experience and one he would surely have to repeat – though not too often, for the lump on his bonce was extremely painful.

'Prof? You there?'

The professor went to the door and opened it to see an old friend standing on the step.

'Scruff? Is that you? Good gracious, how nice to see you.'

The professor tried to shake claws with a cup of tea still in his hand and spilled it everywhere.

'Sorry about that,' he said, mopping it up a little while later. 'Please introduce me to your friend.'

'Maudlin, meet the prof.'

'How do you do, Professor. I'm Maudlin. I used to work for the Muggidrear council, but recently Scruff and I came into the employ of Jal Montegu Sylver, of 7a Breadoven Street, Gusted Manor.'

'Sylver? The famous detective? Yes, I've heard of him, sure. How very fortunate for you both. I understand he's a very astute weasel. Unique in his approach to problems. Doesn't he have an assistant who keeps saying "elementary" or something?'

'*Basic*. She keeps saying "basic". An' she's not really his *assistant*, so to speak,' said Scruff. 'They share the same landjill and they're friends and neighbours. She's a vet.'

Maudlin wanted to cut to the quick. 'Look, Professor, we're in a spot of bother. We've run out of money and we want to get to Muggidrear as soon as possible . . .'

Jyde looked agitated and began pacing up and down, his paws crunching on bits of glass.

'Oh dear, oh dear, but I'm afraid I don't have any to lend you. I'm rather poor myself.'

'Know that, Prof,' Scruff said, 'but we thought

you might have some ideas. You know, things you've invented, like that flyin' bicycle you tried out.'

Jyde blinked. 'That was a failure, as you know, Scruff. An utter failure. You were the pilot. You ended up like that ancient weasel of old – Ikkyrusk – in the village duck pond, after crash-landing. At least, Ikkyrusk didn't end up in the pond, but he did crash when he flew too near the sun and melted something essential. Anyway, I can't think . . . oh, wait a bit, yes, yes, I may be able to help you.'

'Can you?' cried Maudlin.

The professor looked distracted. 'Yes, yes, hmmm. Yes. Out the back. In the old barn at the bottom of the hill. Go down there, ahead of me. I'll be along in a minute.'

Scruff and Maudlin set off down the hill. There was a derelict wooden barn at the foot and, when they opened the doors, they found a basket attached to an enormous colourful cotton pear-shaped sheet lying on the floor. It looked a flimsy set of objects and both the weasels wondered how this assemblage was going to get them all the way to Muggidrear.

A little while later they were joined, not by the professor, but by a grossly warted shrew.

'Well, what're you looking so dopey about, you set of street cobbles?' said the shrew. 'Don't you know what you're looking at?' He sniffed loudly and hawked at their feet.

'Hey!' cried Maudlin.

'Hay's what horses eat,' sneered the shrew. He flicked Maudlin's nose painfully with his claws. 'What a couple of dopes. Name's Lycus Heck, by the way. Dr Lycus Heck. Master of the cane.'

He swung the brass-knobbed stick he was carrying and swiped Scruff across the backside with it.

Scruff stepped forward with narrowed eyes and punched the shrew right on the point of the nose. The shrew fell down and then seemed to go into a frenzied state of activity, thrashing and jerking. Gradually they were amazed to see the shrew's features change into those of Professor Jyde. Jyde sat up and rubbed his nose.

'Ow, that hurts,' he muttered. He looked up at the dumbfounded faces of his friends. 'Oh, dear. Did I change? Of course, I must have. I just put a little of the potion in my tea to spice it up.'

'What's all this about, Prof?' asked Scruff, helping him up.

The professor explained about his new discovery.

'Well, if you want my advice,' Maudlin said, 'you'll leave well enough alone, Professor. No good can come of such scientific stuff as potions which change your personality. It goes against the laws of nature. Mammal shouldn't play Creator, you know. The next thing you'll have is animals being dug up from their graves and brought back to life.'

'What a terrible idea!' murmured the professor, a crafty look coming into his eye. Then he seemed to gather himself together. 'Look, erm, yes – this – this here is a hot-air balloon. You'll need some money for charcoal, to make the fire in the gondola – that's this basket thing on the end of the lines – then the whole thing will fill with warm air and lift you up above the world. Wonderful, eh? Yes, yes.' The intelligent gerbil was darting back and forth nervously, pointing out the different parts of the hot-air balloon. 'Flying high above Welkin. Fields like a patchwork quilt below you. Mammals like ants. Houses like sugar cubes. Wish I could come with you.'

'But first we got to buy the charcoal?' said Scruff.

'Yes, yes, but I know where you can earn some money. The squire's having a sparrow shoot at The Grange this afternoon. If I were you I'd go and offer yourself as beaters. You have to drive the sparrows out of the gorse and into the guns. Finches of all kinds, actually. They shot over two hundred last year.'

Maudlin said, 'I'm not sure I approve of blood sports.'

'Well, the birds do get eaten. It's not like dormouse-hunting, where they simply cut off the bushy tail and leave the rest to rot. The dead birds are distributed amongst the local population, to the poor in their cottages and to the old mammals' rest homes. I'm sure the squire could do with some more help. He was only saying to me the other day that he was running out of beaters.'

'What's bin happenin' to 'em?' asked Scruff. 'The beaters?'

'They get shot. The squire's friends are a bit short-sighted.'

Maudlin cried, 'Oh, yes, that sounds promising,' but Scruff pointed out that they had little choice in the matter.

'We got to get some money from *somewhere*.'

'Oh, all right then,' sighed a resigned Maudlin.

'I might as well get shot as fall from the sky. Either way I haven't got long to live, have I?'

Scruff slapped his friend on the shoulder. 'You're such a joker, Maud,' he said, cheerfully.

They went home to Auntie Nellie's for lunch.

'Jugged woodmouse,' said Auntie, in answer to Maudlin's question. 'Nice and tender. Been hanging for a week.'

Yes, thought Maudlin with a queasy stomach, on the back of the thunderbox door.

CHAPTER THIRTY

Fortunately, the gamekeeper at Squire Miffin's estate was a weasel. Scruff found it easier to speak to weasels than stoats, and presented himself and Maudlin at the tradesmammal's entrance. Cook came forth out of the kitchen, glared at him, wiped her floury paws on her pelt, and sent the kitchen boy off to find the gamekeeper. The gamekeeper's name was Jon Broon, and he was a weasel with a lofty opinion of his place in society. His tail and whiskers were greased with vole lard and his ears stood straight up. You could tell he had been a sergeant-major in someone's army.

'Aye,' he said, looking the pair up and down, 'have ye ever done beating before?'

'Not as such,' replied Scruff, 'but it don't sound a hard job. Not one you'd need to be apprentice to.'

The weasel gamekeeper sucked on his front teeth. 'Not hard? Weel, that remains to be seen. Hard enough it is if you're walking point, ahead of the line. Hard enough on the right flank, where most of the game flies up. Hard enough if one of the squire's shooters aims too low and takes your head off your shoulders.'

'Oh, well, yeah, it's hard *then*,' agreed Scruff. 'But since we're beginners you'll probably put us in the middle of the line at the back, won't you? Till we learn what to do.'

'You'll go where I have a mind to put you,' replied Jon Broon, peremptorily. 'Shillin' an hour, it is, and no argument there.'

'Fine. Where do you want us and when?'

'In the meadow at the bottom of Snake's Lane at two this afternoon.'

'We'll be there.'

At two o'clock the shooting party was ready, lining the end of a long lea. At the top of the lea was gorse bush country leading out of some ragged woodland. The finches were in some ferns between the two. The beaters, mostly villagers, were milling around a little way from the shooters. Both parties wore cloth caps, one lot of which were a bit greasy, the other lot bearing tags from a well-known Muggidrear outfitters. Scruff and Maudlin could hear the conversations of both groups.

'La-di-da stoats,' the beaters were saying. 'Got nothing better to do than blast away at innocent finches.'

'Common-as-muck weasels,' retorted the stoat shooters, 'not good for anything but raising finches for our guns.'

Scruff and Maudlin kept apart from all this bickering. They were there for one reason only: to earn a few shillings. Once they had a bob or two jingling in their waistcoat pockets, they intended never to see this lot again.

Maudlin admired the squire's estate.

'Wish I had a mansion like this,' he said, looking back at the house, and beyond a beautiful box garden full of decorative peacock butterflies. 'I'd have all my friends down for weekends.'

'Nah,' said Scruff. 'You ain't got no friends, 'cept me, and I wouldn't want to come here. Too many seeds in the air. I like the smell of mouse dung on a city street. I likes coal cellars and foggy alleys and vole pie shops. You wouldn't get me up 'ere.'

'Time to line up!' called the gamekeeper. 'Back of the woods, you lot. Got your beatin' sticks? Good, off you go then.'

The weasels filed away. Maudlin and Scruff tagged on at the end of the line. They went through the ferns, which towered above them, keeping them in the shade most of the way. Once they reached the trees the head beater made them form a line.

'Now, make as much noise as you please when you start forward,' said that able weasel. 'Flush out them finches, so's the masters can pick 'em off with their shotguns. Ready? Off you go.'

'This isn't the way we used to hunt,' murmured Maudlin. 'I remember a time when we . . .'

It was the Old Tooth Age, when the smell of blood was close at paw. Maudlin-with-the-eye-of-flint was the singer of the clan. He sang stories of the clan's prowess, of their hunting skills and also of their fears. The songs about fear he sang at night, when the camp fire was low and the darkness seemed to close in around the warriors.

In these black hours they hunched closer to the flames, glancing over their shoulders occasionally into the impenetrable darkness beyond the rock hang which was their home. It was out there that the bad spirits dwelt – the bad spirits of Maudlin's songs – and their fur crawled when they thought of these supernatural creatures who stole the souls of the unwary from their very beings.

Although Maudlin sang the songs, he was still expected to hunt. He went out with the others at dawn, searching for rabbit. In these times the odours of the earth were stronger, especially before the coming of rain, and filled the nostrils of a hunting weasel. In these times his senses were powerful. He was quick and alert, fleet of paw, and sharp to catch the drift of something unusual, out-of-place on the wind. Some called him priest, or shaman, and made him create special pictures, symbols, to protect the clan from harm.

Weasels had predators too. Owls. Hawks. Falcons. Harriers. Wildcats. Creatures of wing and feather, mammals of claw and tooth. A weasel had to be as honed as the edge of a flintstone. The scent of prey and predator were of paramount importance. Of course, if something came out of the air there was no stopping it. An act of the Creator. Falcons fell from the sky like thunderbolts, hurtling down in a second, and there was no defence. But one could be ready for the cat, or the harrier, and avoid them if one could.

Finally, more deadly than all these problems, was an enemy who had just emerged from the darkness of the earth. Its name was Man and it walked on two legs and

284

carried weapons: pointed sticks, flint knives and axes, rock-throwing slings, hand-made fire. Moreover, it was a large animal with clumsy big feet and a small brain. Mustelids wondered how it had survived, and later, how it had managed to evolve.

Man had no pelt, no fur at all except right on the top of its head. It had no claws and no fangs. In fact, the clan would have bet sixteen walnuts against a bushel of hollyhock seeds that the naked, pale, ugly creature known as Man would disappear before the world got any older, so unsuited was it to survival in the harsh world of the Age of the Tooth.

Maudlin found the hollow bole of an old tree, where the turf and moss met and mingled. Here he hid for a time, listening for rustlings out in the grasses which would tell him that prey was about. The bole had many smells, mostly of other predators, but some of frightened fur. He curled amongst them, soaking them into his spirit. All day he waited until the twilight came, and then he emerged with the long shadows. There on the plain before him were the rabbits, grazing. They nibbled, and nibbled, their teeth clicking, trying to eat as much grass as they could before the warning scents went out that a predator was in the region.

Maudlin flattened himself in the meadow grass, crawling under buttercups and daisies, back in the Old Tooth Age. His eyes were bright, his fur was glossy, his muscles superb. He was lithe as any creature on the face of the earth. Closer and closer he crept, stopping dead every few moments when a grazing head came up to stare, then stealing, stalking, sneaking forward when the head went back to eating.

How gradual death moved towards that single rabbit on the edge of the grazers where the grass was lush and dangerous. It slipped forward imperceptibly in the growing gloaming. There was always quiet panic in the rabbit. It could hear its own heart pounding. It could hear its own blood pumping round its body. These drums continually kept it alert, as it stopped to wonder occasionally, to stare at its fellows all nibbling away around it. If one had bolted, for no reason, all would have run. Each in its place kept the others there. Each was an essential part of the whole. Those in the middle felt slightly safer than those on the periphery. But not much. Death could come out of a hole in the ground. Sometimes it had, erupting from a disguised piece of turf, from the heart of a flower, from the leaves of dry, dusty weed. Nowhere was secure.

Closer, closer, crept Maudlin, as the large, blood-red sun began to slice itself in half on the edge of a sharp horizon. Rabbits blinked, wondering if the darkness would come in as an onslaught, sudden and savage, or if it would creep like death over the hills and woods and fields. It could come either way, depending on whether it was carried in on the back of a storm, whips of lightning cracking its flanks, or whether it blew in calmly from a depthless sea of itself, wave on gentle wave.

Darkness like dust began to settle. A chill wind sprang up. The rabbit on the edge prepared to leave, to move closer to the burrow. One last nibble at the luscious grass and . . . a shadow came as a narrow streak out of the ferns. Its demonic eyes were like hot stones. Its mouth and foul-breath odour were on the rabbit before it could even shriek.

Needle-sharp white fangs pierced the jugular. Shock. Nerves, frozen. Mind, numb. The worst of its repetitive nightmares finally at its throat, fixed there, unyielding. There was no hope. The bad dream was real at last.

Horror blanked all. The rabbit stiffened, kicked once or twice, then its eyes glazed. Its fellows were gone, had vanished into the earth. It was alone in its final throes. Now the real darkness came in. *A darkness not seen before. A darkness which would never go away again, which would settle inside as well as out, which was* death.

Maudlin drank of the sweet warm fluid. Red. Red. He tasted the colour as well as the tang. He smelled the colours as well as the odour. Red. Red. He drank it down as it flowed from its source deep inside the rabbit. A great well lay within. The pumping had ceased, but the flow came still, draining onto the dark grass beneath. Maudlin of the Old Tooth Age. This is how they hunted. Death was meted out at close quarters then. Life's succour was taken at the font. There was nothing between: no gathering and bottling, no storing, no barrelling, casking, corking. No drying or salting, even. Taken straight from the heart, the lifeless form of the container left on the heather, to stiffen in the wind, to grow coarse and hollow, to serve as a warning to others who would seek the lush grass on the edge.

Red-mouthed and satisfied, Maudlin made his way back to the camp fire. His eyes were red, his brain was red, his dreams were red. If there was guilt, it was buried beneath a sea of red. He had eaten. 'I have eaten,' *he sang to his clan.* 'I have washed my weapons in the blood of my prey.' *They too had eaten, had washed their teeth in scarlet waters, but they had not words, the music, the poetry of the singer.*

They left it to him to tell them how they had felt, how they felt now. They listened to the fear of the prey, for whom they had a great respect, for they knew fear just as deeply as their quarry. They were amazed at what they had done and how they had done it. They felt mighty and powerful, great and magnificent!

Then came the songs of ghosts and they felt small again. They peered over their furry shoulders, beyond their tails, and stared out into the blackness. Out there were other hunters, too fearsome to even contemplate: yet here they were listening to the song which told of their existence. It would be good to go into the cave, once the songs were finished, and curl up with one's neighbours and friends. It would be good to get out of the night. Frightful creatures, horrible fiends, lurked, waiting for the last hunter on his or her way home. It was good they were all back, around the camp fire, safe as safe could be.

Maudlin finished his songs and licked his soul, and then poked his pink tongue between those two fine front fangs, for the residue of the day's red . . .

'Keep that line straight there!' yelled the head beater.

Maudlin jerked himself out of a reverie. Finches flew up into the air, clouds of them, peppering the sky. Ahead, the guns blazed in the hot afternoon. The sun was full of fluttering. *Bang! Bang! Bang! Bang!* Birds flew, birds fell. The blast of shotguns was relentless. The beaters kept their heads down. One weasel more or less would not injure the reputation of those stoat shooters. The noise of the shooting knocked the hollow out of the air. It was a damning sound. Death did not creep in at close quarters here, but thundered from a distance. A daffodil lost its head right next to Maudlin's, showering him with yellow shreds. Time to drop to the ground, cover one's ears with one's paws, and think of being somewhere else, somewhere less monstrously loud.

At the end of the day the shot birds were lined up on a grassy bank. There were two hundred of them in all. Maudlin and Scruff were paid.

'You did a good job,' said the gamekeeper weasel to Scruff as he paid them their wages, 'while some of us was on the ground, coverin' our ears.'

He looked hard at Maudlin when he said this, but Scruff would have none of it.

'He wasn't scared, he was *bored*,' he told the gamekeeper. 'He'd done the job and he was bored. *I* was bored too. Anyone would be, watchin' that lot blatter away with their toys.'

With that the two Muggidrear weasels went back to Auntie Nellie's cottage.

CHAPTER THIRTY-ONE

The day after the shoot Scruff went into the village to buy firelighters, charcoal and matches. Then he and Maudlin said goodbye to Auntie Nellie. That good jill sniffed into her pawkerchief and bid the two young jacks a fond farewell.

'Nice to have a visit,' she snuffled. 'Sad when yer go away. Gives me the melancholy riders.'

'Never mind, Auntie, we'll come and visit again,' said Scruff.

'Took yer I don't know how many years this time,' she said, sharply. 'I'll be dead before the next one comes.'

They assured her they would not wait until she was dead before they came to visit once again. Scruff talked about the following spring. That seemed to cheer her up a little. They left her dusting the flowers in the front garden. Auntie Nellie kept a spotless house.

At the barn they met with Professor Jyde, who had already unravelled the hot-air balloon. He took the charcoal and firelighting implements from the two weasels and showed them how to light the fire in the bucket provided. This was placed in the gondola – the basket – and the two weasels climbed in with it. They held open the entrance to the cotton balloon so that it could fill with hot air. Once it had begun inflating, the balloon looked very pretty. It was like an upside-down pear – or to be more accurate – a fresh green fig hanging from the tree.

Professor Jyde took a tiny weathervane out of one of his many pockets and held it up in the breeze.

'Wind direction is perfect,' he said. 'Sou'-sou-east. That should take you right down to Muggidrear. Now the only thing I'm worried about is the landing. It can be dangerous amongst buildings. Is there a large park you can head for?'

'We'll find a green patch,' Scruff assured him, 'won't we, Maud.'

Maudlin said, 'Will we?'

'Course we will. Come on, Maud. Jump in, she's getting a little frisky.'

Indeed, as the balloon filled it was blowing this way and that in the air, tugging at the guys and restraining lines. The gondola was bouncing on the ground. Maudlin climbed reluctantly over the edge of the basket and joined his friend. Once he was in, Professor Jyde made ready to release the balloon from its moorings. At that moment there was a loud moan from the hay loft in the barn. Professor Jyde glanced anxiously in that direction. Scruff said, 'What was that? Sounded like someone was waking up.'

'From quite a long sleep,' muttered Professor Jyde. 'I have to get to him before he wanders off.'

Maudlin said, 'Who is it?'

'Some bits and pieces I found in the local burial ground,' replied Professor Jyde, letting slip the guys. 'At least, his body came from there. I found his brain in a jar in the local antique shop. The lady said it was over a hundred years old! Pickled, of course. Belonged to one of the warders in the Bedlam Institute for the Criminally Insane, so she said. Personally I think it probably came from a lunatic, a murderer no doubt. It was a funny greyish-green colour and had some unhealthy-looking purple bumps.'

Another groan, followed by a crashing sound.

'I can't believe it!' cried Maudlin, looking towards the barn. 'You did it! You raised a mammal from the dead. You're not only irresponsible, you're crazy. What is it? A stoat?'

The balloon was beginning to drift upwards, with Scruff frantically fighting with the rigging, to stop it tangling with the loose guys.

'No, of course not. It was the brain of a mink. At least, I think it was a mink. It looked remarkably like a pickled walnut, but how can you tell . . . ?'

The doors to the barn flew open with a crash. Out staggered a jerky-moving multiple-pieced creature. The forelimbs were those of a weasel sewn onto a mink's body. The hind legs were those of a badger. The head had belonged once on an otter's neck. The moth-eaten tail had obviously been owned by a squirrel. Goodness knows where the heart had come from, but the brain, as they had been told, was mink.

Mad, murdering mink.

Waving its forelimbs in a threatening manner the monster stumbled forwards. The mild Professor Jyde ran towards his creation, shouting, 'Back inside, Stampenstone! Back! Back! Bad mink. What have you done with your chains? You've broken the manacles again, haven't you? How many times do I have to tell you . . .' They last saw the professor arguing with the slow-moving monster he had made out of bits of bodies, trying to herd it back into the barn using a stick to prod it with.

'I'm not sure we'll be seeing the professor again,' said Maudlin, as they went up into the clouds. 'That *thing* has just bitten his stick in half.'

However, the two weasels had more important things to worry about than the dead brought back to life. Their hot-air balloon was now sweeping across the world. Below them the fields whipped by in patches. There was no danger at the moment as they were well above the treetops and there were no mountains in their way. All they had to do was enjoy the view. Maudlin tried doing that but it made him feel sick. He was not good with heights. Scruff seemed all right.

Birds wheeled about the balloon, but not in a threatening manner. All that could be heard above their wild cries was the swish of the wind in the rigging. Inside the gondola the fire burned brightly. Scruff occasionally used bellows on the charcoal to bring it to a greater heat. In fact the fire was keeping them quite warm, because the higher they went the colder it became. They became friends with the earth, which was now like a huge bladder below them, covered in green and brown patches.

They drifted over villages and towns and could see mammals looking up at them, pointing. They were causing quite a stir in the world below. Whole markets stopped trading to watch them go overhead. Farmers in their fields enjoyed the respite of watching them, as one might watch a butterfly. Sometimes they went lower than they intended and whole fields of vole and mouse herds were driven into a panic, charging this way and that, following some blind leader. Once, the balloon almost hit a water tower, but they managed to heat the coals quickly so that it rose above the structure.

In the late evening the dreaming spires and lofty towers of Muggidrear came into view. It was still light. It had recently been raining, but now the dying sun was leaving a clear sky behind it. The bronze beams sparkled on buildings which were normally dreary-looking places with little to recommend their architecture. The mouths of stone gargoyles gaped and gushed silver rain-water. Carved angels glistened, their blank faces and blind eyes showing animation for once. Traffic could be seen in the city streets: coaches, wagons, carts, lone pack-mice. Scruff began to get excited. There was the fruit market, the meat market, the long winding street containing the stalls from which bric-a-brac could be obtained seven days a week, fifty-two weeks a year.

'Makes yer old heart thump, don't it,' he said to Maudlin. 'I missed my dirty old city, I did.'

'Not me. I think I could live in the country.'

'Ah, you wouldn't like it, Maud. Not all the time. It's all right for a visit, but not to live.'

'I would. I would.'

'Nah, you wouldn't.'

'I WOULD!'

'All right, no need to shout – but I bet you wouldn't.'

Maudlin sighed and let it go. There were more pressing things to worry about, like where they were going to land.

'Maybe we should make for Whistleminster Palace,' he said. 'There's a big park at the back, Scruff.'

'Oh, we don't want to land on that side of the river. The *human* side. We'd have to walk all the way back across the bridge, or take a ferry. Nah, we'll put her down in one of our own parks.'

'But they're so much smaller.'

'Oh, I think I've got the hang of this now. Look, you just tug on these rope things, then chuck a bit of coal over the side every so often, to let the fire go down.'

'You can't throw live coals on a city!'

Scruff nodded. 'I suppose you're right. We'll chuck 'em into the river. Look, the wind is taking us along Mother Bronn now. I'll throw some out.'

He took the iron tongs and reduced the size of the fire. The red-hot charcoal fell thirty or so metres, flaring like meteors on the way then sizzling and steaming when they hit the river. The balloon began to go down. Scruff yanked on the rigging. The balloon veered crazily to starboard, heading out over the animal side of the river.

'There you are! Told ya,' cried Scruff, triumphantly. 'I've got this down to a fine art, I have.'

'We're heading towards Ringing Roger!' shrieked a terrified Maudlin.

True enough, the clocktower was swinging up fast in front – four-square and formidable. Its clockface was white and gleaming in the sunlight. The hands stood at quarter past nine. Nearer and nearer it came with Scruff pulling and wrenching on stays and lines, hoping to divert the balloon from its present course. Green parks flowed beneath, but there was no time to throw out coals now, even at the risk of bombing the populace below. It was as much as the pair of weasels could do to steer the balloon and they were not doing a very good job of that.

'We're just going to miss it,' cried Scruff. 'We'll just scrape by on the left.'

'No we won't. We're heading smack dead in the middle.'

'If I just give this one a pull – no – that didn't do it – what about this one? – nope, no good either.'

'We're swaying! We're swaying!' screamed Maudlin. 'I'm going to fall out.'

'Don't be so dramatic. You're all right.'

But they clearly were *not* all right, either of them. The mammals in the streets below had stopped now, to watch them. There was a kind of fascinated hush as they followed the wayward balloon with their eyes. It hurtled towards a certain crash with Ringing Roger. Just as they swept over City

Hall, Scruff noticed something about the flowerbeds in the gardens of one of the factories owned by Mayor Poynt.

'Will you look at that!' he murmured, his attention diverted for a few moments. 'All the time it was *him*.'

'WHAT ARE YOU BABBLING ABOUT?' yelled a frantic Maudlin. 'WE'RE GOING TO DIE A HORRIBLE DEATH.'

'Nah . . .'

At that moment the balloon hit the stumpy spire on top of Ringing Roger. The folds of the balloon wrapped themselves around the weathervane and the whole upper-storey of the craft collapsed. The gondola swung violently downwards, glancing off one of the corners of the tower. Two weasels were flung out of the basket: one this way, one that way. Both managed to catch hold of something on the clockface. The gondola continued to swing around the tall structure, finally hooking itself up on one of the four carved figures which jutted from the corners of the tower.

Quarter-past-nine. Fifteen minutes past the ninth hour.

'You all right, Maud?' asked Scruff.

He was hanging by his forelimbs from the hour hand.

'No, of course I'm not,' squeaked Maudlin.

He was dangling from the end of the minute hand.

'We'll be fine,' said Scruff.

'You might be. Your hand is going upwards. Mine's going down.'

'Yes, there is that, I s'pose. Can't you edge along

297

and climb onto my hand? It feels quite sturdy.'

'Are you serious?'

'Well, if you don't, Maud, at precisely half past nine you're going to slide right off the minute hand and drop onto the point of King Redfur's lance. His bronze statue's right underneath you. So make up your mind. I'd edge along to middle, if I was you. Otherwise you're going to get it right in the . . .'

'I think I get the picture,' muttered Maudlin, growing madder by the second with his best friend. 'Look, I'm edging. I'm edging.'

CHAPTER THIRTY-TWO

'What time is it?' asked Bryony.

Monty replied, 'Half past nine. Why?'

'I don't know. I just thought I heard something. Like a scream followed by a thud.' She shrugged.

Monty said, 'What's that got to do with the time?'

'Well, as it gets dark the magpies fly in and steal balls, then bomb the squirrels with them.'

'Wouldn't that be a thud followed by a scream?'

'Depends if the bombed squirrel saw the bomb coming.'

'Look,' said Monty, 'it's getting late. It's twilight. I can hardly see the ball. Don't you think we'd better be getting home now? I keep looking at that patch of daffodils, thinking Sveltlana's lurking in there somewhere. I'm sure if my ball goes into the rough and I go in there looking for it, I'll never come out again.'

'It's all right,' murmured Bryony, concentrating on her stroke and not really listening. 'Just one or two more holes. We've got them on the run.' Bryony was a very competitive weasel.

'You think we stand a chance of winning? How do you come to that conclusion?'

She looked him in the eye. 'Basic, my dear Monty, basic. Mechanical devices *always* go wrong at the most crucial time. It's a law of the universe. It never fails.'

'Come on,' cried Lord Haukin, having taken his shot. 'We're here to play, not to natter. There's a hundred guineas on this game if you haven't forgotten.'

Lord Haukin's partner, a stiff-looking stoat, seemed to confirm this view by huffing and hissing steam from his mouth.

They were on the flog course, just outside the city. Flog was very similar to golf, except that the holes were played backwards. 18 first, then 17, and so on, back to 1. Flog was invented by the mustelids, who loved golf just as much as humans, but didn't want to appear as if they were copying the two-legged creatures who inhabited the other half of Welkin. So they turned the game backwards, in more ways than one, and called it their own. In fact, some mustelid historians were now saying that flog had actually first been played by ancient mustelids, back in the Old Tooth Age, and humans had pinched it and changed it. There was some evidence for this in some flog-club-shaped rabbit bones found in a cave, along with round wooden objects that could have been balls.

Bryony was obsessed with the game. She loved it. It helped her relax from her veterinary practice. There was nothing she liked better than whacking a little white ball down a fairway. Monty, on the other hand, only played to please his friend. He was useless at the sport. It infuriated him. Bryony claimed it helped her to think more clearly while Monty simply became frustrated, believed he was wasting his time, and felt he could do a better job of hacking at the turf if he was behind a plough.

'Good shot,' said Monty, as she whacked the ball up the fairway.

Bryony had persuaded Monty to play with her against Lord Haukin and 'one other' as Hannover had put it. The 'one other' turned out to be a steam-driven automaton, a mechanical flogger who hit the ball precisely every-single-time and was now helping Hannover to win the match.

Monty now took his shot at the green. He mis-hit the ball, which flew off to the left. It struck Hannover's companion with a loud *clang* on the side of the head. The automaton's head spun round on his neck. There was another loud sound, this time a *thwunk* and a metal plate flew off the chap's chest, followed by a few nuts, bolts and springs. He then began throwing his flog clubs like spears at some magpies who were idly watching the game. Finally, with an ominous *hiss*, he started off over the next hill, to vanish beyond it, running towards the river.

'*Now* look what you've done,' cried the

brussoned Hannover, thumping angrily at the fairway with his number seven iron and hacking out a divot the size of the next county. 'You've gone and clobbered my partner.'

There came the sound of a distant muted explosion.

'Jumped into the river,' said Bryony with a nod. 'Best place for him.'

Lord Haukin grumbled. 'We were winning, too. It's not fair. You'll have to forfeit the game.'

'Null and void, that's the rules,' said Bryony. 'It was *your* partner who quit.'

'Only because he got a ball on the bonce!' And he stomped away towards the clubhouse.

Monty too, had had enough.

'Can we go home now?' he said to Bryony. 'I'm still worried about Scruff and Maudlin. I think they should have been here by now.'

'I'm not worried about Scruff. He's a very resourceful weasel. He'll come through, you wait and see. I expect he's on to something, that's why they're late in coming back to the city.' She chipped on to the green next to the pin and one-putted. 'There, par on that one. What's happened to your ball?'

'Lost it,' grumbled Monty, digging around in a clump of clover with his nine iron. 'It's hiding from me.'

'Flog balls are not alive. They can't hide.'

'Ha! So you say.'

Someone came running across the flog course at this point. It was the stoat secretary of the club. He was waving his paws in an agitated manner.

'Jis Bludd, Jal Sylver. There're two weasels

302

hanging from the hour hand of Ringing Roger. It's a wonder they haven't fallen, they've been clinging there this last quarter of an hour. A lamplighter and a watchman. They arrived in a monstrous balloon. They say they work for you.'

'Why didn't you say something earlier?' cried Monty, flinging away his bag of clubs.

The secretary simpered. 'I know how Lord Haukin hates to be interrupted while he's playing a match for money. Then I saw him storm into the clubhouse. I take it you won? He's kicking his locker at the moment. If it hadn't been Lord Haukin I would have come sooner. He does own the club, you know.'

'But this was an emergency,' said Monty. 'Here, take my clubs and those of Jis Bludd, too. Leave them in the locker rooms.'

Outside the course they hailed a hackney cab. It took them straight to Ringing Roger. The cab-driver wanted to go there as much as they did themselves. He had heard about the two weasels hanging from the clockface and wanted to see them for himself.

'There they are,' cried the cab-driver excitedly, reining his mice to a halt and pointing upwards. 'Looks like they're getting tired. Shouldn't be surprised to see one drop in a minute. King Redfur's waitin' underneath, ain't he? Sharp, that lance. Bronze, y'know.'

Bryony and Monty looked out of the side window to see their two friends and employees hanging from the hour hand of the clock. It was a few seconds to ten o'clock. By the time they had climbed out of the coach, Ringing Roger was chiming, the whole tower shuddering with the notes. Scruff and Maudlin trembled from ears to tip of tail.

On the blunted spire there were two or three workmammals, trying to get the pair on the clockface to take the end of a rope they were dangling over the edge. But Scruff and Maudlin couldn't let go of the hour hand to grab the rope, or they would fall. It was a most frustrating and suspenseful spectacle which had the crowd holding its breath. Every mustelid spectator was waiting in hope; that either they would be saved; or failing that, that they would fall. There were even humans watching, from the other side of the river. It was a win-win situation for them. The entertainment was going to be great either way it went.

Monty ran towards the tower with Bryony close on his heels. They opened the door at the side and found a spiral staircase. This took them to the level below the clockwork. There was another set of steps to go up to reach the clock itself. Thirty-nine steps. Once inside the clock housing they could see through the frosted-glass clockface.

TICK-TOCK-TICK-TOCK-TICK-TOCK

The sound of the clock in the confined space was loud, as was the clicking and whirring of wheels and springs, and levers and escapements, and all the other clockwork parts.

As well as the clock hands and figures, two silhouettes were visible through the glass face of Ringing Roger. Monty was one of the most resourceful weasels in the land. Bryony, too, was never without her intellect close behind. They both saw the clips around the edge of the huge circular clockface, simultaneously. The glass was in two halves, a hairline join running vertically up the middle from six to twelve o'clock. When the clips were off, it would fall apart, allowing them to reach the two stranded hangers-on, whose forelimbs must have been aching.

'The clips,' said Bryony, moving forwards.

'The glass,' agreed Monty.

The pair of them began unclipping the two halves of glass from their frame. There were twelve clips in all. When the last two clips were undone, the two separate halves fell inwards, away from the spindle to which the hands were attached. They were carefully lowered and laid flat on the floorboards of the mighty clock housing. This exposed the two creatures on the outside of the tower.

'Wotcha, guv'nor!' cried Scruff, delightedly.

'So pleased,' murmured a strained-looking Maudlin.

Scruff slid down the hour hand to the spindle, climbed along it, and then dropped gratefully onto the floor of the clock housing.

Maudlin did the same. His left paw slipped once, causing the crowd below to go 'OOOoooooo', but eventually he too was inside the home of Ringing Roger. No-one was disappointed. It had been a breathtaking time and a clever rescue. Ice-cream sellers and purveyors of toffee gooseberries did good business afterwards as the spectators wandered off, heading for their homes, their entertainment complete.

The glass was replaced. The workmen above descended, offered their congratulations, and went home. Scruff and Maudlin, their forelimbs dangling as if quite sore, followed Bryony and Monty back to Breadoven Street, where a hot bath and some buttered toast put them back into sorts again.

'So,' said Monty, when they were all settled, 'tell Bryony and I about your adventures.'

Scruff and Maudlin did as they were bid. The story was interesting enough, but Scruff had something important to say at the end.

'Listen, as the balloon was goin' over the city, I looked down, and guess what I saw?'

'What did you see?' asked Bryony.

'Crossed cricket bats,' cried Maudlin, excitedly. 'We saw crossed cricket bats.'

Monty sat up. 'The coach which carried Prince Miska. The heraldic set of arms. You've found it?'

'Except that it ain't a coat of arms,' said Scruff. 'Not at all. It's a whatchamacallit – a trademark – for a firm makin' cricket bats. We saw the crossed cricket bats made out of flowers, in a factory flowerbed. An' guess whose name was cut in the lawn beside that bed. Guess who owns the factory what makes those cricket bats . . .'

'Jeremy Poynt,' breathed Bryony.

Maudlin nodded. 'Dead on the nail, Bryony.'

'Of course,' murmured Monty, sucking his chiboque. *'Poynt's Cricket Bats! Art and Science shaped in willow!'* He was quoting from an advertisement in the newspaper. 'So, the mayor took away Prince Miska – but was it with or without the consent of the Prince Imperial? My guess is that the prince has been kidnapped, taken somewhere against his will. Sveltlana is looking for him too

306

but, as we deduced, she wishes to assassinate him. I have no doubt about it. None at all.'

'Why do you say that, Monty?' asked Bryony.

'Because Slattland is going through a change. A quiet revolution. There are the royalists, who are gradually losing favour, and the democrats, who want a parliament like ours. I believe the Prince Imperial is willing to give way to the democrats, on the understanding that he is allowed to stand for election himself. If he sheds his royal title, he would be allowed to do that. On the other paw, my enquiries have led me to understand that Sveltlana is an anarchist. She wants Slattland to collapse and then grab total power for herself from the ruins. She wants to become a dictator and rule the way the royal family once did, without having to answer to a populace or a government of any kind.'

'Why would the prince come here?' asked Maudlin.

'Ah, there you have it. For advice. Advice on how to step down as Prince Imperial and launch a political career. There's someone in Welkin who's done just that. Who else do you know who has let go of his royal title in order to make a bid for power? Who else has shed his royal rank in order to be elected? You get only one guess.'

Chapter Thirty-three

Falshed was not feeling very pleased with himself.

He was at City Hall, in front of the mayor's desk. On his way into the office the chief of police had passed a female lemming who had just had audience with the mayor. Her musky perfume still lingered in the air. She had looked particularly pleased with herself. Falshed wondered what had gone on between the mayor and that jill lemming, whose eyes had been of the softest dewy brown with a glint of something highly venomous behind them.

'Falshed!' The shivering and brussoned mayor had just thrown some coals on the fire, though it was a warm day. 'Sylver was at the Hannover Flog Club, playing Lord Hannover himself. Why hasn't he been arrested? Why isn't he, at this very moment, dangling from the end of a rope on the gallows? Speak, stoat, speak!'

'Er, um, didn't know he was at the flog course, Mayor.'

'Nor, I suppose, that he was inside Ringing Roger for at least an hour.'

'I wasn't aware of that, Mayor.'

'That's because you're a halfwit – in fact, no you're not – you're a quarterwit.'

Hoping to redeem himself, Falshed said, quickly, 'We've caught the leader of the shrew gang who have been plaguing the north of Welkin. Orgibucket. I have him on remand at the moment. Shall I set a date for the trial?'

'No, throw him in proper jail,' growled the mayor. 'I'd rather it was a weasel, but a shrew will get me just as many votes. As long as I'm being seen to be tough on crime.'

The chief of police was in a bit of a quandary over this decision.

'Er, don't we have to commit him to trial? Twelve just mammals, and true? That's the law, you know. Even a mayor can't tamper with the wheels of justice.'

'You don't need a trial to throw him in *debtors'* prison. He probably owes you a hundred guineas. He can't pay, can he? So throw him in jail until he *can* pay. Which will be never. Therefore he'll rot and die in a prison cell and won't ever be able to get out to challenge our decision to put him there. Who's going to believe a debtor, anyway? Save the city a whole lot of money, not bringing him to trial.'

'There's just one catch,' said Falshed, miserably. 'He doesn't owe me a penny.'

'Are you going to argue with me, Chief?'

Falshed shook his head. 'No, but if my enemies should get wind of the fact that I'm falsifying evidence, they're likely to have *me* thrown into jail. I can't go to jail, Mayor. I've put too many of the occupants there. I'll be ripped to shreds within a few minutes.'

The mayor half-rose from behind his desk. This was in order to get to his waistcoat pocket to look at his pocket watch. 'If we're not arguing, why are you still standing there? Lord, look at the time. Go and see if Thos. Tempus Fugit and Wm. Jott are waiting outside.'

The chief knew the subject was closed. He had to throw Orgibucket into debtors' prison. The only way he could safely do that was to let Orgibucket go, lend the creature a hundred guineas, give him a night to spend it on the town, then demand its return. When the shrew announced he could not pay, Falshed would arrest him again. That's the way it would have to be. In which case, Falshed would lose the hundred guineas, for ever. He was not a rich stoat and the idea of losing so much money grieved him. Yet the mayor had given him little choice in the matter. Falshed would also have to follow Orgibucket every step of the way, in case he simply ran away with the money instead of spending it.

He poked his head outside the mayor's office. Sure enough Jott and Fugit were waiting, frostily ignoring each other.

'The mayor wants to see you now,' said Falshed. 'Hop to it, you two.'

The stoat and the weasel got up and entered the office together.

'Ah,' said Poynt, looking up. 'You two. How's my wonderful city heater going? Is it installed yet?'

The two jals in question were having to combine their steam and clockwork skills in order to build the great engine below the streets – it would be able to heat the whole city, both summer and winter.

'The engine is in place,' said Fugit, stiffly.

'We just need to start it up,' added Jott.

'Good, good.' Jeremy Poynt rubbed his paws together. 'Excellent. Now, Falshed, have you caught that anarchist, Spindrick yet? If we can't throw his cousin Sylver in the jug, at least we can get rid of one weasel from that horrible family.'

'Can't find him,' said Falshed, stubbornly, feeling the mayor had put upon him enough for one day. 'If you want him, you'll have to look for him yourself.'

Jeremy Poynt's eyes narrowed.

'Am I hearing things?'

'No,' said Falshed, 'I've had it up to my neck fur. If you want me, I'll be down the nearest inn, getting drunk on honey dew.'

With that, he marched out of the mayor's office, and straight into Sybil Poynt, who was coming in.

Falshed's legs immediately turned to jelly. His stomach filled with warm melted butter. His jaw fell open in a most unbecoming manner. Princess Poynt did that to him. It was her beauty, or her

311

poise, or the haughty way she tilted her chin. She regarded him with large brown eyes and he sighed, deeply.

'Hallo, Princess.'

'Hallo yourself, Chief Falshed. Made any false arrests lately?'

He coloured slightly under his fur. 'I never make false arrests, your highness.'

'Oh, really? I just took it that if you worked for my brother, you would naturally be corrupt. Most of his minions are.'

'I'm not a minion.'

'Glad to hear it. Look, what are you doing this evening, Chief? I have two tickets to the opera. Gravelotti is singing *The Bat*.'

Falshed hated opera. 'Why, nothing,' he babbled. 'I would *love* to go to the opera.'

She handed him the two tickets. 'Here you are then. Find a nice friend to go with; I can't stand it myself. All that wailing and bellowing, and when you understand the words, they're so silly, aren't they? *Your tiny paw is frozen.* And there she stands, a great gallumphing soprano with badger-like proportions and a paw the size of a frying-pan. The disbelief can't be suspended under those circumstances, can it? Or perhaps you don't think so, since you like it so much. Let me know how you get on. I'll test you later, to make sure you didn't fall asleep.'

Sybil drifted past him in a cloud of musky perfume, leaving him with two tickets in his paw. Falshed choked on the entrancing fumes and gnashed his teeth. Oh, Princess Sybil, you angel in stoat fur. You divine mustelid form. Your tail is the

312

riding whip of the gods. Your fangs are sun's white flames. Your pelt was spun by silkworms in the far Orient. And you smell so *super*. Falshed groaned. Find yourself a nice friend? That was a tooth-click. How many friends does a chief of police have? Especially a corrupt chief of police who works for a corrupt mayor? None, that's how many. Life was a rotten joke at the moment.

He stumbled out on to the street, hoping the wind would blow the tickets out of his paw, and whisk them up to the chimney pots.

'Are those tickets for the opera?' said the voice of a passer-by.

It was Vet. Bryony Bludd.

'Yes,' said the chief, looking down at them. There was something in her voice which made him ask, 'You – you wouldn't want to go, would you?'

'The opera? Gravelotti? And Calmli Domino? Oh, and the wonderful diva, Shue Brown. I'd *love* it.'

'Here,' said Falshed, thrusting the tickets into her paw, 'take 'em. Next time you see me, tell me the plot. I'm supposed to go but – but I'm on duty.'

Bryony was left standing there with two tickets for the opera in her paw. The Chief of Police was disappearing around the next corner. She winced. What she had been hoping for was that Falshed would come with her and she could talk to him and pump him for information. Now she was stuck with two opera tickets she didn't really want. Oh well, Texrose Tuttle or Honeysuckle Jones would come with her. They both liked opera. It was a shame to waste tickets as rare as badger's rubies.

It turned out that Honeysuckle Jones was free

that evening and the pair of them dressed up to the nines and went to the opera. It was a grand affair with mammals – mostly stoats it had to be said – in evening dress, mostly arriving my coach. It wasn't often that two vet weasels managed to mingle with the upper classes and Bryony was determined to make the most of it. They had with them their opera glasses and some bon-bons – without wrappers so they would not rustle sweet papers. The seats were in a private box overlooking the stage: two of the poshest seats in the whole opera house!

'Where did Chief Falshed get these tickets?' whispered Honeysuckle. 'Even *he* hasn't got that much influence.'

'I don't know,' replied Bryony, looking over the balustrade at the other patrons and matrons, 'and I don't care. This is really good. Look, there's the owner of the Blackden and Crookstone Bank, and over there Jis Grindslow Ho, who owns the Star of Otterbrook diamond. And down there – look – a jill with enough stoat bodyguards to fill a cesspit. She looks a tough old dowager, doesn't she? Look at the size of the shoulder pads she's wearing under that glitzy-looking dress! Hey, this is really, really posh, Honeysuckle. I'm glad we dressed up.'

At that moment the curtain went up and Shue Brown pierced the still air of the opera house with her lancing notes.

After the performance, which both weasels thoroughly enjoyed, Bryony continued to quiz the audience through her opera glasses and was suddenly arrested by the sight of a female lemming in the stalls. Was it her? Yes it was. Sveltlana! She was wearing a scarlet, fur-lined cloak, fastened at the throat by that monstrous dagger-pin brooch.

The lemming saw Bryony at the same time and stared coldly up at her. Bryony left the box, flinging an apology at her friend, and raced down the red-carpeted stairs to catch Sveltlana.

The lemming looked about to run when she saw Bryony, but then seemed to change her mind. She waited until Bryony caught up with her.

'So,' sneered Sveltlana, 'no nearer to finding Prince Miska, eh?'

Bryony replied, 'Nor you, by the look of it.'

Sveltlana clicked her teeth. 'I don't actually *need* to find him. I just have to ensure he never returns to Slattland. I'm inclined to think that someone else has done my job for me. I think he's dead. If he was going to be anywhere, it would be here, tonight. He loves opera more than he loves his life. And Gravelotti is his all-time hero. If Miska was alive he would have been at this performance.' She sniffed. 'I shall be leaving myself on the boat tonight, for Slattland. You can tell your friend, Jal Montegu Sylver, that he is just about the worst detective I have ever had the misfortune to employ.'

'I'll pass on your message, though I think you're entirely wrong.'

Sveltlana sniffed. 'Think what you like. I'm leaving . . .'

Bryony stepped forward. 'Not if I make a citizen's arrest, here and now.'

Sveltlana's turned flinty. Her claws flew to the dagger-pin in her brooch. Then she clicked her teeth. Her paw dropped back down by her side, without drawing the pin from its sheath.

'There's no need for all this,' she sneered. 'Your mayor has given me diplomatic immunity. I can't be arrested, by you or anyone else.' She waved a piece of paper in front Bryony's nose.

Bryony was aghast. 'He couldn't do that!'

'Oh, but he has,' cried Sveltlana. 'I simply looked him in the eyes and said that once I was elected president of Slattland he could look forward to certain rewards for his hospitality. I told him a poor, helpless female like me could not possibly harm anyone. I told him his firms would be given most of the contracts for the rebuilding of Slattland's docks and towns, roads and bridges, ships and railways.

'I think it was those last few words which convinced him. He just buckled at the knees, that fat white-furred fool, and simpered, before filling out the form and stamping it with his personal seal. How weak you Welkinites are. When I am president of Slattland . . .'

'Dictator more like!'

'As you will. When I rule Slattland, my armies will be visiting this green land of yours. Then we shall meet again, in circumstances more favourable to me. You will be begging me for your life.'

'I never beg.'

The female lemming gloated. 'We'll see.'

With that Sveltlana turned on her paws and made her way into the crowd leaving the opera house. Honeysuckle caught up with Bryony.

'What was all that about?' she asked.

'Oh, nothing,' said Bryony, fuming quietly. 'Just some icy creature stepping on my grave.'

Honeysuckle said, 'Hey, come on, let's get home.

Look, the fog is already nosing at the doors. It's going to be a damp walk through the cobbled streets. See, the street lamps are already disappearing in the mist. I don't like this time of night. There'll be pawpads about, you mark my words. Look, there's that tough old dowager you saw in the opera house, getting into that coach. Wait a minute. Isn't that the mayor's coach? Those are the mayor's musclemammals, Bryony. What's going on!'

Bryony suddenly realized *exactly* what was going on.

'Hi!' she called, trying to reach the coach through the crowd of mammals pouring from the opera house. 'Stop! Where are you going with that lemming! Stop, I say.'

The stoat musclemammals helping the elderly dowager into the mayor's coach looked across at Bryony and scowled. Two of them shook bunched claws at Bryony. Before she could reach them, they were all inside the coach and the coachmammal had whipped the mice into motion. The vehicle rattled away at great speed, along the street towards the river.

CHAPTER THIRTY-FOUR

'So you think the prince was dressed as a jill?'

It was Monty who had asked the question, while sucking on the stem of his chibouque. He was in his flat, accompanied by Bryony, Scruff and Maudlin. The question had been directed at Bryony, who was sitting on the edge of the table since there were not enough chairs to go round. Her tail was tucked under her and she swung her legs forwards and backwards under the edge of the table. Unknown to her or anyone else, for they were all too intent on questions and answers, Scruff was watching this backward-forward movement with glazed eyes.

'I'm certain that the mammal in the dress was a male lemming. He got into a coach – actually he was more or less pushed into it by the mayor's

318

bodyguards – and was driven away at high speed. Towards the Bronn. Honeysuckle and I followed, but by the time we got to the river's edge both the stoats and the lemming were in a boat and travelling downriver towards the government buildings. They seemed to be heading towards the Tower of Muggidrear.'

'Traitor's Tower, eh?' This was the royal prison where the Prince Poynts and King Redfurs of the past had jailed those they did not like. Most of the occupants had been executed and hung on public gibbets. Some had died there of old age. However, the tower had not been used for a long time now and was lying idle, waiting for history to change course again. 'Well, we can check that out with the otter, Jaffer Silke. He notices most things that go on along the river. What do you think, Scruff?'

Scruff's eyes were still following the mesmeric movement of Bryony's hind legs.

'*Woof!*' he said. '*Woof! Woof!*'

Maudlin groaned. 'Not this again. He's gone into one of those trances. Your cousin Spindrick is a really good hypnotist, isn't he? Whenever Scruff sees something going backwards and forwards, I lose him to his doggy brain. That's why I have to keep him away from clocks with a pendulum.'

'SCRUFF!' Bryony had stopped her leg-swinging exercises and had yelled into his ear.

'What?' he cried. His eyes returned to normal. 'What's up?'

'Never mind,' said Monty. He got his sword-cane and hat. 'Let's go down to the river and see if Jaffer's there.'

It was early evening. They went out into the streets. It was a grey twilight, murky and damp, giving a blueish tinge to the buildings, and making them appear as if they were built from solid slate. Overhead, the sky was in chunks, hanging like heavy blocks of suspended red sandstone. The group walked through alleys and courtyards enclosed by buildings which hardly ever saw the light of the sun.

When they left Gusted Manor and entered Poppyvile, these locked-in spaces tended to fill up with urchins, fishjills and other poor mammals. There were weasels in rags, begging coppers from passers-by almost as poor as themselves. Jack weasels with shallow chests and deep coughs haunted the doorways of hovels. They watched the four pass by through ringed, hollow eyes. Here and there were thin weasels selling bootlaces and matches. A jack with a dancing mouse had a small crowd around him, but when he held out his hat for coins, the ragged jill and jack watchers melted into the shadows of the street. A mousemeat pie-seller carried his wares on a tray balanced on his head, walking down the middle of the street, keeping well clear of upstairs windows.

A knife-grinder pushed the cart bearing his sandstone honing-wheel over the cobbles, singing out in his traditional cry, *'Bring out your scissors, bring out your knives, I'll sharpen the blades 'til they're bright as your eyes!'* It was a mournful cry, which for the most part went unheeded, for few weasels in this district could afford such posh things as knives and scissors, and if they had such luxury items they sharpened them themselves, on the front steps of their hovels. The knife-grinder's cart rattled on over the cobbles, passing the debtors' prison, where the half-moon windows had the forelimbs of occupants poking through the bars. These windows were down level with the street and the occupants of the jail were trying to steal the laces out of passing footwear.

Monty stopped to get his bearings and felt claws fiddling with his shoes.

'Hey!' he said, looking down. 'Leave those, if you please!'

He stared down at the grille and instantly recognized the creature whose dirty claws were attempting to undo his laces.

'Orgibucket!' cried Monty. 'What are you doing there?'

The miserable shrew looked up at the speaker for the first time. He had been too intent on stealing the laces to do so before. It was not often that a mammal stopped right in front of his cell window and it was difficult enough stretching out through the bars to try to whip out the laces before the owner knew what was happening. There were those in the prison who could do it just like that! Magically. But they were skilled shoelace thieves and had been doing it for years. Orgibucket was still at the apprentice stage, having been in prison only a few days. He had yet to earn a farthing from the shoelace-sellers who bought the stolen goods.

'Ah,' said the chagrined shrew, 'you find me in reduced circumstances. Click your teeth in merriment, if you will. Ridicule a mammal when he's down. Tell me you told me so.'

'I will do no such thing,' replied Monty. 'So,

where's your gang now that you're in debtors' prison?'

'Gone, gone,' replied the shrew, wearily. 'They were caught robbing a pie-seller's tray from an upstairs window and were transported to the colonies. My own younger brother amongst them! I promised our mum I would look after him and now he's gone to do hard labour in a place where he'll most probably die of mosquito bites or swamp fever. You can be amused at his plight too, if you wish. We are sorry shrews now, I admit, all come to terrible ends. This is punishment for a life of crime. Though in truth, I'm not here for any crime I have committed, but because of the police chief.'

'Did he catch you at something?' asked Maudlin.

'No, he loaned me a hundred guineas. Me! Ha! Of course I went out and spent it straight away. Got drunk on honey dew. Gambled it away at White's. Bought a yellow-necked mouse to sell on at a profit, only to have it drop dead at my feet three minutes after the sale. Bought fancy clothes only to spoil them with spilt drinks. Ended up with thruppence-farthing, which I squandered on food, being starving by that time. Falshed then found me scraping around in the gutter, searching in the muck for cabbage stalks to sell in Poppyvile. He demanded his money back and when I couldn't pay, he threw me in here.'

'He did that?' cried Bryony.

'Yes, yes, but I deserve it,' moaned the mournful shrew. 'I've been bad all my life. I never thought it would come to this, but I can't say I'm not to blame. Oh why did he have to lend me so much money? If it had been ten shillings, instead of a hundred guineas, I would have bought myself a fancy waist-coat and a pint of honey dew, then would have taken the night train back to Howling Hill. Instead, I ruined myself. My liver is swollen like a sponge. My brain is reduced to a pile of mush. A hundred guineas' worth of booze does a lot of damage, I can tell you. I could hardly see, hear or move after that binge. He had me dead to rights. I couldn't run, I couldn't hide, I could only stand and whimper.'

Scruff said, 'You were a proud shrew once. A bully, a cheat and a thief. But, I have to admit, I feel very sorry for you.'

'Proud? True. A cheat? Also true. A thief? So very, very true. What can I say? I shall die within two or three days. I've sold most of the hair from my pelt for a biscuit.' He stepped back to show them his bare coat. 'I shall starve and die. None shall mourn. I would not want them to. My passing deserves only contempt. My fate is just. I am full of remorse, but it's much too late for that.'

'It's not too late,' said Monty, suddenly making a decision. 'I shall pay your debt. I have need of your services, my shrew'd friend.'

That good weasel then went to the prison gates and demanded entrance. He was followed by his three friends. The crafty-looking stoat jailer let them in once a bright coin was in his grasp. All four went in and saw such sights as to make any mammal wince. The occupants of the jail were poor, yellowy-toothed creatures with faded pelts and dull eyes. They drifted around on the mucky straw-covered stone floors like ghosts. When they saw the four well-fed weasels they moved in like gnats, begging for farthings. Monty could not help

323

them all. It was an impossible task. He passed out what he had in his pockets, but once it had gone he could do no more. Had he emptied the prison with his generosity, and thus emptied his own bank account, it would have filled again before the week was out. There would always be debtors in Muggidrear.

They found the shrew in an open cell crammed with creatures of every shape and size. Most of them seemed to have some sort of mange complaint and there was a lot of coughing and spluttering going on. Those who did not were covered in sores. There were fleas everywhere, the straw on the floor and beds thick with them. It was a sorry place and unworthy of a great city like Muggidrear.

'The mayor and his council are responsible for places like this,' said Bryony. 'It's disgusting.'

'Perhaps he does not know what conditions are like in here,' Orgibucket said.

'Well, he should do,' interjected Scruff. 'It's his job to know. When I was a lamplighter I made sure every lamp in my part of the city was lit and doused, every night. The mayor should inspect places like this and sort 'em out if there's somethin' wrong.'

'If you think this is bad,' said Monty, 'you should see Bedlam.'

Monty left a surety with the prison governor, promising to pay the hundred guineas ('and interest') within twenty-four hours.

'If you don't,' warned the stoat governor, 'you'll be in here in that shrew's place.'

'My bank will send you the money directly,'

324

murmured Monty, trying to keep his temper.

The five creatures then left the foul-smelling debtors' prison. They purchased Orgibucket a good breakfast from a street vendor and then continued towards the river. Once there it took a little while to find Jaffer Silke, but when they had him, the otter confirmed Bryony's ideas.

'Yup! I saw a boat of big jacks carryin' a lemming. Strappin' jill she was. Shoulders like a stevedore. Went dahn towards the Tower. Moored up against it and more or less carried her onto the jetty then into the tower. I was goin' to have words with 'em, when they came out. Shouldn't be handling jills like that, no matter what they done. But they never did come out. Then I had to fish out this body in the water. Leastways, I thought it was a body, but he was still alive. Full o' water. I pumped his chest and it came out like water from a village pump. Fair gushed all over the bottom of me boat. A shrew, like that one there, he was,' Jaffer paused before adding, ' 'cept he had more hair on him. Jumped off the prison ship, he said. Took his chance and went over the rail when the guards wasn't looking.'

Orgibucket's eyes lit up.

'Was he *just* like me? Did he have a white patch like this one behind my left ear.'

Jaffer stared at the spot offered for inspection.

'Come to think of it, yup. He did. Feisty little beggar he was. When we got to the shore he upped an' ran like a rabbit with a weasel at his tail – beggin' your pardon, Monty.'

'That's all right, Jaffer. Thanks for all the information. You've been a great help.'

'My brother!' whispered Orgibucket, with great relief in his voice. 'My brother escaped the convict boat to the colonies. I expect he's back in Howling Hill. Oh, thank goodness. I won't get into trouble when I have to face my dear old mum in shrew heaven. I was quite prepared to do something which would land me up in the other place rather than face Mum having failed to keep my brother out of trouble.'

'All's well that ends well,' said Bryony.

CHAPTER THIRTY-FIVE

Monday and Saturday had been arrested. They were caught in possession of illegal gunpowder and were awaiting trial. They had got a note to Tuesday and asked him to blow up the human jail instead of the whole of the animals' side of the river. Tuesday had refused. He was not interested in the human side. He was battling against authority on the animals' side of Muggidrear. To that end he had got himself a job as one of the clock-work engineers on the mayor's new city heater. This got him legitimately down in the sewers, below the city streets.

Thus Spindrick had put himself in a position to plant his gunpowder bomb. In his garret in a Wimper Street boarding house, he rubbed his paws together and worked steadily by the light of the candle. There was no gas lighting in his garret. He did not believe in modern inventions, and anyway he was testing out various fuses for his bomb and it was easier to have a candle handy to light the fuse and time how fast it burned down.

'String soaked in a solution of salt petre's the best,' he murmured to himself, 'with just a dash of sulphur to make it sparkle.'

He lit a half-metre-length fuse and timed it with his grandfather's pocket watch.

Halfway through there was a banging on the door.

'You want stickleback kippers for your breakfast or not?' yelled the landjill's voice, through the door. 'I can do scrambled wren's eggs, just as quick.'

Breakfast? Spindrick pulled back the blinds and sunlight streamed into the previously dark flat. It was morning. He had been working all night! Well, that was one of the compensations of this type of employment. The interest level was high. It was thoroughly absorbing. Of course, there were boring bits. Scraping match-heads off Coot Vista Matches into a shoe-polish tin lid wasn't a great deal of fun, but when you mixed these with iron filings they made a wonderful primer to set off the gunpowder. Spindrick (a.k.a. The Weasel Who Was Tuesday) loved messing about with explosives. It was dangerous. It was exciting. The burning smells were great and the vision of the explosion was inspiring.

'Kippers or eggs? Or some vole-blood puddin'?

Come on, I ain't got all day. I got the washing to do, the ironin', the front step to scrub . . .'

'Kippers, Jis Loganbelly. Thank you, stickleback kippers will be fine. They're not too smelly, fishwise, are they?'

'Smell like flippin' stickleback kippers always smell.'

'That's lovely. Yes, that's excellent. I'll be down in a minute.'

He heard her paws thumping on the wooden stairs as she descended six flights down to her part of the house and the dining room. Now he had lost his timing! The fuse had burned through and he hadn't been watching the seconds tick by. Never mind. He could do it again later. He leaned back in his chair and scratched his whiskers. The time was getting very close now. He thought about the panic he would produce in the city streets and he felt slight apprehension. Spindrick was not a blood-thirsty anarchist by any stroke of the imagination. He valued animal life. But drastic times needed drastic measures to deal with them. He had to convince the whole of the mustelid population that they were wrong and he was right. There was no question of his being wrong. Everyone else was wrong. He, Spindrick, was right.

He looked around his garret. Hanging from the ceiling were several different types of bomb fuse, all carefully labelled and documented in his little pocket book as to the amount of salt petre and sulphur they contained. In the far corner, under the bed, were the empty gunpowder barrels, marked

XXXXX HIGHLY EXPLOSIVE: NO NAKED LIGHTS WITHIN TWENTY METRES XXXXX. Seeing this, he remembered, and blew out the candle. In several saucers by the window was his combustive and highly inflammable mixtures of match-heads and iron filings. His primer materials. They looked nice and red and glinty in the sunlight now streaming through the dusty window. He frowned. There was a dead spider in one of the dishes. It looked untidy. He picked it out of the saucer and popped it into his mouth. Dry. Bristly.

A thumping on the ceiling six floors down interrupted his reverie. Jis Loganbelly, banging on the ceiling with a mop handle.

'Coming, Jis Loganbelly,' he yelled. 'Be there in a minute.'

He unbolted the inside of the garret door, took off seventeen padlocks, and fitted them to the outside of the door. Then he put the ring of seventeen keys into his pocket and descended the stairs. On the way down he met the jill from the flat beneath his garret. She was a weasel actress currently in a play at the Royal Daggerwobble Theatre. She clicked her teeth at him as he came up behind her.

'Morning,' she said, brightly. 'Such a nice day.'

'Wonderful,' he agreed. 'Look, Vivia, are there any parts for a hypnotist in that new play of yours. What's it called?'

'*Lady Fandamere's Wind*'. It's by the new writer, Ostler Tame. Brilliant play. I don't think there's any hypnotist in it though. There's a piano player. Can you play the piano?'

Once the ordeal of breakfast was over, Spindrick

left the house in the grey dawn. He made his way through the streets which were already full of urchins and vagabonds and other Muggidrear street life. These creatures seemed to have emerged from holes in the shadows. They dragged their miserable forms through the alleys and byways, looking for scraps to eat which had been missed by the birds. Spindrick weaved his way through this poor underclass, promising them under his breath that, come the revolution, they would all be bank clerks.

Finally, Spindrick came to a jackhole with the cover off and protected by a circular barrier. A watchmammal stood at the entrance to this hole.

'Mornin',' said Spindrick. 'Anyone else here yet?'

'Nope, you're the first. You're always the first at work. You must be keen. Hopin' the boss will see you, I s'pose?'

'Well, yes. I need promotion,' lied Spindrick, 'so's I can earn enough to feed my litter of kittens. Seventeen of them me an' my mate have got now. Don't know where the gruel's coming from to go into their darling little mouths.'

'Rather you than me,' said the watchmammal, who was an unseemly fat stoat with twitching whiskers and tail. 'Can't says I envy you.'

Spindrick descended the ladder to the great heating machine below. The previous evening he had entered the sewers by another hole and brought along the last of his kegs of gunpowder. Unknown to Jott or Fugit he had filled some of the shiny pipes with the explosive black powder and now it was ready to ignite. Spindrick inspected the area in the light of day from the jackhole, making sure there were no tell-tale signs of gunpowder on or around the monstrous device. The area was clear. He could relax. Now it was just a matter of lighting the blue touchpaper and retiring. He needed just the right time to do that. A symbolic day! The day was coming nearer and nearer.

The mayor's annual garden party!

CHAPTER THIRTY-SIX

'MAYOR'S ANNUAL GARDEN PARTY' said the banner over the door leading to the gardens of City Hall. 'ENTRANCE BY INVITATION ONLY.'

The garden party was in three days' time. It was Sybil's day, really, though the mayor used it to pay back favours. Sybil loved arranging treats like this. Falshed, on the other paw, loved helping Sybil. She had him running backwards and forwards, carrying chairs on to the lawn, ordering weasels about, posting policemammals at the entrance to stop any inquisitive citizens peeking in and spoiling surprises.

'What's happening to the crime in the city?' growled the mayor at Falshed. 'Stopped altogether, has it?'

'Mayor?'

'Well, it must have done, if you've got time to chase around running errands for my sister. What have you done about my scheme for apprentice steeplejacks and jills? The council have now passed a law that they have to climb Ringing Roger to qualify. Remember? The crowds, paying to watch? The funeral scam, where we collect money for fallen weasels and skim the top of it? Come on, Falshed, there's proper work to be done.'

'But Mayor, what work?'

The mayor flicked the ear of a passing work-weasel with his claw in irritation.

'You have to muster up the crowds, Falshed. The first exam takes place in an hour. I want your police out on the streets, herding tourists and citizens towards Ringing Roger. I want you to set up barriers so that traffic can't get through and passengers of coaches and hire cabs have to get out and walk in that area. I want you to *organize* things, Falshed. That's what I pay you for, isn't it?'

'But you don't pay me, Mayor. I'm paid out of public funds.'

Jeremy Poynt's eyes half-closed and a shiver went through his white pelt which shimmered in the strong sunshine. 'Public funds . . . which *I* control, Falshed.'

'Yes, Mayor. I understand.'

Falshed left the laying of the tablecloths to the weasel and stoat servants, and made his way out of the gardens. Princess Sybil was just coming in. The divine Sybil! His heart did a hop, skip and jump. She was the Creator's most perfect form of a stoat. If the Creator had a mate, she would be in the mould of Sybil Poynt. Her extraordinarily slinky walk, when she occasionally went down on all four paws, made his head spin with silken dreams.

'Oh, Chief, you're not leaving, are you?'

Falshed melted to a pool of grease on the paving stones. Out of this grease came a smarmy voice. 'Oh, Princess, I'm sorry but I have important work to do for the mayor. There's – there's a gang operating in the fruit market. I have to organize a raid and head it myself of course, to make sure it's done correctly.'

Sybil sighed. 'Well, if you must. But can you come back straight away once they've been arrested? I need you, Chief. I need you desperately.' Her musky scent overpowered his will. Her whiskers brushed his face as she passed. Falshed's legs almost gave way.

'I'll return as soon as I can,' he promised her. 'Once affairs of the city have been settled, nothing could keep me away.'

She gave a little wave of her paw, indicating that this was as satisfactory as it could be, under the circumstances.

Once Falshed was outside the influence of the princess's perfume and adorable body movements, he filled his mind with grit. There was work to be done. He did it well. He managed to herd a huge crowd of mammals to the streets and squares below Ringing Roger, where the mayor's men were walking about with collection tins. They would stand square-shouldered in front of mammals and glare at them until a coin was produced and the tin rattled within. Business was brisk.

Around the base of Ringing Roger, the young

apprentice weasels were arranging their equipment. They had ropes spun from spider's-web silk, which as everyone knows is one of the strongest materials known to mammals. They had proper boots. They had thick gloves with sticky clawtips. They each had a prayer book in their top pockets, which they occasionally touched with a paw for reassurance.

There were half-a-dozen of them – three jacks and three jills – ready to make the climb. Once the crowd had swollen to its maximum, and filled the area around the great clock, the first four began to ascend. They went up one on each corner. The crowd held its collective breath, watching them move from brick to brick. Only a short while ago they had seen two weasels hanging from the hands of this clock. Now they were watching it being scaled from below for the first time. Ringing Roger was becoming important in the rock-climbing and mountaineering world. Instead of mountain-climbing, famous munro baggers were now talking about taking on the south face of Ringing Roger in winter.

Moving amongst the crowd, the mayor's stoats were collecting money for the privilege of watching the weasels climb.

The apprentices were worthy of their teachers. They scaled the clocktower steadily and with confidence. Despite his boss's desires, Falshed was secretly pleased no-one had yet fallen. He kept whispering out loud, 'Slip, slip, fall off, weasel, drop to your death with a horrible scream,' so that his policemammals could hear. He hoped this would be reported to Mayor Poynt. When the weasels were only halfway to the top the clock had chimed in the noon. Midday in Muggidrear! *Dong! Dong! Dong!* . . .' The tower shuddered with each stroke of the great mechanical clapper striking the bell. Bits of mortar fell. A old bird's nest, loosened, plummeted to earth. The crowd let out a gasp.

But the four weasels bravely held on, their claws gripping the brickwork, and managed to live out the chimes. Once Ringing Roger had stopped shaking, they scrambled the last few metres to the top. A great cheer went up, under which could be heard the grinding of a worried Falshed's teeth. Triumphant, the four clung there, waving to the crowd, before abseiling down to where their two comrades were waiting.

One of these now decided he was not going to climb. The other, a young jill and the smallest of the group, was going to have to go up alone. This was quite different from going up in company, where there was someone to help if your paw could not quite find a firm hold. A lone climb. This brave young jill, Daphne by name, could not be roped to other ascending weasels, nor receive the comfort of their presence and voices. It was twice the task now. Yet, she steadfastly refused to put it off to another day. She wanted to graduate before the day was over. Her bold little heart was set on it.

Daphne began climbing. Thirty minutes had now passed since noon and the Ringing Roger had struck the half hour with a gentler note than it used for the full-blooded hour. The quarter-hour chime was even less vicious than the half-hour, so she had at least twenty-nine minutes to reach the top without being shaken like a leaf in the wind. It was still a difficult climb, completely vertical, and without her friends.

'Please let her fall,' whispered Falshed, but without conviction behind his words. He knew the mayor would be angry if no body hit the pavement with a sickening thud and lay still and mute. Mayor Poynt would certainly not be still and mute. He would be active and loud. Yet, deep inside him, Falshed was not the blood-thirsty creature he pretended to be. This was forced on him by his superior. 'And if you do, let it be quick, without any pain. A simple *splat* will do. No horrible cracking of bones. No scattering of waste material. No piercing screams.'

Gradually the little form of Daphne the would-be steeplejill weasel ascended the side of Ringing Roger. Her little claws found holds in cracks in the mortar. She used her teeth too, when the going was precarious, to grip the brickwork. Her tail went from side to side, to act as a balancing weight. Her ears twitched this way and that, and were good indicators of her emotional state.

Down below, her companions – those who had already been where no weasel had been before – were watching and waiting. They had faith in their fellow apprentice, knowing her to be a skilful climber.

Not so the crowd. The crowd knew nothing of her skills, had no knowledge of her dexterity, her nimbleness. They murmured amongst themselves, gripped each other's forelimbs with their claws, and closed their eyes when Daphne seemed to falter. *Don't let her freeze*, they thought to themselves. *Don't let her look down*. They had visions of her stopping, the terror gripping her heart as she looked back, and of her eventually tiring and dropping off the side of the building like ripe fruit from a vine to splatter on the cobblestones below the tower.

She moved slowly.

When she was seven-eighths of the way to the top the hour hand suddenly clicked onto the 1. No-one had been watching the time. All had been so intent on Daphne's progress skywards. Daphne felt the machinery inside the tower begin to growl and rumble. All on the outside heard it click and whirr. Suddenly Daphne was at crisis point. The clock was going to strike. True, it would only be once, but she was at a place where she was clinging on by her very clawtips.

'*Doooonnnggg!*'

The note was deep and cold, coming not from the heart, but from the very stomach of the ancient clock. It was as if the timepiece were waking from a hundred-year sleep. It shook itself. It shuddered from roots to flagpole tip. Daphne's hind paws slipped. She quickly sank her teeth into the brickwork as she was left dangling with only one pawhold. Someone in the crowd screamed. There was a universal sigh of dismay. Falshed (it was he who had screamed) cried out that he had not meant her to fall and to hang on tightly. There were many who copied him then in stuffing a paw into their mouths to stop themselves from whimpering. There were many who did not, however, and as Daphne hung there, between life and death, someone started singing a song, very softly at first, which gathered strength as more mammals took it up.

'*Hickory, dickory, dock, the weasel climbed the clock, the clock struck one, but the weasel still clung, hickory, dickory, dock.*'

It didn't rhyme *exactly* but no-one cared about that. What was important was that it gave Daphne encouragement. Indeed, it seemed to work. She scrabbled about with her hind legs and eventually they found new pawholds. Finally she was stable again. She steadied herself, then after a short rest, continued the climb. She reached the top of Ringing Roger by ten past one, and the crowd went mad.

Jeremy Poynt was incensed.

Falshed was standing before him in the mayor's office, cap in paw, wondering if he was going to die himself. Sometimes the ermine figure of Jeremy Poynt took on the proportions of a polar bear in Falshed's eyes. The mayor was certainly as ferocious as that noble beast.

'You mean *none* of them fell?' spluttered the mayor, viciously hurling a whole scuttleful of coal on the already roaring fire. 'Not one of them dropped to their death?'

'No. There was this one weasel, a jill, who *almost* did, but everyone started singing a song to give her heart.'

'I hope you didn't join in?' growled the mayor, with an ugly look.

'No,' lied the chief of police. 'I didn't.'

'But you didn't stop it?'

'It was all over within a minute or two. There – there was no time to think about it.'

Mayor Poynt sighed. 'I always said you were a

slow thinker, Falshed, and times like these prove me right. Never mind. There'll be other apprentices wanting to pass the exam. Other climbs. I supposed it was too much to expect that one should fall on the first day. Off you go. Arrest someone. Throw someone in jail. Earn your living.'

'Yes, Mayor,' said Falshed, much relieved, backing out of the office, 'and if you see your sister, please give her my kindest regards.'

'Don't push it, Falshed.'

'No, no. Sorry, Mayor. Er, bye.'

Chapter Thirty-seven

Bryony had witnessed Daphne's miraculous climb
to the top of Ringing Roger. Her heart had been
with the little weasel all the way. Now it was over
she approached the newly qualified steeplejill.
She had a proposal to make to her. Once they
had chatted the pair of them went back to 7a
Breadoven Street, Gusted Manor, where Monty,
Scruff, Maudlin and the shrew, Orgibucket, were
waiting for them.

Those waiting at the flat greeted the two jills and
then looked at the new steeplejill with some
misgivings.

'You think you are able to climb Traitors'
Tower?' asked Monty. 'Forgive me, but you don't
look much more than a kitten.'

Bryony said, 'I've just seen her scale Ringing

Roger with hardly a slip, and here she is – even though it chimed the hour and did its best to shake her free of its walls. This little jill,' she put her fore-limb around Daphne's shoulders, 'is a brilliant climber.'

'We'll 'ave to do it in the dark,' reminded Scruff.

'No problem,' said Daphne. 'I was going to do it with my eyes shut anyway.'

This was a joke of course, but it took the four silent jacks a while before they got it.

'Oh, right,' said Maudlin. 'Yes – good one.'

Bryony sighed. 'They're very slow,' she said.

'Well, they're *only* jacks, after all,' replied Daphne.

Monty nodded. 'Fine, you've had your fun, now gather around the table and have a look at these architectural plans. I found them in Lord Haukin's library. They're of the towers of Muggidrear in general and Traitors' Tower in particular. See, here's where we ought to scale the outer wall, and if you look closely you'll see a cell on each landing . . .'

Jis McFail poked her head around the doorway. 'Can I get anyone tea and hot buttered crumpets?'

Every paw shot up.

Later that day, when the sun had gone down over the dark chimneys of Muggidrear, and the lamplighters had walked their rounds and lit the gas lamps of the city, and the nightwatch-mammals had risen from their beds, yawned, and changed from pyjamas to outdoor clothing, six creatures made their way down to the river. They carried spider's-web ropes and crampons and grappling-hooks and climbing boots. They had

343

charts and maps and wore dark coats and trousers. One of them at least had a skeleton key in his pocket, with which he could open any door. They were equipped for burglary, yet they were not robbers; they were weasels (and a shrew) out to rescue an imprisoned lemming.

Jaffer Silke, the otter, was at the landing stage.

'Got your message, guv'nor,' he said to Monty. 'Who're these two geezers? Ain't seen them before.'

He pointed a claw at Orgibucket and Daphne, who in her dark coat and trousers did indeed appear to be a 'geezer'.

'Friends of ours,' said Monty. 'Experts in rescuing princes.'

'Oh, well then,' said Jaffer, 'if they're *experts*.'

They all climbed into Jaffer's boat and he took them along the river, though the evening shadows of statues and lampposts thrown down from the street above. Colours rippled on the water where the lights reflected in its black wavelets and ripples. Black, mysterious-looking barges passed them, going down the middle of the river. They were like the funeral ships of ancient kings and queens, slipping along the river of the dead. Occasionally a pleasureboat, lit up with burning torches, cut across their bows full of passengers clacking in merriment. One or two rowing-boats were about, rowed by mammals such as Jaffer, making a living from the seedy side of the river Bronn.

'Here we are,' whispered Jaffer, sliding his craft silently under a stone bridge. 'Traitors' Gate.'

They were now on the narrow waterway which

344

led to the towers down which traitors would be carried in olden times. This was so that the royal prisoners, destined for the chop, did not have to be taken through the streets of Muggidrear where rescue attempts might take place. After dropping Maudlin off on the river bank, Jaffer followed this archaic route to Traitors' Tower, which loomed above the three other towers on the venerable building. Jaffer was just mooring the boat to a grassy patch near the tower, when a voice rang out on the battlements.

'Twelve o'clock and all's well! How say you, first tower?'

'All's well,' came the muffled reply.

'Second tower?'

'All's well.'

'Third tower?'

'Fine, absolutely – eh? – oh, I mean, yes, *all's well*.'

'Traitors' Tower?'

'All's well, captain.'

'Third tower, report to the duty officer after your watch is over, if you please.'

'Yes, captain. Sorry, captain.'

A bell was rung twelve times and a bird squawked somewhere within the courtyards of the ancient prison.

'The Mouse-eaters,' whispered Jaffer. 'They guard the place with pikestaffs and wear them silly-lookin' leggings. Got some birds in there too. Thirteen of 'em. Bullfinches. Traditional, it is.'

The equipment was taken from the boat and laid on the ground. Daphne made herself ready for the climb.

'Now,' whispered Monty to Orgibucket, 'here's where you come in.' He handed the shrew a copy of *The Chimes* rolled into a cone. 'I want you to howl into this like you did before, up north. I want those guards in the tower to think wolves are in the city. I want them to be so scared they'll vacate the battlements of the tower. Come on, then, let's hear you. Let's hear that famous shrew-wolf yowl.'

Orgibucket took the makeshift trumpet and putting it to his furry mouth, he howled mightily. It was a howl loud and mournful enough to chill the backbones of the dead. It was enough to rattle the teeth of the skeletons of executed kings. The guards in the tower above froze in midstep. The howling continued for at least ten minutes. Finally, one of the stoat guards gathered enough courage to look over the edge.

'What can you see?' whispered his friend.

'Nothin'. Blackness. It's quite still now, ain't it . . .'

At that moment Orgibucket let out his most fearful and ferocious yowl of all time.

Maudlin's haunting voice was then heard floating up from the river Bronn, as if on the back of a dream.

'The wolves are coming! The wolves are coming!'

'Right, that's it,' said the shivering guard, lurching back from the edge of the battlements. 'You can stay out here if you want – I'm goin' down to the guardhouse for a cuppa tea.'

'We're safe enough up 'ere, ain't we?' said the other, hopefully.

'Maybe. Maybe not. I'm not waiting around to see, are you?'

346

'Nope,' said his friend.

There followed the slamming of the tower door and then silence. Daphne took this as her cue. She gave the signal that she was prepared to go. Bryony gave her a leg-up and she was on her way, climbing the outside of Traitors' Tower like a fly on a wall.

'Any misgivings I had about her,' said Scruff, 'have just vanished into the night air. She's brilliant.'

Daphne reached the battlements and had to wait there, just below the crenellations, because a Mouse-eater was patrolling the spot where she was going over the top. Once he had gone, she was over in a trice. A few moments later there was a rope dangling down to the creatures below.

'Right, Scruff – you, Bryony and Maudlin stay down here and guard the rope end,' said Monty. 'Orgibucket. How are you at climbing?'

'Not as good as I can tunnel, but I can go up a rope all right.'

To prove it he began climbing first, hanging on with his front claws and scrambling against the brickwork with his hind claws. Monty followed. Soon the pair were halfway up the rope and going strong when a voice came from the tower above.

'You down there!'

Monty and Orgibucket stopped climbing immediately and held their breath.

'You, otter. Yes, the boatmammal. What are you doing in the grounds of the tower with your rowing-boat?'

A stoat was leaning out of a window, calling down.

'Me?' came the voice of Jaffer, strong and clear, 'You talkin' to *me*? I'm empowered to go any-wheres on this river my dooty takes me. I've got my scavenger's licence, I 'ave. This 'ere backwater's part of the river, ain't it? Same water, anyways. I came up 'ere looking for poor drowned souls. You 'aven't seen none, by any chance, 'ave you?'

'The river means the river. You're not supposed to come up this waterway. It's private. Crown land, laddie. Didn't you see the notice above Traitors' Gate? I could have you arrested.'

'Arrested is it?' cried an indignant Jaffer. 'You come down 'ere and I'll arrest your nose for you.'

'Just clear off!'

'Yes,' came a second stoat voice from the battle-ments, 'any more of your lip, snirpy-mouth, and I'll come down there and sort you out myself. It's a good job I've got better things to do than mess around with blind and deaf loopy otters who can't read.'

'You and whose badger colony?'

'Me and my teeth, that's all.'

'Stoats,' grumbled Jaffer, putting the boat into the water and climbing aboard, 'who'd put up with 'em. Give 'em a bit of authority and they think they own the whole animal kingdom.'

He paddled away, grumbling noisily. Soon Jaffer had gone and it was all quiet again. Maudlin, Bryony and Scruff remained tight up to the wall under the lea of the tower where they could not be seen unless someone leaned right over the crenel-lations to look down.

Monty and Orgibucket continued climbing. When they reached the top they found the rope tied around one of the teeth of the crenellations. Daphne had hidden herself somewhere. She came out of the shadows and immediately they clambered over and were on the battlements.

Orgibucket took out his skeleton key. They went to the door leading to the spiral staircase which went down the middle of the tower. It was unlocked. They followed the stairs to the first landing. There was a cell there, but it was empty. The next landing down, some twenty steps, the cell was also empty. But on the third landing they looked through the grille on the door and there he was, the Prince Imperial, lying on some straw.

'*Pssssst!*'

The prince stirred. 'What?'

'Over here. At the door. Friends. Don't make a sound. We'll have you out in a jiffy.'

Orgibucket used his underworld skills to pick the lock. Soon they had bundled the lemming out of the cell. He seemed a little bemused. They hurried him up the staircase to the battlements of the tower. The new watch of Mouse-eater guards had come on duty but they were looking out over the Bronn. Obviously their companions had not warned them of the wolves, because one of them let out a long sigh of contentment.

'What?' asked the other.

'Oh, I dunno,' said his stoat companion, a catch in his throat, 'I was just lookin' at Whistleminster Bridge and the city beyond. It's a sight so – so touching in its majesty. All bright and glittering in the smokeless air. I can honestly say I never felt a calm so deep. And look, the very houses seem asleep, and all that mighty heart is lying still.'

There was a silence then a click of teeth.

'You great wet nanna, you. You jill's blouse. Sentimental? I should cocoa. You great nancy. You wopping great cissy.'

'You callin' me a nancy?'

'Well. You listen to yourself. Anyone'd think you were spoutin' poetry, if they didn't know you.'

There was another silence, then, 'Coming out for a jug or two tonight? Some of the jacks are going to the Prince Poynt Arms. There's a skittle match on . . .'

Monty, Orgibucket, Daphne and Prince Miska managed to slip across the tower and down the rope while the two stoats were trying to prove how stoatly they were. The fleeing group then followed the waterway up to Traitors' Gate, where they found Jaffer waiting patiently in his bobbing rowing-boat. Once everyone was aboard, they set off up the Bronn to the nearest landing stage to Breadoven Street.

CHAPTER THIRTY-EIGHT

On getting back to 7a Breadoven Street, the group first said farewell to Orgibucket, a much changed shrew, who said he was on his way back up north again.

'Me and my brother, well, let's say we're reformed characters now. I never want to see the inside of a prison again, that's for sure.'

Bryony said, 'You realize that Chief Falshed will be tearing his hair out once he realizes he'll never get his hundred guineas back.'

'Oh, but he will. I intend to pay back every penny, even though it was a scheme to get me into debtors' prison. I'm certain the mayor was behind it all, too. But I don't want to live my life owing the chief of police a lot of money. As soon as I can I'll send him my earnings from whatever job I can find in Howling Hill.'

'Good for you,' said Monty.

They all bid farewell to the shrew and he left, slipping out of the house into the early morning fog like a grey ghost.

'Now,' said Monty, as they all settled into fore-limbchairs, 'what's *your* story?'

This remark was addressed to Prince Miska.

Monty, Bryony, Scruff and Mauldin were all ears.

'Well,' said the prince in a slight accent, 'you may have heard, my country is going through a quiet revolution. Until now the royal family has ruled the country, absolutely, with no ifs or buts. Now the peasants – I'm sorry, the *ordinary citizens* – wish for a democracy. Quite right, you say! Well, so say I too, and I came to Welkin to seek advice on how to shed my present royal status and put myself up for election as a commoner who has newly embraced the idea of democracy.

'As you probably know, I came here by ship. When I disembarked one of the mayor's coaches was waiting for me. I met with the mayor who tried to offer to lend me his election team – the stoats who transformed him from a prince into a politician in the eyes of the public – on the understanding that I sponsor his building firms in Slattland once I was elected its first president. I said nothing. Instead I asked if I might be taken across the river to see the queen. Of course, I wished to tell her of my decision, she being a member of one of the last royal families in the islands of our great mother ocean.'

'Of course,' said Bryony, and was glared at by the others for her interruption.

'Again, the mayor's coach took me . . .'

Monty said, 'Was it his personal carriage, or a coach?'

'It was from one of his factories which makes cricket bats for you mustelids. I do not understand this game you call cricket . . .'

'Me neither, and I've lived here all my life,' said Bryony, and received another set of glares.

The prince continued. 'I spoke with the girl-queen, but by then I knew I had been followed here, by a countess from my own country – someone so wicked you would not believe the things of which she is capable.'

'I think we would,' Monty said.

The prince went on, 'The mayor's coach then took me back to mayor. I asked him to hide me from the countess. We agreed I should stay in the towers of Muggidrear – a castle where I would be safe until it was time to leave for Slattland.'

'Towers of Muggidrear,' murmured Monty. 'Not really a castle, prince – more of a prison for royal mammals.'

'So, yes, a prison. Now I know it.'

'And the opera?' asked Bryony.

The prince's eyes lit up at the magic word.

'The *opera*,' he breathed. 'Yes, with Gravelotti singing tenor. Oh, I couldn't miss that, now could I? I would have risked my life to go.'

'You did,' Scruff pointed out.

'Yes, I did. I disguised myself as a *dowager* and went and heard the golden voice. It was worth it. I saw *her* in the audience. The deadly one. She had

353

her minions planted all around the opera house. If she had seen me – well, our friend Jaffer Silke would have been dragging me out of the river now, swollen and very, very dead.'

'What happened after that? Did the mayor finally get you to say you would sponsor his firms?'

'No. He made a deal with the countess instead. I was to be the bargaining tool, the victim. She wanted me dead, but at least he stopped at murder. He promised her he would keep me a prisoner in the tower until the elections were over.'

'That's monstrous,' said Bryony.

'Rotten to the core, those Poynts,' Scruff cried.

'Well, we've managed to free the prince,' Monty said, 'and the mayor will be chewing his paws at this moment. Of course he won't admit to any of this. He'll call it preposterous, as he usually does, and ask us to produce the evidence. All we've got is our word against his.'

'What about the stoats who did his dirty work for him – the guards in the tower?'

'No doubt those poor creatures are now in the army, serving on the front, fighting blood-thirsty hordes of marsh rats. That's the sort of reward the mayor gives to those who do his dirty work and serve him faithfully.'

'The army,' murmured Prince Miska, a dreamy look going into his eyes. 'The front.'

'Ah, yes,' said Monty. 'You like the army, don't you? I believe you're a general as well as a prince? How do you rate your chances of becoming the first president of Slattland?'

The lemming looked serious. 'Good. I would say

good. I have to beat Sveltlana, the Countess of Bogginski, of course. That will not be easy.'

'Yes,' agreed Monty, in a faraway voice, 'she's very clever, isn't she? And quite beautiful. Those eyes . . .' He suddenly stopped himself, and turned away, as if embarrassed by his own revelations.

The prince said, 'She *is* very clever. She speaks seventeen languages fluently, including Humpbacked Whale, which as you must know is a difficult language based on sing-song tones.' He joked, 'She also has three A levels, in Anarchy, Rioting and Civil Disobedience. All Grade A. I think she is a very formidable opponent.'

Bryony said, 'Won't you be in danger from her when you return to Slattland yourself?'

'Not really. She would never dare to have me killed in my own country. Here, yes. There, no.'

Once all the explanations were out of the way, Miska still seemed a bit upset about something.

'What is it?' asked Bryony. 'Are you still angry about Mayor Poynt?'

'That? No, no. He is a very foolish and greedy stoat, but not worth being concerned about. No, I am unhappy because I still don't know how not to be a prince. I think my citizens love me, but they will not vote for me if I look and act like a prince. It's very hard not to be a prince when you've been one all your life. How do I stop? How do I become a peasant? Some of the royal princes, kings and queens have not been so good to the citizens of Slattland. How do I become ordinary, common creatures of the gutter like all of you in this very grubby-looking house . . . ?'

'Let's have a bit less of the *common* if you don't mind,' Maudlin said, indignantly, but Monty silenced any further comments from him with a wave of the paw.

'What you must do,' said Monty, 'is to stop feeling superior to us all and think of us as your equals.'

'Equals?' The prince blinked. This was clearly something that had not occurred to him before now. 'You mean, I must think of you in the way that I think of myself?'

'Something of the sort. We all have our different ways, of course, our individual characters and personalities, but basically we all have a right to expect to be treated equally. We should all respect each other as mammals. One should not expect another to bend a knee, or bow a head in deference to rank. One should not expect privileges, exclusive rights. One should not feel one was born to be preferred.

'If you can be courteous to a beggar and look him or her in the eye, and feel they are as worthy a creature as you to be standing the face of the earth, then you will be making progress. If you can put arrogance behind you, and walk with peasants and feel you are in privileged company, then you will be on your way to shedding your royal status. If, on the other paw, you expect special treatment wherever you go, and believe that other mammals should regard you as better than they are, then you will be failing in your efforts to let go of royal ways.

'If you can do all these things, and feel no sense of loss, then my friend, you will be a mammal among mammals.'

The prince looked a bit shaken. 'Well, that is certainly not an easy thing to do, is it? All my life I have been told I am better than other mammals. I believed it. I must now stop to believe it, yes?' He stopped and thought for a bit, before adding. 'And the mayor, Poynt, has done this? How extraordinary.'

'Ah,' said Monty, 'the mayor. Yes. Well, I think the mayor is a good actor.'

'You mean he pretends such a thing?'

'Let's say there is much of the prince still buried deep within him, which he finds impossible to root out.'

Prince Miska drew himself up. 'I don't want to be a false president of my mammals. My lemming citizens need someone who speaks the truth to them, not creatures like this mayor who *pretend* to be of the mammals. Thank you, Montegu Sylver, for your advice. You, I believe, were also a lord once upon a time? You found it easy to become an ordinary citizen?'

'Ah, but my ancestors were peasants.'

'If we go back far enough,' the prince said wisely, '*all* our ancestors were peasants.'

'Now that kind of thinking is what you need!'

Bryony interrupted. 'Now, we have to get you back to Slattland. I've been studying the shipping schedules. There's a fast sailing ship that leaves in three days' time. Shall I book you passage?'

'Thank you, but as an ordinary citizen, perhaps I should be booking these things for myself?'

Scruff said, 'You're still in danger. You shouldn't be walking the streets on your own. Sveltlana might've left some of her bully-lemmings behind

357

her, just in case. But I tell you what, let's all go to the mayor's garden party, eh? I'd love to see Poynt's face if you walked into his garden. He'd have a fit, wouldn't he? What d'you say, Monty?'

'I think that's an excellent idea, Scruff. We'll give the mayor what he deserves – a good fright. We'll all go. Lord Haukin will get us invitations. He enjoys a good joke as much as anyone. The mayor's annual garden party is quite an event. All the important citizens of Muggidrear will be there . . .'

'Important,' said Prince Miska, gravely, 'but equal.'

'Quite so,' agreed Monty, with a long suck on his curved pipe. 'This will be the talk of the town. You can say you are there, Prince, to ask the advice of the mayor regarding the shedding of royalty. Indeed, I think you *should* ask him. I'll be interested in his reply. Let's see what Poynt comes up with in answer to that question.'

In the lull that followed, Scruff said to the prince, 'You really do like opera, then?'

'Yes.'

'Personally, I prefer the music hall.'

'I *love* the music hall,' cried the prince, fervently. 'I would die for the music hall. I am the devoted servant of the stage – opera, play, music hall, ballet – I have the greasepaint in my blood. When I am president I shall build a new theatre, a *big* theatre, and perhaps one day play in *Hambone* myself. I was a prince once upon a time, after all.'

'Once?' said Scruff. 'That's good.'

'Yes. A prince no more. Except for maybe Prince Hambone, on the stage, when no-one remembers I was once a real prince.'

In the corner of the room, Bryony said quietly to Monty, 'So – you really thought she was – beautiful? Sveltlana?'

He gave her a sidelong glance. 'Yeesss – in a sort of way.'

'What way?'

'Well,' he grabbed his chibouque quickly and began sucking on the stem, before saying, 'in a *classic* way, I suppose. Not the sort of looks I, personally, *really* admire. I prefer the wild, untamed, natural looks of an outdoor jill. I'm the sort of jack who prefers to see the wind ruffling a jill's fur, the hot sun on her glossy pelt, the raindrops glistening in her fur – say, out on the flog course – wild and free. Well-groomed is fine. Glamour, that sort of thing, is for *other* jacks. But I like the touch of a dark storm in a female – a jill with independence . . .'

'Yes, all right,' said Bryony, briskly, 'you needn't go on.'

CHAPTER THIRTY-NINE

Sybil had absolutely refused to use mechanical waiters for her garden party. The steam-waiters and clockwork-waiters were stacked in the coal cellar out of the way. If they could talk they would have said they did not like being crammed in like toy soldiers next to each other. The rivalry between clockwork and steam engine even found its way into these mechanical devices, reached deep into their tin souls, and clockwork-waiters hated being brass cheek by iron jowl with horrid steam-waiters, and steam-waitresses despised being enamel apron-to-apron with clockwork-waitresses. One lot hissed quietly, the other lot let out a low whirr. There were annoyed clicks and clacks, and angry sputters and spits from various parts of the coal cellar. Heavy engine oil mingled reluctantly with light lubricating oil. Had these automatons been able to speak the conversation might have gone line this:

Clockwork-waitress: 'Get yer cheap spiny tin whiskers out of my delicate works, you heavy-metal oaf.'

Steam-waiter: 'Just as soon as you stop plugging my steam outlet with your big bronze nose, cuckoo brain.'

As it can be seen, neither steam nor clockwork would fare well in polite society, but this was a reflection on their inventors who used much the same language with each other.

Sybil therefore had weasels to serve the guests who began to drift in a little after one o'clock in the afternoon. There was a marquee set up in case it rained, but at the moment the sun shone with benevolent brightness so chairs and tables were set up on the lawns. Guests wandered beneath a canopy of daffodils and tulips which overhung the pretty paths. The tables were laden with food and drink. Great cold cuts of mouse joints, legs of vole, mouse-liver pate, mustard and cress salads on dock-leaf platters, hard-boiled turquoise thrushes' eggs, frog and toad spawn, crisp dragonflies on toast, and many other tasty dishes covered the cloths Sybil had embroidered herself. For drinks there was honey dew of course, but also herb robert cordials and campionade.

The mayor looked splendid! His spreading girth was hidden by a magnificent outfit, the crowning glory of which was the waistcoat. This was made of oriental silk embroidered (again, by Sybil) with yellow celandine flowers. It showed off his white pelt to great advantage. He strode around amongst the early guests swinging a great gold watch on a long golden chain. Every so often he would check the time against the chimes of Ringing Roger. To those he needed or wished to keep as friends he called out a cheery greeting; to those who did not interest him or could not do him any favours, he nodded curtly.

By two o'clock most of the guests were there.

A motorized Wm. Jott and Thos. Tempus Fugit crashed into each other as they entered through the gate.

'Watch it, Billy,' said Thos., glaring.

'*You* watch it, Tommy,' said Wm.

Thos. had a clockwork shoes on, while Wm. was wearing steam-driven trousers.

Falshed was trying to tempt Sybil into biting the other side of a biscuit he was praising, in the mistaken belief that she had baked it herself.

Lord Hannover Haukin, his monocle fixed firmly in his right eye, viewed the proceedings with mild disdain.

'Not like the old days, Mayor. Where's the wild-mouse carcass roasting on a spit over an open fire? Where's the Marten dancers with their justling bells? Where are the poets, the singers of songs, the tumblers, the jokers, the players? What's happened to the traditional hairy rock-cress buns, the mountain milk-vetch salads, the navelwort stemen pies? Where are the tame pied-kingfishers fetching tiddlers from the pond for the youngsters to cook on charcoal fires? What's happened to the ornamental garden birds we used to see? The slate-coloured junkos, the bobolinks, the rufous-sided

362

towhees, the *xanthocephalhi* and *locustella fasciolatae*? Gone, I suppose. All gone.'

The mayor, quite rightly believing he was being made fun of, tried to ignore the stoat lord without appearing outright rude.

'Can't afford such luxuries every year,' he let out a false chuckle. 'You should give a party yourself, Lord Haukin.'

Lord Haukin sighed. 'I suppose I should, but it looks such a bore.'

The mayor, who did not wish to appear unsophisticated, gave a wide yawn.

'Oh, yes, it is. But you know, Sybil will have it. She loves to entertain. She's a socialite to the core, is Sib.'

'What do you have for entertainment?'

'Ah,' said the mayor, a little more enthusiastically. 'I've had a few dozen weasel urchins rounded up from the streets. Filthy little beasts. We're going to put them in that roped-off ring over there and then throw farthings.'

'Where's the entertainment in that?'

'Why,' said Jeremy Poynt, 'they'll fight for the coins. It's great fun watching the little tics kick, bite and scratch each other. Haven't you seen it done before? You're in for a treat. They'll tear each other to pieces for a farthing. Ha, ha, ha!'

With that the mayor moved on to his other guests. This was a good move on the mayor's part. Lord Haukin, who had been growing angrier by the minute, had been about to strike his cane on a tender part of the mayor's anatomy and ask him if he found the pain entertaining.

The band was playing. The mayor and Falshed

liked martial tunes: good stirring stuff that sent soldiers into glorious battle with their blood simmering in their veins. But Sybil said she was having none of that raucous stuff. She wanted gentle music which told of streams trickling down mountainsides and wind blowing in tree tops.

However, for some reason the band struck up a cheery little marching song just when the mayor was becoming irritated with the tinkling stuff. He beamed across at them, only to see a rather scruffy weasel conducting them. The mayor marched across to this individual, unable to stop himself keeping in step with the tune.

'Oy! What d'you think you're doing?' he cried at the interloper.

'Me?' said the weasel. 'Puttin' a bit of bounce into the afternoon, that's what I'm doing.'

No matter how much the mayor sympathized with this idea, he wasn't going to have some foul weasel at his garden party.

'Just clear off, before I call the police.'

'Oh, you don't want to do that, squire,' said the scruffy weasel in a low voice. 'Not a respectable geezer like you, old stoat.'

There was something in the way that the weasel said these words that made the mayor uneasy. His confidence evaporated. The weasel was pointing with his baton (actually a twig taken from the mayor's laurel hedge) at the gate to the garden. The mayor frowned. Coming through the gate was that jumped-up blighter Montegu Sylver, the bane of the mayor's life. He was accompanied by several other mammals.

The mayor bristled with delight. Sylver had at

last delivered himself up into the mayor's paws. This was going to be easy.

'Falshed!' he yelled, excitedly.

The chief of police came running. 'Mayor?'

'Do I have to do everything myself? There's that fugitive, Sylver. Arrest him now, for abduction and murder.'

'Oh, you don't want to do that, squire,' said the scruffy weasel who was still conducting the band. 'Not a geezer in your position.'

'Will you shut your blasted trap!' cried the mayor. 'Falshed, why aren't you clapping on the handcuffs? Why are you standing gawping? Arrest Montegu Sylver for the assassination of the Prince Imperial of Slattland!'

The chief of police coughed into his paw. 'Can't do that, Mayor.'

Poynt was incensed by Falshed's lethargic attitude. 'What's stopping you? Apart from stupidity?'

'If you look closely, Your Honour, you'll see that the Prince Imperial is standing at Montegu Sylver's side.'

The mayor's head swung back. 'What?' he said. Sure enough, Prince Miska was accompanying Sylver. The royal lemming was one of the party of mammals. 'Arrghh,' cried the mayor, beside himself with frustration. 'How does that weasel do it? Every time!'

Monty said, 'Allow me to introduce you to the Prince Imperial of Slattland, Mayor – Prince Miska.'

'Not for long,' cried the prince, looking the mayor up and down. 'Soon to be President Miska the First. Anyway, I've already met the mayor. He had me thrown into Traitors' Tower, didn't you, Mayor? That *was* on your orders, wasn't it?'

The mayor almost choked on his pastry and frantically waved for Falshed to come and rescue him.

At that moment there was a fanfare at the gates and to the mayor's astonishment a human – a little girl using a skipping-rope – came in, followed by a retinue of retainers. The child stopped skipping and looked around her excitedly. 'A party!' she cried. 'I love parties.'

'Hi, you, little girl,' cried the mayor, grateful to have a distraction. 'You can't come in here. This is a garden party for mustelids. Go back across the bridge. Go home. You're not allowed.'

The girl's face screwed up. 'My uncle says I am,' she replied, defiantly. 'My uncle says I'm old enough to come out now.'

'I don't care what you're blasted uncle says, you're not going to gatecrash *my* party.'

'Ahem!' said Monty.

'What?' cried the mayor, swinging round to face him.

'I do believe that's the queen, Mayor.'

Mayor Poynt blinked. 'Nonsense,' he said, but his voice was without conviction or confidence.

'I'm afraid it is.'

'The queen – the queen is a fully-grown *woman*.'

'Fake, I'm afraid. Clockwork or steamwork. One or the other, but not *real*. That's the real queen, there. She's six, I think.'

'Six and three-quarters,' said the queen. 'Hello, weasels. Nice to see you again. Any cream cakes? I *love* cream cakes. Oh, and there's you, Prince

Lemming-thing. Have you seen any cream cakes? I would like some lemonade too. And jelly. Stoat, fetch me some,' she demanded of the mayor.

'*Please,*' reminded her nurse by her side.

'Please. And some strawberries.'

The mayor choked again, then scuttled off to find some eats for the queen. Princess Sybil came over and looked up at the queen. They began a conversation with both of them speaking at once, yet miraculously they seemed to understand each other. Guests stood around, bewildered. Finally the mayor arrived back with two weasel servants bearing trays of goodies for the queen.

It was while the queen was entertaining the guests by stuffing a strawberry cream cake in her mouth – a task which amazed the young lady's audience given the largeness of the confectionery and the smallness of the queen's mouth – that Sveltlana finally struck. The evil lemming stepped out from behind a gazebo (she had been hiding there since dawn) in a scarlet-and-black cloak. Her claw was quick and a dagger flashed through the air, heading straight for Prince Miska's chest.

'LOOK OUT!' cried Scruff, who had seen the movement in the shade of the gazebo.

Monty had also seen the quick, shadowy actions of the countess and whipped his top hat in the weapon's path. The dagger ripped through the hat but was fortunately deflected. It spun through the air on the other side, missing the prince, and buried its blade in a marquee pole next to the mayor's ear. There it quivered, while the mayor swallowed several times, nearly choking himself on a vole-au-vent.

Falshed rushed forward and seized Sveltlana. 'Got you, assassin!' he cried. 'Off to the prison with you!'

She sneered and waved her piece of paper. 'Diplomatic immunity!' she cried. 'You can't touch me.'

The mayor, who was still half in shock, had other ideas now that he had almost ended up the target of this assassin's blade.

'Escort her to the docks,' he coughed, still trying to get the crumbs out of this throat. 'Put her on a boat. We can't throw her in jail, but we can deport her. Consider yourself deported,' he told the countess.

She lifted her head and sneered. As Falshed's men marched her past the prince, she said, 'You would be well advised to remain in Welkin, Prince Miska.'

'From what I'm told,' he said, mildly, 'I would be no safer here than I would be in Slattland. Aren't you going to invade if you are elected president? I shall see you at the polling booths, Countess. Lemmings will learn of your deeds here and will be ashamed for you.'

Her eyes flashed in amusement and she left the garden party with a haughty expression on her face.

'Well,' said the mayor, having cleared his throat at last, 'I think we've seen the last of her!'

'Perhaps,' Monty said, staring after her, 'but I wouldn't wager my pelt on it.'

'Now let's hope the rest of the afternoon is peaceful,' said Sybil, coming across and doing her pacifying-hostess bit. 'Let's just keep it quiet and genteel, what with having the queen here and everything. After all, that's what we're here for, isn't it?'

At that moment a policemammal came running through the gates into the garden.

'The rats!' he shrieked in panic. 'The rats are coming!'

Another stoat policemammal was right behind him, screaming, 'They're already here!'

Several of the guests gave out loud whistling shrieks themselves and the mayor clutched at the queen's ankle sock in fright, only to receive a painful rap on the knuckles from her skipping-rope handle. Rats in colourful garb swarmed through the gates into the mayor's garden. There were rats of all shapes and sizes, booted to the thighs, armed with rapiers, and wearing great sweeping feathers in their broad-brimmed hats. They rushed towards the tables on which the food was spread, and flung themselves underneath them, their paws over their ears.

Several stoat matrons swooned. A fully-grown stoat general fainted dead away. Stoat kittens ran screaming under their mothers' skirts. Monty called for calm. Mayor Poynt yelled in sheer panic. Weasel servants dropped their trays. Sybil told them their wages would be docked forthwith. Scruff started barking. Bryony threw a glass of water over him. Maudlin laughed, hysterically. Falshed trod in a jelly as he jumped on the tables to warn everyone that martial law was being imposed. The queen jumped up and down in glee, crying, 'What a *super* party!'

And the band played on. A merry little ditty.

Finally a rat in very flamboyant historical costume – stockings, knickerbockers, padded doublet, wide-brimmed hat with feather, pure white ruff – came striding into the garden. There was urgency in his step. He stopped, surveyed the garden party, then swept off his hat with his right paw and bowed, sticking out a leg in the manner of a Welkin noblemammal three centuries before the present time.

'Duck!' he said.

Then he threw himself full length on the lawn.

This warning was immediately followed by an almighty explosion. The whole city reverberated, shook at its very foundations, and juddered still again. The bomb, for it was certainly something of that sort, had evidently gone off somewhere down in the sewers. Following the explosion there came a creaking sound, then a crash, which terminated in a clatter and clanging of bells. A huge metal spring went whizzing over the heads of the garden party guests. An hour-hand the size of a giant javelin buried itself in the middle of the lawn, narrowly missing an elderly female stoat in flounces. A number six spun over the marquee and hoopla-ed the main tent pole.

Finally a large dust cloud rose from somewhere close to the river.

'What was that?' croaked Mayor Poynt, shaken to the very core of his ermine-covered body. 'What happened?'

CHAPTER FORTY

'Two things, I imagine,' said Monty Sylver, for the benefit of all the guests. 'One, my guess is that Spindrick's bomb has finally gone off in the sewers, am I correct, Toddlebeck?'

'Hmmm, *partly* correct,' replied the leader of the sewer rats, regaining his feet. 'This is why we vacated our homeland below the streets. The bomb was discovered just ten minutes ago. We just had time to evacuate.'

Monty nodded. 'And two, I think the bomb went off right under Ringing Roger and caused it to topple on its foundations. Our famous clocktower has fallen, mustelids. We have lost our sense of time.'

The mayor put his paws in his face.

'Not Ringing Roger,' he moaned. 'I was

371

using that to examine the steeplejacks and jills.'

'Never mind, Mayor,' whispered Wm. Jott in his ear, 'I'll build you a steam clock, just like the one in the colonies.'

Toddlebeck now stepped forward, causing the mayor to move backwards in panic. He did not like rats. Weren't stoats at war with them, or something? Had they been below the city streets all this time, waiting to emerge and take over the civilized world and barbarize it? 'It is worse than thee fear, my mayorial friend,' spake Toddlebeck, his paw on his sword hilt. 'Thy big machine is blown to smithers.'

The mayor blinked. 'Big machine?'

'The one thee built in the sewers. This Spindrick placed his steam-driven explosive device *inside* thy great machine. We evacuated the premises, forthwith and presently. The explosion thee have just heard, and felt, means that the now-many parts of the device are strewn throughout the sewers of the city. I fear my knowledge of machines has grave limits – the modern world passes us *sewer* rats by – but I assume the machine will not function when it is in a million scattered bits.'

'Arrrggghhhhhh!' cried the mayor, falling to his knees.

'*Steam*-driven bomb?' yelled Thos. Tempus Fugit, stepping forwards. 'You mean the anarchist Spindrick chose steam over clockwork for his infernal device?'

'No,' replied Toddlebeck. 'He used both. He is nothing if not fair. A bad weasel, but not a biased one.'

Monty said, 'What do you mean? Was that why you said *partly* correct?'

'Yes,' Toddlebeck said. 'There be a brace of bombs, egad. The first, a steamwork bomb he placed in the heating machine. The second, a much *greater* petard, is of clockwork and has tentacles of gunpowder going out all over the city. Methinks if that one blows, the whole city will be but matchwood and flakes of iron.'

'Where is the gunpowder clock?' asked Monty.

'If thee stick thy head down the nearest jackhole, thee will hear the tick-tock echoes through the sewer caverns.'

Monty ran out into the street, followed by Scruff, Maudlin and Bryony. As he ran he threw off the frock-coat he was wearing, so that it would not encumber him. Down the nearest jackhole he went, into the darkness of the sewers. He stood there for a moment until his eyes adjusted to the darkness, then off he shot, running on all fours along the walkway which followed the sewer tunnels. Every so often he stopped and listened for the ticking of the clock. He could hear it now, echoing through the deep silence of the underground world.

Finally he rounded a bend to find a weasel running on the opposite path – the other way.

It was Spindrick Sylver.

'You'll never make it, cousin,' cried Spindrick in glee. 'There's only one minute to go!'

With that, the anarchist weasel ran up some iron rungs, through a jackhole, and out into the street. Monty guessed his cousin had a hiding-place somewhere above – a bomb shelter – where he would be relatively safe from the explosion.

Monty continued running along the path. Finally, he saw an alarm clock, large with a white face, rodent numerals and a big brass bell on top with its clapper poised. The time bomb! It was on the other side of the tunnel. There were wires and leads running off it in every direction. The hand on the clockface was racing round. Thirty seconds to go! There was no time to swim across the sewer. He had to race over the arched ceiling, exhausted as he already was by his long swift run.

Monty threw himself up the wall of the sewer. Fortunately there was moss and lichen for his little claws to cling to. Only the speed at which he ran prevented him from falling back down into the flow of the sewer and being carried away from the clock. Over the arc of bricks he ran, finding cracks and fissures, managing against gravity and all odds to stay on track, until finally he dropped onto the path on the other side.

Two seconds to go!

He was lying on his back, winded, on the cold damp bricks of the walkway. The back of the clock had been removed. Monty could see the wheels clicking over, the alarm spring gathering its strength to strike, the ratchets and levers flicking back and forth. In there the brass machinery was all but ready to release its final deadly tock.

Monty's limbs were aching with the effort of his run and climb. They had seized in cramp and he had no energy left to move them. His whole body was racked with pain. There was only one part of him which was not utterly fatigued. It was the brave weasel's only chance of saving the city. His little tail. It flashed out.

The tip – the sore tip which had been squashed by the coach wheel earlier – poked into the moving parts of the clock. It went right into the brassy heart, into the mass of wheels that turned the spindle to which the clock hands were attached. A sharp brass cog's teeth penetrated his fur – bit into his wounded flesh – turned one more click – then jammed.

One second to go!

The hand of doom had been halted. Monty remained where he was, still as death, with the clock hand one second away from destruction. He was exhausted, completely unable to move. Finally he heard the others coming along the path. Maudlin was calling out his name.

'Here,' croaked Monty. 'Help, quickly.'

Scruff and Maudlin dashed along the path. They were on his side of the sewer and they ran to pick him up. Bryony yelled, 'NO! Leave him there.' They did as they were told until she had crossed the sewer. There her delicate claws reached round the back of the clock and ripped the leads and wires from the works. The bomb had been made safe. The city would not go up in a cloud of brickdust and sewage.

'Well done, Monty,' Bryony murmured in his ear. 'You're my hero, you know that.'

He nodded and retrieved his painful tail.

CLANG - CLANG - CLANG - CLANG - CLANG - CLANG - CLANG - CLANG - CLANG - CLANG - CLANG

This time it was not only Maudlin who almost

had a heart attack, but it was only the alarm clock going off, nothing more.

When they all got back to the garden party, the queen insisted on giving them some of the cream cakes which she had gathered around her possessively in a great wide circle.

'We are most amused,' she squealed. 'My first party and there's been such goings-on! Bombs and cream cakes and weasels and rats running everywhere and mayors screaming. It's all been such fun. I'm going to come every year.'

'Oh goody,' said a voice, flatly. (Sybil, who liked to be the centre of attraction at her *own* parties.)

Weasels, rats and stoats alike congratulated Monty and his fellow weasels for saving their homes and their lives. The mayor, gnashing his fangs, was pushed into the background. No-one wanted to speak to him. Falshed tried to cheer his boss up, but received a tongue-lashing for his pains, so the chief went and shared a jelly with Sybil.

Thos. Tempus Fugit and Wm. Jott spent the rest of the afternoon arguing about whether the clockwork bomb *would* have worked as well as the steamwork one, if allowed to explode.

Monty and his friends were among the first to leave the party. They did not feel it right to gloat and they felt if they remained any longer, hearing the anguished cries of a mayor in spiritual pain, they would be unable not to. Indeed, it was difficult to feel sorry for the mayor, even though he had undergone a terrible shock.

On the way home they tried to talk of other,

ordinary, everyday, things as they walked back to 7a Breadoven Street.

But now and then a noise which would be recognized by a human as a snigger escaped one or the other of these strolling weasels.

On hearing the sound they all had to turn their heads and look away, for fear of breaking out into one of those bouts of uncontrollable mirth which overcome men – and weasels – at times like these.

CHAPTER FORTY-ONE

Monty and his three friends – Bryony, Maudlin and Scruff – were sitting in the living room of 7a Breadoven Street. There was an air of comfortable satisfaction about the place. Not smugness, you understand, just a warm feeling of companionship and the startling discovery that the world was not all bad, that some good things did happen occasionally.

Of course, out there in the city bad things were happening. Enough to fill a dozen newspapers and some left over. There was poverty, injustice, crime, disease, and many other *bad* things which helped to make a kind of darkness settle on the times like a thick mist. But there were lights out there too, shining bravely, trying to brighten the haze.

'What a nice evening,' said Bryony, glancing at

the window and seeing it clear of fog. 'You can see the evening star.'

There were murmurs of agreement from the others.

It was now eight weeks since Mayor Poynt's annual garden party had been invaded by the sewer rats. Work had begun on rebuilding Ringing Roger, felled like a mighty tree by Spindrick's bomb. Somehow the mayor's own building firm had managed to secure the contract for the work – surprise, surprise, his company had put in the lowest price – but the margin for profit was quite low since the other tenders had been very competitive. Also, not surprisingly, Jeremy Poynt had abandoned his scheme for a heating device below the city streets.

Spindrick himself had disappeared, gone to earth, but Monty knew that sometime in the future his cousin would rise again from the rubble of his misdeeds and attempt a new destruction of society.

'Perhaps we could send Spindrick out there one day?' said Monty. 'To the stars. Or even just to the moon. It would be pleasant to rid this world of him, just to give ourselves a rest.'

Maudlin, who had been reading *The Chimes*, suddenly let out a low whistle.

'What's goin' on?' asked Scruff. 'You win the crossword competition, did ya?'

'No, but it says here that Citizen Miska has been elected the first president of Slattland. Citizen Sveltlana, the opposition, was a close runner-up.'

Monty said, 'So, our friend defeated Sveltlana. But a close runner-up, eh? Well, well. She lives to fight another day.' His eyes went a little misty for a moment.

'Beauty and the beast, rolled into one,' muttered Bryony.

Monty looked away, then sought to change the subject.

'Some sea captain, a marten, was speaking to me in the coffee shop the other day. He has heard a tale that would set your fur on end. Apparently, and this is just hearsay, Slattland is having a great problem with vampires. You are aware that vampires come from that part of the world? It's their natural habitat: dense dark forests, tall gloomy cathedrals, brooding castles. It breeds them.'

'How so?' asked Bryony.

Maudlin's fur was now standing on end and he looked from one to the other with big round eyes. Scruff, on the other paw, seemed not to be listening. He was concentrating on trying to thread a needle in the dim light, so that he could sew a tear in his rather threadbare coat.

'It's in the air, in the stark, bleak winters, in the minds of lemming peasants,' continued Monty. 'It breeds a particular kind of creature that changes into a bat in the foul night vapours. It all began with Count Vlad-the-Spitter.'

'What?' croaked Maudlin, 'he spat a lot, did he?'

'Not that kind of spit,' explained Monty. 'The kind of spit you use when skewering meat. A long thin spike. He used to skewer his victims with such spits and drain them of blood, so that he could drink it by the cupful at his leisure. Of course, these days vampires like to take their succour straight from the artery or vein. They come in at the window during the night hours, silently, and sink their vile teeth into their victims, sucking the very life-blood from their sleeping forms.'

Maudlin gulped and stroked his fingers across his furry throat.

'OWWWW!' yelled Scruff, suddenly. 'Blood!'

'What?' cried Maudlin, jumping up in panic.

'Pricked my paw,' muttered Scruff, holding up the needle.

At that moment there was a crash, as some*thing* came hurtling through the window, shattering the glass pane. The thing, which hissed and bubbled in a vile fashion, bounced across the room and settled between Maudlin's hind paws. He yelped and jumped backwards.

'A vampire!' he cried.

There was a moment's silence, then the others began clicking their teeth in merriment.

'It's a cricket ball,' said Monty, touching the chugging round object with his foot. 'A steam-assisted cricket ball. I bet Lord Haukin has something to do with this. He's always thought the game could do with a bit of pep. I bet he's commissioned someone to make this thing for him – Wm. Jott, or perhaps even Scruff's friend, Prof. Speckle Jyde? How droll. How very amusing . . .'

Maudlin managed to click his teeth too, and tried to see the funny side of it, saying, 'Oh, I knew that. I was just pretending.'

'Then on the other paw,' Monty said, his face darkening, 'it could be one of Spindrick's bombs.'

This was the last straw for Maudlin. His newly acquired sense of humour vanished immediately.

He was out through the door before you could say Dakk Makkintashhh.

A little while later Scruff sighed good-humouredly. He got up and fetched a bowl of water. He put the gasping, grumbling cricket ball into the water and watched as it fizzled itself out. Then he quietly closed the open flat door and went back to sewing the tear in his coat, saying, 'That Maud, he's a card, isn't he? Always pretendin' to be scared. You can't help clickin' your teeth at him, can you?'

THE END